SAVING AVERY

ANGELA SNYDER

Copyright © 2015 Angela Snyder
Cover Art ~ Paper & Sage Design
This book is a work of fiction. Names, characters, places and incidents either are products of the author's imagination or are used fictitiously.
All rights reserved. No part of this publication may be reproduced, stored in retrieval system, copied in any form or by any means, electronic, mechanical, photocopying, recording or otherwise transmitted without written permission from the publisher. You must not circulate this book in any format.
This book is licensed for your personal enjoyment only. This book may not be resold or given away to other people. If you would like to share this book with another person, please purchase an additional copy for each recipient. If you're reading this book and did not purchase it, or it was not purchased for your use only, then please return to the retailer and purchase your own copy. Thank you for respecting the hard work of this author.

SYNOPSIS

Avery Mason had it all: the nice house, the fancy clothes, the expensive cars and the perfect husband. On the outside looking in, her life appears to be perfect. But inside, Avery knows her life is far from perfection as her husband's carefully constructed façade slowly starts to crumble.

Forced to fake a happy marriage while enduring physical and mental abuse from the man who had once been her whole world is taking its toll. And ever so slowly, Avery finds herself slipping into an existence where she is gradually becoming a shell of her former self.

When Dr. Max Harrison transfers from Chicago to North Carolina, his world is flipped upside down the moment he sees Avery. With one glimpse into her blue-gray eyes, he can see the pain she is so desperately hiding from the rest of the world. As Avery attempts to push him away, he becomes convinced that there is more to her than meets the eye. And when he finally uncovers her darkest secret, the pieces of the puzzle slowly start to click into place.

Max and Avery want to be together, but nothing in life is ever that simple. It's not going to be easy to get her away from the powerful Mason family, but Max will risk everything to protect her. His only concern is Saving Avery.

Note: Due to strong language and sexual content, this book is not intended for readers under the age of 18 and not intended for people with any triggers.

AUTHOR'S NOTE

Saving Avery is a work of fiction; but, unfortunately, domestic violence is very real. If you or someone you know is suffering at the hands of another, please get help.

PROLOGUE

AVERY

I THINK THE biggest mistake of my life could be chalked up to naiveté. I was barely eighteen when I had first laid eyes on Nathan Mason. He had all the qualities that a girl my age should have wanted for a future husband. He was rich, handsome and perfectly charming. And on the night we met, his piercing blue eyes captured me in a way that threatened to keep me there forever, never letting me go.

If only I had known back then how true that would ultimately become.

As I sit on the patio overlooking the ocean, I think to myself how perfect my life must appear to an outsider. I'm twenty-three years old. I have a handsome husband, who is one of the country's top plastic surgeons. I have an enormous house on private beachfront property, an array of expensive cars at my disposal, all the designer clothes a girl could ever wish for and more money than I could ever spend in my lifetime. I have the kind of life women dream about. I have the kind of life that women envy.

Anyone on the outside looking in would say I have the perfect life.

But they couldn't be more wrong.

AVERY

FIVE YEARS AGO...

MY FATHER WAS hosting my high school graduation party at our estate. He always threw the most lavish affairs, so my party was no exception. The house and grounds were large enough to accommodate quite a crowd of guests, and so my father invited as many people as he could. Being that he was the mayor of our city, most of the attendees were his colleagues and people I had never met before and, quite frankly, didn't care to meet.

However, I had promised my father that I would make an appearance and at least try to pretend to be enjoying myself. Little did he know that I was planning to secretly ditch early to join my classmates at Becky Weston's party. All of my friends would be at her house, and it was one of the last hurrahs before everyone started to move away for the upcoming college fall semester.

I had been accepted to several colleges, but ultimately decided to take a year off to travel Europe, much to my father's dismay. He fought me tooth and nail at first about my plans for foreign travel, but eventually I wore him down. He told me I was as bullheaded as my mother and that he never won an argument with her either. Having lost my mother at the tender age of eight, I always loved when he told me how much I reminded him of her, even if it was about our similar temperament that he seemed to disagree with.

After getting sucked into a twenty-minute conversation about economic woes with a group of older men, I was desperate to leave and join my friends. My cell phone vibrated in my hand, alerting me via text that my best friend, Samantha, had just arrived at Becky's party. Sam would be leaving for UCLA on the other side of the country soon, and so I wanted to party it up with my best friend as much as I could up until that time. We have been inseparable for almost our entire lives, and I was going to miss her like crazy.

My eyes quickly scoured the crowd and eventually settled upon my father. He was engaged with a few of his colleagues in a cloud of cigar smoke, so I figured my chance to escape had finally arrived. I sent a quick text to Sam to let her know I was leaving. As I made my way to the front door, it suddenly opened before I could reach for the knob. A group of three people stood on the other side under the yellow haze of the porch lights. I recognized Mr. and Mrs. Mason right away. They were long-time family friends, and I had met them on numerous occasions. Mr. Mason was the chief of police, and Mrs. Mason was a lawyer. Together, the Masons were a power couple at the highest rung on the social ladder. Rumor was that they controlled the entire city, including everyone who lived in it. If they wanted something taken care of, then it would be. They were the *it couple*, the couple everyone wanted to be and the couple everyone adored. My father was one of their closest friends, and he undoubtedly considered himself very fortunate about that fact.

"Avery," Mr. Mason said with a smile. "Congratulations."

"Thank you, Mr. Mason."

"Your father told us you're forgoing college and instead going to travel Europe. How exciting," Mrs. Mason said with a smile, but it didn't touch her eyes. I thought she was being sarcastic, but the woman was the queen of masking her true intent. She stepped aside and motioned to the figure in the shadows behind her. "I don't believe you've had the pleasure of meeting our son. Avery, this is Nathan."

Before that night I had only heard of Nathan Mason. In fact, I had heard so much about him, I felt like I already knew him. I knew that he had graduated high school two years earlier than his peers and then from medical school at the top of his class. I also knew that he had finished his residency under the wing of one of the best plastic surgeons in the world and was currently enrolled in one of the country's most prestigious fellowship programs.

His mother never missed an opportunity to brag about her son; and when he stepped forward into the light, I understood why. He was exceptionally handsome with a classic face, blond hair and piercing blue eyes. The dark suit he wore was impeccable, and his blue eyes glittered in the light as they landed on me. With his hand outstretched, he plastered a smile on his face that made my insides quiver. "Hello, Avery," he said with a deep timbre.

I placed my smaller hand in his and watched with rapt attention as he brought my hand up to his mouth. When his lips brushed against my knuckles, it instantly felt like a shock of electricity coursing through my body from his kiss. The party at Becky Weston's house and my friends were completely forgotten in that instant. The rest of the world seemed to blur around us as we stared at each other. I knew at that moment that it would have taken a team of wild horses to drag me away from the company of Nathan.

Mr. Mason took his wife's hand and grinned. "Let's leave these two alone to get acquainted," he said before they walked away.

Nathan stared down at me. "You weren't leaving, were you?"

I shook my head, incapable of speech at that moment.

"Good," he said with a soft smile. "Well, since you're staying, let's go somewhere a little more private, shall we?" Nathan asked.

All I could do was nod. He acted and spoke like he was from a different era, and I was truly captivated by him. I didn't even realize my hand was still in his until he pulled me along after him, leading me outside and around the back portion of the property.

With noise from the party and chirping of crickets in the background, Nathan and I spent the rest of the evening on the verandah talking and sharing stories. Even though a little over a decade separated us in age, we had a lot in common and immediately hit it off like we had known each other for years. The more I got to know him, the quicker I started to fall for him. He exuded confidence in everything he said and did, and we shared an instant connection that couldn't be explained. And when he told me about his love for traveling and how he was planning a trip to Europe, it almost felt like fate had intervened that night and brought us together.

Like most girls, I imagined my future being much like a fairytale. Who wouldn't want to meet the perfect prince and live in a big castle? Nathan was everything a woman would dream about. He was smart, funny, well educated, charming and certainly wasn't lacking in the looks department whatsoever. He was mature and ambitious, with a dream of opening his own medical practice in North Carolina. He had a bright future, and I found myself just wanting to be a part of it.

He stole a kiss at the end of the night right along with my heart.

~

After my graduation party, Nathan and I began to date exclusively. He was my first steady boyfriend, and I fell head over heels in love with him all too quickly. He soon became my everything, the center of my universe.

Nathan lavished me with expensive gifts and a love that I think I had been craving for most of my life, having lost my mother at such a young age. His parents and my father wholeheartedly encouraged the relationship and couldn't have been happier when we announced our engagement. We were married shortly thereafter and ready to spend the rest of our lives together.

It was like a real-life fairytale, but only to those on the outside looking in.

It took some time, but the façade that Nathan had carefully constructed slowly began to crumble…

AVERY

SIX MONTHS AGO...

MY BODY SLOWLY sinks into the warm water of the bathtub. As the steam billows up around me, I feel content. There is a false sense of security within the confines of the mist, and I wish I could hide there forever.

My eyes flicker to the razorblade resting between my fingertips, and I release a shaky sigh from my lips. Anyone who says suicide is the easy way out clearly never tried it. This is the hardest decision I've ever made in my life, and I'm still not even sure if it's the right choice. I just know right now it's my *only* choice. I'm tired of fighting. I'm tired of the pain. I just want to be done with it all.

Swallowing hard as tears stream down my face, I grip the blade hard and cut into my flesh. I wince as pain, which five glasses of wine obviously can't mask, shoots through my arm. I hiss through gritted teeth and manage to carve a jagged line into my left wrist. After I'm finished, the blade falls and clatters to the tile floor. I watch intently as dark red blood begins to bubble to the surface of the wound, seeping out onto my ivory skin and gently dripping to the floor. My arm grows heavier and heavier until it eventually slips from the ledge and into the bathtub. The water gradually turns from crystal blue into a deep red. *So much blood*, I think to myself.

My eyes grow heavy, and my mind begins to wander over the past few years of my life. There is a sharp line between the point of before Nathan and after Nathan. Before Nathan, I was so carefree and vivacious. And after Nathan, I became just an empty shell of my former self. He changed my life so drastically that it sometimes feels like a nightmare that I so desperately want to wake up from.

The abuse started out slowly, gradually growing worse and worse as time went on. The first time he ever hit me, we were newly dating and in the honeymoon phase, as people like to call it. In the midst of an argument, he leaned over and slapped me across the face. I'll never forget the look in his eyes. It was as if he had transformed into a whole other person entirely. He had so much anger built up in him that it seemed to exude from his every pore. It was like he had been waiting an exceedingly long time for that very moment just to snap and lash out.

After the initial shock wore off, I broke up with him, wanting to have nothing to do with him ever again. But Nathan did what he always does best — he apologized and made excuses for his behavior. He talked me into staying in a relationship with him. He told me he was going to go to anger management classes. And being so young and naïve, I truly did believe that he could change, that he *would* change. I thought therapy could fix him. Little did I know that the wrathful monster inside of him was patiently waiting for a chance to escape. There was no help for him. He couldn't be cured. He was irrevocably broken.

For the next several months after that first incident, our relationship really was perfect. Nathan never laid a hand on me again, and he pampered me like a complete princess. Many of the girls in our social circle were envious of me, and I didn't blame them for their jealousy. We were the ideal couple, and everyone wanted what we had. And for a while, I actually felt lucky to have found such a great catch.

After a while, however, his carefully constructed mask began to slip, and the cycle of abuse became a regular routine with us. We would fight and break up. Nathan would apologize, and I would take him back. I didn't know it then, but somehow I had unknowingly allowed him to slither his way into my life and control every aspect of it. I no longer had any friends or family to turn to. He made sure that he was the only one I could turn to. And so I did.

We soon became engaged. And before I could even blink, my father and Nathan's parents were planning the wedding for us. It became an arranged marriage in every sense of the word. I didn't even have a say in what kind of flower arrangements or even what type of cake I wanted. And the more I protested, the quicker the wedding date got bumped up. They didn't realize that I wasn't suffering from a simple case of cold feet. I was afraid to marry Nathan. In fact, I was downright terrified.

My life felt like it was tied to a speeding runaway train that I couldn't stop or control no matter how hard I tried. I pleaded with my dad that I didn't want to marry Nathan, but he wouldn't hear of it. He wanted the marriage to take place, saying it would solidify my spot in the social world with the phenomenal reputation of the Mason family. And deep down I knew my father's real reasoning was because it would benefit him to have ties to the Masons to further his career in the political world. With feeling like everyone was against me, I stood idly by while everyone around me took the reins to control my future.

After Nathan and I were married, everything changed for the worst. He demanded power over every aspect of my life. The physical and verbal abuse and threats steadily became more frequent, more sinister. He was mean and outright cruel at times. I became one of those battered women that I had heard about and had always promised myself I would never become. And no matter how many times I tried to leave, he always found me. I would come back to even more abuse, worse than the last, as punishment for leaving him. My dreams of a brighter future, a future without him were always quickly extinguished and disintegrated a million times over. And then finally...I just couldn't do it anymore. I didn't want to run any longer. I just wanted to be free.

"*Avery, what the fuck have you done!*" Nathan roars as he runs into the bathroom, coming to a halting stop at the side of the bathtub.

His voice shakes me from my thoughts and chills me to the bone. The only thing I can think about is that he's home early. He wasn't supposed to be home this early.

Feeling too weak to move, I stare through heavy-lidded eyes as Nathan bends down and appears in my line of vision. Weariness takes over, and my head slumps forward onto my chest. With the force of the movement, my body starts to slip down into the water. Nathan quickly grabs me and pulls me out of the bathtub. He positions me down on the floor and uses a nearby towel for a makeshift tourniquet on my wrist. "What have you done?" he asks again in disbelief, his voice cracking.

I can hear the heartbreaking sadness in his voice, and for a moment I think he's going to cry. I've never seen Nathan cry before or show any other emotion other than anger or hatred. I can't help but wonder in that moment that, if I live, maybe he will change. Maybe he will start to love me the way he's supposed to love me. Then again, he's fooled me so many times before that I don't let myself hold onto that notion for very long.

His voice sounds so far away as he says, "Stay awake, Avery! Do you hear me? You are not going to die!" He shakes me so hard that my teeth knock together. "You are not leaving me!" he yells.

I almost have the urge to laugh. Even when I'm on the verge of death he's still threatening and trying to control me. I realize in that moment that this is why I'm leaving. His anger and abuse just became too much for me. A person can only handle so much before they break, and I think I reached my breaking point years ago. Everything after that point was just pure and utter torture.

I close my eyes, and the world around me vanishes into a black void. I know he's performing CPR, but I can barely feel the air being pushed into my weak lungs.

I'm numb.

I'm at peace.

I'm finally free.

AVERY

PRESENT DAY...

I STARE AT my reflection in the foggy bathroom mirror. As the overhead fan gradually pulls away some of the steam from the hot shower I took moments earlier, my reflection becomes less distorted. The fluffy white towel wrapped around me is in striking contrast to the multi-colored bruises littering my exposed skin. Pink, red, purple, blue, green and yellow spots mark my arms, chest and legs like cheetah print. Nathan is usually very methodical and careful in the way he hits me; therefore, he rarely touches my face. He's calculated and smart in that sense, because he knows that doing so could lead to questions...questions he wouldn't want to answer to anyone — especially the police.

Before I met Nathan, I was a free spirit that my father was constantly trying to rein in and tame. He allowed me to rebel to a certain extent growing up, knowing that I was, for the most part, just being a typical teenager. However, every day I spend with Nathan I feel that spirit slowly breaking. I wear a constant frown when I'm alone in remembrance of how miserable I really am. Most days I feel like I can't even breathe. It's as if he is literally sucking the life out of me.

I'm not totally broken...not yet anyway, but I don't doubt for one second that Nathan isn't trying to break me down completely. It's only a matter of time until my former self totally disappears, and left in her place will be a lifeless doll without any will or conviction of her own. He likes control, and controlling me seems to be his most crucial conquest in life.

My eyes fall to the jagged scar on the inside of my left wrist. Nathan was able to save me that night no matter how hard I fought to die. After my botched suicide attempt, I was placed on involuntary psychiatric hold and eventually committed to a hospital. I spent forty-five days on mind-numbing drugs under Nathan's authority and control. The memory of him shoving a piece of paper in my face while I could barely hold my own head up still haunts me to this day.

"All I have to do is sign this, and you'll be committed to a psych ward for the rest of your life," he had said. *"Imagine what it will do to your father's reputation. I'll tell every newspaper in the city that you were a drug addict, a whore, mentally unstable. A scandal like that could ruin everything he's worked so hard for."* And then for good measure, he'd added, *"I'll take everything away from you, Avery. You will have nothing. I will destroy you and your entire family. Try to remember that the next time you even think about hurting yourself or running away."*

Nathan always knew the right things to say to make me stay. If he threatened my family, it was like a stake straight through my heart. His threats knew no bounds, and he used them often. My father was in the midst of preparing to run for governor, and I knew how important the campaign was going to be to him. My sister, Allison, was just getting her life together with a new husband and baby. I had always protected Allison no matter what, and nothing would ever change that.

Feeling like I had no other choice, I went along with my husband's plans. But going home to Nathan was like returning to a life sentence in prison. I would have to die before he would ever let me go. And even though deep down I wanted to keep fighting and trying to run away like I had in the past, I just stopped. I found myself slowly dwindling away into someone else, someone weak and docile, someone I never thought I would become. And as long as I'm with Nathan, nothing and no one would ever change that.

Snapping myself out of my reverie, I continue on with my strict routine for the day. After waking up at three every morning, I have to shower, get ready, make sure the house is spotless and have his breakfast ready all before five-thirty.

While running a brush through my long reddish-brown hair, I check my subtle makeup one last time in the mirror. Nathan likes my hair to be down and my eye makeup to be in neutral colors, nothing too dark. And even though years ago I would have rebelled against him, now I just appease him to save myself from the additional pain and anguish. Trying to commit suicide changed me. That last little bit of fight inside of me died, and I wish more than anything that I could get it back. I know the old Avery is in there somewhere, but she has yet to make an appearance when I need her most.

I pull on a pair of dark blue scrubs and instantly feel slightly better. I have been volunteering at the local hospital for the past six years. It actually started out as a punishment from my father when I broke curfew one too many times, but I eventually grew to love it and have been volunteering ever since. I mostly visit with kids who have cancer, and bringing a smile to their face helps me to hurt a little less inside. It gives me a purpose, and most days it's my only reason to get out of bed in the morning.

After Nathan and I were married, I had to fight him tooth and nail to allow me to keep volunteering. He eventually agreed with certain stipulations, and it wasn't without consequences if his rules were broken. I'm on an extremely stringent schedule. I have to be home at a certain time with the house clean and dinner started before he gets home. And if I'm ever late…well, let's just say there's hell to pay. I live my life by the ticking of a clock, my eyes constantly glued to the time. A deep-rooted fear has been instilled within me if I ever run late for anything.

Some days I ask myself if it's worth the punishment, worth the bruises and worth the heartache. But every time I see a child's face light up when I bring them their favorite snack or read them a story, it makes it all worthwhile. And one small spark of light breaking through the darkness that is my life allows me to continue on for another day. And that is all I am able to do right now — find one small reason every day to carry on.

Before I leave the bathroom, I reach into a drawer in the sink cabinet and produce a prescription of anxiety medication. I pop a pill into my mouth and swallow it with a cup of water from the sink. It isn't a miracle drug, but it does help...especially on the bad days.

Tiptoeing into the bedroom so that I don't disturb Nathan, I grab a beige cardigan from the closet and slip it on. Even on the hottest days of the year, I wear a cardigan to hide the bruises on my arms. It's easier than attempting to cover them with makeup every morning when I already have so many other things to do before he wakes up.

I walk into the living room and adjust the throw pillows and rearrange the magazines on the coffee table. I sweep the tiled and hardwood floors, inspecting each room as I go. My hands move quickly to make sure everything is in its place before making my way to the front door. I grab the morning newspaper and place it on the large island in the middle of the kitchen. Then I glance at the breakfast schedule Nathan has posted by the fridge. Today is Monday. He wants two over-easy eggs, one piece of multi-grain toast with light butter, an orange cut up into quarters and half a glass of two-percent milk. I get to work on making his breakfast and barely notice when he comes into the kitchen and sits down at the island. He doesn't say anything; just opens the paper to the business and financial section like every morning.

After arranging the eggs, toast and orange on a large plate, I place the food in front of him. He smells fresh from his shower, and his hair is still slightly damp. I nervously glance at him as he inspects the food before I turn around to grab his glass of milk.

Sometimes my anxiety medicine makes my mind a little foggy.

Sometimes I forget things...like this morning when I forgot how Nathan wanted his eggs, and I made them scrambled instead of over-easy. I don't realize my mistake until I hear the plate shattering against the floor beside my feet. I jump and freeze.

Nathan is up and out of his chair in an instant. He grabs my wrist and whirls me around to face him, his blue eyes piercing into me. "How difficult is it to make eggs the way I want them made?" he yells.

To a normal person, eggs are eggs whether they are scrambled or over easy. But to Nathan, this mistake means insolence and defiance. His hand clamps down on my wrist and the back of my neck as he pushes me to the floor. My face is less than an inch from the jagged pieces of fine china. "I should make you clean this up with your mouth," he says through gritted teeth.

I close my eyes and try to calm my breathing. And then I say the only thing that will make things somewhat better. "I'm sorry."

His fingers tighten their grip, and his thumbnail digs into the scar on my wrist. I wince in pain. "I don't think you are, *Avery*." He says my name as if it leaves a bad taste in his mouth.

"I am. I'm sorry," I plead, cringing at how weak and compliant I sound. *When did I become this person?* I think to myself.

After a few moments, he finally releases me. Standing, he straightens his white linen shirt and tie. "Now I'll have to stop somewhere on the way to work to get breakfast, and I'll probably be late. Some of us have a *real* job to go to in the morning, Avery. Some of us have people that depend on us. Some of us actually *work* for a living. I don't get to volunteer like you do. I make real money to keep you in this nice home."

I stay hunched over, afraid to move, afraid to speak.

He sighs loudly, walks away and slips on his suit jacket. "I have to go." His footsteps pause halfway to the front door. "I expect this mess to be cleaned up before you leave."

I don't move until I hear the door close and his car pull out of the driveway. With trembling hands, I grab a small broom and dustpan from the pantry and clean up the broken plate and food. I scrub any remnants left on the floor and cabinets with some dish soap and a rag. When I'm satisfied that the kitchen is completely spotless, I grab my purse and head out the door.

I climb into my white Mercedes-Benz and snack on a granola bar on the way to the hospital. My neck and wrist are killing me, but the pain reminds me that I'm still alive and I'm still fighting...even if it doesn't feel like it sometimes.

All the tension in my body seems to dissipate the moment I pull into the parking lot. A lot of people hate Mondays, but I love them. After a weekend in hell, Monday is a reprieve for me, a light at the end of a very dark tunnel. Even if it's only an eight-hour escape, it's better than nothing.

As I park the car, the corners of my lips pull up into a grin, something that rarely appears on my face anymore. But when I'm here, I can't help but feel a sense of peace somehow and a sense of worth. This is the only good thing I have in my life. Without it, I would probably shrivel up and die.

I step out of the car, checking out my reflection in the window. I adjust my cardigan and make sure the sleeves are pulled completely down to my hands. When you constantly have something to hide, it becomes easier over time. Everything becomes habitual, natural.

Grabbing my purse and lanyard with an ID badge that has *volunteer* emblazoned on the bottom of it along with my photo, I make my way into the hospital with a smile on my face.

~

I KNOW I shouldn't pick favorites, but out of all the children in the pediatrics wing of the hospital, Jacob is my favorite. His father isn't in the picture, and his mother rarely comes to visit. It's not because she doesn't want to see him or doesn't love him, but the hospital bills are piling up, and she's busy trying to hold down two full-time jobs. I know Jacob misses his mom, and a lot of times I find him alone and crying in his room. But I'm always able to turn his frown upside down even if it's only for an hour out of the day. I suppose that's why I focus a lot of my attention on him at the end of my shift before I leave. Making him happy makes me happy. I just wish the happiness I feel when I'm around him would stay with me a little bit longer after I've gone home.

Jacob just turned six a few months ago and was diagnosed with leukemia shortly after that. I know the chemotherapy is taking its toll on his body; hence, his extended hospital stay, but he always has a smile for me. I knock on his door and enter the room. He's staring out the window with a frown on his face.

"Jacob," I whisper.

He turns, and his freckled face instantly lights up, completely melting my heart. "Did you bring it?" he asks with a big grin. He's missing his two front teeth, which makes him look even more adorable.

"Bring what?" I ask, pretending like I totally forgot.

His face falls a little. And then when I pull the chocolate pudding cup from behind my back, his smile instantly returns. "You didn't forget. You're the best, Avery!" he says as I hand him his favorite snack in the whole wide world and a plastic spoon.

I had promised the snack after a particularly rough chemotherapy session this morning. At least once a week, I sit with Jacob during his therapy. I hold his hand and comfort him if his mom can't be there. He's usually pretty stubborn about letting anyone else be around him when he's not feeling well, so I consider it an honor that the kid likes me. I have to say the feeling is definitely mutual.

Jacob digs into the pudding, eating it greedily. I smile, because it's impossible not to around this kid. "How are you feeling?" I ask.

He shrugs and puts another spoonful of pudding into his mouth. "Little better. I guess."

I don't force the issue. He has his good days and bad days. If he wants to talk, I let him talk. But most of the time he just wants to focus on his mom, sports and videogames. "So is your mom visiting you tonight?"

He nods emphatically. "Yeah. She said she's bringing me that new game I wanted."

"The one with the *Ninja Turtles*?"

Jacob nods again.

"Awesome!" I exclaim. "You're going to have to show me all the different characters and levels tomorrow."

He grins. A spoonful of pudding pauses just before it reaches his mouth, and his brows knit together as if he's thinking about something very serious. Then he turns to me and says, "You know, you're, like, the coolest girl I know, Avery."

"Well, that must make you the coolest boy then," I say, tapping on the brim of his baseball cap. He's been wearing that hat every single day since his hair fell out. I know he wants to look like a normal boy on the outside even if he doesn't feel normal on the inside.

After Jacob finishes his snack, I toss it into the trash. Then I hand him a napkin so he can wipe the chocolate from his face.

We spend the next half hour talking about comic book characters, cartoons, movies and his crush on the girl across the hall. Her name is Bailey, and she's as cute as a button. She suffers from the same affliction as Jacob, and they sometimes go to their chemotherapy sessions together, talking about everything under the sun except for the hospital and cancer, of course.

Yawning, Jacob asks, "Avery, will you read my favorite story?"

My eyes dart to my watch. I'm going to be late getting home if I don't hurry, but I could never say no to Jacob. Spending time with him is one of the very few things in my life that actually makes me forget about the sorrow looming over me. "Sure. There's nothing I'd rather do," I say, and it's the truth.

I grab a storybook about knights, princesses and dragons in a far off land, sit down in a chair and begin to read. It doesn't take long before Jacob is fast asleep. He never makes it the whole way to the end. One of these days I'll have to start from the end and read to the beginning just so he can hear the ending.

Standing, I quietly put the book away on the shelf. Then I turn to

Jacob, and pull the covers up to his chest and fix his pillow so that he's more comfortable. Smiling down at him, I study his little face and how innocent and peaceful he looks. Sighing contentedly, I start to walk around the bed towards the door.

When I look up, my steps slow and then come to a complete stop. A doctor in a white lab coat stands in the doorway, leaning against the doorjamb. His dark gaze is fixated on me as a heart-stopping grin slowly spreads across his face. "Hello," he says with a rich timbre to his voice.

I've never seen him in the hospital before, and I'm sure I would definitely remember a face like his. He's brutally handsome with a mop of shaggy dark brown hair that matches the color of his eyes. He looks like a doctor that belongs on a soap opera in California rather than here in Nags Head, North Carolina.

"The nurses claim you are the only one who can get Jacob to take his medicine and go for therapy. You must be really good with kids." He walks into the room and stops a few feet away from me. He's tall, towering several inches over my five-foot-five frame. "Do you have any children of your own?" he asks.

His question brings back haunting memories that I have tried so hard to push down deep into my subconscious. However, they always manage to bubble back up to the surface. I was pregnant a little over two years ago. I didn't even know I was…until I lost it. As a result of the physical abuse from Nathan, I had a miscarriage. I remember bleeding profusely on the bathroom floor while waiting for him to decide if he should call an ambulance or not. I was covered in bruises, cuts and scrapes, and he didn't want anyone to find out what he had been doing to me. Eventually he decided to call in a favor from a fellow doctor — someone who wouldn't ask questions and who ultimately didn't.

There was no mourning for the baby I lost. Nathan wouldn't allow it. The whole incident was swept under the rug and never talked about again. Devastated and heartbroken, I vowed to never get pregnant again. When I think about having kids with Nathan, I get a sick feeling in the pit of my stomach. I've been on a strict birth control regimen since that day, unbeknownst to my husband. I would never want to bring children into this world with him as their father. I wouldn't wish my life on my worst enemy, let alone an innocent child.

Giving myself a mental shake, I glance up and realize the doctor is staring at me. Under his gaze, I feel exposed as if he's looking right through me to my very soul. His question still lingers in the air, and his left brow quirks up as he waits patiently for my answer. When I say nothing, his eyebrows dip in confusion. "Are you okay?" he asks softly.

As he takes another step forward, I can now see that his eyes are dark chocolate with flecks of gold. He's extremely attractive with strong features, and I can't force myself to look away. Long forgotten need and desire suddenly flood my senses as a shiver runs down my spine, and my fingers itch to touch the stubble lining his strong jaw. I'm very attracted to him, and it scares the hell out of me. It's too dangerous...for both of us. *If Nathan would ever find out —*. I shudder at the thought, and it feels like I've been doused with a bucket of cold water. I know that my only option now is to ignore him. I'm very skilled at pushing people away; and, unfortunately, it's one of the things I'm extremely good at these days.

Smiling shyly, so as to not come off as a total bitch, I give him a small wave goodbye and leave the room hastily. I have to force myself not to run down the hall. Only after I'm a few rooms away do I slowly release a breath that I wasn't aware I was holding. I place a hand over my hammering heart. I'm completely unnerved and trying to get my bearings when I bump right into the back of Rosie, one of the nurses. "Sorry," I apologize quickly.

Rosie turns with a big grin on her face. She's an older woman with more salt than pepper in her hair, rich brown skin and a personality so bright it puts the sun to shame. I've known her the entire time I've been volunteering at the hospital and consider her a friend...

maybe my only friend. "You look flushed, Avery. Are you feeling okay?"

My hand fans my suddenly warm face. I'm sure my cheeks are bright red, and that thought makes me blush even more. "Yeah. I'm just feeling very warm. Is the air conditioning broken again?"

"Nope." She shakes her head and chuckles. "You know, all the nurses seem to be complaining about it being so hot in here, and I think I know the reason behind it." When I raise a brow in confusion, she continues. "Did you just talk to *Dr. Dreamy*? All the nurses are getting flustered over the new doctor in the hospital today."

I realize she's talking about the doctor that was in Jacob's room... the doctor I just completely ignored. "His last name isn't really Dreamy, is it?" I ask.

She laughs. "No, but it should be." She leans in close as if she's about to tell me a secret. "His name is Max Harrison. He's the new pediatrician, and he just transferred here from Chicago." Her eyes glance over my shoulder, and a big grin creeps onto her face. "Speak of the devil," she mutters.

I turn in the direction she's looking and see Dr. Harrison standing in the hallway. His eyes are glued on me, and it looks like he's trying to decide if he should come and talk to me or not. I quickly look back to Rosie, and I can feel the blush rising in my cheeks once again.

"Yep. You're exhibiting the same symptoms as all the other girls today," she says with a knowing look. "If I was about twenty years younger..." Her voice trails off, and then she chuckles and shakes her head. "Too bad you're married, Avery. I bet you wish you weren't," she says with a wink.

"You have no idea," I mumble under my breath. When Rosie asks me to repeat what I said, I simply tell her, "I have to go." I glance at the clock on the wall nervously. I don't want to be late getting home, especially not after what happened this morning.

I run to the nurses' station, grab my purse from under the desk and hightail it out to the parking lot. As I walk quickly to my car, I can't help but question the mixed emotions flowing through me. Dr. Harrison is the new pediatrician. That means I will be seeing a whole lot more of him. I have mixed feelings about that fact. I'm happy that the hospital has a new doctor, but I'm confused and apprehensive about the way I reacted to him. I haven't been attracted to a man in a long time. In all actuality, I've been fearful of almost every man I've come into contact with over the past few years. My aversion to being touched and to men in general stems from years of abuse by the hands of my husband, but there's just something about Dr. Harrison that makes me feel like I could possibly trust him.

Pushing the thought aside, I climb into the car and start the engine. The clock on the radio flickers on, and I freeze. I'm running ten minutes behind. Gripping the steering wheel tightly, I coast the car out of the parking lot. I just hope that I make it home before Nathan.

MAX

I NEVER REALLY believed in love at first sight. My father always preached to me growing up that he knew the moment he saw my mother that they would be together forever. They've been married for almost thirty years, so maybe there is some truth in what he told me.

I'd never had a moment like that where you just look at someone and feel an instant connection and imagine a future with them even though you don't know the first thing about them...that is, until I saw *her*.

I had been on my way to a patient's room when I'd first noticed her in the hallway. My heart skipped a beat, and I almost tripped after my legs suddenly forgot how to work. She was completely out-of-this-world gorgeous with a kind smile that would melt even the hardest of hearts instantly. That day I watched her from a safe distance as she interacted with the children, and it seemed like she had a kind soul to match her sweet smile. Since then, I've only caught glimpses of her in the halls, but never had the chance to say hi and introduce myself.

I've only been at the hospital for a week, but with orientation, meeting the other doctors and staff and getting acquainted with the layout of the hospital, I had barely gotten into the swing of things until today. I'd been kind of admiring her from afar, always hoping for an opportunity to run into her. And when I finally got my chance to talk to her today, I blew it.

I replay our encounter in my mind over and over. I wanted her to say something, anything really. I had an idea of what her voice would sound like in my mind, and I had been dying for a chance to finally interact with her. And then with complete and utter surprise, I watched the pretty brunette grin and wave awkwardly before practically running out of the room without saying a single word.

Perplexed, I stand frozen in place. Did I say something to offend her? I can't remember saying anything beyond normal conversation. But the look in her eyes when I had asked if she had any kids told me that there was a story behind them. I sigh and shake my head. Maybe I was just being too forward.

Finally getting the chance to meet her face to face did something to me. From a distance she had seemed almost like a mirage. Up close and personal she is everything I had hoped she would be and so much more. Sure, on the outside, she's obviously beautiful with long reddish-brown hair framing her pretty face and bangs ending just above a set of stunning blue-gray eyes. But in those eyes I saw something that made my heart pump a little faster. It was as if with one glance into them I could see an open book to her soul. One glance and we connected on some kind of level that I can't explain even though I just experienced it. A myriad of emotions appeared in that one look, and I instantly recognized one — a deep and immutable sadness. Even with the smile on her face, I saw right through her. It's as if she's wearing an impenetrable mask for everyone else's benefit; but, for some reason, I can see through it.

Her guard was down in Jacob's room, and I was lucky enough to catch a glimpse of her in her element, relaxed and natural. I watched her while she tucked him in, her delicate hands pulling up his covers and fluffing his pillow to make him comfortable. And then she looked down at him with the most serene and empathetic look. With the sun cascading through the window at her back, she looked like an angel standing in a heavenly beam of light. It gave me chills.

Shaking my head to clear my thoughts, I venture out into the hallway. The girl's back is to me, and she's standing with a nurse named Rosie. I feel the strong urge to call out to her, but I don't even know her name. I was hoping that her ID badge would reveal what I was looking for, but it just designated that she's a volunteer with a photo. Anyone willing to volunteer their time in a hospital must have a heart of gold, and I didn't doubt for one second that hers was made of twenty-four karats.

I catch Rosie's stare, and her lips move as she says something. And then the girl suddenly turns and looks right at me. I feel the nervousness all over again, and I feel embarrassed that they clearly caught me staring. I want to go talk to her again, but something is holding me back. I'm suddenly feeling very nervous and awkward, and those are not typical feelings that I get around anyone, especially women. I'm not bragging, but let's just say I've never had a problem getting a girlfriend. Usually I am the one getting asked out. But when I'm around this girl, I feel like a bundle of nerves, tongue-tied and lucky to even remember my own name.

Before I can make another move or decide what I want to do, the girl looks at the clock on the wall, grabs her purse and flies out the door.

"Damn," I mutter. I definitely blew my chances today. I've never seen her interacting with any of the staff except for Rosie. Maybe they're friends and Rosie can tell me about this mystery girl. I'm desperate to know more about her, and I really want to put a name to the pretty face. I glance down to the paperwork in my hand. After my rounds are done, I'll find Rosie. Maybe she can shed some light on this situation that I feel I'm knee-deep in already.

AFTER MY SHIFT is over, I walk to the nurses' station in search of the one person who can give me the answers I need. Rosie glances up as I approach. "Dr. Harrison," she acknowledges.

I first met Rosie in my orientation several days ago. She has a reputation from all the doctors for being phenomenal at her job. Besides the praise, what stuck out to me the most were the bright and colorful scrubs she had on that day and every day after that. Today, she's wearing bright green scrubs with a Scooby Doo print. I bet the kids just love them. "Do you know the name of the girl that volunteers here?" I ask her.

She lifts her gaze from a stack of papers and says, "You're going to have to be more specific. There are several volunteers, Doc."

"I saw you with her earlier. She has long dark hair." *And the most gorgeous blue-gray eyes I have ever seen*, I think to myself. " You two were talking just before she left for the day."

Her face scrunches up with a big grin, accentuating the wrinkles around her eyes. "Oh! You mean Avery Mason."

Avery. The name suits her. "Is she mute?" I blurt out.

Rosie chuckles. "No, Dr. Harrison, she is not mute."

My curiosity peaks. I wonder why she wouldn't say even one word to me. Maybe she's just extremely shy. "How long has she been volunteering here?"

"Oh, several years now I suppose. Since she was in high school." She taps her pen against the desk and smiles thoughtfully. "She's a total sweetheart."

She didn't need to tell me what I already knew. Just from seeing her in the hallways and with the kids I know she has a great personality.

"She's married," Rosie says cautiously. "But not happily," she adds in a quiet and tentative tone.

I raise a brow. "Did she tell you that?"

"No." Rosie hesitates, and I can see a pained look on her face.

"She didn't have to." I'm curious as to what she means, but she quickly adds, "My shift is almost over. We can talk more tomorrow if you'd like, Doc."

I nod. "Nice to see you again, Rosie."

"Same here."

My legs feel heavy as I walk towards the exit. I'm no longer knee-deep in the situation. I'm barely keeping my head above the quicksand. I didn't know Avery was married. In fact, I didn't even think to look for a ring on her finger. I had been so mesmerized by being in the same room with her, that common sense just went right out the window.

As I get in my car, Rosie's words come back to me. She said Avery's not happily married. I wonder what she meant by that. I shake my head. It's not as if I even know Avery well enough to pursue anything with her, and I certainly don't need a workplace romance during my first week here. I sigh and scrub a hand down my face. In spite of that, there's just something about her that makes it seem there's more to her than meets the eye, and I desperately want to figure her out.

AVERY

MY STOMACH DROPS when I see Nathan's black BMW sitting in the driveway, and I curse the construction on the highway that delayed my trip home. I can feel my heart attempting to leap out of my chest as I park my white Mercedes beside his car. With trembling hands, I open my purse and find my anxiety medication. I pop two pills in my mouth and swallow hard. I can barely stand when I get out of the car. My legs are shaking as I attempt to make my way to the house. I stare at my watch. Every second that ticks by will only make it worse. Forcing myself to hurry, I will my legs to move faster up the steps to the front door.

Plastering a phony smile on my face, I walk into the living room where I know he'll be waiting. Nathan is sitting in his favorite leather recliner with his eyes glued to the clock on the wall. His three-piece tailored black suit looks impeccable, as always. The charcoal-colored tie is pulled loose from around his neck, and the first three buttons of his white linen shirt are unbuttoned. His blond hair is disheveled as if he spent some time running his hands through it just moments earlier. His expression remains impassive as he states, "You're twenty minutes late."

I can't tell yet if he's angry or very angry. There is a big difference when it comes to Nathan, and it can mean the difference between letting things slide or getting hit. "I-I ran into s-some traffic on the way home from the h-hospital," I stammer nervously.

He stands, and those light blue eyes that I have come to fear so much pierce right through me. "Maybe volunteering at the hospital isn't such a good idea after all, Avery."

Panic begins to set in. He can't take that away from me. It's the only reprieve I have from this glass and metal prison he calls our home. "It won't happen again," I whisper.

"Speak up!" he barks.

"It won't happen again," I say, louder this time.

He nods and walks over to me. I resist the urge to flinch under his gaze and touch as he leans in and gently kisses my forehead. "It better not," he warns. He pulls back and stares at me for a few seconds. "Well, I guess dinner is out of the question since you're —." He pauses and checks his watch. "Twenty-three minutes behind. You're lucky I'm in the mood for Chinese tonight."

"I'll get the menu," I suggest, thankful for the excuse to get away from him.

"Change first into something a little more suitable," he says as he walks into the kitchen.

Nathan has a particular taste for the clothes I wear, and scrubs and sneakers are definitely not part of that particular taste. I rush into the bedroom and change into a beige shift dress. My hands are shaking as I zip up the back. He hasn't punished me for being late... yet. I close my eyes and take a deep breath and say a little prayer that everything stays calm between us until he goes to bed.

When I walk into the kitchen, Nathan is at the breakfast bar pouring a glass of wine. His eyes boldly peruse the length of my body. "Much better," he remarks before taking a sip from his glass.

My lips curl into a tentative smile, and I pull open a drawer to search for the menu. I try to steady my trembling hand as I offer him the tri-folded piece of paper. Instead of grabbing the menu, he grips my wrist and pulls me roughly against him. He stares down at me, his index finger gently grazing my cheek.

I swallow hard and wonder if, or perhaps when, he's going to punish me. Being with Nathan feels like constantly being trapped in a small room with a venomous snake. You never know when it's going to strike, but you know it will eventually happen and that it will hurt.

"When are you going to let me make you an appointment?" he asks. I cringe inwardly. He always brings up the discussion of me having plastic surgery. In fact, it's one of his favorite topics. His eyes dart around my face as he silently picks out all of my imperfections that only he can see, that he always sees when he looks at me. "We could start small with some Botox around your eyes and mouth." His eyes drag down my form. "Definitely need some lipo," he mutters before sighing heavily. "It would take a lot of work, but I could make you better, Avery. I could make you beautiful."

His words slice right through me, and I squeeze my eyes tight to force myself not to cry. Nathan hasn't paid me a compliment since we first started dating when he used to tell me I was the most beautiful girl he had ever met. Since we've been married, his critiques of me get worse and worse. I would never go under anyone's knife, especially not his. I know I'm not perfect, but I used to be secure with my body image. I used to have a sense of self-worth and feel pretty. Now I find myself constantly keeping an eye on my weight, although I never fluctuate more than a few pounds, and the doctor tells me I should actually gain a few. And every now and then, when I'm in front of a mirror, I catch myself absentmindedly looking for the so-called flaws that Nathan sees on my face. My insecurities keep growing and adding up every time he brings up how much work I need to be his version of beautiful.

His fingers drift down to my left wrist, and I inhale sharply. "I wish you would let me take care of this scar. I could make a clean revision, making it more consistent and almost invisible when it heals." His thumb absentmindedly trails over the raised skin. "It would be as if it never even happened."

Yes, he would like that, wouldn't he? Everything is better, in his eyes, when it's brushed under the rug. I like the scar. It reminds me that I survived even if sometimes I wish I hadn't.

When I don't respond, he eventually releases his grip on me and says, "Just order me my usual. I'm going to drink my wine out on the deck until the food arrives."

I nod as he walks away. I release a long, shaky sigh, unaware that I had been holding my breath. Closing my eyes, I clutch the granite countertop. I only have to make it through a few more hours until he goes to sleep. I just hope he keeps the monster inside of him at bay until then.

AVERY

WE EAT IN silence. Nathan's phone buzzes for the fifth time in the past several minutes, and he glances at the screen. A slow smile spreads across his face. I wonder what or perhaps who is making him smile, but then I decide I don't care. I wouldn't be surprised if Nathan is cheating on me...again. I've never had concrete proof of an affair, but there have been several women I've been suspicious of over the years. Most of them have been his numerous secretaries, each one more stunning than the last. I have heard his colleagues make jokes about the revolving door to his office when it comes to Nathan's employees. He changes secretaries more often than his underwear, and I don't doubt that he fired them after growing tired of them sexually.

In the past several months since my suicide attempt, he's barely touched me in the bedroom. I'm sure someone else is fulfilling his needs. Nathan isn't the type to just not want sex. I only wish I knew who was sleeping with my husband so I could write her a thank you note. Feeling his hands on me, the same hands that hurt me, makes me die a little inside. I can't find pleasure with him when he continues to give me so much pain.

He puts down his chopsticks and stares at me from across the table. His smile doesn't waver, and I can't believe my good fortune. I broke one of his *rules* by being late, and he's actually being pleasant. "I forgot to tell you that I've been asked to be a guest speaker and presenter at a national medical conference in Seattle. I'll be gone for a week."

I can't stop the surprise from registering on my face, but I quickly cover up the emotion with a forced frown. All I want to do is jump for joy, but I learned a long time ago how to fake my emotions when it comes to Nathan. He never sees the true me. *Never.*

"I'm catching a flight Friday afternoon and won't be returning until next Saturday."

I just have to make it through the rest of this week, and then Nathan will be gone for seven whole days. On the outside I appear sad, but inside I'm ecstatic. In the back of my mind, I have been planning for an opportunity like this for such a long time — an opportunity to try to leave him...for good this time. He's been limiting his trips for out-of-state clients and watching me like a hawk since I tried ending my life six months ago. But I've been doing everything I could lately to get him to trust me all in preparation for a chance like this.

He places his elbows on the table and steeples his hands, placing his chin on top of them. "I trust that you won't stray while I'm gone," he says with narrowed eyes trained on me.

I stare back at him. I don't know if he's implying I'm going to leave him again or if I'm going to cheat on him. Perhaps both. Nathan has made it very clear as to what would happen if I ever looked at a man, talked to a man or, god forbid, ever touched another man. I can remember when our former pool man flirted with me one day. I wouldn't even call it flirting as much as just a casual hello, a smile and a wink. His actions seemed so harmless to me at the time, but Nathan saw something very devious in those small gestures. The next morning Nathan beat the man so badly that he was in a coma for almost a month. Whatever anger he had left after the beating he took out on me. The lies I spun for the emergency room staff flowed freely while I sat under Nathan's stern gaze. *"I fell down a flight of stairs."* I don't know if the ER doctor necessarily believed me, but Nathan's reputation and his money were very persuasive. I know firsthand that anything and anyone, for that matter, can be bought.

And as for leaving him, he's also made it very clear as to the consequences for my actions. I remember the first time I thought I could run away. After we were married for only a few months, I decided I couldn't take any more of the verbal and physical abuse. I packed a suitcase and hopped a bus at the nearest station. I was halfway across the state when the bus I was in got pulled over by several police cars. Nathan's father is the chief of police, and Nathan filed a missing and endangered person report the moment he discovered me gone. His father put all of the department's manpower into finding me. After my dramatic capture, I endured all I could with Nathan for weeks until I was once again yearning to run away.

I have tried everything imaginable over the past few years to leave him, but nothing has worked. And when I made a last-ditch effort to leave this world physically, even that plan failed in the end. Staring down at the jagged scar on the inside of my wrist, I push my memories back down where they belong. "You can trust me," I say finally.

He clasps his hands together and nods once. "Well, I'm going to bed. I have an early meeting and surgeries scheduled all day." He stands and walks over to me. I don't even have time to react when he suddenly grabs my face roughly, crushing his fingers into my cheeks and jaw until I whimper in pain. He glares down at me and says through gritted teeth, "I expect you to be on time tomorrow evening, Avery. Don't. Disappoint. Me." He enunciates the last three words, making them sound like a threat. Then he releases me and disappears up the stairs to our bedroom.

My fingertips gently massage my sore jaw as I blink back tears from the pain. I cautiously wiggle my mouth back and forth. My jaw isn't broken, but it hurts like hell. And here I actually thought he wasn't mad about me being late or perhaps had forgotten all about it.

I should have known better. Nathan never forgets, and he most certainly never forgives.

After a few seconds of composing myself, a sigh of relief washes over me knowing that he's sleeping in the other room. One more day down. And that is exactly how I live — day by day. I can't look into the future, because all I see is darkness. There is no light at the end of my tunnel. Not yet anyway.

My muscles slowly begin to relax. I'm always so tense around him, constantly on my toes, anxious and waiting for his next move. Without finishing the rest of my dinner, I stand and clean up the dining room and kitchen until it's spotless. Nathan wouldn't have it any other way. Being one of the country's best plastic surgeons, he spends every day making people—mostly celebrities—look perfect. And in that liking of perfection in his work, he expects it at home and everywhere else in his life. If only he practiced that perfection with his own personality.

After grabbing an afghan from the couch, I slip out the back door and onto the deck that overlooks the ocean. The smell of salt water fills my lungs as the soft breeze blows my long hair off of my shoulders. I close my eyes and picture myself in a different place where there is no pain, no sorrow. It's a short-lived bliss, a chance to forget my life for a moment. But the black cloud lingering overhead is always there, always threatening to come down around me at any moment.

I wrap the afghan around myself before walking down the stairs and onto the wooden pathway that leads right to the sandy beach. This stretch of beach is private, and there are only five houses along it. The house to the right belongs to a retired and quite famous restaurant owner. He's hardly ever home, however. The house on the left at the end of the row has been empty for over two years. The asking price is steep, and it's going to be a hard sell in the struggling market. The realtor is constantly trying new tactics, raising and lowering the price and holding an open house every few months, but nothing seems to be working.

Shifting my gaze from the house, I look towards the ocean. The sun is setting, and the sky is filled with purple, blue and orange. I stake my claim on the beach near the water, pull my knees up to my chest and push my feet into the cool sand. I wrap the afghan tighter around me and begin my nightly routine. I can feel the tears welling up in my eyes, and I let them fall freely. My sobs are masked by the crashing ocean waves. This is where I seek solace every night. I cry because I think I would explode if I didn't get some sort of release. With pent-up emotions always running rampantly through me, I have to vent somehow.

Nathan forbids me to cry in front of him. Deep down I think the tears remind him of how much he's actually hurting me, and he doesn't want to face the truth. I used to cry and scream and yell at him, but I learned a long time ago that it only leads to more punishment, more pain and a hell of a lot more tears. I'm conditioned to feel numb around him, and it's easier that way. The only downfall is that I also feel numb around everyone else all the time.

Nathan wasn't always like this. He was so sweet and kind at first, especially the first night we met at my graduation party. I quickly fell in love with him. Thinking back on it now, though, I realize I never knew what love really was. I think I fell in love with the idea of him. I was young and inexperienced as to the cruelties of the world. Nathan portrayed himself as someone completely opposite of who he is now. The man I fell for was nothing but a carefully crafted façade, a myth, a real-life monster in disguise. And there isn't a day that goes by where I don't regret saying *I do* at the wedding. Two years, one month and fifteen days later I'm still regretting it.

Things could have been so different for me if I hadn't met Nathan. I would have traveled Europe, exploring my independence and then headed to college like I had always planned, becoming a teacher instead of a *trophy wife*. I hated that term with a passion, but that was exactly what I had become. I was a piece of eye candy hanging on my husband's arm at every event, every party, every social gathering.

I like to think about the possible *what ifs* sometimes even if it hurts me to my very core. What if I would have met someone in college, someone kind and gentle who wouldn't even think of laying a hand on me? We would have fallen in love, married, had two-point-five kids and lived in a house with a white picket fence in the suburbs. I would be happy.

Sighing, I shake my head, dispelling the notion. The dreams I once had for my life have slowly been destroyed one by one. I try not to think about how different my life could be now, because it only depresses me further. As long as I am here in this *prison* with *him*, I will never have a future — at least not a happy one.

I'm only twenty-three, but I feel like a shell of my former care-free, rebellious self. And I worry that if I don't get out of this relationship soon, the person that I used to be will never come to the surface again. She will drown in self-loathing and depression, and I will be broken for the rest of my life, too afraid to leave and not strong enough to fight anymore.

I stand and wipe away my tears. It's dark now, and the full moon and twinkling stars above illuminate the night sky. As I straighten my clothes, I can feel my mask falling back into place. I'm sick of pretending to be happy, but I have no other choice.

Making my way back to the porch, I glance at the house for sale next door and notice a light is on in the living room. With no blinds on the windows, it's easy to see in. The room is filled with furniture, and I wonder if the realtor is staging the home for another open house. Thinking nothing more of it, I climb the steps of our porch and go inside.

I change into pajamas and lie down on the bed as close to the edge as I can. Nathan stirs in his sleep and reaches for me. I grimace as he pulls me towards the middle of the mattress and wraps his arm around my waist tightly, crushing me against him. Even in his sleep he's possessive.

Closing my eyes, I think about today, attempting to focus on something positive. Dr. Harrison invades my thoughts. When I saw him today, I felt something; and I haven't felt much of anything over the past two years. But the fact that he makes me *feel* means I need to steer clear of him. Until I leave Nathan, until my life is actually my own, I can't bring anyone else into this mess. Max seems really nice. It's too bad I'll never have the chance to get to know him. *In another life*, I tell myself. In another life, I could fall in love with someone who loved me back and have the future I always wanted.

Eventually, sleep takes hold of me. I find peace within my dreams that are permeated with Max's dark gaze and kind smile.

MAX

I SIT IN the living room nursing a beer in a comfortable oversized recliner that the saleswoman at the furniture store picked out. She said I would love it, and she was right. I do love it. It's the best piece of furniture I've ever owned.

I take a swig of beer and sigh. The house is quiet. Too quiet. The satellite company is coming tomorrow, so at least I'll have TV for the upcoming weekend. Chuckling to myself, I shake my head. I can't believe I'm actually looking forward to watching television on the weekend instead of going out, but I pretty much left all my friends behind when I moved from Chicago to Nags Head.

My fingers dance around the screen of my cell phone. I consider playing some music to break the silence, but then decide not to bother. After this beer, I'm hitting the sack anyway. It was an exhausting day. The hospital isn't as large as the one I left, but I had a routine there. It was familiar. It was home to me. I did my residency there and was hired into a full-time position right away in the pediatrics department. I knew my way around. I was comfortable. Now I'm completely out of my element once again, attempting to learn all new protocols and procedures and trying not to step on any toes in the process. And if I didn't have a pretty brunette distracting me, maybe I could learn everything the first time around.

A smile tugs at the corner of my lips. Avery. I can't stop thinking about her. She looks like she stepped out of some sort of fairytale. I almost expect birds to be flying around and singing and fluffy bunnies hopping behind her at the hospital. But this fairytale won't have a happy ending for me, because she's married.

Sighing, I slump down in the chair and glance around my new pad in an attempt to distract myself from thinking about her. The house is huge and on a private beach, to boot. I still can't believe how I lucked into it. I'm only renting as of right now. The realtor worked some magic and convinced the desperate owner that month-to-month rent was better than letting it sit empty. The rent isn't cheap, but to be able to stick my toes in the sand and swim in the ocean in my downtime will outweigh the cost. And it's definitely much roomier than the hotel room I've been crammed into for over a week when I first got into town.

The house is still on the market; and if they get a seller, I'm out on my ass. But I'm going to enjoy it while I can. I think buying this place would have been a bigger jump than I wanted to take considering the hefty price tag. And plus the thought of settling down here makes the reason why I left Chicago seem even more real, and I want to live in denial for just a little bit longer.

I still can't believe I actually went through with the move. I had a lot going for me back home at one point in time. I had a beautiful fiancée, a great job and wonderful friends and coworkers. But once I found out my fiancée Gretchen was cheating on me, I decided I needed a change of pace and that I needed to put as much distance between us as was humanly possible. She broke my heart into a million pieces, and I would never be able to forgive her or my so-called best friend that she slept with.

So I returned to the one place that had always made me happy as a kid. My parents often took my sister Megan and I on vacation to Outer Banks. My family still lives in southern Virginia, and Nags

Head is a hell of a lot closer than Chicago. In my mind it's a win-win situation.

I bring the bottle of beer to my lips and take a long pull on it. I was never much of a drinker, but having one in the evening when I'm alone helps to numb the hurt I've been feeling since I called off my engagement. Gretchen really turned my world upside down in the worst possible way. I was going to spend the rest of my life with that girl. She was the one woman who finally tamed the *ultimate bachelor*, as my friends called me, and she stomped on my fucking heart.

I run a hand through my hair and chug the last of the beer, setting the empty bottle on the end table. Tired of sitting in silence, I get up and walk out onto the back porch. I stand in almost complete darkness, having forgotten to hit the switch for the outside lights. There are a lot of things I need to learn about this house, but so far I just haven't had the time.

I move to the edge of the deck and close my eyes. The sound of the waves crashing onto the shore is soothing, and it reaffirms my decision to move here. I most definitely could fall asleep to the sound of the ocean. It's so damn peaceful.

As I concentrate on the waves, I faintly pick up on another sound. It sounds like...someone crying. My eyes snap open and search the beach. They almost instantly settle on a figure sitting in the sand. Her long dark hair is whipping in the wind, and her back and shoulders are slouched forward as if the weight of the world is upon her at that very moment. Her hands cup her face as she sobs into them.

My heart instantly aches for this girl, and I wonder what happened to make her cry like that. I don't know if she's one of my neighbors or not since I haven't really made a point to introduce myself to any of them. The realtor was in such a hurry for me to the sign the lease that she didn't really expound on the neighborhood either.

I watch the woman from the shadows of the deck. She cries for a long time, and I'm unable to tear my gaze away. It's as if I'm mesmerized. Her sobs are heartbreakingly sad, and I feel a deep ache inside of me that I have never felt before.

After several minutes, I watch as she slowly stands, carefully wiping the tears from her eyes and straightening her clothes as if nothing happened. She turns and walks up the pathway towards the house next door. It's only when she's within a short distance from the porch that I can make out her features under the lamppost. A small gasp escapes my lips as the realization sets in that I know her. *Avery.* Her piercing blue-gray eyes stare in my direction as I say her name in my mind, and I stand stock-still, holding my breath. I know she can't see me, but I would hate for her to know that I was watching her. Her eyes float over the outside of the house and lock onto the living room where I left the light on. Her eyebrows knit together, and then she continues up the steps and vanishes inside the house next door.

Releasing a breath, I lean against the railing and stare out over the ocean. Avery's life is like a jigsaw in my mind, and the pieces are slowly falling together as I learn more about her. I find myself wanting to complete the puzzle and see the whole picture, because I think there is much more to her than meets the eye. I have a compelling urge to protect her, and I have a feeling deep down that's exactly what she needs right now.

AVERY

*I*T'S WEDNESDAY AFTERNOON, and Jacob is showing me how to build an awesome array of Lego vehicles, airplanes and castles. I am so excited about Nathan leaving on Friday for his weeklong conference in Seattle that I am in a better mood than usual. Jacob must have been able to sense it, because he insisted on going to the activities room to play. He hardly ever wants to leave his room, so this is a big deal for him. He pulls a portable IV pole behind him as he floats his newly built stunt airplane in the air with his other hand. He mimics engine noises with his mouth, and I can't help but grin.

"Wow, Jacob. That is the coolest plane I have ever seen."

"Really?" he asks with wide-eyed innocence.

I chuckle. "Yes, really."

He smirks and continues to fly his plane around the room. My eyes follow him before catching a glimpse of two figures in the hallway. My eyes lock onto Dr. Harrison as he talks with Dr. Benson. Max throws his head back and lets out a hearty laugh at something funny the other man said. His laugh is infectious, and a smile tugs at my lips.

His dark shaggy hair falls in front of his eyes as he leans forward; and he's quick to give his head a slight shake, so that the hair returns to its natural and sexy just-got-out-of-bed style. I can't seem to drag my gaze away from him no matter how hard I try. For the first time in a long time, I feel attracted to a man and not fearful of being around him. I guess Nathan hasn't stolen everything from me after all.

For the past couple of days, I've been seeing Max more and more around the hospital. He always says hi or tries to strike up a conversation with me in the halls. I usually just smile or wave. And for the past two days, we've eaten lunch together in the cafeteria. I think I maybe said a total of five words to him as he jabbered away about the hospital and the weather. It's not that I don't want to talk to him, but I have a deep-rooted fear instilled in me that both of us will end up getting hurt in the long run. Until I am free from Nathan, I can't even think about being with anyone else. If Max would get hurt because of me, I'd never be able to forgive myself.

In all actuality, I doubt if I even have any real chance with Max. I'm sure he's just trying to be friendly. Nevertheless, he always seems nervous around me, for some reason; and it's undeniably sweet and cute. I've seen him talking to the nurses, who are all clamoring to get his attention. It's against hospital policy to date coworkers, but people do it all the time anyway. I'm sure he'll have no problem finding a willing nurse to keep their relationship on the down low. A pang of jealousy hits me hard when I think of him being with someone else, but I have no reason to be jealous over a relationship that I could never have.

As if sensing my gaze, Max turns and looks at me. He caught me staring, and I feel the heat rise to my cheeks. His lips curl up into a big grin. He gives me a wave, and I wave back. He takes a step towards the doorway, but Dr. Benson says something and points down the hall. I watch as a deep frown appears on Max's face before he nods and follows the other doctor.

I wonder if he's upset because he didn't get the chance to talk to me. My heart beats a little faster at the thought. Even though I know we would never stand a chance, it's still exciting to think about the possibility.

"Avery, can we come back in here some other day and build a rocket ship?" Jacob asks, diverting my attention from the now empty hallway.

"Sure, Jacob. Whatever you want."

"Awesome!" he says enthusiastically.

Jacob is having one of his better days, and I hope that he does feel up to playing in the activities room again. His condition is so touch and go at the moment while he goes through treatments. It breaks my heart when he's sick, but he lights up my life when he's having a good day like today.

I keep an eye on the time. Nathan's threat is still fresh on my mind from the other night. I cannot be late. I'm looking forward to when he's gone next week, and I won't have the compulsive need to glance at my watch every few minutes. "Okay. I think it's time to clean up."

It's a team effort putting all the tiny Lego pieces back into the appropriate boxes. Once we're done, I walk Jacob back to his room and tuck him into bed. "Did you have a good day?" I ask.

"The best!" His little arms reach out and hug me tight.

I can feel my emotions getting the better of me as I hug him back. "I'm so happy to hear that." My eyes roll up at the ceiling as I try my best to keep the tears at bay. If he only knew how much his small gesture means to me.

"I'll see you tomorrow, Avery," Jacob says, pulling away.

"Okay, buddy. See you tomorrow." I am overwhelmed with happiness when I leave his room. I grab my purse and make my way to the parking garage.

On the way home, my happiness is slowly replaced with sadness, tension and worry. I park the car and rush into the house. Nathan is not home yet, fortunately.

I quickly pull my hair up into a ponytail and change out of my scrubs and into a simple, but expensive gray tank dress and matching flats. My hands are a blur as they move quickly to prepare dinner and set the table. Half an hour later I hear Nathan's car pull up and the door slam shut. An instant feeling of dread creeps upon me. I always get that sinking feeling when he comes home.

Nathan enters the house with a smile on his face. He reminds me of Dr. Jekyll and Mr. Hyde. I never know who is going to be walking through that door and what kind of mood he is going to be in.

With a forced smile on my face, I ask, "How was your day?"

"Good," he says. "Very good actually." Coming up from behind me, he wraps his arms around my waist. Then he stills. "Something you're forgetting?" he asks in a low voice.

I scramble to think of what I could have forgotten. It could be something as little as a dish I left in the sink or something he told me to do and I didn't remember. I'm in panic mode as I try to think. My heart pounds hard against my ribcage with an erratic rhythm. Think! I scream in my head.

He steps away, and I feel my entire body automatically tense in preparation for retribution. "Your apron," he whispers in my ear as he puts the loop around my neck and ties it around my waist. "We don't want to ruin these beautiful clothes I work so hard to buy for you, now do we?"

"I'm sorry," I say quietly. I hate apologizing all the time, but it comes so naturally to me now.

"No need to be sorry, Avery. Just learn from your mistakes." His hands gently massage my tight shoulders. "You're so tense," he whispers against the shell of my ear. "Maybe I can help you with that." He kisses my neck as his hands trail down the length of my body.

I force myself not to cringe from his touch. "I'll never be able to finish cooking if you keep doing that." I try hard to make my tone lighthearted so that he doesn't sense anything's wrong. It's not that Nathan isn't aware of my displeasure towards him and especially towards his abuse. It's just easier if I play along with his sick game. He likes to pretend that we have the perfect, happy marriage, but that couldn't be farther from the truth.

He grins against my throat. "All right. I'll save it for later," he promises.

My stomach drops at his promise, but I continue on with the task of making dinner in an attempt to distract myself.

~

*L*ater that evening, we eat in silence, as usual. Nathan received a phone call while dinner was in the oven, and his mood drastically went from good to bad. He glances at his phone every time it buzzes. A deep frown is set on his face, and I can feel the anger coming off of him in waves.

I take my time eating, hoping that he'll get tired and just go to bed without touching me. As I'm lifting a forkful of food to my mouth, he says, "Go brush your teeth and put the black and pink chemise on that I like."

I stare down at my plate. "But I'm not done eating." My voice sounds so weak and small, and I cringe inwardly.

He glares at me from across the table and slowly stands. His eyes look wild. His inner Hyde is back in full swing. "Don't test me, Avery," he says in an unnervingly soft tone. "Get up and do what I told you to do. Now!" he commands, slamming his fist down on the table.

I jump, and my fork clinks down on the plate as it falls from my grip. I stand up from my chair and hurry into the master bathroom. My hands are trembling as I fumble with the toothbrush and toothpaste. I manage to squeeze a small amount onto the brush and stick it in my mouth. I can see the tears welling up in my eyes, but I don't dare let them fall. If he sees them, he'll be even more upset with me. I hum to myself, a calming method I have been using since I was a child after my mother died. Slowly the tears dry up, and I quickly spit and rinse my mouth.

I walk into the adjoining bedroom. In another life, I would dream of a bedroom like this. The floor-to-ceiling windows on the far wall overlook the beach and ocean. The plush carpet is ivory, and the furniture is dark in stark contrast to it. The focal point of the room is the four-poster mahogany king-sized bed. The sight of it always makes my stomach tie into knots, and tonight is no exception.

Feeling nauseous, my fingers scramble to pull open the doors and top drawer of the armoire. After a few seconds, I spot the babydoll chemise Nathan was talking about. I undress quickly and slip into the lacey material that leaves nothing to the imagination.

"Lovely," Nathan says from the doorway.

Startled, I turn to him. I had no idea he was watching me.

"Come here," he demands, as his eyes greedily sweep over my form.

Reluctantly, I slowly walk over to him. His fingertips graze down my sides, and I shiver in response to his touch. Then his hands wrap around my waist and pull me roughly against him. He puts a finger under my chin and makes me meet his gaze. "I want you so bad right now," he breathes against my lips. His mouth slants over mine. The kiss is soft at first, but grows demanding far too quickly. He snakes his fingers into my hair, gripping tightly and pulling until my scalp is throbbing in pain. Locked into his grasp, his lips press harder against mine in a bruising kiss.

His hands release my hair and move to my wrist. He abruptly twists me around and shoves me over to the bed. His hand is on my back, forcing me facedown on the mattress and pinning me down. I don't dare resist even though every fiber of my being is screaming at me to do just that. Instead, I turn my head to the side and stare out the tall windows at the dark ocean beyond, wishing that I could disappear into the water and not face what is about to happen.

The sound of him unzipping his pants fills the room, and a shudder runs through me. My breathing is shallow through the web of my long hair covering my face. Once he's undressed, he pushes my thighs apart. He always takes me like this, from behind. With another man, it might be an enjoyable position. But with Nathan, it feels degrading, as if he can't bear to look at me. We've never had sex any other way. And since he was my first, I don't know any other way.

I can feel his hard length poised at my entrance. I tell myself to breathe through the pain, to try to relax so it hurts less, but my body tenses up from knowing what's coming next. He's done this before so many times — taken me when I wasn't ready...violating me...*raping me*.

"Wait! Please!" I cry out.

But he doesn't even hesitate. He parts my lips and enters quickly, brutally spearing me. With no lubrication, it feels like I'm being torn in half. I turn my face into the mattress to muffle my screams. He continues his brutal assault, pumping in and out of me inch by inch until he completely forces his way inside.

"You. Are. Mine," he says, enunciating each word with a powerful thrust.

Tears fill my eyes and spill over onto the sheets below. The pain is excruciating, and I know he won't stop until he gets his fill of me. I try to steady my breathing, but silent sobs wrack my body as he continues to assault me. His hands grope their way up the length of my body and tightly encircle my wrists, holding me in place as he thrusts savagely. His fingers are forming new bruises over the old ones that barely had a chance to heal. The bruises are his marks of ownership, his way of displaying his power over me.

I don't fight back. I've been conditioned with years of mental abuse to learn not to fight back. When you fight back, it's worse. My brain goes into hibernation mode, not being able to handle the overload of sensory abuse on my body. And so I quietly drift into another state where I'm calm, unaware of my surroundings. I stare out the windows at the dark water, and I picture myself as a bird flying over the waves. I feel so free and happy, gliding through the night without a care in the world.

I want to disappear.

Let me disappear.

I close my eyes and repeat those two sentences in my mind over and over again. I withdraw into myself, barely feeling any pain now. I block out his heaving pants and grunts. And then it's quiet. I'm in a different place, and anywhere is better than here. It's amazing what your mind is capable of when you're in a situation you can't escape physically. The more time that passes while I'm with Nathan, the more withdrawn and numb I become. Soon I wonder if I'll be able to feel anything ever again.

My face sinks down into the cool cotton sheet now wet with my tears as he grunts one final time. He collapses on top of me, his hot breath on the back of my neck. "That was so good, baby," he whispers and kisses my tear-stained cheek. He slowly pulls out of me and walks to the bathroom. "I'm going to take a shower and go to bed. Are you staying up?" he asks sweetly.

I'm always surprised by the way his personality is like an on and off switch. He can change his demeanor in an instant. I never know what mood he is in or will be in, and that is what scares me the most. It takes all of my willpower to keep my voice steady as I manage to say, "Yeah. I think I'm going to clean a little."

"Okay. Goodnight."

After the door to the bathroom closes, I curl into a fetal position and tremble. This time was worse than all the others combined. I feel completely and utterly gutted. Silent sobs wrack my body as I hear the shower turn on in the next room.

After a few minutes, I manage to stand. I grab a change of clothes from the armoire and make my way to the guest bathroom. I'm so sore I can barely walk, but I force myself to move. Very gently, I clean myself up and change into a pair of gray lounge pants and a black sweatshirt.

As I'm getting ready to walk out of the bathroom, I catch a glimpse of myself in the mirror. My eyes aren't as bright and full of life like they used to be. They look dull and vacant. I barely recognize myself anymore. The girl I once was is slowly slipping away day by day. A year ago I would have fought back. I wouldn't have let him do that to me. I would have kicked and scratched and yelled. But over the years I have learned that the punishment is so much worse than what I'm actually subjected to. Nathan owns me in every sick sense of the word, and he's always quick to remind me of that fact.

Tearing my gaze away, I walk out and begin to clean up the dining room and kitchen. I concentrate on the sounds coming from our bedroom as I load the dishes into the dishwasher. Nathan is done with his shower, and then I hear him climb into bed.

I grab a bottle of painkillers from the cupboard and a bottle of water from the fridge. My entire body is covered in a thin sheen of sweat from the pain currently running through my body. I pop a few pills and swallow them down with the water. It hurts to move, but I know I can't stay in this house another second. I need my release. I need to hear the ocean waves crashing around me, and I need some sort of solitude to offset this hell I'm living in.

A stray whimper escapes my lips, and I clasp a hand over my mouth to silence the sound. I hurry to the back door and slip into a pair of sneakers.

And then I run.

I don't stop running until I reach the ocean. My knees buckle as emotions overcome me, and I fall to the sand below, sobbing so violently I have trouble breathing. "I can't do this anymore!" I howl into the crashing waves. "I can't live like this." I stare into the dark water, and I wish it would just swallow me up and take me away from this place.

The realization slowly settles down upon me. I need to leave him. Nathan is going to be gone for a week, and I know that something has to be done while he's gone. He's left for weekend trips before, but never for an entire week. It almost seems like fate is intervening just when I need it to the most and just when I was beginning to think I couldn't handle anymore.

I can't stay married to someone who treats me like this. If I can't run away, maybe I can hide. I need to talk to my father. He is the only one who can help me now. I don't have anyone else. Nathan saw to that a long time ago when he slowly put a wedge between my friends and myself until we stopped speaking and I was all alone. I realize now why he did that — it was so when the time came when I was ready to leave him, I would have no one to turn to. He knew exactly what he was doing. He's always ten steps ahead of me and completely methodical.

If he won't let me go, I might need to take drastic measures...again. I stare down at my wrist and the scar from when I attempted to take my life six months ago. I thought Nathan would change after that. If anything has changed, it's the frequency of his violence. It's gotten worse over the past few months, and I'm getting the urge to reopen that wound on my wrist...except this time I'll make sure no one will be around to stop me.

After my tears are done falling and my breathing returns to normal, I stand up and slowly make my way back to the house. It feels like I'm walking into a black hole that is slowly sucking the life out of me, but now I have a little glimmer of hope shining through the darkness. I just hope my father listens to me this time and helps me when I need him the most.

MAX

I SAW AVERY on the beach again last night. She cried harder than the night before, so whatever happened at home must have really been bad. The sound of her tortured sobs was like a cold, metal spike running straight through me. It was so hard to just sit and watch her and not do anything. It's not that I don't want to help her. I just don't have enough information to know the cause of her pain. Is she crying because she lost someone, or is she crying because of something being done to her? I don't know the answers, but I intend to find out.

It's busy at the hospital for a Thursday. I'm attempting to concentrate on my work, but my mind keeps straying to Avery. She seems really off today. Every time I've tried to approach her or talk to her, she either ignores me or flashes me a grim smile. And when I tried to sit with her at lunch, she stood up and left without saying a word. We have been eating lunch together for the past couple of days and talking. Well, it's mostly me talking while she just listens and says a few words here and there. I thought we were starting to make some progress, but then she threw me for a loop once again.

I still haven't told her that I'm her neighbor. I know I will have to tell her eventually, but I'm waiting until the time feels right. But if she keeps ignoring me the way she is, maybe I'll never get the chance to tell her. I don't think she's ignoring me because she doesn't like me. I think there is another reason, and perhaps it's because of whatever happened last night.

I've caught her talking with several kids and Rosie today, and she doesn't seem to have a problem chatting it up with them. When she's around the children, she looks happy and the complete opposite of how she is with me. I figure my best bet is to catch her when she's visiting with Jacob. Maybe I can get her to talk and tell me what happened to her last night.

In the afternoon, I make my way towards Jacob's room. I have Avery's daily routine pretty much down pat, and I know she always stops at Jacob's room before she leaves for the day. She adores that kid, and the feeling is totally mutual. I can tell how much she cares for Jacob as if he were her own son.

My footsteps slow as I near the room. Avery's voice floats out into the hall. I can't really hear what she's saying, but Jacob giggles. A grin pulls at the corners of my mouth. I want to talk to her again and see if she responds with more than just a smile. It's not that I mind her usual engaging smile that seems to instantly turn me to mush; it's just that I love to hear the sound of her voice.

"Hey, Avery," I say as I walk into Jacob's room.

She looks up at me with those hauntingly beautiful blue-gray eyes. Her dark hair glistens in the sunlight cascading through the window, highlighting the deep shades of red. Her smile dims a bit, and I feel a profound sense of sadness radiating from her. I just can't quite shake the feeling that she's constantly on edge around me. I just wish I knew why.

Avery remains quiet, barely acknowledging that I'm even there. I know she was just talking to Jacob right before I entered the room, so I wonder why she won't talk to me. Maybe her foul mood is because of something I've done and has nothing to do with last night at all. The thought of me upsetting her in some way puts me into a panic. "How are you?" I ask, trying to strike up a conversation.

Her eyes go to the floor and dart left and right as if she's trying to decide. I wonder what's going on in that pretty little head of hers. She opens her mouth, but closes it almost immediately. I can see the tears in her eyes as she runs out of the room. I look at Jacob, and he just shrugs.

I dart into the hall and see Avery disappearing into the break room. I follow her, catching the door before it can close. Her back is to me, and she's slumped over the sink with her hands gripping the counter. "Avery," I say as the door shuts behind me.

She immediately straightens her spine, and it reminds me of what she does on the beach after she's let out all of her emotions. It's as if she's rebuilding a hard exterior around herself that no one can penetrate. "I'm sorry," she says so low it's barely above a whisper.

She's sorry? For what? I don't even know what she's apologizing for. Confused, I walk over to her. "Hey, if I did something to offend you, just tell me." I'm behind her now. She's staring straight ahead out the small window above the sink. Her breathing is shallow, and her shoulders are bunched up around her ears from being so tense. "Did I do or say something wrong? Is that why you've been avoiding me? Is that why you won't talk to me?" I'm asking a lot of questions, but I'm desperate to know the answers. There is some kind of connection between us, and I need to know that I'm not imagining it. I just want her to tell me that she feels the same way. Even if it's just friendship, I'll take it. I just want to help her with whatever it is she's dealing with.

She turns and looks at me for a fraction of a second, but it's long enough to see a million emotions flash behind those piercing eyes. She steps around me to leave. She's always running away, but I'm not going to let her today. I'm going to get to the bottom of this right here, right now. "Wait a minute," I say as my hand darts out and grasps her wrist in a firm, but gentle grip.

Crying out in pain, she jerks away from me quickly. In the

process of pulling away, the sleeve of her cardigan slides up her arm, revealing purplish-blue marks on her exposed skin. Even though I don't want to frighten or upset her, I reach out and gently pull the sleeve up a little more. I quickly inspect her skin before she pulls away. She has bruises the whole length of her forearm. Some are fresh, and some are old based on their color. My brows furrow as I meet her gaze. "Who did this to you?"

Her eyes are wide as she looks up at me, and I realize I just saw something I wasn't ever supposed to see. "I...I fell," she says, her voice catching.

She's lying right to my face. Those bruise patterns are not from a fall. And I bet if I placed my fingers over the elongated bruises around her wrist, they would almost match. What is she trying to cover up? Who is she trying to protect?

I watch her closely as she pulls the sleeve of the cardigan down to her wrist, concealing her skin once again. She tugs at the sleeves in an obsessive manner. Come to think of it, she has worn a cardigan every single time I've seen her since I started working here. Another piece of the puzzle clicks into place in my mind. This isn't a one-time thing. She's been hiding these bruises for a while now. "You said you fell. Oh yeah? Where? How did you fall?"

Avery hesitates for only a split second before saying, "I fell down the basement steps the other day. I was bringing down a basket full of laundry and slipped on the next to the last step from the bottom."

She's obviously used to practicing her lies to tell people. She's so good at it that I almost believe her. *Almost.* "Some of those looked at least a few days old. Did you fall more than once?" My tone is demanding and impetuous, and I instantly regret it when I see the tears welling up in her eyes.

I watch as her tough exterior slowly begins to crack. She releases a shaky breath before saying, "Please. Please don't tell anyone."

"And what exactly am I not telling anyone?" I want to hear her say it. I want to hear the words.

The look in her eyes is of pure, undiluted fear, but what or, more importantly, who is she afraid of? "Please," she pleads. Her eyes dart to the watch on her wrist. "Oh no!" she gasps. "I'm going to be late again."

"Late for what?"

"I have to go," she says in a panic.

I want to reach out for her again, but I'm afraid to hurt her. I keep my hands balled in fists at my sides to resist the temptation as I watch her run from the room. We barely got the chance to talk, and then I find out in those few moments that she's being abused. But by whom? I'm determined to find out.

Leaving the break room, I manage to catch a fleeting glimpse of Avery rushing out the exit. Rosie is at the nurses' station when I walk up to her. "I need to speak with you." My voice sounds a lot sterner than I intended, but I'm upset, and my emotions are at war with one another in my mind. I'm angry, confused and fearful for Avery's safety. I just want to know what the hell is going on with her. If she needs help, I need to know that, so I can do everything in my power to get her the help she needs.

Rosie follows me into an empty room. "Did I do something wrong, Dr. Harrison?" she asks.

"What?" I ask, distracted. "Oh, no, you didn't do anything wrong." I hesitate. How can I put this out there without telling her what I saw? Obviously Avery covers her bruises for a reason. She doesn't want anyone to know, and I don't intend on spilling her secret to anyone until I know the truth behind it. "This is about Avery."

"What about her?"

"What's wrong with her?" I blurt out. Shit. That sounded so much better in my head. Frustrated, I scrub a hand down my face. "I mean is something wrong? She was very upset today, and I'm concerned."

"She's always upset. There's no happiness in that girl unless she's with those kids."

"Does she cry a lot?" Maybe she needs medication for depression, but that still wouldn't explain the bruises.

"Well, she never cries in front of me or anyone, for that matter, but you can tell that she's carrying a huge burden on those little shoulders of hers. Avery's such a lovely girl. I don't know why she stays with him."

"Him? Her husband?"

She nods with a frown.

And then the question is out of my mouth before I can even process it. "Does he hit her?"

Rosie hesitates like she isn't sure whether she wants to tell me. "Well, I mean how clumsy can one person be? Over the years I've seen the bruises she tries so hard to cover up. And believe me, she does one hell of a job at covering them up. Even when it's a hundred degrees outside that girl will wear long-sleeved cardigans and turtlenecks." She blows out a long breath. "Listen, Dr. Harrison, I was in an abusive relationship. I know the signs, and she has all of 'em." She shakes her head sadly. "I've known Avery for six years, back when she was still in high school and started volunteering as a way to please her father and pad her college resume. The girl she was before she met her husband is not the same girl you see today. She used to be so spunky and full of life." She stares into the distance. "The complete opposite of who she is now," she says softly.

I try to imagine Avery as her old self, being vivacious and cheerful. What I wouldn't give to see her like that once more.

Rosie sighs deeply and continues. "I tried to bring it up once, about her leaving him. Avery didn't talk to me for weeks on end. Her bruises aren't the only things she's covering up. For some reason, she's protecting him. I see it like this — if she doesn't want to help herself, then how can I help her?" A deep frown sets on her face. "Avery is a strong girl, but she's been more withdrawn lately. Something happened about six months ago, and Avery hasn't been the same since. I can see a change in her, and it scares me. She's good at pretending, but that hard armor of hers is starting to crack, and I think maybe he's finally breaking her down."

Her words sink in slowly. My mind fills with images of Avery being hurt, and it kills me inside. I really don't know her that well, but I do know she doesn't deserve that kind of a life.

"Anything else you need, Doc?" Rosie asks, breaking through my thoughts.

"No. Thank you. You've been very helpful."

"If you think you can help her, please try, because that girl needs saving. She just doesn't know it yet." She offers a small smile, pats me on the shoulder and leaves the room.

I run a hand down my face and over the stubble on my chin. Rosie gave me a lot of information to take in. Instead of getting over this little crush I have with Avery, it is actually growing into more of an obsession. I need to find out more about her and what's going on in her life that would make her stay with someone who hurts her. I wouldn't exactly label myself as a knight in shining armor, but maybe she needs me to be hers.

MAX

*I*T'S LATE WHEN I arrive home. There was an emergency at the hospital, and so my shift lasted a lot longer than usual. I set my things on the kitchen counter and immediately make my way outside onto the back patio. I step into the darkness and instantly spot Avery on the beach. This is definitely a ritual with her. This has happened every night this week, and somehow I sense that this is the only way she can deal with her emotions for the day. I think the ocean is her therapy, a catharsis.

I resist the urge to go to her. I need to find out more before I start interfering in her life. For all I know, I could make things much worse for her by intervening.

My hands clench into fists, and my gaze drags to the house next door. It's impressive, even more impressive than the one I am currently renting. There is a hot tub and a pool built into the lower level of the back porch. And like mine, floor-to-ceiling windows cover the back of the house overlooking the ocean. The house looks perfectly normal from the outside, but I have a feeling what's on the inside is completely opposite.

I haven't met Avery's husband yet, but I don't doubt that he is probably very successful and charming. Everyone who knows him probably thinks he's a great guy too. *If they only knew what I'm slowly learning.*

Tomorrow is Friday, and I intend on inviting them both over for dinner. I want to meet Avery's husband and feel him out under my own terms. Then I'll decide where to proceed from there, although I have a feeling my decision might involve my fist meeting his face.

I watch as Avery slowly walks back to the house. Her gait is rigid and sluggish. She stops at the porch steps, and I can see the grimace on her face as she eases herself up onto the first step.

He hurt her again. I know he did. My hands curl onto the railing, my knuckles turning white from the tight grasp. I remember the fear in her eyes when she looked at the clock. She said she was going to be late again. I wonder if he punished her because of that or for another infraction. I feel horrible. I am the one who cornered her in the break room and then confronted her. I made her late. *It's my fault.*

Even though I want to yell out to her, I don't say a word. There must be a good reason for her not to seek help herself and for her to continue to stay with him. I'm going to bide my time until I can talk to her and figure out what needs to be done. And if I need to take matters into my own hands, then I will.

Avery eventually makes her way inside. I run a hand through my hair and look up at the twinkling stars littering the night sky. "Avery, I'm going to help you," I whisper. "I promise."

AVERY

*A*S SOON AS I arrive home Friday afternoon, I start packing Nathan's suitcase while he jumps in the shower. My emotions are running high as I think about a week without him being here, a week for me to plan on leaving him.

My mind replays the day at the hospital as I fold clothes neatly on the bed. Max attempted several times to talk to me, but I ignored him as best I could. It's awkward between us now simply because he saw the bruises that I try so hard to keep hidden. He knows the truth or at least assumes to know what is going on in my life. And when he tried to bring it up today, I had to brush him off even though I didn't want to. He may think he can help, but he's wrong. No one understands the extent of my husband's power except for me. People that try to help me just end up getting hurt, and I won't let that happen to Max.

"Are you almost done?" Nathan calls from the bathroom. "I don't want to miss my flight."

Me either, I think to myself. The punishment I received last night for being late is still fresh in my mind. The moment I walked through the door, Nathan grabbed me from behind and shoved me into the island in the middle of the kitchen. My ribs and right knee bore the brunt of the impact. He left me lying on the floor for a long time before he finally told me to get up and make him dinner.

The only thing that kept me sane last night was the fact that I knew he would be leaving the next day. Even though my knee and ribs are killing me, I am more than happy to pack his things. I walk around the room gingerly, favoring my right leg. It feels a lot better than it did last night, but it's still tender. I finish packing his dress shirts and zip up the suitcase. "It's all packed," I call back to him.

"Good," he says as he walks into the bedroom. He fixes his tie one last time before slipping his arms into his suit jacket and putting on a pair of shiny black shoes.

He looks at me for approval, and I give a slight nod and a phony smile. Nathan looks good in whatever he wears, but he looks best in a suit. My attractiveness to him, however, fizzled out long ago after I learned that his appearance is all smoke and mirrors, hiding the monster underneath. He may be handsome on the outside; but on the inside, he is repulsive in every way imaginable. He is a real-life monster in an expensive Armani suit.

Nathan turns to me and puts a finger under my chin, lifting my gaze to his. "Are you going to miss me?"

I nod once. He has a boyish grin on his face, and this is one of the rare moments when he reminds me of the man I fell in love with. At one time he was the sweetest guy on the planet, and I considered myself lucky to be called his girlfriend. And then he changed into a cruel, vindictive monster almost overnight. I think the darkness was always in him and hidden behind a carefully constructed façade, waiting for just the right moment to appear and lash out. I don't know if he actually realizes how much he hurts me and that he just doesn't care or if he's completely oblivious to my misery and pain. I may never know the truth.

He frowns and wipes a stray tear away that I didn't even realize had fallen. "Don't cry, Avery. You know I don't like that," he complains with a stern voice.

"I'm sorry," I mutter.

His smile slowly returns, and he kisses my forehead. "I'll be back before you know it."

I almost laugh at the notion that he thinks I'm upset because he's leaving. If he only knew that I'm upset because of the man he has become and for the longing of the man he used to be...or used to pretend to be.

Nathan steps back and grabs the suitcase handle. "Don't make me regret leaving you here alone," he warns before wheeling the case behind him out of the room.

When the front door closes behind him, I release a deep, shaky breath. I breathe in and out deeply, desperately trying to control my emotions. My ribs are killing me with every breath, but I don't care. A burst of joy escapes my lips before I can contain it. No rules, no stress, no abuse and no pretending for an entire week. I suddenly feel free...even if it's only temporary.

I have a lot planned for this week while he's gone. The first step is to meet with my father and tell him that I want a divorce from Nathan. I have hinted around to my father before about our marital troubles, but I have never used the *D* word. I'm sure my father will be upset. He likes to keep the image of the perfect, happy family for the press releases on his campaign trails. At this point, though, I don't care if it upsets him. I'm telling him how I feel, and that's final.

I have to wonder if Max has a little bit to do with my sudden need to escape. The feelings he stirred up made me realize that I can have more in life, that I want more in life. I could have a bright future, but I will never know just how bright while I'm stuck here under Nathan's thumb.

Grabbing the house phone from the charging dock, I carry it outside onto the deck. The afternoon sun beats down on my face, and I close my eyes and relish every second of it. I feel a sense of freedom already without the ever-demanding, oppressive presence of Nathan. For a week, the house will actually feel like a home instead of a prison, and I'm going to enjoy it immensely.

Smiling at the renewed energy coursing through me, my fingers press the numbers for my dad's cell phone. I walk down to the swimming pool on the lower level deck and wait for him to answer. He picks up on the third ring.

"Hello?"

"Dad."

"Avery. I haven't heard from you in a while, sweetheart. How you are you? How's Nathan?"

I cringe when he says *his* name. "Fine," I state simply. My voice is shaky as I ask, "Dad, do you think we could meet for lunch tomorrow?"

He hesitates, and I can hear papers shuffling in the background. He's checking his schedule, and it makes me roll my eyes. It's pretty sad that my own father has to pencil me into his life, but I should be used to it — he's been penciling me into his life for the last twenty-three years. "Sure. That should be fine. I can move some things around," he mumbles. Then a little louder he asks, "How about noon at our usual place?"

Stepping to the edge of the porch, my hand wraps around the railing as I stare out over the water. "Sounds good, Dad." A flicker of movement to my right catches my eye, and I turn to see a man jogging. He's wearing navy blue shorts and a gray hoodie with an iPod strapped around his right biceps, the headphone wires bouncing as he runs. His legs are muscular and tan, and I can't help but wonder what the rest of him looks like under his clothes. The hood is pulled down low, shadowing his face, and he stares straight ahead, not noticing me at all.

"Listen, Dad, I'm going to go. I'll see you tomorrow."

"Okay. Bye, sweetheart."

I hang up the phone and stare at the mystery man, watching him attentively. I've never seen him before, and I wonder briefly if he realizes this is a private beach. To my surprise, he jogs past my house and up the porch steps next door. I thought the house was still empty.

Maybe the real estate agent wasn't, in fact, staging it like I had thought. Maybe he's my new neighbor.

I can't seem to tear my gaze away from him as he jogs up the steps and stops on the deck. He raises his arms above his head, revealing a couple inches of rock hard abs, and a low groan escapes his lips as he stretches. The sound reverberates through me, and my lips part with a gasp. I've never been so turned on by a single sound before. Feeling instantly flushed, I watch intently as he leans down, stretching his fingertips down to each foot.

Our porches are only several yards apart, so I get a clear view of him. I can't help but stare. There's something about him that seems so familiar. And when he straightens and lowers his hood, my heart stutters. Max. His eyes lock with mine in surprise. He quickly reaches for the cord to his ear buds; and with a swift tug, they fall. "Avery. Hi."

My hand raises and does some sort of awkward wave. I am in complete shock that he's my new neighbor, but he doesn't seem all that surprised to see me. I wonder how long he's been living there and how long he's known I'm his neighbor. "Hello," I say, and it sounds like a throaty whisper. I quickly clear my throat and say, "Dr. Harrison. Hi."

"Please. Call me Max." He runs a hand through his sweat-slicked hair and flashes me a killer smile. My mouth goes dry. He is dangerously beautiful. "I wanted to tell you at the hospital that I moved in next door, but I didn't get the chance. You're always too busy running away from me," he says with a grin.

The realization slowly sinks in that the man who invades my thoughts and dreams is going to be less than a hundred feet away at all times. It was hard enough to ignore him at the hospital, and now he's going to be running up and down the beach like a fitness model getting ready for a fashion shoot. I don't know whether to be delighted or completely terrified. "So...you bought the place?" I ask in an attempt to act nonchalant even though I'm a nervous wreck on the inside.

"No. Just renting for the time being."

"You didn't have a few million lying around to buy it?" I joke. I'm surprised I'm being so casual with him. I spent the day ignoring him. But as long as he's acting friendly, I will too.

He chuckles. "No. My piggy bank doesn't hold that much, unfortunately."

I grin. Hot, nice, sweet *and* funny. I grimace inwardly. It's going to be so hard to keep ignoring him. I know I should turn around and go back inside, but my legs won't cooperate with my brain. I stay rooted where I am. There's one question that I need to ask and know the answer to. "When did you move in?"

After a brief hesitation, he answers, "Monday."

So he's been here all week. My stomach drops as I worry my bottom lip between my teeth. I wonder if he's seen me on the beach at night. I never noticed him watching me, but that doesn't mean he wasn't. Maybe that would explain his sudden interest in me. After all, seeing a woman bawling her eyes out on a beach every night would raise some suspicion.

He wipes some sweat from his forehead with the back of his hand. I suddenly feel a little hot myself. I touch my fingertips to my cheeks, and I can feel the warmth there. His eyes are trained on me, and I suddenly feel uncomfortable under his dark gaze.

Clearing his throat, he says, "I thought I saw someone leaving your house a little bit ago. Was that your husband?"

I nod and try to keep a frown from appearing on my lips. I fail miserably. "Yes. Nathan. He has a medical conference in Seattle. He'll be gone for a week."

Max's brows quirk up. "I see. Well, I was going to invite you both over for dinner tonight." He shrugs and then says, "I guess now I'll just have to invite you."

Dinner. Alone. With Max. Nathan would kill me if he ever found out. I stare down at my knotted fingers and try to think of a quick, believable excuse.

Perhaps sensing my hesitation, Max quickly adds, "I'm not the best cook in the world, but I make a mean spaghetti."

My head snaps up. "Spaghetti? That's my favorite," I blurt out.

"Really? Well, I guess that means you can't refuse my invitation then."

Grinning, I reply, "Well, I could refuse...but I don't want to." I hear the words coming out of my mouth, but I can't believe I'm actually the one saying them. I didn't even know I remembered how to flirt. My brain seems hell-bent on tuning out my subconscious, which is the one and only thing that wants me to say no and realizes that this isn't a good idea.

His smile widens. "Okay. How about six o'clock?"

After hesitating for a few moments, I finally nod. "Sure."

"See you later then, Avery." He walks backwards toward the patio doors, his eyes never leaving mine until he disappears inside.

After he's gone, I turn and amble up the steps to my house. I put the phone back on the charging dock and collapse onto the couch in the living room. *What have I done?* I know I should have turned Max's invitation down. I also know I should probably feel guilty about having dinner with Max when my husband isn't home, but I don't. I actually feel excited and happy. And it's been so long since I've felt that way. Far too long.

AVERY

IT'S ALMOST FIVE o'clock when I step out of the bathtub. I take my time blow-drying my hair and putting on makeup. I do my eye shadow a little darker than normal since I don't have Nathan here dictating over every choice I make. The smoky look really makes my blue-gray eyes pop, and I get a thrill from rebelling just a little. I finish the look off with a pale pink lipstick that has a hint of gloss in it. My lips look totally kissable, and I suddenly find myself fixated on whether Max will try to kiss me or not.

No. He was going to invite both Nathan and I over tonight, so clearly he has no romantic intentions. Whatever I think I'm feeling for him is probably all in my head. But fantasizing about being with him in another life, a happier life is better than facing my harsh reality.

Standing in the walk-in closet, I rummage through outfit after outfit trying to find the perfect thing to wear. I settle on a white, blue and gray tier sundress. It's a modest cut, fitted through the chest and waist and then flaring out to just below my knee. I walk over to the full-length mirror and frown. Dark bruises litter my skin. The worst is the large one, which is an angry shade of purple, covering my knee that is partially visible under the hem of the dress.

Sighing with sadness and frustration, I return to the bathroom and dig my most prized possession out of my beauty bag — tattoo cover-up concealer. This stuff works wonders for bruises, and I have relied on it for the past few years. At one of the women's shelters I ran away to, a battered woman, not much unlike myself, told me that she used the stuff religiously. Her husband often bruised her face and neck, and so she needed the makeup to convince her family and coworkers that she was in a perfect, happy marriage. She reveled in the moment that she had had enough and threw the makeup in the trashcan, leaving her husband and the abuse behind. If only I could have a moment like that in my life. What I wouldn't give to leave all of this and Nathan behind.

The bathroom clock ticks loudly, as my eyes fixate on it. It's ten minutes until six o'clock, so I do my best to apply the makeup as quickly, but as evenly as I can. I feel like Picasso or Rembrandt, attempting to create a masterpiece with my skin as the canvas and the concealer as my medium. The bruises on my arms virtually disappear right before my eyes. The makeup is waterproof, but it doesn't stay on forever. After several hours, it will start to rub off. I have to be careful when I wear it and make sure I reapply it or wear something that doesn't require much cover-up.

Once I'm finished, I put on some jewelry and a watch on my left wrist. The band of the watch covers my scar, and so it serves a greater purpose than just allowing me to keep an eye on the time. I slip into a pair of wedge sandals and walk to the patio door. My hand stops when I grip the knob. My wedding ring glistens in the light, and I can't tear my eyes away from it.

I'm cheating on my husband.

The realization hits me hard.

Theoretically, I haven't committed adultery, and I don't know if things would even go that far between Max and me. But I would never tell Nathan about this dinner, and hiding it from him is essentially cheating. Right?

My fingers clench around the doorknob as I force myself to think about the hell Nathan has put me through the past five years. Even though we're technically married, I haven't loved him for a long time. And I don't think he has ever loved me. I'm planning on getting divorced as soon as possible. I try to tell myself that there's no reason to feel guilty. So then why am I hesitating?

I pull my hand back and close my eyes. "You deserve to find some happiness in your life," I say out loud. I don't know if I truly believe that, but I know deep down that I should. I've just been numb and drowning in pain for so long that I don't know if I can bring myself some peace and break through the surface again.

Fighting down the mixed emotions I'm reeling from, I glance at my watch and hurry outside. I don't know what the future with Max holds, but I know it has to be a lot brighter than the dark hell I'm living in now.

MAX

*L*OOKING AROUND THE back patio, I hope that I haven't overdone it. Candles and tiki torches are burning everywhere, casting a nice glow around the deck. On the round, glass table, I had placed some fine china that my mom had given me a while back when I got my own place after college. I never used it before tonight, but I have to admit it does look nice. A bottle of wine is on ice in a bucket, and two wine glasses are by each plate. The spaghetti is warming on the stove, and the breadsticks are baking in the oven. Feeling content, I sit down and wait.

I don't remember ever being this romantic with my ex-fiancée. Don't get me wrong. I sent the occasional flowers and took Gretchen out on a lot of dates, but I never made this much of a fuss over dinner with her or anyone, for that matter. Especially not a *friend*, which is exactly what Avery will be to me until she hints at wanting something more. And I desperately hope she wants more.

She said her husband is out of town for a week, and I can't help but feel as if fortune is intervening at the exact moment I want it to. This will give me an opportunity to get to know Avery better and find out what is really going on in her life instead of trying to squeeze information out of Rosie every day. Rosie always has a smile on her face, but I know she's getting annoyed with my numerous questions.

It's a little after six, and I'm beginning to worry if Avery will show. I guess I didn't consider that she might not feel right about dinner alone with a coworker and neighbor while her husband is out of town. I know the situation is complicated. I'm not stupid. She's married. In any other situation, I wouldn't even pursue a married woman. But this isn't a typical situation, and this is Avery I'm talking about. She is one of the most selfless people I have ever met, and she's being abused. I constantly see the unhappiness and fear in her eyes. I don't know what is going to happen between us, but I just want to try to help her in any way that she needs me to. There's just something about Avery that makes me forget about the rest of the world and just focus solely on her. She's like a breath of fresh air slowly bringing me out of my rut and back to life.

My head turns at the sound of Avery running up the porch steps, nearly tripping in the process. "I'm sorry I'm late," she apologizes quickly while trying to catch her breath.

Standing, I watch her carefully. "Avery, it's fine if you're late. I would have waited all night out here for you," I say, and it's the honest-to-God truth.

She seems to slightly relax, but the look on her face is as if she doesn't believe me. Realization creeps over me as I remember her panicking from being late yesterday. And then that night she was crying on the beach and limping. Her husband must punish her when she's late.

My hands clench into fists at my sides over the thought of him hurting her, but I quickly calm my emotions. I don't want her thinking that I'm anything like Nathan. I'm going to do my best to prove to her that people can be kind and that she deserves their kindness.

I focus my attention back to her. The dress she's wearing suits her and shows off her legs. Her long hair falls down her back in soft waves, and I find myself wanting to run my fingers through it. "Avery, you look beautiful."

I watch the flush of crimson slowly rise to her cheeks. "Thank you, Dr. Har — Max," she says, correcting herself with a shy smile.

Pulling out a chair, I tell her, "Have a seat. I'll bring everything out."

She hesitates before sitting down. "Are you sure?" she asks.

"I'm sure," I tell her. I have a feeling she's not used to being waited on either.

I take the spaghetti pot out first and set it on a trivet. Then I go back in the house, take the garlic bread from the oven, place it in a basket and bring that outside as well. While I'm pouring the wine, I glance over at Avery. The candlelight bathes over her beautiful features, and she takes my breath away.

As I dish out the spaghetti onto her plate, I grin and ask, "Is this really your favorite, or were you just saying that to be nice?"

"It really is. I can remember my mom making it a lot when I was a kid. I think it might have been one of the only things she could make," she says with a grin. "It always reminds me of her when I eat it, so I guess maybe that's why I like it so much," she says reflectively.

"She doesn't make it anymore?" I question.

"She died from cancer when I was a little girl."

I grimace. *Way to bring up a sore subject, Max*, I chide myself. I have a knack for putting my foot in my mouth when I'm around her. "Oh, Avery, I'm so sorry. I wouldn't have brought it up if I had known."

She waves her hand, dismissing it. "It's fine."

I set the plate of spaghetti down in front of her and dish out my own before taking a seat. I watch in anticipation as she takes the first bite. Her eyes roll up to the heavens as she groans, "Mmm!"

A smile spreads across my lips. She is completely charming without even trying. "Is it good?"

"Better than good. It's perfect."

"My dad's recipe," I say with pride.

"Your dad?" She sounds surprised.

"Yeah. He was the cook of our family. He actually taught my mom how to cook." I take a bite of the spaghetti. It turned out just right, and I couldn't be happier. "Pretty darn good. I was so worried I would ruin it and we would have to get take-out." She grins at my confession, and it's contagious. I can't stop smiling when she's around.

"So do you cook more than just spaghetti?" she asks.

"Yes, but not much more. How about you? Do you like to cook?"

She gives a slight shrug. "I suppose I enjoy it." She takes a sip of wine. "Neither one of my parents really cooked, so they hired a chef from California. I learned all the basics from him. He was a great teacher."

"So you must be a pretty good cook then?"

"I have to be," she answers. I can tell right away that she didn't mean to say it, and I watch her fingertips touch her lips as if she wants to stuff the words back into her mouth. I want to ask her what she meant by that, but she quickly changes the subject. "So how long have you known I was your neighbor?"

I take a sip of my wine, stalling. She's anxiously awaiting my response, and I don't know whether to tell her the truth or make something up. But I decide that I don't ever want to lie to her. "I saw you the first night I stayed here actually."

Avery fidgets in her chair, and her eyes nervously dart down to the table. I don't have to be a mind reader to know she's worried about me seeing her crying on the beach. I decide not to divulge that secret just yet. "So how long have you been married?" I ask, trying to redirect the conversation.

"Two years, one month and nineteen —." She stops abruptly and looks up at me.

My God. She didn't finish, but she was going to say nineteen days. She has it down to the very day, and I wouldn't be surprised if she knows the exact hour as well. The manner in which she speaks about it sounds like she's counting down a prison sentence rather than an amorous marriage. And I have a feeling that's exactly what Avery's life is like — a prison.

"Have you ever been married?" she asks. Now *she's* attempting to redirect the focus of the conversation.

I shake my head. "Came close to it once," I confess.

She says, "Oh," and then becomes very quiet.

"Sometimes things don't work out the way you plan or want them to."

She nods. "I know the feeling," she whispers.

We settle into a comfortable silence while enjoying our meal with the ocean waves breaking in the distance. The more I'm around Avery, the more I pick up on her idiosyncrasies. She always wears a watch, and her eyes continuously peek at the time. I think it's almost a subconscious thing, because I don't think she actually realizes she's doing it. She avoids eye contact with me whenever possible. I wonder if this is a habit her husband instilled in her. At the hospital she ignores all of the male doctors, but has no problem talking to the female nurses and doctors and kids. I'm assuming she's not allowed to talk to men in general. She also bites on her bottom lip when she's nervous, which is almost all of the time. She's a very nervous person in general and always seems to be on edge. I can't help but think of how Rosie described the *old Avery* — spunky and full of life. That is not the girl sitting here before me, although I can tell she is breaking out of her shell little by little the more I'm around her.

I'm so angry that Nathan could control this sweet girl like he does, breaking her spirit at any cost. More of Rosie's words come back to me about how maybe Nathan is finally breaking her down. I worry about Avery. I want her to know there is a better life out there for her. And even if it's not with me, she deserves to be with someone who cares for her, someone who loves her.

As Avery reaches for a breadstick in the middle of the table, my eyes flicker to her arm. Her perfect skin is highlighted by the candlelight. Just yesterday she had dark bruises the whole way up her arm, and now they are gone. Something's not adding up here. I lean forward, and now I can see that the perfection in her skin is not natural. She's wearing some kind of makeup on her skin to conceal the bruises. Some of the darker bruises are peeking through a little, and I frown.

I lift my gaze to her face, and she's staring back at me. The look in her eyes tells me she knows exactly what I was looking at. She places the bread on her plate and sighs softly. "Max...I..."

I wave my hand dismissively. I don't want the night to turn awkward and force her to tell me things when she's not ready. "Tell me something about you, Avery. Anything."

"There's really not much to tell," she says quietly.

Shaking my head, I say, "I don't believe that for a second."

She meets my gaze for a moment before looking away once more. "You already know all there is to know about me, Max. You know where I live, that I'm married and that I volunteer at the hospital."

I nod. "Yes. But what do you like to do? What are your hobbies? What are you good at?"

A frown graces her lips. "I don't...I'm not really good at anything at all."

"Not even one thing?" I question in disbelief.

Her lips quirk up a bit as she says, "Well...I like to sing."

For some reason I feel like this is a little-known fact, and I'm happy that she shared it with me. "You sing?"

"Only in the shower."

"Are you any good?" I ask.

"I haven't heard any complaints," she says deadpan.

I chuckle, and she grins. I'm starting to get a sense of the real Avery, and I'm enjoying her immensely. "I would love to hear you sing sometime."

She grows quiet suddenly, and I grimace inwardly. Perhaps I'm being too pushy when it comes to trying to get Avery to come out of her shell, but I just can't help myself. It's so easy to let everything blur into the background when I'm around her. When I'm with her, it's like the rest of the world fades away. It's just us together in the moment.

We finish our dinner in companionable silence. After refreshing our glasses with wine, we move to the far corner of the patio overlooking the ocean. Avery wraps her hands around the railing and closes her eyes. A soft breeze blows, whipping Avery's hair behind her shoulders. Her soft, flowery scent washes over me, and I have the sudden urge to be closer to her.

Hesitantly, I walk up from behind and wrap my hands around the railing in front of her. Her back is pressed against my front. Almost instantly, I feel her entire body tremble as she recoils from my touch. With panicked breaths, she breaks away from me. I step back quickly, not knowing what I did wrong. Her eyes search mine for a minute, and then her face contorts with a myriad of emotions — confusion, torment, shame, embarrassment. "I'm sorry, Max," she whispers.

I'm not sure what caused her to react the way she did, but I can easily figure it out. I know it has something to do with a history of abuse at the hands of her husband, no less. My hands clench into fists. I want to take my anger out on Nathan. But he's not here, and I don't want to scare Avery away. I take a calming, deep breath. "Why do you stay with him?" I blurt out the question before even mulling it over in my head, but I desperately want to know the answer.

Her bottom lip trembles, and I know she's trying to hold herself together. I've only ever seen her crying alone on the beach, and I have the sense that's the only place where she releases her pent-up tears.

After a few moments, she lets out a long sigh, and her features slowly relax. "I've tried to leave him." Her gaze moves to stare out over the ocean. "Things started getting really bad about two months after we got married. I packed my things and got on a bus. I don't even remember where I was going. I just knew I couldn't stay here with him." She closes her eyes briefly and swallows hard. "His dad is the chief of police, and so Nathan made up a story to his father that I was a danger to myself. I didn't even make it out of the state before the bus was pulled over by every responding police officer in the county. Nathan had me committed to a mental institution soon thereafter." She wraps her arms tightly around herself as a chill seems to pass through her. "Three months of my life I don't even remember because of the drugs. He told me if I ever tried to leave him again that he would send me to an institution permanently. He not only threatened me, but my entire family. It doesn't help the situation that my father is in politics and that the Mason family basically has him in their back pocket. Nathan and his family donate a lot of money to my father's campaigns," she explains.

I shake my head slowly. It's starting to make sense now. I'm getting more pieces to the puzzle, and soon I'll be able to see the whole picture. Everything she tells me about Nathan makes me loathe him with a passion. "So you never tried leaving again?"

Her shoulders slump in defeat. "I've tried. So many times. He found me." Her eyes move to the flickering flame of one of the tiki torches. "He always finds me," she adds. "Nathan is a very powerful man with a lot of resources." Avery's voice sounds lost, haunted, and it sends a shiver through me. She glances down at her wrist as her fingers absentmindedly run under the watchband, stroking her wrist. "The last time I tried was about six months ago. He found me in a run-down motel in South Carolina. I thought I had finally escaped, but I was wrong. When he brought me back here, I kind of snapped. I waited until he left for work, and then I..." She swallows hard and tears form in her eyes.

I stare at the vertical scar on the inside of her wrist. She isn't talking about just trying to run away. She attempted the ultimate escape. She tried to kill herself. My heart breaks for her that she felt like she had no other way out. I just want to take her into my arms and hold her, but I don't want to scare her away. She obviously doesn't like to be touched in certain ways, and with time I'll learn which ways are acceptable to her. For right now I'll give her the only thing I can — support.

"I...I haven't tried again." She releases a shaky sigh. "But I've just... I've given up hope."

I reach for her, and my thumb gently skims over the scar. I hear her sharp intake of breath, and I look up to meet her blue-gray eyes. "If you ever feel the urge again, will you promise to talk to me first?" I ask, my voice insisting.

She hesitates, and then nods once.

"You have so much to offer. I see it in those kids' faces every day at the hospital and especially with Jacob. What would he do without you, Avery? You're the only one who can put a smile on his face." I stroke her soft skin. "I would hate to see a world without you in it."

Tears quickly fill her eyes, and she pulls away from me. "I-I should go," she says with an unsteady voice.

"I'm sorry if I upset you, Avery," I say quickly. "That wasn't my intent."

She turns her back to me, but doesn't walk away. "You didn't upset me." She wrings her hands nervously. "I'm just not used to someone being so nice to me."

Even though I don't want to scare her, I just need to feel her in my arms. I want her to feel safe with me. I stand and walk around to face her. Her gaze is to the floor. "Avery..." My voice trails off. I want to hold her, but I don't know if she'll let me. So I decide to simply ask. "I want to hold you. Will you let me do that?"

She bites her bottom lip nervously. Then she looks up at me and gives me a small nod.

I pull her into my arms and gently embrace her. Our hearts beat rapidly in competition with each other. I have to wonder if she's feeling the same connection that I feel. God, I hope so.

My nose sinks into her soft hair, breathing in the scent of coconut with a hint of a flowery perfume. Everything about this moment feels right. She feels so damn good in my arms, and I don't ever want to let her go. My mouth moves to her ear as I whisper, "Every night this week I've watched you go down to the beach and cry." I feel her stiffen against me at my confession, but she doesn't attempt to pull away. I continue and say, "I understand the release you need after the mask you have to wear all day long. But you don't have to pretend with me, Avery. You don't have to hide your tears from me...or the bruises."

Ever so slowly I feel the walls tumbling down around her. Tentatively, she curls her hands into my shirt, and I hear the first break in her breathing as she starts to sob.

"It's okay," I whisper as my hand soothingly strokes her long silky hair down her back. "It's okay to cry, Avery."

Her fingers grip my shirt tighter and pull me impossibly closer. I wonder how long it's been since someone held her. It breaks my heart to think that it's been far too long. She is so strong and yet so fragile, and I just have an overwhelming need to protect her from everything bad in this world.

I hold her for a long time until her breathing returns to normal and the tears stop. Then I pull back and stare down at her tear-stained face. "Avery, I feel this indescribable connection to you. Tell me I'm crazy. Tell me you don't feel it too."

She closes her eyes for a few seconds. When she opens them, they are glittering from the candlelight. "I feel it," she whispers. "Max...you're the first person to make me *feel* anything in such a long time."

Her words hit me hard, and I stare down at her gorgeous lips. I want to kiss her, but I hold back. And then she surprises me by leaning up and brushing her mouth lightly over mine. I take that as an invitation and gently cup her face in my hands before deepening the kiss. Her lips are just as soft as I had imagined. The kiss is brief, but it's meaningful.

We slowly part, and my heart feels like it's going to leap out of my chest. I have never experienced what I'm experiencing right now with her. I know it's too soon and maybe even wrong to feel this way, but I can't stop myself even if it's against my better judgment. She's married, unattainable, but I don't want to stay away. I can't stay away.

I think she does need a knight in shining armor after all, and I want to be that for her. I want to protect her.

My thumb tenderly glides over her bottom lip as she gazes up at me. She looks so beautiful it hurts. "Your husband will be gone until next weekend?" I ask.

She nods. "Next Saturday."

"Let me spend time with you this week, Avery. I want to get to know you better."

She doesn't answer right away. "Max," she starts.

"I know it's wrong to want this, but it feels so damn right. I feel so connected with you, and I know you feel it too. I'm not expecting anything to happen between us, Avery. Just spend time with me...as a friend. We'll let fate decide where it goes after that."

I can see numerous emotions flicker across her face. I would give anything to know what she's thinking right now. But before I can make another plea to her, she whispers, "Okay." Then she slowly steps back out of my reach and says, "I should go. Thank you." She hesitates before adding, "For everything."

"I'll see you tomorrow, Avery." I watch her walk off the porch and into her house. Even though we just met a few days ago, I feel like I've known her forever. Avery is so easy to love. I just wish she could understand that. Nathan clearly doesn't deserve her, and I intend to spend our time together this week proving that to her.

AVERY

I RUN INTO the house and close the door. Letting out a long breath, I lean against the cool glass and press a hand to my chest. My erratic heartbeat thumps loudly under my palm. I close my eyes, and the only thing I can think about is Max. When he had invited me over spaghetti, I never could have imagined the evening we would share together. It was more than just dinner. It was a glimpse into another life, a life where I could have more than just heartache and pain. Everything had been absolutely perfect.

My fingertips graze over my lips as I relive our kiss in my mind. There was an instant spark there that I never experienced before. I didn't want the evening to ever end, but that is exactly why it had to. Being around him is dangerous in every sense of the word, but I can't help but feel this strong, inexplicable connection to him.

The house phone rings, snapping me out of my daydream. A sense of alarm floods over me as Nathan's name pops up on the caller ID. He always calls a lot whenever he's gone. He likes to keep a constant tab on me, especially from afar.

My hand moves to pick up the receiver, but then I stop myself. Nathan is in Seattle. *He can't hurt me right now.*

Deep down inside I know the consequences that will come from me not answering, but at the moment I just don't care. My arm falls back down to my side, and I let the phone continue to ring while I walk to the bedroom. The handset on the nightstand rings and rings and rings. Without hesitation, I grab the phone and take out the battery. With a nod of satisfaction, I change into pajamas, wash my face, brush my teeth and then nestle into my side of the bed.

I close my eyes, but sleep escapes me. I can't seem to stop thinking about Max. And as our dinner replays for the fifth time in my head, I throw back the comforter with a sigh. Climbing out of bed, I move to the windows and glance over at Max's house. He's cleaning up from our dinner on his porch, and I watch him from a shroud of darkness. I know I shouldn't spy on him, but I can't help it.

Dinner with Max felt like a first step for me in the right direction for once. I let him touch me, and he held me as I cried. I haven't cried in front of anyone for years, and I can't even remember the last time I let someone hold me. Just the thought of it makes me nervous. I've been shown nothing but pain and cruelty for so many years that an act of kindness is abnormal to me now. But there's just something about Max that makes me feel safe, and I want to hold onto that feeling for as long as I can. Even though I instinctively want to keep my guard up when I'm around him, he's been easily knocking down all my walls without even trying. He sees me. He really sees me. I'm not just a possession or a trophy to him. I'm someone. And I think I might be someone he cares about, even if it's just as a friend.

Max told me he wants to spend time with me this week. He wants to get to know me better, and I feel exactly the same way. I want to know everything about him — where he grew up, about his family, why he chose to be a doctor, his hopes and dreams. I don't know what the future holds, but it's suddenly looking brighter than it ever has before.

I watch Max until he douses the tiki torches and candles and retreats inside his house. I return to bed and close my eyes. With thoughts of Max running through my head, I slowly fall asleep with a smile on my face.

AVERY

THE NEXT DAY I meet my dad at our usual place, a seafood restaurant in Rodanthe. The owner of the restaurant and my father grew up together; and so even though the place is packed, we're able to secure our favorite table right near a large window overlooking the Pamlico Sound.

For the primary portion of the meal, I listen to my father talk about his upcoming campaign for governor. "It's almost a lock. With the Masons behind me, I don't see how I couldn't win," he says smugly.

Nathan's family has money and power. If they want strings to be pulled, they will be pulled no matter the cost. I think back to the first time I met Nathan. I often wonder if that night had been planned by our parents to get Nathan and I together. I can't say I really blame my father. He probably thought he was helping out by introducing me to one of the wealthiest bachelors in North Carolina. He couldn't have known about Nathan's dark side. I don't know if Nathan's own parents even know. The only person who knows the absolute truth is me...and now Max. And I haven't even told Max that much. He somehow figured some of it out on his own. For years I felt like I was standing in a crowded room screaming, but no one could hear my cries. And then Max gives me one look and instantly knows me inside and out. It scares me more than anything, but it also gives me hope for something I haven't felt in my life since my mother died — love.

I stare down at the fancy linen napkin I'm nervously twisting in my trembling hands. I've never been able to have a conversation with my father without him making me feel like a child. With as much courage as I can possibly muster, I say, "Dad, I want to divorce Nathan."

My father sputters in his glass of water, nearly choking. He coughs violently and looks at me with flared eyes. "What?" he asks as if he cannot believe what I just said.

He's as blind as the rest of them. He has no idea what happens behind closed doors. No one ever does. On the outside looking in, we are the perfect couple. Nathan is a rich and successful doctor, and I am a trophy wife who lives a life of luxury. A perfect fairy tale with a happily ever after. The end. What they don't know is the hell I am put through day in and day out and the torture he inflicts on my mind and my body. I would trade everything — the money, the social status, the clothes and the cars to get away from him. *Every single thing.*

"Now, Avery, you know I'm in the middle of a campaign. Nathan and his family are a very big part of this. They have donated a *lot* of money, and I owe them tremendously for their support. If you two are having a little tiff, I'm sure it will blow over soon. No sense in stirring the pot if we don't have to. Right?" he asks eagerly.

I wring the napkin tighter in my hands. "What if it's more than a little tiff?" I ask.

"Whatever is going on between you two, I'm sure you can work it out," Dad says, reaching across the table and patting my hand.

"I don't want it to work out," I say sternly, standing my ground even if my voice is wavering, a telltale sign of my true emotions. "Dad, I need your help. I can't do this on my own." I look at him pleadingly. I am almost to the point of begging.

"Avery," he says in a scolding tone that makes me scowl. "I need this campaign to go off without a hitch. Do you understand how important this is to me...to our family?"

In just the matter of a few words, he has dashed my hopes and dreams away. I can feel the panic rising in my chest. Swallowing hard, I simply nod, not trusting myself to speak. With tears trying to force their way into my eyes, I stare out the window and watch the kite surfers on the water.

"That's my girl." He gives my hand a light squeeze and then releases me. His fork digs into the seafood on his plate. Before the scallop reaches his mouth, he asks, "Now, are you sure it's nothing you can't work out with Nathan?"

I waver. I want to tell him everything, but I am so afraid of him not believing me and casting me off for the sake of his career. And I don't think I could handle that reaction right now from him. How do I tell my father the truth when he doesn't even want to hear it? "I wish mom was here," I whisper.

"I know, sweetheart. I miss her too." He chews slowly and then takes a sip of water. "My fundraising event for my campaign is in a few weeks. Nathan told me you will both be attending," he says, changing the subject. That was always something he was good at doing — deflecting attention away from the real issue.

"I guess so," I mutter.

"Avery, I *need* you and Nathan there. And I need your sister and her family there as well. Have you talked to Allison recently? My secretary can't seem to ever catch her at a good time to discuss the fundraiser."

I shake my head in response. He doesn't actually need us there. He wants us there solely because if I'm not there for a potential photo op, it will make him look bad. My sister Allison and I have to appear with him like the all-American family with our handsome and rich husbands and her perfect baby while the photographers snap pictures. What a joke.

When Allison and I were young and he was a single father running for state representative, we were pawns in his campaign. We were told to smile pretty for the press and pretend like everything was perfect when, in reality, my sister and I were struggling every single moment of our lives without our mother and with the fact that we had a father who was never around. Even as an adult I'm still pretending to be happy on the outside when I'm dying inside, and deep down that makes me so angry. I'm so damn tired of pretending.

"So you'll be there?" he prompts.

I turn my attention from the water and back to him. "Wouldn't miss it," I say with lucid sarcasm dripping from my tone.

He tips his chin towards my plate. "You barely touched your lobster."

I stab my fork onto my plate and push a forkful of lobster in my mouth to appease him. He smiles and resumes talking about his campaign and the upcoming fundraiser.

When I finally leave the restaurant, I am disheartened. Lunch didn't go exactly as I had planned in my head. I thought my father would at least hear me out, but that obviously isn't going to happen. If he won't help me, there is only one person I can turn to — my sister. I don't know what it's going to take to actually leave Nathan and file for divorce, but I know I need help. He would never let me leave willingly. I know that for a fact.

I will need a place to stay where he won't be able to find me no matter how hard he looks. And I'll need some cash to get by. Nathan was able to track me by my credit card usage before, so this time I know I can't leave a paper trail. I will also need protection in case he would find me, but I know I can't turn to the police for help. Nathan has too many ties with his father being the chief of police, and I don't want to risk being placed in a psych ward again.

There are three important things I need from my sister, and I hope she doesn't turn me down as easily as our father. Allison is my last resort on a very short road of opportunity. It's going to take a lot to leave Nathan once and for all. And it's not just something I need to do. It's something I *have* to do.

MAX

IT'S IN THE late afternoon when I hear Avery's car pull up to the house next door. I'm lounging on the back porch soaking up the afternoon's sunrays after a run on the beach. Several minutes later, she emerges onto her back patio. I turn my head and wave. She looks upset, but she attempts to hide it with a smile. It's the fake smile that she puts on for everyone to show them that she's fine. But, in reality, she's not fine.

I stand and move to the edge of the porch. "Everything okay?" I ask.

"Yeah," she says quietly.

I've been waiting all day for the chance to ask her out tonight, so I'm hoping her sour mood doesn't affect her answer to my question. "Do you have any plans later?"

She shakes her head slowly.

I rub the back of my head with my hand. Why am I always so nervous around this girl? I never had this much trouble asking out anyone before I met Avery. "How about dinner and a movie?"

A real smile cracks through the fake one and spreads quickly across her lips. It's a smile that I see so rarely on her, and she wears it well. "Sure. What movie are we going to see?" she asks.

I'm stunned by her answer, and it takes me a while to register that she actually said yes. I was mentally prepared for the exact opposite. Something definitely changed between us last night. "Your choice. We'll leave at six."

"Okay. I'll meet you out front then." she says before disappearing back into her house.

A big goofy grin is plastered on my face and stays there while I get ready for our date tonight — our first real date out in public. After a long shower, I slip into a pair of dark deconstructed jeans and a light blue button-up shirt with the sleeves rolled up on my forearms. Socks and sneakers are next. I decide to wear my favorite pair of black and white Vans. I have no idea how Avery is going to be dressed, so I hope I'm not too casual.

When I lay my eyes on her as she walks to my car, I no longer care whether we are both casual or not. She looks hot as hell in dark skinny jeans, heels and a black blazer over a white sequin shirt that glitters like diamonds in the sunlight. Her long hair is pulled back into a high ponytail, and her bangs are swept to the side so I can get a full view of those lovely eyes of hers. Her makeup is dark and smoky again, and I love it. It makes her look hotter, if that's even possible.

Noticing my stare, her step falters. She glances down at her outfit and then back up to me. "Do I look all right?" she asks nervously.

It's hard to imagine a girl that gorgeous being so self-conscious. It's as if she doesn't even realize how beautiful she is. I scowl inwardly when I think that maybe she doesn't know because her husband never tells her or perhaps tells her the exact opposite. Pushing that terrible thought aside, I grin and tell her, "You look amazing."

She looks relieved, but still a little nervous. I'm glad I'm not the only one who's feeling that way. My stomach feels like I just stepped onto a roller coaster. I don't think I've ever been this nervous about a date before.

Stepping around the front of my silver Escalade, I open the passenger side door for her. She climbs in, and then I slip behind the steering wheel. Turning the key, the engine roars to life. "All set?" I ask. When she nods, I pull out of the driveway. Coasting down the highway towards the main strip of restaurants and businesses, I ask, "What are you in the mood for?"

"How about Big Fred's Burger Joint?" she suggests.

I stare at her in disbelief before turning my attention back to the road. I thought she was going to suggest some fancy place where you have to wait an hour to get in and the bill is the amount of someone's rent check. Instead, she chooses a small diner with a menu that consists of greasy food and milkshakes. "Have you eaten there before?" I ask. I'm insanely curious for her answer.

"Years ago," she says. "They have *the* best burgers."

I chuckle and shake my head.

"What?" she asks, obviously confused by my reaction.

"You just don't seem like the type of girl to go to a place like that. I figured you would want lobster or sushi or —."

Before I can finish my thought, she cuts in with, "Well, I guess you don't know me well enough yet."

Grinning from ear to ear, I reply, "I guess not." I glance over at her and see that she's smiling. "But I want to get to know you, Avery," I say with sincerity. My hand finds hers and lightly squeezes.

Her eyes meet mine, and she whispers, "Ditto."

MAX

WE GET TO the burger joint, and Avery surprises me by ordering a greasy burger, fries and a chocolate milkshake. What she ordered sounded so good that I decided to order the same exact thing.

While we eat, I make small talk by asking about her favorite things. Her favorite type of music is oldies from the '50s and '60s because it reminds her of her mother. Her favorite movies are all classics as well. "What's your favorite season?" I ask.

"Winter," she says without any hesitation.

Everything about this girl throws me for a loop. I would think that summer would be her favorite season since she lives right on the beach. I ponder her answer before asking, "Is there a reason for that?"

"I think I like it so much because it feels like everything has a chance to start over." She catches my gaze for a moment and continues. "Everything is dead and cold, and then a few months later in the spring it all gets to be reborn. Winter is cleansing in a way. A fresh coating of snow is the purest thing, covering everything in a sparkling blanket of white, making it beautiful no matter how dirty or impure it was before. Even the ugliest weed can look pretty when it's covered in snow. And then in the spring, everything has a chance to grow again and start over. Winter is like a clean slate, so to speak."

I have a feeling there is a deeper meaning in what she is saying, but I try not to overthink it. If she thinks she is impure or ugly in some way, she is wrong. She is beautiful both inside and out, and I've only just begun to scratch the surface.

Avery takes a sip of her milkshake from the thick straw. I try to avoid staring at her, but that proves to be extremely difficult. When her plump pink lips wrap around the straw, I feel like I'm going to spontaneously combust. I can still remember how soft those lips were against mine and the way she tasted. I stifle a groan and force my eyes to my plate and try to focus on something other than her mouth.

We're able to finish eating without any combustion on my part, and I pay the check before we head out the door. "The movies are starting in about twenty minutes, so we should probably head there now," I say as we get into the SUV. When I start the engine, Lynyrd Skynyrd's *Free Bird* comes on the radio. I reach for the volume knob at the same time she does, and our fingers bump against each other.

"Sorry," she says quickly.

"I was just going to turn it up."

She grins. "Me too."

I crank the volume and glance over at Avery. She closes her eyes and sways gently to the music. "You don't strike me as a Lynyrd Skynyrd fan," I say as I pull the SUV out of the parking lot and onto the highway. *Although she didn't strike me as a burgers and fries kind of girl either*, I think to myself. She's definitely full of surprises. I'll give her that.

She laughs. It's a breathy, genuine laugh, and it sounds wonderful. "Who couldn't possibly love this band?"

"That's very true." I listen to the lyrics of the song, and it kind of reminds me of Avery. She's like a beautiful, rare bird, and her husband has clipped her wings. He keeps her steeled away in his gilded cage, never allowing her to be free, never allowing others to see her true beauty. I'd love to see her be able to leave him and be free to do whatever she wants to in life. She deserves so much more than she has right now.

Avery softly sings along, and I strain to hear her over the radio. I remember she told me last night that she liked to sing in the shower. Losing herself in the music, she starts to sing a little louder, and I can clearly pick up on her voice. She sounds incredible. "You should do karaoke," I suggest, glancing over at her. I would love to hear her voice secluded with only music in the background.

She laughs again, and it's music to my ears. I can see a slight blush creep onto her cheeks. "That is something I've never tried."

"Really? Never? Well, you should. You'd be very good at it," I say confidently.

Her smile slowly fades. "I would be too embarrassed to be on stage in front of people," she confesses.

"What could you possibly be embarrassed about? You're gorgeous, funny, smart, and you can sing."

She worries her bottom lip between her teeth and stares out the window. I know that's a habit she has whenever she's nervous. Immediately I regret saying what I did. She really has no idea how amazing she is, and her constant self-doubt tugs at my heartstrings. I reach over and pull her hand into mine. My thumb skates over her soft skin, and I'm struck with the realization that she's not wearing her wedding ring. I grin. She's giving this a chance. She's giving us a chance. Even if we haven't spelled it out or put into writing what we're doing, I feel like there is something between us, something more than just friendship. This feels like a real date, and everything else doesn't matter when we're together.

"Have you lived in North Carolina your whole life?" I ask in an attempt to cut through the tension still lingering in the air.

"Yes. Well, I was actually born in California."

"California. Wow." I look over at her and see she's staring at our joined hands as my thumb caresses her skin. When I first took her hand, it was balled into a tight fist; but now she's slowly relaxing. I take that as a sign of trust.

"My mom was actually an actress. Her stage name was Olivia O'Dell, and she met my father while he was on a business trip in Cali. They fell in love, and nine months later I came into the world. They moved to my father's estate in North Carolina when I was only two months old. And a couple years later my sister Allison was born. My mom always wanted to return to Hollywood, but..." Her voice trails off as she returns her gaze to the window. She's instantly in another place, another time.

I give her hand a gentle squeeze, and it seems to bring her back to the present.

"She never got the chance," she says with a small sigh.

"Was she in any big movies that I would know of?" I ask.

"*Live Again* and *One More Time* were her biggest hits. She starred in romantic comedies mostly, so I'm sure you haven't seen them. You don't strike me as the romantic comedy type," she jokes, squeezing my hand playfully.

I chuckle and squeeze back. "I would definitely take a De Niro movie over a romantic comedy any day, but I would love to watch your mom's movies sometime with you."

A huge smile appears on her face, and she says, "I'd like that."

We reach our destination, and I'm actually kind of disappointed that the ride wasn't longer. I love talking to Avery and hearing her throaty laugh and little sighs. Just being around her, in general, makes me happy. It's a scary thought when I think of how miserable I'm going to be after this week is over.

I shake my head, dispelling the thought. I have this entire week with her. I'm really enjoying her company, and I think we get along great. I'm not going to mope around and constantly think about it ending. Instead, I'm going to revel in the time we have together, no matter how short it may be.

When we walk into the theater, there are three movies playing. One is a horror flick, which Avery immediately says no to. I'm totally fine with that since I'm not big on scary movies...although I wouldn't mind her jumping into my arms if she got scared. The other two movies are complete opposites. The one is a total guy's pick with non-stop action, guns and fighting, and the other is a total chick flick.

I glance at the posters. "Well, there's only one way to settle this."

She looks at me with apprehension.

"Rock, paper, scissors," I say deadpan.

She giggles, and it makes me smile. "Best two out of three," she suggests.

After three quick rounds, she wins by covering my rock with her paper. And so I buy the tickets to the romantic comedy. Most guys would probably complain about seeing a chick flick, but I'm just happy to be here with her, no matter what we watch.

"I think you let me win," she says as we walk to the concession stand.

I feign shock, and she laughs.

"Come on, Max. You picked rock three times in a row."

"Did I?" I ask, nonchalantly. She's right. I did let her win. I don't really care what movie we see as long as I get to spend time with her.

After we get our drinks, I reach for her hand. It feels so damn good in mine, and I can't stop grinning like an idiot. She leads the way into the theater. We sit in a dark back corner of the theater in what I refer to as the 'make-out seats'. While I wouldn't mind making out with Avery, I'm not going to push my luck. If this is going to work, we're going to have to move at her pace. And at this point, I don't care if her pace is as slow as molasses. Just being around her makes me happy. Anything else that might happen is just the icing on the cake.

We chat quietly through the previews and talk about each movie that looks interesting. I'm quick to find out that Avery and I have pretty much the same taste not only in music, but in movies as well.

"Oh, I want to see this one," she whispers in my ear.

I grin at how close she gets when she wants to whisper to me, and I'm secretly hoping that she talks through the whole damn movie. Another preview comes on. "This one looks good too."

She grabs her drink from the cup holder and says, "We should come see this when it comes out." She catches herself, and the hand bringing the drink up to her mouth halts suddenly. "I mean...I..."

I lean over to her and whisper, "We'll come see it. I promise."

A smile tugs on the corners of her lips. Before she can say anything else, the movie starts. The basic plot is about a woman whose husband is cheating on her, and she falls in love with a guy that she works with. *How fitting.*

Avery is completely engrossed in the movie; however, my eyes keep straying from the screen to her face. I love to watch her reactions to different parts of the movie. And when her pink lips part as she gasps, I find myself just wanting to kiss her again.

As if she can sense my eyes on her, she turns her head. Our lips are only inches apart. I can't stop staring at them and thinking about what they felt like pressed up against mine last night. I reach up and gently run my fingertips along her jaw line. My thumb skates over her bottom lip, and I can feel her soft breath on my skin. Her lips gently kiss the pad of my thumb. It's a simple gesture, but it's meaningful and incredibly sexy coming from her.

She smiles a heart-stopping smile that takes my breath away. Then she slides under my arm that's draped over the back of her chair, resting her head on my chest. My nose is in her hair, breathing in her flowery scent. She smells wonderful. I wrap my arm around her, pull her close and run my fingertips casually up and down her arm. She's tense at first, but quickly relaxes. I can feel her sigh with content, and it makes me happy to know she's comfortable with me. She stays in my arms for the rest of the movie. With any other girl, it wouldn't be a big deal. But with Avery, I know she's starting to open up to me and trust me. And I can't help but start falling for her, although I think I already tripped and fell head over heels days ago when we first met.

AVERY

MAX HOLDS MY hand as we walk out of the movie theater. It's as if he's afraid of letting me go. And in all honesty, I don't want him to let me go.

He opens the car door for me, and I climb in. He gets in the driver's seat and navigates us out of the parking lot and down the strip of businesses and neon lights along the stretch of highway.

We're riding in comfortable silence when he says, "Hang on," before suddenly veering off the road. He pulls the SUV into a dirt and gravel parking lot in front of a brick building and parks near the front entrance. I look over at him curiously and see that he's staring straight ahead with a big smile on his face. I follow his gaze. We're in front of a little dive bar. Through the cloud of dust that the SUV stirred up, I see a lighted sign by the front entrance with the words *Karaoke Tonight*.

I turn back to Max and instantly protest. "No. No way."

He smiles and says. "You have to, Avery. It's fate that brought us here. I was telling you earlier how you should do karaoke," he says, sweeping his hand towards the building, "and now here we are."

"I...I can't," I argue.

"Why not?"

I hesitate. I can't really think of a good reason besides the fact that I am completely and utterly terrified. Before I can say another word, he gets out of the vehicle, walks around the front and opens my door. He holds his hand out, but it seems like it's more than just an invitation to get out of the car. It feels like it's an invitation to jump into deep water with him and trust that he won't let me drown.

Closing my eyes, I take a deep breath. *Just jump*, I tell myself. I put my hand in his, and he pulls me out of the vehicle with a big goofy grin on his face. I can't resist that grin.

We walk into the bar. A cloud of cigarette smoke floats in the air, and multi-colored lights flash sporadically through it from the stage and DJ booth near the back wall. I grab Max's hand and lead him straight to the bar. The bartender looks at me expectantly. "Two tequila shots," I say with conviction. Max shoots me a look, and I shrug and say, "If I'm going to do this, it's not going to be sober."

He laughs. "So you *are* doing it then?"

I pinch my lips together and stare up at him through my long lashes. He looks so damn happy. How could I ever say no to him? I nod once, and his smile widens.

The bartender brings back the shots. I slap money on the counter and down both of them one after the other. The alcohol burns my throat and leaves a warm sensation trailing down to my stomach. I gasp for air and shake my head at the taste. It's been so long since I've had straight liquor. It definitely hasn't improved in taste.

Max's jaw drops. "And here I thought one was for me," he jokes.

I laugh.

His dark gaze is on me as his fingers gently cup my jaw. "I love to hear that," he says softly. My heart stutters in my chest. "I wish I could make you happy all the time."

I stare into his dark eyes and instantly get lost. He always says the sweetest things to me, and I know he has no idea how much his words mean to me. I lean up on my tiptoes and kiss him. I intended for the kiss to be short, but my lips linger. He's the one that breaks it off first. He has a heated look in his eye, and I know he's trying to restrain himself. I respect that he's not trying to push me, but I don't know how much longer I will want him to hold back.

The bartender returns and asks, "Another?"

I shake my head and say, "No. I'm good."

While Max orders a beer, I turn to face the back of the bar and focus on the person on the stage. It's an older man, and he's singing a Johnny Cash song. His voice cracks, and it sounds like he's moaning...or maybe dying, but the audience doesn't seem to mind. I'm hopeful that they won't mind my singing either. I have never sung in public before and definitely not in front of a crowd. I know I'm not tone deaf, but I don't know if I would classify myself as being good at singing either.

The song ends, and the DJ announces, "We need more people to sign up. Come on up here, sign the book, and I'll call your name when it's your turn." He pauses and then calls Tiffany to the stage. Tiffany looks like she's had twice as much tequila as me. She staggers on the stage, throws up a pair of devil horns with both hands while simultaneously sticking out her tongue. She grabs the microphone, and her friends in the crowd cheer her on as an upbeat country song about getting revenge on an ex blasts through the speakers.

Everyone seems to be singing country, but I don't know any country songs. I listen to the radio on the way to and from the hospital, and it's usually tuned in to a pop or rock station. If I sing something different, will they boo me? What if I get up there and can't sing at all? What if I stand there frozen on stage like a moron?

Anxiety slowly crawls its way into my body and roots itself deep into my bones. I can feel sweat starting to form on my forehead, and I quickly wipe it away. Just as I'm ready to tell Max I can't do this, he says, "I'm going to go sign your name." Before I can object, he disappears into the crowd with a beer in his hand.

My heart is racing. I don't know why I'm so nervous. *It's just a bar*, I try to tell myself. *No one knows you here, and they're probably all drunk.* I can't seem to shake the feeling from my stomach, and soon I'm in a full-blown panic attack. I rush to the women's bathroom and lean over the sink. My head is pounding, and I know it's probably from the tequila. I reach into my purse for my pills, but then I realize I didn't bring them. I didn't think I would need any. "Shit!" I hold a hand on each side of my pounding head and try to relax. "It's okay. You're okay," I tell myself. But I don't feel okay.

I hear a knock on the door. "Avery?" It's Max.

"Yeah. Just a minute," I call, and I can hear the tremor in my voice. My breathing becomes shallow, and I press my hand to my chest, willing my heart to stop its erratic beating.

"Are you okay?" He must have heard the fear in my voice too.

I go to the door and open it. He takes one look at me, and he instantly rushes forward, his hands cupping my face. "What's wrong?"

"Panic...attack," I say between short pants.

"Okay. We're going to get through this, Avery." He grabs my hands and says, "Close your eyes."

I do as he says.

"Breathe nice and slow for me. Nice and slow. That's it. Breathe, Avery. Just breathe."

My chest rises and falls with shaky breaths. I relish in the comfort of my hands in his. I have never been able to calm myself down before without medication; but if anyone could make me feel better, it would be Max. He always seems to know just what I need.

"Right now I want you to pretend that you aren't you and I'm not me. We're just two people having fun for one night. Forget the past, forget the future and just focus on right here, right now. Can you do that for me?"

I nod and continue to breathe in and out slower and slower.

"Concentrate on my voice. Breathe, Avery. It will all be better soon. I promise."

Before I know it, my breathing and heart rate have returned to normal. I open my eyes and gaze into his dark chocolate stare. "Thank you," I whisper.

"You're welcome."

I lean up to kiss him, but stop abruptly when the DJ announces my name. My eyes grow wide.

Max whispers against my lips, "You can do this, Avery. Remember, just focus on the moment. Only here. Only now. With me."

"Only here. Only now. With you."

He crushes his lips to mine for a swift kiss. Then he grabs my hand as we walk out of the bathroom. The crowd parts as we make our way through it. I reluctantly pull my hand from Max's hold as I hop up on the stage. The DJ smiles and says, "Pick a song from the list."

Flipping through the book quickly, I find a song that reminds me of my mother. She used to sing it when I was a little girl. I show the DJ the song, and he shakes his head with an amused expression on his face. "Okay. Make sure you blow them away," he says, handing me the microphone.

I step to the edge of the stage and stare past the blinding random patterns of multi-colored lights. There are at least fifty people sitting in tables surrounding the stage and even more at the bar and on the dance floor to the left of me. I've never sung in front of a crowd before. I'm more of a singing-in-the-shower kind of a girl. The only person who knew about my love for music and singing was my mother. I used to sing to her all the time, especially when she was sick from the chemotherapy.

For some reason, I was comfortable enough to sing in front of Max in the car. There's just something about him that brings out the *old Avery* and makes me want to open up to him and...love him.

Before I can even decipher my feelings for him, the song begins. I close my eyes, focus my thoughts on Max and instantly feel a calmness sweep over me. The opening to the song starts as I bring the microphone to my lips and begin to sing.

MAX

AT LAST BY Etta James filters through the speakers. Leave it to Avery to not pick a country song like ninety-nine percent of everyone who went before her. She told me she likes the classics, whether it's music or movies. I think she developed a lot of her tastes from her mother, and I would bet money that her mother was just as sweet and kind as her oldest daughter.

I make my way through the crowd and stand towards the edge of the seating area. I'm so anxious to hear Avery sing that I can barely stand still. Her eyes are closed as the intro plays, and she swings her hips slowly, delicately in time with the music. She looks like she's in her own world, and it is a beautiful sight. She appears completely calm and relaxed when just moments earlier she was having a panic attack right in front of me. I know me helping her through that was a major deal. I just hope it helps her to trust me and open up to me even more. I want her trust more than anything, because I know she doesn't do so easily.

Avery's lips part over the microphone as she begins to sing, and I can tell within the first few words that her voice is incredible. All the noisy conversations around me begin to die off almost instantaneously, and a hush falls over the entire bar. People turn their attention towards the stage to stare. Everyone is mesmerized by her, and I am totally beguiled.

Avery belts out the Etta James song almost better than the original. My God, she can sing. Like a siren calling me, my feet start moving towards the stage. I stand just a few feet away from her as goose bumps break out over my skin from her sultry voice. She sings just like an angel.

I am completely enraptured as I watch her. And as if sensing me, she opens her eyes and locks them on my gaze. I smile as she sings to me, and I feel like the luckiest bastard in the world. It's in that moment that I realize I've fallen for this girl. Hard. She has me under some kind of spell, and I never want her to break it.

The song finishes, and the bar is so quiet you could hear a pin drop. Suddenly, an explosion of whistles and applause roars throughout the crowd, and Avery's eyes grow wide. She looks shocked and amazed by their reaction. She has no idea how talented she really is.

I hold my hand out to her, and she jumps off the stage and into my arms. She looks up at me under the colored lights, and everything in that moment just feels right. I lean down and kiss her, and we are instantly rewarded with catcalls and clapping. Avery tentatively grips my shirt into her fingers, pulling me closer. The kiss grows heated as the world around us melts away.

It's after the third person yells, "Get a room!", when I finally break away.

I chuckle and grin, leaning my forehead against hers. "You were amazing." Taking her hand in mine, I say, "Let's get out of here."

We run out of the bar and don't stop running until we reach the SUV. She's laughing hysterically, and I know I would never get tired of hearing that sound. "I can't believe I just did that!" she exclaims.

"You were amazing. Everyone was completely captivated by you, Avery."

She bites her lower lip. "Even you?"

"You left me breathless." I put my hands on either side of her as she leans her back against the passenger's side door. "You're incredible."

Her blue-gray eyes narrow as if she doesn't believe me.

"You. Are. Incredible," I say, emphasizing each word.

She leans into me, and her lips meet mine in a scorching kiss. Her delicate hands slide up my torso, and I lose myself in her touch. My fingers itch to feel her, but I keep them planted on either side of her on the Escalade.

She tastes like mint and smells divine, and I just can't get enough of her. It feels like my senses are on overload. My tongue plays with the seam of her lips until she parts them, inviting me inside to explore her mouth. I sweep my tongue over hers and swallow the groan that escapes her throat. Forgetting myself, I press against her, pinning her to the car. Suddenly, she begins to tremble under me, and I feel a slight pressure on my chest as she gently pushes me back. I take a step away from her immediately. "I'm sorry," I say quickly. "I got carried away."

A crimson blush is on her cheeks as she sadly says, "It's okay. I should be the one apologizing."

I cup her face in the palms of my hands. "You never have to tell me you're sorry, Avery. For anything. We'll move at your pace... however painfully slow that might be," I joke. She smiles, and my heart melts. "Let's go," I say as I open the door for her. As I'm walking around the SUV, I take a deep breath and exhale. Avery has me so turned on, but I have to take things slow with her. I can't run when all she wants to do is walk. But I know when she's finally ready for me, I'll be there waiting no matter how long it takes for us to get to that point.

On the way back to the house, Avery asks, "So why did you leave Chicago?"

I grimace. It's a sensitive subject for me, but I want to be as forthcoming and open with her as I can. "It's complicated," I say finally.

"Short version?" she suggests.

"My fiancée cheated on me," I say with a huff. Then, as an afterthought, I add, "With my best friend." I glance over at her and see a shocked expression flash over her face. "Yeah. I had to get away from that mess." The revelation of Gretchen telling me she was sleeping with Kenneth still haunts me. My best friend of almost twenty years slept with my fiancée, the girl I was going to spend the rest of my life with. I lost the two most important people in my life within a matter of a few minutes. I shake my head to clear my thoughts. "My parents took my sister and I to Outer Banks for vacations a lot when we were young, and I was always happy there. I needed a place to go where I could be happy, so I thought why the hell not? I called the hospital, had a couple of my colleagues pull a few strings, and, well, here I am."

Then Avery surprises me by reaching over and placing her hand over mine and giving it a light squeeze. "Even though I'm not happy you had to go through all of that, I am happy that it led you here."

I stare at her for a few seconds before turning my attention back to the road. "Me too," I confess. When Gretchen cheated on me, I felt like my world was going to end. But fate has a funny way of working, and it brought me to Avery. I believe wholeheartedly that I'm here for a reason, and that the reason is, without a doubt, Avery.

Pulling the vehicle into my driveway, I park and kill the engine. The radio stays on, and Sam Smith's *Stay With Me* filters through the speakers. How very fitting.

Avery and I sit there, absorbing the lyrics. He's saying the words that I somehow can't muster up the courage to say. I want Avery to stay with me tonight. I don't know what she's thinking, but I'm not ready to let her go yet. I just hope she feels the same way.

AVERY

WE SIT IN the car, and the song playing on the radio is almost like fate smacking us right in the face. *Stay With Me.* I want to stay with Max, but I don't want to say what I'm really feeling. And since I pushed him away earlier, he probably doesn't want to say or do anything to ruin the evening. We've both been holding back. Me especially. And unless I take some control, this night is not going to end the way I want it to.

His words from earlier come back to me now. *Only here. Only now. With me.* Swallowing hard, I decide to take the leap. I'll deal with the consequences later. "I don't want to be alone tonight," I whisper, and it's the truth.

Max looks over at me. "You don't have to be," he whispers back.

With an unspoken agreement, we both climb out of the car, and Max leads the way to his house. My heart is thumping against my rib cage. I'm so nervous. I don't know what will happen between Max and me. Maybe nothing. Maybe something. But I haven't been intimate with anyone other than Nathan. We met when I was eighteen, and he was my first steady boyfriend. He took my virginity, but he never made love to me. It was always rough from the very beginning with him getting all the pleasure and leaving me with nothing but pain. I wonder if it's always like that. I wonder if it will be like that with Max. I can't imagine Max being rough with me, though. He's too gentle, too sweet and too kind — the exact opposite of Nathan.

Perhaps sensing my apprehension, Max turns to me and says, "Avery, you can leave at any time you want."

I put my hand in his and squeeze, needing to make sure he's actually real and here with me. He's almost too good to be true, and he has no idea what his kindness does to me. It's like every word he speaks fills my empty soul little by little, and he is slowly mending my ruined heart.

We walk into his house. It's big, quiet and smells like pine. I look at the dirty dishes on the counter and half unpacked boxes scattered throughout the living room and smile. Just one more reminder that he is nothing like Nathan.

Max catches my gaze and shoves his hands in the pockets of his jeans as he rocks back on his heels. "Don't mind the mess," he says nervously.

"Oh, I don't mind at all. Trust me."

He gives me a quick tour of the open layout. While he's showing me the big things like the fireplace and his new furniture, I focus on the little things. There are pictures of Max with his friends, souvenirs from Chicago to remind him of home, family photos and so much more that give me a little glimpse into his life. My fingertips linger on a photo frame, and I briefly wonder if someday we will have a picture of us to add to the collection. Hope for something more in my life suddenly blooms in my chest.

He stands in front of the patio doors that lead to the back porch and stares out the glass. "Do you ever get tired of this view?" he asks quietly.

"Never," I answer honestly.

"Do you spend much time on the beach?"

I frown. "No, not really. Not recently." I've been so depressed that all the things I used to enjoy just seem trivial when I'm completely miserable with almost every aspect of my life. When we first moved here and things weren't so bad, I would spend hours collecting seashells, walking, running and swimming. The only time I spend on the beach now is when I need to vent and release my emotions.

He opens the French doors and takes a step out into the cool night air. I follow him outside. "Do you hear that?" he asks, his expression serious.

Listening intently, I shake my head. "No. What is it?"

"The ocean is calling us," he says with a grin on his face.

I glance to the water and back to him. "I didn't bring my bathing suit," I whisper.

"Who says you need one?"

Before I can even think of a response, he's stripping off his shirt and shoes and running down the steps towards the sand. I watch him as he makes his way into the water, crashing through the waves. A few seconds later he comes running out, yelling at the top of his lungs that the water is freezing.

A laugh escapes me, and I realize I have been laughing most of the night. I don't remember the last time I laughed so much or been so happy. My fingertips trace the smile on my lips. I haven't smiled this much in ages either. *Only here. Only now.* His words echo through my mind. Before I can second-guess myself, I'm stripping out of my heels and pulling my blazer and jeans off. Clad in only my shirt and panties, I run down the steps and to the water.

Max's eyes are wide as he stares at me. He didn't think I would do this. Actually I didn't think I would either. It's so unlike the *new Avery*, but something the *old Avery* would have done in a heartbeat with no hesitation. I pass him and run into the strong waves. The water comes up to my chest, and the feeling is exhilarating. It gives me such a rush, and I feel truly alive for the first time in a long time. Squealing and laughing, I run out of the water. "I-I-It *is* f-f-freezing!" I yell, shuddering from the cold.

Max catches me in his arms and spins me around. I hold onto

him tight until we collapse onto the wet sand. We lie on our backs laughing and panting. Our laughter slowly dies down as we take in the beauty of the scene above us. The clear night sky is bright with a full moon and millions of tiny twinkling stars. It looks like an exquisite painting, and I want to remember it just like this forever.

"Beautiful," I whisper.

"Very beautiful," he whispers back.

I look over at him and realize he's staring at me with a lopsided smile on his handsome face. Even though we've only known each other for a short time, I feel like I've known him forever. The way he looks at me makes me shiver. It's like he's looking right into the depths of my soul, a place no one else has ever been before. I want to get to know him better, so I ask, "Why did you decide to become a doctor?"

He gets a thoughtful look on his face before he answers. "Well, my dad's a doctor and so was my grandfather, so I guess you could say it runs in the family. My mom and dad are pretty laid back, though. I think they would have been just as proud of me if I had been a professional snowboarder. As long as I'm happy, they're happy. That's all that matters to them."

"They sound wonderful."

"They are," he responds.

I look up at the stars once again. "My mom used to tell me that stars are the souls of everyone on earth who have died and that they twinkle every time they are thinking of their loved ones here on earth. Before she passed away, she told me she would always be up there in the stars watching over me. I was only eight when my mom died, but I remember every single thing about her. She was the sweetest person I have ever met." I feel Max's fingers interlace with mine, and I hold his hand tightly as if he's my lifeline. "I think my dad tried to overcompensate after she was gone. I know he was trying to manage a successful career in politics and had his hands full with two little girls. At some point, though, he lost sight of what was important. We didn't need the big house and the expensive toys. We just wanted to eat dinner and play in the park and go on vacation with our father instead of nannies and babysitters. I feel like he pushed us away when we needed him the most. Even today at lunch when I went to talk to him about divorcing Nathan, he wouldn't listen to me. He's too busy with his campaign and —." I stop talking when I feel Max's hand tighten around mine. I turn to him, and he has a look on his face that I can't decipher.

"You're divorcing Nathan?" he asks, incredulously.

I bite into my lower lip nervously. "Yes. I want to, but it's not going to be easy." I release a shuddering breath. "He'll never let me go willingly."

Max sits up and stares down at me. "Are you going to talk to your father again about it?"

"I can try. I just don't think he'll understand. He's very good at brushing things under the rug as far as anything that might affect his career."

He nods slowly. I hate how the conversation turned to Nathan and put a damper on our evening. I want things to be how they were before I brought up the heavy stuff. Slowly, I place my hands on his shoulders. His gaze slides from my eyes down to my lips, and I feel butterflies instantly erupt in my stomach. I haven't felt emotions like this in a long time. Gently, I trail my fingertips down over his muscular chest and rippled abs. His body screams perfection, and I want to feel every inch of it.

He leans into my touch, and his lips brush softly over mine. He's waiting for me to make a move. And so I do. Inclining my head, I press my lips against his. He tastes and feels so good. He's like a drug, and I am totally addicted.

The kiss grows more and more demanding as his tongue dips into my mouth. It's velvety soft and slides over mine. My fingertips curl into his shirt, and I pull him even closer to me. I can't get enough of him. I can't get enough of this feeling. I felt empty for so long, and he makes me feel so alive.

Suddenly, he pulls back. We're both breathing hard, and it takes me a while to catch my breath. "I don't want to push my luck," he whispers.

I don't want him to stop, but I know we should probably take things slower even though my body is trying to tell me otherwise.

He stands and offers his hand down to me. When I place my hand in his, he gently hauls me to my feet. His hands linger around my waist, and he gazes down at me with a look of adoration on his face.

"We're both covered in sand," I say, my voice barely above a whisper.

"Yeah," he agrees.

"Maybe we should take a shower." *Oh, God. What did I just say?* "N-not together," I stammer. "You can take a shower, and I can take a shower, but not in the same shower," I ramble on even though I try to force myself to stop. Mortified, I say, "I'll just stop talking now."

He chuckles. "You can shower in my master bathroom, and I'll take a quick shower in the guest bath."

I just nod so I don't risk saying anything else embarrassing.

AVERY

AFTER HANGING UP my wet clothes on a rack in the master bath, I scrub my teeth with my index finger and a dollop of his toothpaste I found in the medicine cabinet and rinse with mouthwash. Then I climb into the amazing shower that has two glass walls with a door and a backsplash of brown and beige tile. I turn on the water, and the spray comes out of a large showerhead centered in the middle of the ceiling. I swear that thing is made for elephants, because the spray almost hurts with the amount of force and water that comes out of it.

I lean partially out of the spray, not wanting to ruin my hair and makeup. My eyes flicker over the small assortment of soaps and shampoos, and I grab a bottle of body wash. Opening the lid, I take a whiff. *Mmm.* This must be why Max smells so good. It's a very clean scent with a hint of sandalwood. It's very manly, and I have to smile that I'm going to use it and smell like him. I lather up the soap in my hands and set out to rid myself of any trace of sand.

When I'm done, I rinse off and step out. Max had laid out a few white, oversized, fluffy towels before he left, and I grab one. I dry off and stand in front of the partially steamed mirror. After pulling the bobby pins and clip from my hair, I run my fingers through the long strands and glance at my reflection. What I see makes my stomach drop. "Oh no!" I gasp.

The tattoo concealer washed off, and in its place are all the bruises I so desperately tried to conceal. Dark purple, blue and green splotches trail down my arms, stomach and legs. I can feel my breathing pick up as I begin to panic. I had gotten lost in the moment and forgot about my past that is so clearly mapped out on my body. I can't let Max see me like this. I grasp onto the sink and try to calm myself down.

A knock sounds at the door, and I jump. "Avery, did you find everything you need?"

"Yeah!" I call out, and I can hear the panic in my voice.

"Is everything okay?"

I take a deep breath. "Yeah. Just give me a minute."

"All right," he says, sounding unsure.

I hang the wet towel up and wrap the other dry towel around me, twisting and tucking the end between my breasts. Tearing my eyes away from my reflection, I open the bathroom door a few inches. I can see Max sitting on the edge of his king-sized sleigh bed. He's only wearing a pair of pajama bottoms, and my mouth instantly dries.

"Can you...Can you turn off the lights?" I ask. I squeeze my eyes shut and groan inwardly. I hope I don't sound as awkward as I feel.

He hesitates for only a moment before saying, "Sure." And then he moves to switch off the lamp beside him.

I turn off the bathroom light and walk out. The room isn't pitch-black because of the full moon shining through the floor-to-ceiling windows, but it will do. I can hear my ragged breaths as I make my way to his bed. I don't think I've ever been so nervous before in my life.

I stand before him, and Max rests his hands on my hips. My entire body trembles under his touch, and he slowly draws back and buries his hands through his hair. "Avery, we don't have to do anything tonight. I had one of the best nights of my life tonight, and I don't want to ruin it. We can just lie here, or I can walk you home if you'd like. Even though I really don't want you to leave," he says with a grin, "the decision is yours. I don't want to scare you away. And I definitely don't want to hurt you."

He's afraid of hurting me, and that is exactly what is holding me back. *Fear.* Fear of being hurt. But Max is not Nathan. Max is sweet and kind and gentle; and even though it sounds crazy since we haven't known each other for that long, I'm falling in love with him. "You won't hurt me," I say out loud for his benefit as well as mine. I close my eyes for a moment and take a deep breath. "I trust you." The words are surprisingly easy to say, but I doubt he has any idea of the power behind them and the strength it took in order for me to say them.

He stands and his hand cups my cheek. "We'll move at a pace you can handle. If you want to stop, we'll stop." I lean into his touch, and his thumb skates over my bottom lip. His eyes stare at my lips as he licks his own. "Right now I really want to kiss you."

I know in that moment that I don't want to stop any of this. I wrap my hands around his neck and pull him down to me. "Then kiss me," I whisper.

His lips slant over mine in a tender kiss. His hands rest on my hips, unmoving, and I know he's afraid to touch me. I pull back from him and swallow hard. I have never been in the position where I could take control of a situation, especially one like this. The fact that he's not forcing me or hurrying things makes me want him even more.

I search his eyes with mine. "Touch me, Max."

"Where, Avery?" he asks, breathlessly.

"Everywhere," I whisper.

His fingertips hesitantly trail up around my waist before grasping the material of the towel and pulling me against him. Our bodies meld together, his growing erection digging into my belly. His mouth is on mine again, and a small moan escapes me. His kiss and touch are slow and deliberate. He's not trying to rush anything or take things too far.

"I want to make you feel good, Avery," he says. "Will you let me do that?"

"Yes," I answer, my voice throaty.

His fingers tangle into my hair, and he pulls me closer for a deeper kiss. I hold onto his muscular arms for support as I stand on unsteady legs. His biceps tighten under my touch, and my fingers ache to explore the rest of his body.

He presses a gentle kiss to my shoulder before pulling away from me. "Lie down," he gently commands.

Slowly, I move to the middle of the bed. He stands at the edge, looking down at me with hooded eyes. My fingertips are wrapped around the top of the towel so tightly that I have no doubt my knuckles are white.

I glance down to where his eyes are focused, and I can see that the lower half of my towel has opened, exposing me. I don't know what possesses me at that moment, but I part my legs to give him a better view.

I can hear his sharp intake of breath. He wants me. And at this moment, I can't think of anything else in the world I want more than him. I don't speak a word. I let my body do the talking.

His gentle hand grabs my left leg and raises it to rest on his shoulder as he kneels on the bed. His lips trail kisses down my ankle to my inner thigh, leaving licks of fire in their wake. When his mouth nears my apex, my entire body is shaking with need. Self-doubt slowly creeps in the back of my mind. I've never had anyone do this before, and I start to worry. What if it doesn't feel good? What if he doesn't like doing it to me? The worry builds and nags at the back of my mind, as his mouth grows closer. "Wait. Please," I call out in between pants.

He stills and lifts his head.

"I've never...No one has ever..." My voice trails off, and I close my eyes as I can feel my face flush with embarrassment.

"Hey," he says softly, and I meet his eyes. "It's okay." He plants a soft kiss on my mound, and I shudder. "Don't think. Just relax."

He plants another kiss before his tongue darts out and laps at my swollen little nub. I groan loudly. It feels exquisite, and he only licked me once.

"Is this okay?" he whispers.

All I can do is nod. I don't trust myself to speak, because I don't want him to stop. Ever.

The moment his tongue trails its way up the length of my slit I involuntarily lift my hips and gasp harshly. He pauses, staring at me. "Avery," he says hoarsely. The way he says my name almost makes me gasp again.

"Please," I beg him. My voice sounds strange and needy.

He smiles and settles down on the bed between my legs. He parts my lips with his fingers, and then his tongue laves at my most sensitive area. Just a few licks, and it feels like fireworks are going off in my brain. I moan loudly as he begins his deliciously torturous assault on my clit. My head falls back onto the mattress, and I screw my eyes shut. My fingers curl into the bedding, threatening to rip the sheets underneath me.

Nonsensical words flow from my mouth with gasps and moans as he continues to pleasure me. And then just when I think it can't get any better, I feel his finger slip inside of me. He curls the tip and massages my front wall gently, and I can feel myself falling into a downward spiral as my body shivers in anticipation of what's to come.

It's been so long since I have felt this type of pleasure. I haven't had an orgasm in such a long time, and I didn't realize how much pent-up sexual tension I had...until this moment.

"Please. Max. Please," I beg again between pants. I don't think I could form a full sentence even if I tried. My body feels like it's going to overload on pleasure.

Max slips another finger inside of me alongside the first one, and they methodically rub over that magic area that I had only ever heard of, but didn't know existed until now. I release the sheets, lean up and thread my fingers through his thick, dark hair. Our eyes meet, and I watch him lick and suck on my throbbing nub. I can't stop watching. This is the most erotic thing I have ever witnessed.

I sink my teeth into my bottom lip as I try to hold back the inevitable. I don't want this to ever end. But within a few seconds, I feel like I'm on the edge of a precipice and ready to fall over.

"I want to feel you shatter," he whispers against me.

I gasp at his words and groan in response. And then I watch as his other hand reaches down and grips my backside, pulling me even closer to his mouth, closer to the burning pleasure. His mouth encloses around my clit, focusing all the attention there. Suddenly, it feels like an emotional dam bursts inside of me. I shatter around his mouth, gasping his name as the orgasm spreads through every nerve ending in my body. I grip his hair tighter, and his eyes never leave mine as my body is wracked with ecstasy. It's the most powerful orgasm I ever remember experiencing. It goes on and on, wave after wave hitting me again and again until I'm completely and utterly spent. Releasing my fingers from his hair, I fall back onto the bed, panting as if I had just run a marathon.

Max licks me one last time, causing me to tremble, before moving to stretch out next to me. His fingertips trail down the side of my face as he says, "That was the most beautiful thing I have ever seen."

I can feel a blush rising to my cheeks, and he chuckles. His dark eyes pierce mine in the darkness, and I am instantly lost in them. My hand adventurously moves down his chest, and his abs tense as my fingertips brush lightly over them. He catches my hand in his before I can go any lower. Then he brings my hand up to his mouth and kisses my knuckles. "Let's go a little slower." He leans down and kisses me sweetly. "From here on out," he adds with a grin. He pulls me into his arms and plants a kiss on the top of my head. "Sleep, sweet Avery," he whispers. "I'll meet you in a few minutes in our dreams."

Resting my head against his chest, I listen to his heartbeat. The steady rhythm lulls me into a rare, peaceful sleep.

MAX

I WAKE UP the next morning with Avery curled up against me. Her head rests on my chest, and I can feel the wet spot from a tiny puddle of drool running from her mouth. It makes me smile knowing that she slept so soundly. She clearly feels safe with me, and I couldn't be happier about that fact.

Sunlight filters through the room, highlighting the delicate, dark lashes fanned out over her pink cheeks. I honestly think I could stay in bed and stare at her all day. I've never felt this way about anyone, not even Gretchen, and I knew Gretchen for a hell of a lot longer. There's just something about Avery that draws me to her like a magnet. I have an overwhelming sense of wanting to protect her from all the evil in the world and to make her happy. I want to own her heart just like she already owns mine.

Her eyelids flutter, and I stop breathing. I don't want her to wake up just yet. I love watching her beautiful face when she's completely relaxed and her guard is down. It's very rare and an incredible sight to behold. Her eyelids stop moving, and I breathe gently, not wanting to wake her. I just want to savor this moment with her for a little while more. Our time is limited, unfortunately, and I can't deny the fact that I've been counting down the days when her husband returns. The weekend is almost over, and then I know the week will go fast at the hospital. I don't want to focus on what little time we have left, but it's like a ticking time bomb just waiting to explode.

Nathan doesn't deserve her, and she definitely doesn't deserve to be treated as an object, a possession. I wish I could have met Avery back when she was strong-willed and care free. I caught a glimpse of that girl last night, and I only want to see more. If she were my girl, I would thank God every day that she's in my life; and she would know just how thankful I truly was.

It's easy to imagine a future with her, but it's just a dream. It's not reality. *Not yet anyway.* I'm still torn over the fact that she's planning on divorcing her husband. That gives me some hope and a sense of peace, but the fact that her family won't help her makes me doubtful that it's going to be easy for her. I know deep down that if she could have left Nathan, she would have already. And the fact that she can't leave him scares the hell out of me.

I sigh and feel her stirring. When I glance down, her eyes are fluttering open. She looks confused at first as if she doesn't know where she is. But then when her eyes meet mine, her expression changes and she flashes me that heart-stopping smile.

"Good morning, beautiful," I whisper.

"Good morning." Her voice sounds sleepy and so damn sexy.

"How did you sleep?"

"Really great actually."

Her brows furrow a bit, and I wonder if she has a hard time sleeping with Nathan. My best guess would be yes. I doubt she's ever truly comfortable around a bastard like that.

In an attempt to lighten the mood, I point to the puddle of drool on my chest. "Yeah. I would say you slept pretty good."

Embarrassment flickers over her face, but then she laughs. "Sorry," she says shyly.

I chuckle. "Don't be sorry. I think it's kind of cute."

She playfully hits me in the chest. I catch her hand in mine and bring her knuckles to my lips. I kiss her tenderly and trail my lips down to her wrist. That's when I notice the bruises dappled over her ivory skin not covered by the sheet. I quickly sit up beside her. My fingertips gently trail down the bruised and battered skin of her arm, and I can feel her tremble under my touch. "This is why you wanted the lights off last night," I murmur. I thought she was just being shy, but she didn't want me to see her like this. She moves to pull away from me, but I hold her firmly in place. "Avery." I shake my head back and forth. She doesn't need to hide from me. I wish she would realize that.

A wounded expression appears on her face. "Don't. Don't look at me like that."

The pain that flashes through her gaze is too much to bear. I pull her to my chest and hold her. We sink back onto the bed together and just lay there in a comfortable silence for a while. There's so much I want to say to her, but I don't want to upset her more than she already is. We had such a great night together, and I want our happy moods to continue through today, the last full day I have with her before my workweek begins.

Her breathing is labored against my neck as I run my fingers through her soft hair. "Nathan has no idea what he has. He has no fucking clue as to how special and incredible you are." Her breath catches, but I continue on. "If he did, he would never lay a hand on you."

She exhales a shuddering breath, but doesn't make a move to get away. So I just hold and comfort her, running my hand over her back.

I don't know the full extent of the abuse, and I'm not sure I even want to know the full extent of it. What I do know is that Avery will tell me when she's ready. I'm not going to force her to talk about things that upset her.

"You stay here and go back to sleep. I'm going to make a few phone calls." I kiss her forehead and crawl out of bed, leaving her behind to rest. My cell phone is on the kitchen counter, and I scoop it up. First, I make a special order online as a surprise for Avery. The overnight shipping is a bit pricey, but it should be arriving sometime tomorrow afternoon, so it's totally worth it. After placing the order, I do some searches on Google and then make several calls to various places in the area. Once I find the perfect way to spend our day, I put my phone down and go back to my bedroom. Avery is sound asleep, and I can't help but stare at her peaceful expression for a few moments before waking her.

I climb into bed and gently kiss her lips. A smile appears on her face, but she keeps her eyes closed. "Wake up, Avery," I whisper.

"I don't want to," she says with a sexy little pout. "I was having the most amazing dream."

"And what were you dreaming about?"

"A really hot guy who's a great kisser." She peeks up at me with one eye. "I think he told me his name is Max."

"Oh yeah?" I lean down and kiss her soft lips. "What else is Max good at?"

She releases a small sigh against my lips. "Everything," she breathes.

"Sounds like I should be jealous," I say with a grin. I kiss her chastely once more before standing up. She groans in displeasure, and it makes me chuckle. "It's almost lunchtime, sleepy head, and I have a whole day planned for us. Can you be ready in an hour?"

She nods and crawls out of bed with the sheet wrapped around her. She disappears into the bathroom and emerges a few minutes later in her clothes from last night. "I'll be back later," she says.

I walk over and pull her into my arms. I kiss her softly before pulling away. "I'll just be here. Missing you," I say with a wink.

She flashes me a shy smile before walking out of the bedroom. Sighing, I sit down on the bed. I'm overcome with the feeling that I miss her already. What is it going to be like when Nathan gets back into town and I can't see her whenever I want to? We've only just begun this relationship or whatever you want to call it, and she's already caught me, hook, line and sinker. I have a feeling I'm on a short road that ends in heartbreak, but I'm willing to risk the chance.

I would risk everything to be with Avery. And although that should scare the shit out of me, it actually makes me feel the exact opposite. Call it fate, destiny, serendipity or whatever else, but I know that we're meant to be together. And I believe in my heart that we're going to make it...no matter what stands in our way or who tries to keep us apart.

AVERY

THE FIRST THING I notice when I walk in the house is the answering machine's blinking light. I hit the play button, and the computerized voice says, "Fifty-two new messages." My heart hammers against my chest as message after message from Nathan plays. At first he sounds cheerful, even saying that he misses me already. After about the tenth call, his messages become more clipped with instructions for me to call him back right away. By the end of the message string, the tone of his voice has grown sinister as he spits threats over the line.

The last message plays. "If you don't call me in ten minutes, I'm sending my father to come over to check on you, Avery." He takes a moment and releases a long sigh. "If you aren't hurt or lying in a ditch dead somewhere, you're going to wish you were when I get home." He ends the call, and the machine beeps, signaling the final message.

I stare at the clock on the wall. He left that message a half an hour ago. Almost as if on cue, the doorbell rings. "Shit!" I curse in a hushed whisper.

Scrambling, I run into the bathroom and scrub my face. Some of my black eyeliner remains around my eyes giving me a raccoon look, but it's perfect for what I'm about to pull off. I throw my hair into a messy updo before running into the bedroom. Wrapping myself in a robe and a heavy blanket, I hurry to the front door just as the bell rings again. A loud rapping comes from the other side, and it makes me jump. "Avery!" I hear my father-in-law call. "Are you in there?"

I steady my breathing, slowly unlock the door and open it. Nathan's father stands in full uniform on my doorstep. He looks like an older version of Nathan with salt and pepper hair and a moustache. "Nathan said you haven't been answering his calls or texts. He sent me over to check on you."

I cough violently and press the back of my hand to my forehead. It's sweaty from running around just before I answered the door, so it makes my act even more believable. "I'm sorry. I have been sleeping almost non-stop since Nathan left. I must have slept right through the phone ringing."

"You don't look well, Avery," he comments.

"I think it's the flu. I probably caught it from the hospital."

Richard grimaces and takes a step back. "Yeah, those places are breeding grounds for germs." He pulls his phone out of his pocket and taps on the screen for a few seconds. "I sent Nathan a text that you are all right, but you should still call him. I'm sure he'll want to hear from you. He's been worried sick."

I resist the urge to roll my eyes. "Of course. Sorry you came all the way out here, Richard, for nothing."

"Well, I better get back to work. I hope you feel better soon. Call me if you need anything."

I wave at him as he walks away. "Thank you," I call after him. After I close the door, I press the heel of my hand against my pounding heart. I can't believe I pulled that off.

The house phone rings, and I hurry to answer it. I keep my voice hushed in a whisper when I ask, "Hello?"

"Avery," Nathan says in a clipped tone. "Dad said he swung by. He said you're sick."

"Yes. I think I have the flu."

"I called a million times. You didn't have the phone near you?"

I roll my eyes. It's good to know he's concerned about me not picking up the phone and not the fact that I'm sick...or at least pretending to be sick. "I must have left it in the other room. I've been sleeping almost the entire time you've been gone." I bite my lip nervously. I desperately need him to believe me, because I can't even imagine the punishment I would receive when he gets home.

"Well, keep your cell phone with you. I need to know where you are at all times, Avery." I almost ask why, but decide not to. "I want you to pick up whenever I call."

"Okay," I say softly.

"I'll call later to see if you're feeling any better." He hesitates and then adds in a stern voice, "Make sure you pick up the phone."

"I will," I say bitterly.

He hangs up. I find my cell phone on the kitchen counter. Thirty-seven missed calls, twelve voice mails and sixty-five texts await me. The staggering amount makes my knees feel weak, and I quickly sit down on one of the stools. This is what it will be like when I try to leave him again. He'll become obsessed and threaten to hurt me like all the other times. I swallow hard at the thoughts creeping through my mind. I worked so hard to build his trust, and I don't want to ruin it now. I need to keep his false sense of security intact until I can leave him when he's least expecting it. Putting him on edge and making him not trust me and constantly question where I am is not going to work in my favor.

After several minutes, I finally get up to go get ready for whatever Max has planned for us this afternoon. I can't help but smile when I think of him. With Nathan away, it's easy to imagine how my life would be if I wasn't married. It would be so simple to fall into a pattern with Max. I love being around him, and I can't stop thinking about him when I'm not. I'm going to make the best of our week together, because I don't know if we'll ever get this chance again. Hopefully, when I call Allison tomorrow, she can help me when I tell her of my plans to divorce Nathan. Maybe she will even let me stay with her until I can get everything sorted out. I don't let my hopes get too high, however, because my relationship with Allison has been strained lately, to say the least. Something is going on with her that I can't quite figure out, and it seems like all of her anger is directed at me for some reason.

Clearing my thoughts and focusing on the rest of the day with Max, I take a quick shower and get ready. My long hair falls down my back in loose waves. I give my eyes a dark and smoky look, the way I like. And I revel in the fact that Nathan is not here to protest and order me around.

As I stand in front of my walk-in closet, I wish I had asked Max where we were going so that I knew what to wear. I'm pretty sure he wanted to keep our destination a secret, though, so I don't think he would have told me anyway.

My fingers latch onto a hanger, and I pull out a navy blue wrap dress. I slip into the soft material and meticulously cover any visible bruises with the tattoo cover-up. Most of the bruises are lighter in color now and easier to hide. By the end of the week I probably won't have any at all. It's been so long since I've seen my skin free of bruises, and that thought makes me want to cry. I feel like for the past two years my mind has been in a fog and running in endless circles with no end in sight. Max is the light at the end of a very dark tunnel for me. He gives me a glimpse into a world I could be in. He gives me hope, and that is something I haven't had for a very long time.

I pull on a pair of matching ballet flats and grab my cell phone and purse before leaving the house. My phone rings almost immediately, and I cringe. I'm quick to answer it.

"Avery," Nathan says. "I'm glad you decided to start answering your phone when I call."

"Is there something you want, Nathan?" I ask, and I'm surprised at the tone I'm taking with him.

He doesn't say anything for almost a full minute, and I wonder if the connection is lost. Then he says, "I think it was a mistake for me to leave. Suddenly my wife is turning into a disobedient little bitch."

"I'm hanging up now, Nathan."

"Don't you dare hang up on me, you fucking —."

I don't let him finish. I end the call and stare down at the phone in disbelief. Did I just do that? Maybe it's the fact of knowing he is thousands of miles away and can't hurt me that is making me bold. I look up as Max steps out onto his deck. Or maybe it's *someone* making me bold. He's wearing a charcoal blazer over a white v-neck shirt and dark jeans. The shirt clings to his chest and outlines all his defined muscles, and I can't help but stare. He looks gorgeous as he slips a hand through his mussed hair, and I can't believe I get to spend the whole afternoon with him.

My phone rings again, and his eyes dart from me, to my phone and back to me. "Everything okay?" he asks.

I switch the phone to vibrate and toss it into my purse. "It is now," I say with a smile.

Grinning, he pulls on a pair of mirrored aviator shades and says, "Good. Let's go."

MAX

THE DRIVE TO the Manteo Waterfront on Roanoke Island only takes about fifteen minutes. Even though Avery's phone is not ringing, I can hear it vibrating every few minutes. She doesn't speak a word about it, but I know it's Nathan who is calling her. Her expression is a telltale sign of who is on the other end. She had the same look on her face before we left when she had just ended a call with him.

Avery catches my gaze and gives me a rueful smile.

"Want to talk about it?" I ask.

"It's Nathan. He's been calling me nonstop ever since he left. I just didn't realize that until I went back to the house this morning since I didn't take my cell phone with me last night." She sighs. "His dad showed up on my doorstep a few minutes after I walked in. I feigned having the flu and told Nathan the same. Nevertheless, he won't stop calling me." She hesitates and frowns. "I gave him a little attitude and hung up on him earlier." She shakes her head gently and murmurs, "He's going to kill me when he gets back."

I park the car and wrap my hands around the steering wheel, my knuckles turning white. I know she didn't literally mean what she said, but even the figurative sense of it makes me terrified. If Nathan can put his hands on her, he most certainly could go too far one of these days.

Avery reaches out and places a hand on my thigh. "I don't want to talk about him. You told me to live in the here and now, remember? It's just you and me. Nothing else and no one else matters in this moment."

I smile as she repeats my words back to me. "You're right." I slowly release the steering wheel and pull her hand up to my lips. I kiss her skin softly and say, "Let's enjoy our day together."

We make our way down to the dock where an older gentleman is standing in front of a sailboat and waiting for us with a warm smile. "You must be Max and Avery," he says, greeting us with handshakes. "My name's Lee, and I'll be your captain this evening." He holds his hand out to Avery. "Come aboard, young lady." He helps her onto the boat. I climb in next, and steady myself on the railing with Avery as the boat gently rocks in the water.

As Lee makes some last minute checks, Avery and I explore the sailboat. It's a newer model, white with deep blue sails, almost the same color as Avery's dress. There is a table in the center with bench seats along each side of the boat leading back to the stern, cockpit and hatch for the cabin below. Avery takes a seat by the steering wheel and pats the cushion next to her. I sit down and wrap my arm around her shoulders. She nestles in close to me, and I breathe in her flowery scent as a cool breeze blows over us.

Lee jumps onto the boat and asks, "All set?"

I nod, and he steps behind the wheel in the cockpit. After a push of the button, the engine starts. He grabs the line connecting us to the dock to release the boat and maneuvers the vessel out onto the water. I can tell by Lee's mechanical movements that he's had a lot of experience.

"How long have you been sailing?" I ask.

"Oh, almost thirty-five years now." My uncle taught me how to sail." He turns the boat into the wind and kills the engine. The blue sails puff out with the force of the air, and the vessel cruises against the calm water of the sound.

I look down at Avery. She looks enthralled with the beautiful view surrounding us. "Have you ever been on a sailboat?"

She shakes her head. "I've been on a few yachts for parties, but they were either docked or moving very slowly. Nothing like this." She breathes in deeply as a gust of wind blows over us. "What about you?" she asks.

"My dad owned a boat when I was young, and we went out on the water a lot. I loved being on and in the water way more than being on land. My dad used to joke and tell me that I was part fish."

She smiles before turning her attention to the lighthouse that we're passing by. My gaze darts to the lighthouse and scenery, but it mostly stays affixed on Avery. Her walls are clearly down, and she seems to be really enjoying herself. Her being happy is quite a rare and precious sight to see, but it also makes my chest ache with a feeling I've never experienced before. I want her to always be happy. I never want her to hurt again, but deep down I know I can't truly protect her. After this week is over, things might revert back to the way they were; and I don't know if I can handle that. And I really don't know if I will allow it.

She turns to me as if sensing my stare. "Max, what's wrong? You look upset."

My knuckles gently stroke her cheek. "I just —." My words trail off as my lips find hers. She's tense at first, but slowly loosens up in my arms, completely succumbing to me. I hold her close and kiss her fiercely. I'm afraid to tell her how I really feel, so I pour all of my emotions into that kiss. I desperately want her to know how much she means to me. When we part, she's breathless. "Avery." I swallow hard, trying to gather my courage. "These past few days with you have been some of the best of my life. I'm glad you're giving us a chance. And I'm glad that you're here with me now."

Her fingertips graze the stubble of my jaw, and her eyes meet mine. "I wouldn't want to be anywhere else right now, Max."

I kiss her innocently, more aware this time that we have an audience. It's so damn easy to forget the rest of the world around us when I'm with her.

Lee clears his throat and says, "I'm sure you two are starving." He opens the hatch to the cabin. "Why don't you go down to the cabin and have a look around for something to eat?" he asks me with a wink.

Taking Avery's hand, I lead her down the stairs and into the spacious cabin below. The area has an open layout with a living room, small kitchen, bathroom and bedroom. It's decorated with various shades of blue and white that contrast nicely against the deep, rich wood of the teak furniture and cabinets. A bouquet of flowers sits in the center of the coffee table along with a smorgasbord of food, a bottle of wine and two flutes. Avery turns to me with a big smile on her face, and it takes my breath away. "Did you plan all of this?" she asks while sweeping her hand around the room.

I nod. "Do you like it?"

Her smile grows. "I love it." She walks over to me and wraps her arms around my waist. "This is the nicest and most romantic thing anyone has ever done for me, Max. Thank you."

My arms envelop her, and I kiss the top of her head. "You're welcome." We stand like that for a few moments before I say, "Now, let's eat before my stomach decides to eat itself."

"Okay," she agrees with a giggle.

AVERY

MAX SITS BESIDE me, and we eat heartily while making small talk. He really went all out to make today romantic, and he has no idea how special that makes me feel. No one has truly cared about me for a long time, and it feels good to be wanted and to be taken care of.

After we're completely stuffed from the delicious food, we sit back on the couch and sip our wine. "Are you enjoying yourself?" he asks.

"Immensely." I turn to him and grin. "Are there any other surprises that you have planned for me this week?"

"Oh, wouldn't you like to know?" he teases.

"Yes. I would actually."

"Well, you'll just have to wait and see." He sets his glass down, and I repeat the action.

My tongue darts out of my mouth to wet my lips, and he intently watches the movement. Before I can blink, his mouth is on mine. His fingers snake through my hair as he pulls me closer, deepening the kiss. He swallows the groan that escapes my throat. Our tongues tangle together, and the sweet taste of wine invades my senses. My hands roam over his strong back, and I ache to feel his skin against mine.

He breaks the kiss on the moan. From his expression, I can tell he's struggling with an inner battle. I've caught glimpses of the same expression off and on all evening, and I need to know what he's thinking. "Max, talk to me." My fingertips run through his thick hair. "What are you thinking about?"

He sighs deeply. "I forget about the rest of the world when I'm with you. It's so easy to forget the situation you're in, but it's reality, Avery. You're with him, not me." He shakes his head slowly. "Not me."

"Don't you think I would change that if I could?"

"Then leave him. Be with me, Avery."

Even though I knew Max had strong feelings for me before that moment, it was still a shock to hear the words come out of his mouth. He wants me, and I want him, but it's not that easy. Nothing in life is ever easy. "If only it were that simple, Max."

"But why can't it be?"

I groan and put my face in my hands. "You don't understand. No one ever understands." I stand and walk to the other side of the cabin with my back facing him.

"There has to be something you can do, Avery." He doesn't speak for a few minutes. "What about a women's shelter? I know it's not ideal, but couldn't they protect you?"

"I've tried that," I mutter. "He found me the same night. All three times," I state sadly.

"What about a police station in another jurisdiction or another state?"

"I've tried that. I've tried everything. Don't you get that?" I yell, exasperated. "Don't you think I have tried everything I could to try to leave him? Do you think it's easy for me to stay with him? Do you think I want to live like this?" I cry. He stands and reaches for me, but

I take a few steps away. "I'm sorry. I didn't mean to yell at you." My hands fidget nervously with my dress. "It's not you. It's this situation I'm in that I just can't get out of."

"Let me help you, Avery," he says softly.

I shake my head vehemently. "No, I can't ask you to do that."

"You don't have to ask. I want to help you. Please," he pleads.

I close my eyes. If Nathan ever found out that Max helped me, he would ruin him. No one understands the power the Mason family holds. Everyone is under their thumb. If they want to ruin someone's career, they will. I won't let Max risk everything he's worked so hard for. Even if he did help me, Nathan would find me. He always does. Then what would happen? He would most definitely hurt Max... maybe even kill him. I shake the thought from my head. "No," I say again. "I'm going to talk to my sister tomorrow and see if she will help me."

"And if she won't?"

I bite my lower lip as I think about that possibility; and, unfortunately, I know there's a big possibility Allison will not agree to help me. "Then maybe I can talk some sense into my father, or maybe she will help me talk some sense into him." Frustrated, I drop my hands to my side. "I don't know, Max. I just don't know what I'm going to do."

He rakes his fingers through his hair. "I'm sorry I brought it up. I feel like I'm constantly ruining our time together by bringing up things I shouldn't."

I reach out and take his hand into mine. "You didn't ruin anything." Glancing out the window, I say, "The sun is starting to set. We should go enjoy it on the deck."

He nods and follows me up the steps.

As the sky turns different shades of red and orange and Max holds me in his arms, I close my eyes and wish that the day didn't have to come to an end. I would spend forever with Max if I could. The thought terrifies me and thrills me all at the same time. I'm falling too fast and too hard, but I can't stop my heart from wanting what it wants. Max would never hurt me, but it's not him I have to be worried about.

AVERY

AFTER THE SUNSET cruise on the water, we return to Max's SUV. I text Nathan back on the way home — one text in response to his twenty or more. He's very angry with me, but I refuse to let it upset me. He's still in Seattle; and at this point, it feels like a million miles away.

Max parks the vehicle outside of his house. He gets out, walks around to my side and opens the door for me. I place my hand in his, and he pulls me into his arms. "I know we both have to get up early tomorrow, but I would love for you to stay," he whispers in my ear.

A thrill runs through me as I nod.

He pulls back with a grin on his face and leads me inside his house. We spend the rest of the night watching TV and talking until I end up falling asleep in his lap.

When I wake up the next morning and we part ways so we can both get ready for the day, I am more determined than ever to talk to my sister.

During my lunch break, I call my sister and ask her to meet me at a diner nearby. I really need to talk to her about divorcing Nathan, and I just hope that she'll be more understanding than our father.

"Thanks for meeting me here," I say.

"Sure, Avery." My younger sister is bouncing my niece Sophia on her knee. Sophia just turned two and is cute as a button with curly blonde hair and bright blue eyes. "So what's up? You sounded depressed on the phone."

I stare down at my half eaten turkey sandwich. "I talked with Dad yesterday." If I would tell anyone about my secrets, it would be my sister. We haven't really been close over the past few years, but we were when we were younger. We had to be once we lost our mom.

"About what?" she prompts, sounding impatient.

"About leaving Nathan."

Allison stops bouncing Sophia and gapes at me with wide eyes and open mouth. "What?" she gasps. "Avery, you can't do that!"

Frowning, I ask, "Why not?"

"Think about everything you're giving up. Nathan is a plastic surgeon with more money than everyone in this entire restaurant put together. Not to mention he's like sex on a stick. Do you know how many women dream of marrying a doctor and living the life you do?"

They wouldn't if they knew the truth, I think to myself. And since when does Allison think of Nathan as sex on a stick? Shaking my head to clear my thoughts, I ask her, "What if I told you that everything isn't as perfect as everyone likes to think it is between us?"

She rolls her eyes. "Then fix it."

"You sound just like dad," I grumble.

"Well, at least he's the voice of reason. Leaving Nathan would be stupid." She starts bouncing Sophia again on her knee.

"Since when are you on Team Nathan?"

"I'm not on anyone's team!" she says, defensively. "You just don't know how good you have it," she mutters with bitterness lacing her tone.

I know Allison isn't exactly happy in her marriage right now. She has told me numerous times about Todd barely touching her since Sophia was born. She thinks Todd is cheating on her, and I'm beginning to wonder if she's doing the same thing to him. Allison had been so depressed over the whole thing, but now she seems different. She seems happy even though her marriage is falling apart behind closed doors.

"So what are you going to do?" she asks.

Sighing, I finally say, "I don't know."

"Nathan would give you the world. Who wouldn't want that?"

This conversation isn't going like I had envisioned. I can't even count on my own sister for help. With all of the courage I can muster, I reach across the table and grab her hand. When her eyes meet mine, I whisper, "He hits me, Allison."

She stares at me for a few moments, not speaking. "So what? Todd has laid his hands on me a time or two. A lot of couples go through that, and then they regret what they did." She takes a sip of her iced tea. "Kiss and make up," she suggests.

"You don't understand. I mean he really hurts me. He hits me a lot, Allison. He's mentally and physically abusive."

She rolls her eyes. "Marriage isn't perfect, Avery," she says with a condescending tone. "There are women out there who have it a lot worse than you."

I pull my hand back and stare at her in disbelief. I just confided in her, and she's making me feel like *I'm* the one who's done something wrong. "Thanks for meeting me for lunch, but I should get back to the hospital."

"You don't even work there," she scoffs. "Why would you want to volunteer when you can stay home and do nothing?"

"Because I like doing it. It's rewarding in so many ways," I state. *God!* She is like a horrifying mixture of my father and Nathan combined. "Being a *trophy wife* is not rewarding, believe it or not," I say sarcastically.

"Women would kill to be in your shoes, Avery. Me included," she says in all seriousness.

I narrow my eyes at my sister. "The grass isn't always greener, Allison. Just remember that."

She huffs in disagreement. "Well, in your case, I think it is," she retorts.

Holding back my emotions, I stand and put a twenty-dollar bill on the table to cover my sandwich, coffee and tip. I give Sophia a kiss on the head. With a glance to my sister, I say, "I'll talk to you later." Then I turn to leave.

I'm halfway through the diner when Allison calls my name. When I look back at her, she says, "Think about what I said."

I give her a curt nod. What she said is already forgotten, because it doesn't help me in the situation I am in whatsoever. I need to find a way to get away from Nathan...before it's too late.

MAX

I'M ANXIOUSLY AWAITING Avery to return from lunch with her sister. My eyes are glued on the glass window in front of me, and I can barely sit still as my knee bounces up and down under the cafeteria table.

"Dr. Harrison?"

I look up at the waitress. She has a worried look on her face, and I wonder how long she's been standing there. "I'm sorry. Did you say something?"

"I asked if you wanted anything else...more than once," she says with a small smile.

I glance down at my half eaten sandwich and plate full of chips. I'm too nervous to eat. "No, thank you." I stare out the window and sigh. "I'll just take the check."

"Sure thing." She leaves and comes back a minute or two later with the bill. I leave my money and a tip on the table and head for the exit. Just as I'm on the way out, Avery is walking in the automatic door at the entrance. The look on her face tells me it's not good news. She looks like she's trying not to cry. I walk over to her, but keep a safe distance. "Not good news I take it?"

She shakes her head and walks past me, not bothering to even glance my way.

"Avery, wait!" I call after her.

I catch her in the hallway and pull her into a nearby utility closet. Once the door is closed and we're alone, I plead with her and say, "Talk to me."

She crosses her arms in front of her chest and stares at the ground. "My sister isn't going to help me," she says solemnly. "I even told her that he hits me." She sucks in a deep, shaky breath. "It was so hard for me to confide in her like that, but she didn't even care. In fact, she turned it around on me like I should be grateful to be married to him and that the abuse is just a tiny, dark cloud in a bright, sunny sky."

I close my eyes and release a sigh. How can one girl have the entire world against her? That's exactly what it feels like when it comes to Avery. Everyone is willing to turn and look the other way while she lives a life of hell. Well, I'm not giving up on her. I'll never give up. "Let me help you."

I can almost feel the temperature in the small closet go down a few notches. She holds herself tighter and shakes her head. "No. I can't let you get involved."

"Avery," I say, reaching for her, but she backs away out of my reach.

"You don't understand."

"Then make me understand!" I cry, exasperated.

Her eyes meet mine, and I can see the fear inside of them. "He would kill you if he ever found out about us."

So she's trying to protect me when she clearly is the one who needs protection. "Let me make a few phone calls. Let me get in touch with some people who can help. We can find a place for you to go, Avery. You can get away from him. You can —." Her entire body trembles the more I talk, and so I just stop.

"Please, Max. Don't." She shakes her head sadly and says, "I have to go."

Before I can say another word, she's running out the door. I curse under my breath and rake my hands through my hair. This past weekend had been a dream, almost too good to be true. Nathan will be back in several days, and everything will go back to the way it was. Avery will stay in that house with him. He will abuse her, and there's not going to be a damn thing I can do about it.

I decide in that moment that I can't sit back and watch from a distance for very much longer. I'll give Avery a chance to take the help I'm offering. But if she keeps refusing, I'm going to have to take matters into my own hands. And then Nathan will be the one who will be afraid, because I will do everything in my power to protect her.

AVERY

MAX HAD STOPPED me on my way out of the hospital and asked me to come over to his place later. I reluctantly agreed. Our little tiff in the utility closet is not far from my mind as I step onto his front porch and knock on the door. I expect him to still be angry; but when he opens the door, he is grinning from ear to ear. In fact, he looks like he's about to burst with happiness. "What's your good mood about?" I ask.

"Well, mostly because of you." His words melt my heart, and the argument we had earlier instantly fades from my mind. "And also because I have a surprise for you." He holds his hand out, and I take it. He pulls me into his arms and playfully kisses my neck. I can't help but laugh. "Love that sound," he whispers. He pulls back and stares down at me, his face growing very serious. "Let's not fight or talk about anything that will make us fight. Let's just enjoy tonight. Okay?"

"Okay," I agree.

He takes my hand and leads me into the house. A package is resting on the kitchen counter, and he scoops it up with a big grin on his face.

"Is that part of the surprise?" I ask.

"Yep." We stop in the living room and he says, "Make yourself comfortable. I'm going to get everything ready."

I plop down on his comfortable sofa. I can't help but smile at the photographs scattered around the room. I stare at one picture in particular on the stand beside the couch. Max is a splitting image of his dad, and his mom and sister are gorgeous too. "Good genes," I murmur.

"What's that?" he asks as he walks into the room.

"Oh, I was just saying how beautiful your family is."

He grins at my compliment. "Thanks."

I notice that he has two DVDs in his hand. But when I try to get a glimpse of the movie titles, he conceals them. "Hey, no peeking," he teases. After he sticks one of the movies into the DVD player, he grabs the remote control and sits down next to me. "I had to special order these and get them shipped overnight."

I stare at him curiously. And then when the music for the opening scene begins to play, tears instantly fill my eyes. I turn to the TV and see my mom staring back at me. "Oh, Max," I manage to say. "I haven't watched her movies in so long." I swallow hard past the lump in my throat. "Too long."

He puts his arm around me and draws me back to him. We watch in silence for a while. The movie is called *One More Time*, and it's about two high school sweethearts who lose touch when they go to separate colleges and then are reunited years later after they both are divorced. Their love never died, and they get a second chance. It takes place in the fifties, and my mom's wardrobe is to die for. I know every song in the movie by heart, because she used to sing them to me every chance she got.

When the credits are rolling on the screen, I say, "I can remember my mom boasting about all the old-fashioned dresses and shoes that she had to wear. After she was gone, some of the dresses she kept from the set stayed in her closet. Whenever I needed to feel close to her, I would wrap the fabric around myself. Her perfume lingered in the material, and it made me feel close to her and loved...if only for a few moments."

Max turns to me, his brows knitting together. "Avery," he whispers in a soothing tone.

I don't even realize I'm crying until his hands gently cup my face and he wipes away tears with his thumbs. "You don't know how much this means to me, Max. I've never watched my mother's movies with anyone but her. Seeing her and hearing her voice just brings back such wonderful memories. Thank you for doing this."

He wipes away a few more stray tears and smiles. "I'd do anything for you, Avery," he says sincerely. "Do you want me to put the other movie in?" he asks.

I shake my head. "Let's save the other one for another night." There is something I've been wanting to do, and I can't wait any longer. My lips find his in a fevered kiss. He pulls me closer to him and I practically melt from his touch. There is so much emotion in the kiss that it scares me. I understand now what Max means when he said it feels like the world around us melts away when we're together. It feels exactly the same way for me too.

He pulls back and starts to talk, but I don't let him finish. My mouth presses against his again, and I move on the couch until I'm straddling his lap. His fingers dig into my hips as he pulls me down against his growing erection. A moan escapes my lips; and when they part, his tongue delves into my mouth, tangling with mine.

His fingers begin to move up my back and then stop. His touch is deliberately slow but also hesitant. He's testing my limits, but I don't want anything stopping us. Not tonight. I break away from his lips long enough to say, "Bedroom."

After hesitating for only a fraction of a second, his hands cup my bottom; and he stands with me in his arms. I wrap my legs around his waist as he carries me back the hall to his room. We fall down onto the bed together, our lips never breaking their bond.

Max moves on top of me, supporting himself on his elbows. He stares down at me for a moment before his lips begin to trail kisses down my face and neck. I gasp as he pushes his denim-covered erection against me. "Yes," I purr.

His fingers interlace with mine and move my hands above my head as he kisses me sweetly. But the pressure of his arms pinning me down on the bed brings back a flashback of Nathan. I try to swallow it down and force my mind to think of something else, but I can't. I lose focus and break away from him as a strangled whimper escapes my lips.

"Avery?" I can hear the confusion in his voice.

I screw my eyes shut as a sob wracks my body. He instantly pushes up and climbs off the bed. I curl into a fetal position and whisper, "I'm sorry. I'm so sorry."

"No. Don't be. I'm the one who should be sorry." He runs a hand through his hair, tugging at the ends. "Just tell me what I did wrong. I need to know so I don't do it again by mistake."

I don't want to tell him. I don't want to spoil the mood. So I just lie there, unmoving, not speaking.

"Please, Avery."

His voice sounds so sincere and desperate, and I break. "I've only ever been with Nathan." I swallow hard past the lump forming in my throat. "It's always been rough...forced. He...He holds me down."

Max curses under his breath, and I open my eyes. He looks upset, angry, and I don't want him to be. I need to fix this. Right now. I sit up and grab his hand. It takes me a while to find my words; but when I do, I really mean them. "I'm tired of being afraid." I close my eyes for a moment and take a deep breath. "I want to be with you, Max. I want you."

My words seem to help. His features relax a little. After a while he says, "Let's try something." I watch him lie down on the bed. His hands hook around the headboard. "We'll do whatever you want to do, Avery. You take control."

I stare at him for several seconds. He doesn't realize what he's offering me. Ever since I was a little girl I have never had control of my own life. My father controlled everything I did from the violin and piano lessons to what friends I was allowed to have and what sports I played. And then when I was actually old enough to be an adult, Nathan came and swept the rug out from under me. He was a thousand times worse than my father. I never had a say in any aspect of my life...ever. I have never had control of *anything*.

I fight back the tears stinging my eyes and take several deep breaths to calm myself. A shiver of anticipation runs down my spine as I slowly climb onto the bed. I want this more than anything. I need to do this to feel some sense of normalcy. It's not normal to fear the things I do. And if anyone can help me through this, it's Max.

I slowly plant my knees down on either side of his thighs, straddling him. My tremulous fingers hesitantly inch their way under the material of his t-shirt and feel his heated skin. I run my hands over his muscular chest, and his abs quiver under my touch. Leaning forward, I kiss him softly as my hands explore his body. My lips trail over the stubble on his strong jaw as he swallows hard.

"Tell me what you want, Avery," he whispers in my ear.

I lean back and say, "Take off your shirt."

He leans up and strips out of the t-shirt. Then his hands immediately return to the headboard as my eyes rake over his torso, taking in every detail. He has a light dusting of hair across his chest and a single line of hair that disappears under his jeans. My fingertip glides along the happy trail and stops just above his jeans that sit low on his hips. I lick my lips at the sight of his well-developed pelvic V. Arousal flows through my body until not a single trace of fear remains.

I gently start to move back and forth over his hard length under me, and his lips part as he releases a low moan. The sound reverberates through me. My fingers continue their exploration of his body, and Max's breathing pattern drastically changes from calm to erratic the more I touch him. When I lean down and plant a kiss on his chest, I can feel his heart pounding under my lips. He's just as nervous as I am, if not more.

With one swift movement, I sit up and pull my dress off over my head. His eyes overtly peruse my lingerie-clad body. "Fuck," he whispers as he involuntarily lifts his hips to grind up against me.

His hands squeeze the headboard hard, and I know he's itching to touch me. The thought of his hands on me doesn't scare me, and now I know it's time to try. It's time for more.

"Touch me. Please, Max," I beg.

His right hand moves between us, and he gently caresses me with painstakingly slow, hypnotic strokes through the lacey fabric of my panties. I gasp at the sensation and watch as his other hand moves to my breasts. He teases my nipples through my bra, and I throw my head back as a moan escapes my lips. I suddenly wish I had decided to not wear anything under my dress. I want his hands on me. Skin on skin.

I reach back and unclasp my bra, letting it slide off onto the bed beside us. He gazes up at me and whispers, "You are so fucking beautiful."

His hand continues to touch me between my legs, and I almost come apart from his gentle touch. "Max," I gasp. "I need you," I cry.

I climb off of his lap and watch as he slips out of his jeans and boxer briefs. I remove my panties and toss them over with the rest of my clothes. With no boundaries between us, he lies down. I stare greedily at the sight before me. His sculpted body is definitely a beautiful thing. It should be a sin to look that good. My mouth is practically watering for him, and I don't think I've ever been so turned on in my life.

My eyes finally land on his impressive length resting on his stomach, just begging to be touched. I hold his gaze as I move between his legs. My eyes don't leave his as my hand touches his soft flesh. I can feel him pulse beneath my fingers. Tentatively, I wrap my hands around him and stroke the hardening length up and down. His mouth is slack as his breathing picks up. "Oh, Avery," he groans.

I smile. I'm actually enjoying this. It's nice to have power over someone for a change, and I'm thankful that Max allowed me to have control over him. He has no idea how much that really means to me...

or maybe he does. We haven't known each other for very long, but Max knows me better than anyone. I don't know how that's possible, but it just is.

He calls out my name again, and hearing my name on his lips gives me even more incentive to make him feel good and give him satisfaction like he gave me during our first time together. My tongue flicks over his swollen head, the salty taste of him hitting my tongue as he moans. Feeling bold, I watch him through my eyelashes as I sheath my teeth behind my lips and slide his velvety length into my mouth. He watches me with parted lips as I take as much as I can into my mouth and throat. A long hiss leaves his lungs between clenched teeth as I bob my head up and down his thick shaft.

"Yeah, that's it, baby," he begs.

My fingernails gently graze up and down his thighs as I lick and suck him. His hips flex upwards, thrusting lightly into my mouth as he grows closer and closer to climax. The headboard creeks as Max's hands tighten around the frame. "Avery. I need to be inside of you. Now," he begs.

I give him one last lick before moving up to straddle him once more. His breathing is deep and uneven. I smile at the idea that I could make him come apart like this.

He motions to the nightstand. "Condom," he says softly.

I lean over and reach into the drawer. My fingers shake as I tear open the foil packet and gently ease the condom over his length. He's so big, and I wonder if it's going to hurt. Perhaps sensing my uncertainty, Max says, "We'll go slow."

My gaze meets his as I position myself above him with my knees on the bed on either side of his hips. His length presses against my entrance, and I can feel how wet I am for him. Apprehension has me hesitating for only a moment before I begin to sink down onto him. Max lets out a low growl, and it's the sexiest sound in the world. His head falls back onto the pillow, and I watch the steady pulse thump in his neck. I slowly take every tantalizing inch of him inside of me until I'm completely seated. Placing my hands on his muscular chest,

I begin to gently rock up and down. Amazingly, there is no pain like I have come to expect. To my surprise, there's only pleasure. And it feels so damn good.

My rhythm begins to pick up speed as I ride him faster and faster. The pleasure increases with every up and down movement, and I can't stop the moans coming from my mouth. It's never felt like this before. It's never felt good, and I didn't know it could feel like this.

I watch Max's hands clench on the headboard as he stares up at me in awe. "Fuck. Avery," he whispers.

I stare at his hands, and I suddenly want them on me. "Touch me, Max."

He hesitates with an uncertain look on his face. "Are you sure?"

"I trust you," I tell him, and it's the truth. I've never trusted anyone as much as I trust Max. "Touch me. Please," I beg.

His hands release the headboard and grip my hips. Holding onto me, he thrusts upwards and begins a punishing rhythm that has me panting. He feels so good inside of me, and I don't want the feeling to ever end.

His fingertips trail over my flat stomach and up to my breasts. He kneads my flesh softly and pulls at my taut nipples, making me moan loudly. "Max," I say through a shuddering breath.

"You're so goddamn beautiful," he whispers. "You're the most beautiful thing I have ever seen."

One of his hands trails down between my legs. It only takes a few flicks of his finger against my clit to drive me over the edge. The pressure builds inside of me quickly, and I can't stop it. I cry out and fall forward, collapsing onto his chest. Max holds me, his hands stroking my back, his cock thrusting up inside of me and his breath on my ear as my entire body trembles through an explosive orgasm. My legs quake against his hips, and I whimper from the intense pleasure. The feeling is too much, too great, and I hear myself starting to sob against his chest as my wetness floods and coats him.

Max kisses my cheek and gently rocks in and out of me as I come down from the high. My cries quiet down until my ragged breaths are the only sounds coming from my mouth. I slowly sit up, and Max stares up at me. His thumbs wipe away my tears, and he instantly looks worried.

"Did I hurt you?" he asks.

"Never," I reply. "I just...I didn't know it could feel like this," I whisper. I lean down and kiss his sweet lips. I have an emotion building up inside of me that I can't describe, but I think this is what being in love feels like. And I like it.

Slowly, I crawl off of him and lie down next to him. He looks over at me, and I take in his dark features. My dark knight in shining armor. I wonder again what I did to deserve someone like him in my life. He is the only light in my gloomy world. "Make love to me, Max," I say softly.

This time he doesn't even hesitate. He doesn't ask if it's okay. Because he knows, just like I do, that something passed between us just a few moments ago. I trust him wholeheartedly, and he knows that now.

I spread my legs for him, and he kneels between them. He enters me slowly, and I enjoy every single inch of him all over again. His course cheek lightly brushes against mine as his pleasured groan vibrates against me. I lift my hips to meet him. And in return, he thrusts deeper into me, stealing my breath away.

My hands fist in the sheets as the pressure begins to build inside of me once more. "Max, I —." A loud moan cuts off my voice.

"Come for me, Avery."

His words are my undoing. All of the tension inside of my body slowly beings to unravel as the overwhelming feeling of pleasure takes over me. I cry out as Max picks up speed. His cock thrusting in and out of me quickly has me losing my mind. My hands grip his shoulders, my fingernails biting into his skin as I allow the orgasm to rush through me. I'm just starting to moan when Max joins in. His muscles tremble under my touch as we reach ecstasy together, riding out wave after wave with moans and gentle kisses. His rhythm becomes uneven until he finally stops.

Max stares into my eyes as the last moments of our bliss are shared. His lips find mine, and we share a soul-searing kiss. I know in that moment that my life has changed forever. Never again will I see a man in the same light. Never again will I see a relationship in the same light. There are good people in this world like Max. I have a chance to be happy. And I'm not going to let him slip through my fingers because I'm afraid.

Max gently pulls out of me, lies down and draws me into his arms. I sigh contently because this is where I want to be. This is where I always want to be.

AVERY

THE NEXT MORNING I wake up to breakfast in bed. "You made all of this yourself?" I ask incredulously as I stare down at the tray of bacon, eggs, toast, pancakes and orange juice.

"Yep," he says with a proud expression.

I grin and instantly dig in. "I've never had breakfast in bed before," I say around a mouthful of eggs.

He frowns, but tries to cover it up well. "I'm going to go for a run before work."

I now notice that he's bare-chested, showing off his incredible body. Dark gray sweats cling to the lowest point of his hips, and my heart instantly speeds up.

He catches my gaze and grins that heart-stopping grin of his. "Eat. I'll be back soon."

I watch him disappear as I continue to feast on the incredible food he prepared. It's early. We still have over an hour before we have to be at the hospital, and I'm thankful for every moment I get to spend with him. It's Tuesday, and that means that Nathan will be home in only a few days. I'm dreading his return, but I refuse to let it spoil my time with Max. After our little argument yesterday, I don't want to spend any more time fighting. I want to enjoy every single second with him.

After I'm done eating, I slip into my dress from yesterday and walk outside onto his back deck. I spot Max on the beach in the distance running. I walk over to the railing and watch the beautiful orange and red hues in the sky as the sun rises.

I close my eyes and revel in this moment. This is what life could be like for me. Breakfast in bed after a night of amazing sex with a caring and sweet husband.

Who knew life could be so grand?

I certainly didn't.

And now that I've gotten a taste, I never want to let this dream go.

MAX

My FEET POUND into the sand as I run. All I can think about is Avery. She invades my every thought, and I wouldn't have it any other way.

Last night was incredible. Actually it was more than incredible. It was the best night of my life. Seeing her coming apart in my arms was a thing of beauty, and I want to witness that moment again and again. If I had it my way, I would never let her out of my sight. I would never let her go.

I finish my run and jog up the steps to the patio. Avery's dress whips around her legs in the gentle breeze as she overlooks the ocean and the sunrise. It's beautiful, but it pales in comparison to Avery.

"How was your breakfast?" I ask her as I stretch out my aching muscles.

"Divine," she replies over her shoulder. She flashes me a smile. "Thank you."

"You're welcome." I wrap my arms around her from behind and ease her against the railing. My lips kiss the exposed skin on her neck. Suddenly, I feel her entire body tense and begin to shake.

Immediately, I pull back and turn her around in my arms. She looks scared...lost. Whatever I just did triggered something inside of her.

Wounded bird, I remind myself. She had the same reaction on our first date when I tried to hold her from behind. I make a mental note to remember every trigger so that I don't make the mistake ever again. It will take some time, but I will learn what she can and can't handle.

She flies into my arms, crushing her cheek against my chest and wrapping her arms around me. I hold her and rest my chin on top of her head. "I hate what he's done to you," I say vehemently.

"He ruined me," she whispers so faintly that it takes me a few seconds to realize what she said.

"No." I lean back and meet her gaze. "You're not ruined, Avery. You're just wounded. And I'm going to be here every step of the way to put the pieces of your life and your soul back together. I'm not going anywhere until you're whole again."

She wraps her arms around me tightly like she's afraid to let go...or maybe afraid that I'll let her go. That's not going to happen. Ever.

After a few minutes, she suggests, "Let's take a shower. I haven't had my fill of you yet this morning, Dr. Harrison."

I instantly perk up at the idea, and I can't help but grin. The once shy Avery who couldn't even talk to me is suddenly turning into this bold and sexy creature. And I wouldn't have her any other way.

AVERY

After our lovemaking session in the shower caused us to almost be late, we both pull into the hospital parking lot just in the nick of time.

I climb out of my car, and Max instantly pulls me into his arms. His face is buried in the crook of my neck as he says, "I wish we had more time together. I don't want to let you go."

"I know," I say in agreement. If I could possibly stay in his arms all day, I would. There is no other place I would rather be.

"You shouldn't have to ever feel pain, Avery. You should know only kindness and happiness in this world, because that's exactly what you give back to it." He pulls back and stares into my eyes. His hands gently cup my face as his thumbs caress my bottom lip. "I know we just met, but I have a strong connection to you."

"I feel the same way about you," I confess.

He closes his eyes a moment as if relishing in my words. "I want to protect you. I want to make you happy."

I want that too, but I can't tell him that, because it will never happen — Nathan would never let that happen. If Nathan found out about Max and I, he would do everything in his power to ruin Max. I would have to get away from Nathan first before beginning anything with Max. But we have this week together with no interruptions, no consequences, no rules. And I intend on sharing it with Max and cherishing it and holding onto it like it's my lifeline.

I keep my emotions in check, not letting on that I'm secretly falling apart on the inside. My mouth finds his, and I put all of my emotions into that kiss.

And it's then that I make a silent vow to myself. I will find a way to leave my husband. And then I will find my way back to Max.

AVERY

THE DAYS GO by quickly, and I can't help but see the impending darkness that is to come when Nathan gets home. Today is Thursday, and for the first time in years, I'm able to forgo wearing a cardigan to the hospital. I stare at my almost perfect skin in the mirror. I only had to cover up some of the fading bruises, but the rest of my skin looks flawless. It's been so long since I've been out of the house without long sleeves on or completely covered in makeup that it makes my eyes sting with tears. A part of me can't believe I've actually been able to live with the abuse that I've grown accustomed to for so long. I'm so much happier without Nathan, and I've only had a taste of what my life could be like.

On my way to work, I relive the past few days I've had with Max. We've spent almost every waking moment together. We see each other off and on all day at the hospital. We have lunch together where we sit and talk for almost an hour about everything under the sun. Then we go home separately, only to reunite a short time later at his house. We've made love a countless number of times, and each time it gets easier for me to open up to him. There is no more hesitation, no more fear. I feel like a new person. I feel content. I feel happy.

Later that afternoon, Rosie hip bumps me as I stand at the nurses' station. She has a big smile on her face as she looks at me over the rim of her glasses. "You look happy, Avery." She taps her finger against her bottom lip for a moment before saying, "I think having Dr. Harrison here is having an effect on more than just the hospital."

I feel my cheeks instantly flush with heat. Somehow Rosie knows about Max and me. "You won't say anything, will you?" I ask in a panic.

She gestures as if she's zipping her mouth shut. "My lips are sealed. You can count on me."

I squeeze her arm gently for reassurance. "Thank you, Rosie," I whisper before turning away. A few feet down the hall I pass by Max. He smiles and winks at me, and I smile back at him. We try to keep everything on the down low, but I'm sure the hospital staff has noticed our frequent conversations and us sitting together at lunch every day. And according to Rosie, I look happy. I feel happy, probably happier than I've ever been. And I owe all the credit to Max. He makes me want to be a better person. He makes me want more out of life, and there's nothing I want more than him.

Jacob is patiently waiting for me when I enter his room. And when I produce his favorite snack, he gives me the biggest smile. Max said Jacob's doing better. He might even be able to be released soon if his leukemia goes into remission like they hope.

Jacob and I are in a serious conversation about which Ninja Turtle is cooler when Max walks into the room. He has a face-splitting grin on his face, and I can't help but return the expression. "Hey, Jacob," he says.

"Hey, Dr. H."

"Hi, Avery," he says with conviction behind his tone.

With a wink, I reply with, "Hello, Dr. H."

He chuckles and shakes his head. He turns his attention to Jacob.

"Your white blood cell counts are looking good. You just might be able to get out of here soon."

Jacob frowns a little and nods.

Max's brows dip in confusion. "You don't want to leave?"

"I do, but..." Jacob looks up at me. "I won't be able to see Avery if I leave."

His words hit me hard, and I have to fight back the urge to cry. "Maybe I can talk to your mom about coming to visit," I tell him.

Jacob instantly lights up. "Really?"

I nod and tap the brim of his baseball cap. "Sure."

"I'll ask her tonight!" he says, full of enthusiasm.

"Okay." I stand and say, "I'll see you tomorrow, Jacob." I walk to Max, and he's wearing an expression I can't decipher.

He steps closer to me and takes my hand in his. "You don't see how much you affect everyone around you," he whispers in my ear. "You emit this aura of kindness around you. I just wish you could see your full potential."

"I'm starting to see it," I whisper back and kiss his cheek sweetly. "Thanks to you."

"I'll see you tonight," he promises as we both leave the room and part ways.

MAX

I WAIT PATIENTLY for Avery to come over. She said she was cooking dinner and would bring it over around six. Every minute that ticks by I miss her, and I'm half tempted to march over there and show her how much.

A knock at the door has me grinning, and I hurry to answer it. Avery stands on my doorstep with a covered dish in her hands. She looks beautiful in a flirty dress, and I am so happy to see that she's wearing hardly any makeup on her arms. The bruises are almost completely gone; and, in turn, she exudes a renewed self-confidence. She holds her head up high instead of constantly looking to the ground like before. And it makes me so damn happy that I played a part in her newfound resilience.

I take the covered dish and lead her into the kitchen. "I bought some homemade Italian bread on the way home. I hope that goes well with whatever you made." She never told me what she was making, just that she would whip something up when she got home. But having learned to cook while under the supervision of a professional chef, I'm sure it's going to be great.

Avery pulls the lid from the dish and says, "Chicken, spinach and mushroom casserole."

"Smells good." I put the dish down and turn, pulling her into my arms. I press my forehead against hers and stare into those beautiful blue-gray eyes. "I missed you."

Laughing, she says, "You just saw me at the hospital two hours ago."

I bury my face into her neck and gently kiss her. "I know, but I missed you anyway."

She sighs contently and whispers, "I missed you too."

I break away from her to gather plates and cups. As I'm cutting the Italian bread, I ask her, "Red or white wine with dinner?" After no response, my eyes flicker to Avery, and I see that her attention is on my stack of mail on the counter. Something has caught her interest. I walk over and notice the first thing on top is an invitation to some political fundraiser. I pick up the postcard and hold it up. "Did you get one too?" I ask.

She hesitates before saying, "That's my father's campaign fundraiser."

"Your father is the mayor?" I stare at the card in disbelief. Avery had mentioned her father being in politics, but I didn't realize he was the mayor of the city I'm currently living in. "So I guess it would be a stupid question to ask if you're going," I remark.

She cringes, and I realize it's a sore subject. "I'll be there even if I don't want to be. It's not really a question of what I want when it comes to my choices in life."

Her words slowly sink in. "But it shouldn't be like that, Avery. If you don't want to do something, you shouldn't have to."

"If only it were that easy..." Her voice trails off as her expression grows reflective. I don't know about her, but this week has me fantasizing about what our life could be together. I would never make her go to some stuffy party if she didn't want to go.

I put the card down and set the table. Avery walks over to help. "So do you think you'll go to the fundraiser?" she asks.

"Thinking about it," I answer honestly. It would be nice to see Avery on a weekend that Nathan is home, but I don't know if I could bear seeing her with him in that kind of element where she's pretending. Seeing them together might break me. "I haven't made up my mind," I finally say.

We sit down and have a nice dinner. The casserole she made is excellent, but I had no doubt in my mind that it wouldn't be. Avery's great at everything she does. If only I could make her see that.

After dinner, we watch the other movie that I bought. Her mother is great in this one too, and I hold Avery close, relishing in the moment with her. Even though I'm having a great time, it's hard not to think about tomorrow being our last day together. Saturday, Nathan will return, and everything will go back to the way it was. I don't want that, but I don't think I have a say in the matter.

When she falls asleep in my arms, I hold onto her tightly like she's my salvation. I don't want to let her go, and I wish I could convince her to stay with me. But I know that's a losing battle. She's afraid of me interfering and possibly getting hurt, but I'm not afraid of getting hurt. I'm afraid of what could happen to her if I don't interfere.

I lean down and place a kiss on the crown of her hair. And when I'm sure she's in a deep sleep, I whisper, "I love you, Avery." The words shock me a little, but they also feel natural. I do love Avery. There is no doubt in my mind about that. I'm not ready to speak the words to her face to face, and I know part of that is out of fear — fear of rejection. Even though I can feel the almost tangible connection between us, she might not feel the same way about me.

She's so damn easy to love.

I just wish saying the words out loud would break the hold that Nathan seems to have over her, but I know that's not realistic. She's been broken too many times by him to think that there's happiness out there for her, but I intend on putting the pieces back together even if it takes the rest of our lives together.

MAX

FRIDAY GOES QUICKER than I would like it to. Seeing Avery in the halls of the hospital with a real, genuine smile on her face makes my heart do weird things. It makes me happy to see her so happy, but also sad at the same time because I know this will be all short-lived. I have so many mixed emotions that it's hard to keep them all in check.

After work, we go to the park for a picnic. She kicks off her sandals, as she sits down on the checkered blanket, and sinks her feet into the cool, thick grass. She looks up at me with a heart-melting smile, and I grin like an idiot. I can see a life with Avery. I can see us together in every way possible, but tomorrow this will all feel like a dream. Reality is only hours away, and I wish we could live in this fantasy for just a little while longer. I'm not ready to let her go just yet.

My expression must have changed, because her eyebrows suddenly furrow. "What's wrong, Max?"

"Just thinking," I reply. I quickly replace my frown with a smile and reach out to tuck a stray piece of hair behind her ear. My fingertips trail along her soft cheek as my thumb caresses her full bottom lip.

She plants a kiss on the pad of my thumb. Her eyes meet mine, and I can feel the heat passing between us. "This has been the best week of my life," she says softly. "I just wanted you to know that."

"Ditto," I tell her before leaning in and kissing her sweetly. "I wish it didn't have to end," I whisper against her mouth.

"Ditto," she whispers back.

After we pack up the picnic, we walk to a small ice cream stand in the middle of the park. She orders a chocolate and vanilla twist with sprinkles, and I order just plain old chocolate. We sit on a bench side by side and watch kids run, jump and swing in the giant playground area. She laughs when the kids do silly things, and I can't help but be captivated by her. I want to ask Avery about the first day we met and why her thoughts went somewhere else when I asked her about kids. Avery surprises me by broaching the subject herself and saying, "I was pregnant once."

I wrap my arm around her, my thumb stroking her sun-kissed shoulder. "I was just thinking about the day we met and when I asked you about kids. The look on your face..." my voice trails off as I recall her devastating expression. I still remember the agonizing pain behind those beautiful eyes.

She nods solemnly. "I didn't even know I was pregnant...until I lost it." She pauses and bites into her bottom lip so hard I fear it might split open. "It was his fault that I lost the baby, and I made a promise to myself to never get pregnant by him again." She sighs softly. "He doesn't even know I'm on birth control."

Her words chill my blood to the core. *It was his fault that she lost the baby.* I try to reign in my temper, but I feel myself close to losing it. "You shouldn't have to live like that, Avery. No one should make you feel that way. Ever."

She closes her eyes and snuggles close to me. I wrap my arm around her, and instantly my anger fades. She softly says, "Let's not ruin our last night together by talking about him and things in the past."

I nod. And just like that, the conversation is over. We continue to watch the kids play until the sun goes down. And then I take her home — my home, the home I wish I could call ours.

AVERY

I'M FILLED WITH such mixed emotions. On the one hand, I'm on cloud nine because of Max. On the other hand, Nathan is coming home tomorrow; and I am terrified.

This past week with Max has been incredible. It gave me hope. Hope for a better life. But all of that might come crashing down the moment I return home and see Nathan. I have been ignoring him. I hung up on him numerous times. And I know the punishment will be great. Just when my body had gotten used to the gentleness of Max, it will have to go back to the torment of Nathan. And, mentally, I don't know if I can handle it.

Max enters the kitchen. "Hey, do you want to have some wine out on the back deck?"

"Sure," I say, but even I can hear the tremor in my voice.

Max turns me to face him. His brows draw together, and he has a serious look on his face. "Are you all right?" he asks.

I nod, but all I want to do is break down and cry. "I wish we had more time," I tell him, my voice breaking.

He pulls me close. "Don't go home to him, Avery," Max whispers in my ear.

I still in his arms. "But...I have to."

"No, you don't." He holds me even tighter and kisses my forehead. "I don't want you to get hurt anymore. Don't go back to him. We'll find a way to hide you so that he won't ever find you again."

"That's impossible," I say, and it's the truth. No matter how hard I've tried, Nathan always finds me. He has resources that most people don't have and connections I probably don't even know about. And if he found out that Max helped me..." No," I say adamantly. "I'll figure out a way, but now isn't the time."

He pulls back and stares down at me. "Will there ever be a time?"

My palm cups his cheek, and he leans into my touch. "Yes. I promise."

He closes his eyes and nods once. "If anything happens, will you come to me? Will you let me protect you?"

I nod, because I don't want to lie to him. I won't let Max get hurt. No matter what happens.

Snaking my hands around Max's neck, I pull him down to me. Our kiss is urgent as if our time is going to run out, and I guess that's because it is. Our little world that we have been living in for the past week is going to come crashing down all around us tomorrow. Our little bubble that we have been safely contained in is about to burst, and I may never be able to be with Max like this again. The sinking feeling in the pit of my stomach tells me that I'm not wrong.

I pull back and say, "Go out on the deck. I'll bring the wine."

"All right," he agrees.

I pour two glasses and walk out onto the back deck where Max is reclining on one of the chairs. He's staring up at the night sky, and he looks completely content. A sliver of the moon keeps the deck from being consumed in total darkness. I set down the wine glasses on a small table, and the soft, silvery light cascades over both of us as I approach him.

He looks up at me with a grin, and I wish I could stay in this moment forever. This might be our last night together. And while that thought scares the shit out of me, I also want to make it count. I want to treat it like our last night together, so that I have something to hold onto forever.

Without fear or trepidation, two of my normal reactions to situations such as this, I reach for the hem of my dress and pull it up over my head in one sweep. Max watches with rapt attention as I remove my panties and bra and throw everything into a pile on the porch.

I climb onto his lap on the chair, straddling him. Leaning down, I place a kiss on his full lips. My fingertips reach for his shirt, and he helps me to remove it. We toss it aside, and then my fingers greedily reach for his pants. I unbutton and unzip, and he lifts his hips to pull them and his boxer briefs down and off his legs. With nothing left between us, his fingers find my pulsing clit, and I find his growing erection.

No words are exchanged between us as we stare into each other's eyes. I stroke his velvety length, and he closes his eyes for a moment and groans. He dips a finger into my channel and then adds another, pumping into me as I shudder in response. He makes me feel so good. I never thought it would ever be like this with anyone, but Max knows just how to touch me.

"You're so wet," he says with a husky tone. And I watch in awe as he brings his fingers to his mouth and sucks my juices from them. "You taste so damn good, Avery," he whispers.

His words have me practically melting, and I pull him close for a hot, searing kiss. His fingers return to my slit, finding my swollen, little nub. I gasp, and his tongue accepts that as an invitation. Our tongues tangle together, and I can taste myself mixed in with his own minty flavor.

Breaking the kiss, he leans over and pulls a condom out of his jeans pocket. "I need to be inside of you," he confesses. After tearing open the package, he rolls the condom down over his rock hard length. Then he looks up at me as his thumb sweeps over my bottom lip. "Ride me, Avery," he begs, his voice rough with desire.

I slowly lower myself onto him, allowing my body to adjust to his girth. Max's teeth clench, and he lets out a long hiss as I take my time.

When I quickly seat myself down to the root, he lets out a resonating growl. The sound echoes through me, making me even hotter. He cups my face in his hands, kissing me fiercely.

We establish a steady rhythm as I rock back and forth and he plunges in and out of me. The feeling is indescribable. His hands lock around my back, and he holds me as we make love out on his deck with the cool night air caressing our bodies.

And when I finally collapse onto his chest after our orgasms have subsided, I feel a sense of love, but also loss. I don't want to lose Max, but that's all I can focus on. I'm not going to get to experience this with him for a while...or perhaps ever again. And the feeling grows inside of me until it overwhelms me.

MAX

WE GET DRESSED slowly, and I can almost feel the overwhelming sadness radiating off of Avery. I hate to see her like that. After she slips on her sandals, I pull her into my arms. "Hey," I whisper. "Everything's going to be all right tomorrow."

"What if it isn't?" she asks before releasing a shaky sigh. "I don't think I can go back to the way things were with Nathan. I feel like my blinders have been lifted, and I don't think I can live in the dark anymore."

"Let me take you away from here. Let me protect you." As soon as the words leave my mouth, I can feel her begin to tense.

After a long pause, she finally says, "I can't let you risk everything for me, Max. It's just not right."

"What's not right is living with a person who abuses you. That's not right!" I say, exasperated. We stand there in silence for a long time. I don't want the last moments of our amazing week together to end on a sour note. Sighing, I pull her closer to my chest and breathe in her soft scent. "I don't want to fight. Let's just focus on the here and now. That's all we can ever do until something changes. And, God, do I hope it changes soon."

"Me too," she breathes.

I close my eyes. I don't know why she is so stubborn about this. I want to help. I love her even though I haven't spoken the words out loud yet. I need to do it when the time is right, and it doesn't feel right at this moment. Maybe I'm waiting for her to say it first since I feel so damn vulnerable in this situation.

"Wait here," I say before disappearing into the house. I return a few moments later with a small box. I hand the box to her, and she looks at it apprehensively. I watch carefully as she opens it.

She pulls out the small cell phone and looks up at me.

"It's a burner phone. With only my number programmed into it," I explain. "You can call me anytime you need me."

Her bottom lip trembles, and I suddenly doubt my idea. I thought the phone would give us a way to communicate in secret.

"Thank you, Max." She holds the phone to her chest tightly.

I put my finger under her chin, and raise her teary gaze to meet mine. "If you don't like it —."

She shakes her head softly. "I love having something that will give me a chance to talk to you whenever I need to."

I sigh in relief and pull her into my chest. I kiss the top of her head and whisper, "If you ever need anything, call me. I'll be there. I'll always be there."

She swallows hard and wraps her arms around me tightly. "What did I ever do to deserve you?" she asks.

I pull back and look down at her. "I ask myself that same question every day." Before she can put any self-doubting thoughts into her head, I grab her hand and say, "Let's go to bed. I want to hold you in my arms tonight." *And never let you go.* But I don't say that last part out loud even if it's the truth.

AVERY

I WAKE UP early and crawl out of bed slowly so as to not disturb Max. I leave a quick note on his nightstand telling him *thank you for everything*, and I kiss him sweetly one last time before I quietly leave.

I'm not sure what time Nathan's flight is landing, but I want to make sure the house is in perfect order before he comes home. I already know his temper is going to be flaring based on the number of phone calls and texts I never returned. Mentally, I'm already trying to prepare for the backlash, for the punishment, but it's so much harder this time. My entire body shakes as I attempt to get back into my normal, robotic, passive mode.

After taking a shower and getting dressed, I decide to run to the store for groceries. I haven't cooked in over a week, and most of the fresh fruit and vegetables in the fridge have spoiled. I leave a note on the counter for Nathan in case he returns before I get home, and I set out for the store.

Concentrating on shopping and sticking to the list I made proves to be difficult when my mind keeps reverting back to the memories of the week I spent with Max. It's hard to believe that so much has happened in that short amount of time. It's a whirlwind romance for sure, and I have loved every single second of it. I find myself smiling as I shop, and I don't stop smiling until I pull in front of my house.

My lips pull into a frown as I see Nathan's BMW in the driveway. I try to steel my nerves for the confrontation that's bound to happen. I tuck the burner phone Max gave me into a little zippered compartment inside my purse. The charger is safely hidden inside the house, and I left the box at Max's house. I don't want Nathan to ever find any connection to Max.

I pull out my anti-anxiety prescription and pop two pills in my mouth, swallowing them quickly. I haven't had the need to take my pills in almost a week, and I'm sure the numbing effect that will eventually kick in will hit me like a ton of bricks. However, I know I'll need to feel some numbness after my talk with Nathan.

Taking a deep, calming breath, I climb out of the car, grab a few bags of groceries and carry them up the sidewalk. With a trembling hand, I open the front door. Nathan is nowhere in sight, but I see his car keys hanging on one of the hooks on the wall. I know he's in here.

"Nathan?" I call out with a tremulous voice.

The moment I step into the kitchen, I can sense him. Every muscle in my body begins to tense. It's almost like my mind is trying to prepare my body for the inevitable pain.

He walks from the living room into the kitchen. His eyes never even glance in my direction as he takes a bottle of water out of the fridge. He practically tears the cap off, and I can almost feel the anger radiating off of him in waves. "I called the phone company," he says in a low voice. "They said there's no problem with the line. Cell phone company said the same thing. So I know you were ignoring my calls and texts on purpose."

I swallow hard. "I was sick. I didn't even hear the phone ringing half the time," I explain, sticking with my lie. I place the grocery bags and my purse on the counter, stalling for more time.

He slowly turns to look at me. His eyes peruse my body. "Funny how you don't look sick. You told me you were practically on your deathbed, and yet not one single phone call to Dr. Seiger."

I realize Nathan has been checking up on me even from afar. I wonder who else he called. Closing my eyes, my tongue darts out to lick my suddenly dry lips. "I started to feel better a couple of days ago, so I didn't bother making an appointment."

He takes a long drink of water and sets the bottle down on the counter. "I didn't know you could still volunteer at the hospital if you were that ill. I would think they would want you to stay home and get some much-needed rest. You know, not infect the other patients." His eyes dart to me, and the look is murderous. "I almost came home early. But then your sister said she had lunch with you the other day and that you appeared fine."

My stomach twists into one giant knot. *He talked to Allison? Why?* My heart pounds hard against my ribcage. *Did she tell him what I said? Did she tell him that I want a divorce? Does he know?*

"Did you not worry at all if I made it to Seattle in one piece? Did you not worry if I was all right, Avery?" When I don't answer, he continues by saying, "You are so fucking selfish. You always have been. You only think about yourself." He shakes his head solemnly. "Sometimes I wonder if I married you before you were ready. The age difference has definitely come into play more than once in the past several years. You are so immature, *Avery.*"

The way he says my name is like a curse on his tongue. "I'm sorry," I say, because it's the only thing I can do to try to placate him.

"Sorry," he spits. "You're sorry?" I watch the rage suddenly build within him, and I automatically take a step back. My move irritates him. "Come here," he whispers.

A shiver runs up my spine as I stay where I am. My emotions drain from my body, and I can almost feel them pooling at my feet and bleeding out onto the floor. All of the happiness that Max has created over the past week is gone within an instant.

"Come. Here," he demands, menacingly.

It's a double-edged sword at this point. If I go to him, he'll hurt me. But if I turn and run, he'll hurt me perhaps even worse. I'm screwed either way, and my feet refuse to budge. I can't willingly walk to pain. I just can't.

"I won't ask you again, Avery." He folds his arms in front of his chest, his muscles clenching under his t-shirt with pent-up anger.

"Please, Nathan. I'm sorry for not answering the phone. I told you I was sorry. How many times can I apologize?"

He stares at me in disbelief. I usually listen to him the first time he tells me to do something, and I think he's shocked that I'm not obeying his commands. "Avery." He jabs his finger towards the floor in front of him. "Come here. NOW!" he screams.

"No." I hear the word leave my lips, but I can't believe I said it. My time with Max changed me. I know that now. A small part of the old me has been rebuilt, and I'm standing up to Nathan just like I did years ago.

Nathan stalks towards me, and I quickly back myself away from him to the wall. "I think my time away was a mistake. You are reverting back to your old ways, Avery. And I don't like it," he hisses.

"I don't care what you like," I hiss back.

The smack from his hand hits my cheek before I can even blink. The force of it causes my head to whip around, and the back of my head smacks hard against the wall. My hand instantly goes to the hot skin on the side of my face. It's painful to touch, and something inside of me instantly changes. Instead of crying, instead of wanting to tell him that I'm sorry, I get angry. In fact, I'm seething as I stand before him. My brain is screaming for me to fight. *Don't just stand there and take it! Fight!* I glare at him and scream, "Fuck you!"

Nathan stares at me for a few moments, unmoving, and the room grows eerily quiet. "Say it again." He's breathing hard, and I know he's trying to control the beast inside of him. "I. Dare. You."

I stand my ground, not backing down this time. "Fuck. You." I spit out the words with as much gusto as I can manage. I find myself feeling suddenly empowered. This has been a long time coming. I should have never stopped standing up to him. I should have never let him lay a hand on me. But the past is in the past. I can't change what was.

His eyes never leave mine. "Oh, I see you've grown a backbone while I was gone." His lips curl up into a sinister sneer. "Well, I guess I'll just have to break you down all over again."

The blows come in succession. One hit to my face has me crumbling against the wall behind me. One punch to my stomach has me doubling over in pain. His hands keep striking me, and I can feel my resolve slowly leaving me piece by piece.

I'm cowered down on the floor from the last punch to my ribs, and I desperately hold my trembling hands up. I can't handle any more. "Please. Stop," I sob.

He smiles. "There she is. There's my Avery." He crouches beside me and strokes my hair. I recoil under his touch. "You always were so easy to fucking break."

He pulls me against him and holds me tightly. I struggle against him, but he's too strong. The more I struggle, the tighter his grip gets until I can't breathe. My bruised ribs scream out in pain, and I suddenly grow limp in his arms as the room around me fades away.

AVERY

THE SUNLIGHT IS creeping in the windows and shining onto my face. For a moment I think I'm in Max's bed, and it makes me smile. But when I open my eyes and see where I really am, my contentment dramatically switches to pure and utter terror. The memories of Nathan coming home and hitting me flash through my mind. He squeezed me until I passed out from the pain. That's why I can't remember getting into bed.

A sob threatens to escape my lips, but I hold it in. Slowly, I try to sit up in bed, almost screaming in pain from the movement. My stomach rolls, and I almost retch from the feeling. Groaning, I lie back down and close my eyes.

Even with my eyes closed, I can sense him. My hair stands on end. And as if right on cue, Nathan strolls into the bedroom carrying a tray of food. I glare at him as he walks over to me. He smirks as he places the tray down on the nightstand and then moves to the bed. I recoil when he reaches towards me. "Easy," he says softly. Placing some pillows behind my back, he asks, " Can you sit up?"

I try to move, and that's when I feel the excruciating pain wracking my body. I cry out as he helps me to sit up.

Once I'm propped up on the pillows, he places the tray of food on my lap. He points to the two white pills beside a tall glass of water. "For the pain," he explains nonchalantly.

I stare at the smorgasbord of eggs, toast, bacon and strawberries in disbelief. "What...why are you doing this?" I ask.

He says nothing, but instead grabs the remote control for the television and taps the power button. He turns it to a news station, and immediately a breaking news story runs across the screen. I see my father's name, and my heart stops beating. A reporter is on the screen, and I listen to her every word while my entire body quivers in disbelief.

"It was a close call for Mayor Andrew Bennett this morning. The Mayor was giving a speech at the opening ceremony for the new downtown historical society when an unknown suspect fired a shot into the crowd. The bullet grazed Mayor Bennett's arm and earned him a trip to the hospital. We are told that the Mayor is now at home and resting. He is said to be in excellent condition and in high spirits after the scare. The shooting suspect still remains at large. Mayor Bennett recently announced that he is running for Governor of North Carolina, but police do not believe this incident was politically motivated. Please stay tuned for more on this story later today on our twelve o'clock news hour."

My head slowly turns to look at Nathan. He has a smirk on his face, and suddenly I know exactly who's responsible. "You. You did this!" I hiss.

"Now, now, Avery. Don't start making accusations you can't back up with any real evidence."

The telephone rings, and Nathan picks it up before I can even reach for the receiver. His conversation is brief and ends with, "Of course. We'll be there as soon as we can." He hangs up and looks at me. "Eat, take your pills and get ready. We're going to see your father."

I stare at him in disbelief by his candor. "Why did you do this? Why did you try to have my father killed?"

"I didn't try to have anyone killed, Avery," he scoffs. "I respect your father and want him to be governor of this state. If anything, this little stunt will gain him even more popularity. An otherwise dull and not so known event turned into quite the news story." Then he leans down and stares into my eyes. His voice lowers as he says, "Your sister told me you're questioning our marriage, thinking about leaving me." His words turn the blood in my veins to ice. "I did this to prove a point. When you disobey me, I will hurt the ones you love," he sneers. "Next time it could be your sister. And I won't hesitate to tell my man to blow her pretty little brains all over the pavement." He stands and straightens his tie. "This was all an act to show you how far I'm willing to go, Avery. How far I will go to show you that I own you. I will always own you. And I will never let you go. *Never*," he says, stressing the last word. "I hope we have an understanding of how things are going to go from now on." The smile on his face falters when I say nothing in return. "Do you understand?" he asks through gritted teeth.

I nod once.

He points to the tray. "Eat. We have a busy day ahead of us."

And with that, he leaves. After he's gone, I allow the tears to fall freely. Nathan tried to have my father killed. My own sister betrayed me. And all I can think of is what he would do to Max if he ever found out about us. My dreams of being with Max are suddenly evaporating before my eyes. No one can help me. Not even Max. I know that now. I would never risk his life for mine. I'll be stuck in this prison forever.

Until death do us part.

AVERY

$\mathcal{A}$FTER GOING THROUGH a rigorous security check at my father's estate, I am finally able to enter the office where my father sits at his desk. He's working, of course. The sleeve of his shirt is rolled up to his shoulder, and his arm is bandaged. He stares at the computer screen and looks tired, stressed.

"Dad?" I call out from the doorway.

"Sweetheart," he answers, turning and opening his arms wide for me.

Nathan stays in the doorway as I rush to my father, gently embracing him. I fall apart in his arms as he hugs me tight and soothes me with whispered words while stroking my back. It's been such an emotional day already, and I can't hold back my tears any longer. "Nathan, would you give us a minute alone, please?" he asks.

Nathan hesitates before saying, "Of course, sir."

"I'm fine, Avery. Everything's all right."

I give him one last gentle squeeze before pulling back. I dash the tears from my eyes. "I was so worried."

"It was a close call and it scared the hell out of me, but I'm okay." He brushes a strand of hair away from my face. "Avery, I've been wanting to talk to you about something. I just didn't know how to begin. But I guess now is as good a time as any." He takes a deep breath. "Your sister told me you came to her asking her for help. She said you were making some pretty wild accusations about Nathan." His face grows worried. "I want to know the truth, Avery. What is going on between you two?"

I hesitate, but only for a moment before plastering a blank look on my face. Allison ratted me out to Nathan and my father. A few days ago I would have been elated that she told our father, but now I'm going to have to do some backpedaling to quench the situation before it can escalate any further. "Nothing, Dad. I just —." My voice falters. "None of that matters right now. All that matters is that you're okay."

"Avery," he says in a reprimanding tone. "If something bad was happening, you would tell me, right? You would come to me?"

I nod, unable to say the lie out loud. There is no confiding in my father or trying to enlist his help now. My chance of doing that is over. Nathan showed me his power and his will to ensure I stay with him. There has to be another solution that doesn't involve my family. I can't be responsible for anything that Nathan might do to them because of me.

I wrap my arms around him and hold him tight, trying to control my emotions. "I'm just glad you're okay, Dad," I whisper against his chest.

"Me too, sweetheart. I don't want to leave my girls just yet. I'm not ready."

MAX

I STARE AT my cell phone.
No calls.
No texts.
Nothing.
Not a single word from Avery.

I glance at the television screen as the news story about her father comes up once again. Maybe she is so absorbed with that right now that she hasn't even thought about me. I know that I haven't been able to stop thinking about her, but I don't have anything else on my plate right now.

I'm worried about what happened when Nathan returned home. If he hit her again, I don't know if I'll be able to control my actions.

I can't stand seeing her anything but happy, and I need to figure out a way to get her out of the situation she's in. I know we shared a connection this past week that could never be replicated. It's a one-of-a-kind feeling, and I want to feel it always with her.

Sighing, I turn off the TV. I'll see Avery at the hospital tomorrow. This weekend has been a living hell without her. I got so used to having her in my arms that I now feel lost without her.

I feel like a piece of me is gone, and I can't wait until we can be together and I can feel whole again.

AVERY

I CAREFULLY CLIMB out of my car Monday morning. I adjust the sleeves of my cardigan in the reflection of the window and stare at the frown on my face. My lower lip trembles, and I'm on the verge of tears. The weekend was a nightmare, and I am physically and emotionally drained from it. It was extremely difficult to even get out of bed this morning. And when I saw the fresh bruises littering my skin, I nearly had a breakdown.

It's amazing how Max was able to almost erase my past with just one week of being with him. I almost forgot what it was like to be sad all the time. I almost forgot what it felt like to be abused. Almost.

I'm in a fog when I walk into the hospital. People say *good morning* to me, but I barely hear them. The anxiety medication I'm taking again is clouding my thoughts, but it's the only way I can stay sane. Without the pills, I wouldn't be able to cope with my life right now.

"Avery," a voice says.

"Good morning," I say like a robot.

"Avery," the voice says again.

I'm about to say good morning once more, but then I feel a hand gripping my arm. I'm suddenly pulled into an empty hospital room. With a hushed voice, Max begins to ask a million questions. "Are you okay? I heard what happened to your father on the news. I haven't been able to see you or talk to you in almost two days. I've been going insane. What happened when Nathan got home? Did he hurt you?" The words come flooding out of his mouth, and I can hear the fear in his voice. He's scared. He's scared for me. And he has every right to be.

"I'm fine," I answer. "Everything is fine."

"What happened with Nathan? Did he hurt you when he got home?"

I stare at the floor, refusing to meet his gaze. I'm not going to lie to him, but I don't want to tell him the truth in fear for what could happen to him.

"Why won't you talk to me, Avery? What happened between Friday night and today to make you act like this?" He reaches out and attempts to drag my sleeve up my arm.

"Don't!" I cry, rearing back. "Don't touch me!"

"Did he hurt you?" he asks, seething.

His hands are reaching for me again, but I push him away. Suddenly, he pulls me into his arms and holds me. I fight against him, but he doesn't let me pull away. "Please don't push me away, Avery. Please. I can't bear it," he whispers into my ear, and I can hear the desperation in his voice.

My resolve slowly deflates, and I stop fighting him.

"Tell me what I can do, Avery, and I'll do it. I'll do *anything*."

And therein lies the problem. Max would do anything to help me, even if it meant him getting hurt in the process. And now I know the true extent of the power Nathan has. He would undoubtedly hurt Max...maybe even kill him. And I would never forgive myself if anything happened to him. I squirm out of his arms, and this time he lets me go. "You can't help me! Don't you see, Max? You're only going to get hurt if you try to help me."

"I don't care about getting hurt. I only care about you," he protests.

His words cut through me like a knife to my very core. How did I deserve someone this special in my life? Out of all the darkness and torment, he is my only light. Max is so pure with a big heart, and he would be willing to do anything to protect me. And that is exactly why I need to let him go. Before it's too late. Before he gets hurt. "I can't allow you to be involved any more, Max. You need to just...you need to forget about me."

"Forget about you?" he practically yells.

My head hangs in defeat. "You need to move on. We can't be together. Not now." I swallow hard before adding, "Maybe not ever."

His hands reach out and hold onto mine for support. "Avery," he whispers. When I finally meet his gaze, he continues. "I want to help you, and I don't give a damn about the consequences. You don't deserve this life. You deserve so much more."

"It's not about what I deserve, Max. It's about reality and what I have now. And right now I am married to a terrible man with very destructive means to get what he wants. And he wants *me*. If he's willing to shoot my father, what do you think he would do to you?" The words are out of my mouth before I can stop them. "Shit," I mutter.

Max's brows furrow in confusion and then his eyes narrow. "Nathan is responsible for what happened to your father?" he asks, incredulously.

I bite my lip and then release an unsteady sigh. "Don't you get it? Until I can leave him for good, there is no future for us." I pull my hands away from him. "Please. Just leave me alone," I say, barely able to speak the words out loud.

As I'm walking away I hear him say, "I won't give up on you, Avery."

My chest aches with pain as I stop walking and whisper, "You have to."

"I can't lose you. I won't," he vows.

I glance back at him one last time. I take in his every feature, memorizing his face and etching it into my brain forever. If life were a fairytale, he would be my knight in shining armor, saving me from the evil king like in Jacob's favorite book.

Unfortunately, life isn't as easy as written words on a piece of paper with a happy ending.

"You already have," I tell him before leaving the room.

MAX

AFTER THAT MOMENT with Avery on Monday morning, the rest of the week at the hospital dragged on. She ignored me in the hallways. She changed her schedule so that I wouldn't know where she was during the day. She refused to eat lunch in the cafeteria, because she knew I'd be there. And she arrived early and left early to avoid me altogether. And every night I sat on my back porch watching the house next door and dreaming about the girl who was trapped inside of it.

She stopped going to the beach every night, and a part of me began to wonder if that was because she didn't need to. What if Nathan had come home a changed man? Maybe she's not pushing me away to protect me at all. Maybe she's finally happy with her husband. That thought alone kills me and drives me crazy. I got a taste of what life could be like with Avery, and I'm not letting her go without a fight.

By Monday, I am more determined than ever. I wake up early and make sure I'm one of the first ones there for the day shift. A few minutes after I arrive, Avery's car pulls in. My hands clench the steering wheel as I think about all the things I'm going to tell her. I'm upset. I'm angry. And if she really is going to just dump me like yesterday's trash, then I have a right to know.

But all of my anger and attitude vanishes the moment she steps out of the car. She looks exhausted, broken and utterly and completely defeated. She straightens the sleeves of her cardigan, making sure they're pulled down to her hands and stares at her reflection. Her watery eyes fixate on her reflection, and I think for a moment she's going to have a breakdown right in the middle of the parking lot.

I carefully climb out of my SUV and make my way towards her. The only thought on my mind is that *she needs me*.

AVERY

I HAD BEEN numb for so long that I forgot what it felt like to feel something. Max made me feel a lot of things. And now that I've experienced that glimmer of hope, it's hard for me to go back to the way things were. I'm no longer numb to the physical and mental abuse bestowed upon me by Nathan. In fact, I'm quite the opposite. I'm sad. I'm depressed. I'm angry. I talk back. I fight. I kick. I scream.

And in return, I get twice as much abuse back from Nathan. Bit by bit, I'm slowly breaking to pieces. And I don't know if I will ever be whole again.

I feel like giving up. I miss Max so bad it physically hurts much more than the bruises. I miss everything about him — his dark eyes when they would look upon me with a burning gaze right before we would make love, his infectious laugh and his goofy grin. And I miss how he treated me and how he touched and kissed me like I was the most precious thing in the world.

I hate the fact that he lives right next door and that I can't even talk to him. I've watched him from the window running on the beach, pushing his body to physical extremes. If he's hurting half as much as I am, the feeling of loss must be unbearable.

It's been a week since we last talked. Max had desperately tried talking to me, but I ignored him. He'd even tried confronting me, only for me to just run away from him like the plague. I keep trying to remind myself that I'm doing this to protect him, but I know I'm hurting him — maybe even more than how Nathan could hurt him.

I stare at myself in the reflection of my car window, and I feel broken. I honestly don't even know how I'm holding myself together anymore. Every second of every day I feel like I'm going to break into a million pieces.

I hear footsteps approaching, and I quickly dash the tears from my eyes. When I look up and see Max walking towards me, my heartbeat falters.

His dark gaze doesn't leave mine as he says, "Don't walk away from me, Avery." When I don't make a move, he runs a hand through his thick, dark hair and sighs in relief. "You don't have to say a word if you don't want to talk. I just...I just want to be close to you without you running away."

I give a small nod, and his features instantly relax. He looks worn out, tired. Dark stubble lines his jaw, and his eyes are bloodshot. "Are you getting enough sleep?" I ask.

It's the first time I've talked to him in a week, and he closes his eyes for a moment, as if savoring my spoken words. "No, I haven't been sleeping very well lately. Not at all actually," he confesses.

"Max, if this is about me —."

"Of course it's about you," he says, raising his voice. My eyes widen, and he immediately lowers his tone. "Avery, I miss you. And it kills me to not be able to touch you or, at the very least, talk to you every day. Tell me I'm not alone here. Tell me you feel the same way. Tell me you miss me too."

My walls slowly start to crumble around me, and I can feel the tears welling up in my eyes once again. "I tried so hard to move on...to forget you...but I can't," I say, my voice breaking. "I do feel the same way, Max. It's killing me too every single second of every single day."

He reaches out and takes my hand in his. "I'm not letting you go."

I stare at our joined hands. He gives mine a gentle squeeze for reassurance. I look up into his eyes, and I find a peace there that I can't find anywhere else in this world. "I don't want you to let me go," I confess.

Max gently pulls on my hand, and I fall into his arms. He holds me, and I can barely contain my emotions. After all the pain and abuse this week, it feels so damn good to be held and comforted. The tears that I had so desperately tried to hide earlier come flooding out, spilling over my cheeks. Max strokes my hair and hushes me. "I'm here, Avery. I've always been here, and I'm not going anywhere. You were just too damn stubborn to see that."

"It's too dangerous for us to be together, Max," I whisper, but I can't seem to force myself to leave the safety of his arms. "We shouldn't even be talking right now."

He pulls back and meets my stare. "We don't know what the future holds, Avery, but we can embrace this moment. Only here. Only now. Remember?"

I nod.

He swallows hard, his Adam's apple bobbing in this throat. "Tell me you want to be with me, and we'll figure the rest out. We'll find a way to be together."

Fear keeps me from answering right away. I take a couple of steps away from him, needing the distance to think. "I want to be with you. I miss you so much it hurts. But, Max —."

He shakes his head, stopping me. "No buts. We'll worry about everything else later. Right now the only thing that matters is that we care for each other and that we want to be together no matter what. We'll get through this, Avery. I promise."

I want to ask him how or when, but I don't. A big part of me wants to believe that everything will work out for the best. Maybe we'll figure it out. Maybe we won't, but I know I don't want to spend another minute without Max and worrying about the *what ifs*. I want him. I want to be with him. But it's not going to be easy. "I'm scared," I confess.

"Don't worry. We'll be careful. He won't find out about us," he says, as if he's reading my mind.

I close my eyes, wishing I had just an ounce of his strength and determination. "I hate that it has to be this way."

"It won't always be like this, Avery."

I open my eyes, and they lock onto his. "Promise. Promise me, Max."

"I promise," he says with all the confidence in the world. He takes a step towards me, but stops abruptly. "I want to hold you so bad right now and show you how much I've missed you." He steps back and clenches his hands into fists at his sides. "Meet me tonight on the beach. I need to see you, Avery. I need to be with you."

Hesitating for only a moment, I nod my head in agreement. "Okay. I'll meet you."

He flashes me that familiar grin of his and walks away. I instantly feel a million times better, and I know I can thank Max for that. He is like a breath of fresh air when I feel like I'm so close to suffocating. I don't know how we'll make it work, but I'm more determined than ever to try for Max...for me...for us.

AVERY

*D*URING THE DAY, Max and I get back into our regular routine. We eat lunch together. We visit Jacob together. I finally have a real smile on my face after a week of being in complete misery. It feels so good to feel happy again. The feeling is beyond words.

After dinner, Nathan goes to bed early. He has a lot of surgeries scheduled for the next day, and so he wants to be well rested. The timing couldn't have worked out any better. I can barely refrain myself from running out the door when he goes to bed, but I make myself wait until I know he's sound asleep.

I pull on a pair of sneakers and make my way outside. The ocean breeze gusts over my face, and I feel rejuvenated. I feel alive for the first time since Nathan got back. I jog down the steps and walkway. As soon as my feet hit the sand, I see him. Max is standing right by the water, facing the ocean. My heart practically leaps out of my chest as I run towards him.

He turns, as if he could sense me coming, and opens his arms. I gladly run into them, and he squeezes me so tight it almost hurts. He kisses my face, raining kisses on my forehead, my cheeks, my jaw and my mouth. "I've missed you. It's insane how much I've missed you, Avery."

We find a spot behind a sand dune at the end of the row of houses that is secluded from any prying eyes. I lean against the hill as Max's lips tease me into a frenzy. His tongue licks my heated skin at the base of my neck. My fingers itch to touch every single inch of him. But when I reach out for him, he shakes his head. "Tonight is all about you," he whispers.

His hands grip the bottom hem of my dress and pull it up over my head in one sweep. I stand before him in a bra and panties, and he licks his lower lip as his eyes peruse me. He growls in approval before putting his lips on me once again.

My head falls back against the dune as Max's mouth trails kisses down my chest. He licks and nips my taut stomach, and it makes me quiver in anticipation. He kneels down in front of me and says, "Look at me, Avery."

My eyes find his. I swallow back a moan just from the sight of him. It feels like it's been years instead of just a little over a week since I've felt his touch like this. I didn't realize how much I truly missed him until this moment. I didn't know I could ever feel like this with someone.

"I'm going to show you how much I've missed you, and I want you to watch me." He grins that panty-melting grin of his, and then his attention focuses on my body. His index finger slides up the length of my sex, and I can feel the moisture pooling in my panties. "So wet for me already," he says with a growl.

Hearing Max this turned on has my body on overdrive. I'm literally panting in anticipation of what's to come. And when he strokes me again, I find myself begging, "Please."

His fingers hook onto the waistband of my panties, and he draws them down my legs. I kick them off and stand there bare in front of him. A soft breeze blows against my exposed sex, and I bite my lower lip to keep from crying out. I'm so turned on that I know the lightest of touches is going to have me falling apart.

Max's hands wrap around the back of my thighs, and he parts my legs slightly. He gently kisses my right thigh and then the left. I squirm in his grip and try not to scream out in frustration. "So eager," he says with a lopsided grin as he stares up at me.

"Please, Max. I need you," I whisper. My voice sounds strained and needy.

The moment his tongue hits the apex of my thighs, I cry out. I forgot how good his tongue felt. He laps at my clit, and my legs shake in his hands. My eyes fall closed and my mouth falls open, but Max abruptly stops. "Watch me, Avery," he commands.

My gaze locks onto him. Max is so different tonight...controlling and hot. But he is the type of controlling that I don't mind. He's not hurting me in the process. He's making me feel desired, and it's a whole different side to him that I am able to love.

Once he's satisfied that I'm watching, his mouth returns to my clit. I can feel every movement of his lips, his tongue and his teeth as he gently nips my most sensitive area. It doesn't take long for me to build up to a precipice. My body trembles against him, and I call out his name as the orgasm washes over me. Wave after wave flows through me, and the roar of the ocean behind him masks my cries of pleasure.

After I come down from my high, Max helps me to get dressed. And then he holds me in his arms without saying a word. He just strokes my back and kisses my neck every so often. He holds me tight like he's afraid I'll disappear.

I realize in that moment that Max is my only reason for surviving at this point.

If we have to keep sneaking around, I will do it if it means just one more moment with him. I need Max as much as he needs me, if not more; and I'll do anything not to lose him again.

AVERY

*O*VER THE NEXT couple of weeks, Max and I spend every second we can together. We usually only get a few minutes here and there, but we take them and cherish them. The abuse from Nathan doesn't get any better or less frequent, but being with Max allows me to continue on, to forge through all of the tough times.

It's Thursday night, and Nathan and I are enjoying a hearty beef stew that I had prepared when he says, "I'm leaving tomorrow afternoon. One of my patients in California needs some work done before a movie premiere. I won't be home until Sunday night. Late."

I quickly oppress my elation. I force myself to just nod in answer to his statements. This is the first time he's left for the weekend since the conference in Seattle. And I can barely contain my excitement that I will have a whole weekend to be with Max.

"Avery," Nathan says, sternly, bringing my attention to him. "I wouldn't go if I had any other choice. I don't like the thought of leaving you here alone again considering what occurred when I was in Seattle. It's been tough getting things back to the way they once were, and I don't want to leave knowing that it's going to happen again." He straightens in his chair. "It won't happen again, will it?"

"No," I say meekly.

"And what will you do when I call you?" he prompts firmly.

"Answer the phone."

"Good girl," he replies. "I expect you to answer. Every. Single. Time," he says, drawing each word out for emphasis. "Do we understand each other?"

"Yes," I say without hesitation. I hate how I sound so obedient, but it's better for me in the long run to just comply with whatever he says. I've learned that the hard way over the years.

Satisfied, he wipes his mouth with a linen napkin before standing. "You outdid yourself with dinner. I think it was actually better than my mother's recipe."

"Thank you," I say, surprised by his compliment. It's been so long since he's said anything nice to me that I'm almost in shock.

"I'm going to do a little packing before I go to bed. Will you help me?"

I stare at him with skepticism. He's actually asking me to help? This is so unlike Nathan that it's almost scary. "S-sure," I stammer with apprehension. Warning bells are going off in my head, but I try to tell myself that everything is okay. Maybe he's just in a good mood...for once in his life. "Let me clean up in here, and then I'll come help," I suggest.

"No," he says. "Let's go pack now, and then you can clean up."

My nervousness instantly wears off. He's back to his bossy, demanding self. At least he dropped the nice guy act. "Okay," I agree, following him to the bedroom. Once I enter the room, I notice that his suitcase is sitting in the corner of the room. "I thought you said you needed help pack—?" The rest of the question doesn't even make it out of my mouth before he suddenly grabs me and pushes me to the bed. His body pins me down as he says through gritted teeth, "I want you to know without a shadow of a doubt before I leave tomorrow, Avery, who the fuck owns you."

"Nathan, no! Please! No!" I cry, pleading with him.

The fabric from my dress stretches and rips as he tears it from my body. His compliments and kindness were all a ruse. He was purposefully trying to lure me into the bedroom so that he could rape me and assert his dominance before his trip. He wants me to know how bad it can get, as if I could ever forget. "No!" I scream, fighting him as best I can.

His knee digs into my back, and it's hard for me to breathe. "Don't fucking move, or I'll make this ten times worse, Avery. Don't. Test. Me!" he roars.

My body instantly stills. His fingers grab the hem of my thong, ripping the material until it falls around me in a shredded mess like the rest of my clothes. He mounts me from behind, and I do everything in my power not to scream. Fat tears fall from my eyes as I stare out the window at the dark ocean. I withdraw into myself, not wanting to mentally be present in this moment. I focus on the water lapping against the beach as I withdraw even further.

I no longer hear my cries. I no longer hear his grunts and malicious insults. And I no longer feel the pain emanating from my core.

The ocean is my sanctuary, and I focus every single inch of my mind on it. It seems like hours pass, but maybe it's only a few minutes. I don't know. But Nathan eventually leaves the room. I stay on the bed and curl up into a ball. The tears still fall from my eyes, but I don't even feel like I'm crying. In fact, I don't think I can feel anything at all.

And that scares the hell out of me.

AVERY

THE NEXT DAY at the hospital is nerve-wracking, and I'm second-guessing my decision to come in to volunteer. I'm running on autopilot, barely comprehending the world around me. I spend most of my time hidden away in the bathroom, crying to myself. I can't seem to stop crying over last night. I feel used and irrevocably broken. Nathan has raped me before, but this time was different. This time I felt like a part of me was lost in the process.

The past few weeks with Max have opened my eyes. I'm no longer a living, breathing doll incapable of feeling anything. I am finally alive; and, in return, feeling everything.

Now that I know what it can be like in a loving relationship, everything to the contrary affects me a million times worse. I just never knew it could be so good.

I was living in a world with tunnel vision, unable to see the true extent of the abuse until now; and all those walls I built up over the years to be incapable of feeling anything have suddenly crumbled. Every bruise that Nathan places on my body sears its memory into my brain, causing more and more damage each and every time.

I'm falling apart, and I don't know what to do. I want to rebuild my walls, but yet I don't want to shut Max out. I like feeling his adoration for me. I like being able to express my love for him without trepidation. But I don't know how long I can live like this without shutting everything and everyone out again. In the past, it was always better that way for me. Feeling numb was the only way I could cope with life.

Still feeling in a fog, I walk out of the bathroom and straight into the hard chest of someone. "Excuse me," I apologize quickly.

Large hands envelop my shoulders, and I look up into a pair of piercing blue eyes. My heart stutters into a terrible rhythm. "Nathan," I whisper, all my breath leaving my body. In the five years that I have volunteered at the hospital, he has only been here a handful of times. And definitely not in the recent years — only in the beginning of our relationship when he was trying to put on a front and make me think that he actually wanted to get to know me better and was interested in my life.

"Hello, sweetheart," he says with a sickening sweet tone. He pulls me in for an embrace and a kiss.

It takes every ounce of my willpower not to recoil in disgust. After last night, I can't bear to have him touch me. He glances over my shoulder, and I follow his gaze. The nurses at the station are watching us. Nathan is putting on a show for them.

"W-what are you doing here?" I ask, finally pulling out of his embrace.

He frowns at my sudden departure. "I thought we could have lunch together before I leave for the weekend. My flight is in two hours."

My eyes dart to my watch. My regular lunch hour is approaching, and that is always spent with Max in the cafeteria. I need to talk Nathan into eating in a nearby restaurant. Plastering a fake smile on my face, I say, "Oh, that sounds great. Where were you thinking of going?"

His expression matches mine, but there is something sinister under it. "I was thinking of staying here. How's the cafeteria food?"

My stomach slowly rolls into a tight knot. He wants to eat here? Max will be expecting me there, and we are sure to bump into him. No. I won't do that to Max. "It's not that great," I lie. "You would probably like the diner down the street...or there is a restaurant a few blocks from here that we could —."

"Avery," Nathan says, cutting me off. He eyes me suspiciously. "The cafeteria will be fine."

Maybe my mask wasn't fully eclipsing my real emotions. Maybe Nathan sensed something was wrong and my hesitation towards staying here to eat. I swallow hard and smile wider. "Sure. Okay," I concede.

He nods, steps back and holds his hand out. "Shall we then?"

I tentatively put my hand in his, and we make our way through the halls and to the cafeteria near the entrance of the hospital. We choose a table by the large window overlooking a small garden with a gazebo and benches scattered around the property. I purposely sit on the side facing the cafeteria door and anxiously wait for Max to walk in. It's a few minutes before our regular meeting time, and he's never late.

Forcing my eyes to the menu, I skim over the meal options. It's probably futile to decide what I want, because I'm sure Nathan will decide for me. He has the tendency to do that.

The waitress comes over to the table. "Hello, Avery," she says.

I smile up at Pam as best I can. "Hi, Pam. How are you?"

"Doing just fine. And who's this?" she asks, gesturing to Nathan.

"This is my husband." My leg bounces under the table nervously as Pam raises a brow. I just hope Nathan doesn't catch her surprise of my introduction. Pam works every day during the week, and I know she has seen me here with Max on numerous occasions. She's probably caught sight of our flirtatious behavior, the way he watches me and the way we speak to each other. Pam has never mentioned anything about our relationship, but I have no doubt in my mind that she knows it's more than just two colleagues eating lunch together every day.

Nathan stretches out his hand, and Pam shakes it. "Nathan," he says with that smooth voice of his. "Pleasure to meet you."

Pam isn't immune to his charms, and I see her eyes twinkle as she grins. If she only knew the monster that hid behind that handsome face. "Nice to meet you too." She pulls out a notepad and pencil. "So what did you decide?"

"We'll both have the turkey sandwich on wheat with light mayonnaise, a pickle on the side and two unsweetened iced teas."

"Coming right up," she says before disappearing back to the kitchen.

Groaning inwardly, I put the menu aside. Nathan sits quietly with his fingers interlaced on the table. "So is there any particular reason why you decided to meet me for lunch today?" I ask. "You haven't visited me here for years."

He sits back in his chair. "I knew I would be gone by the time you got home, so I decided to say goodbye to you here." He reaches across the table and takes my hand in his. I stare at him, waiting for a sudden mood change or anything that would cause concern. "And also I just wanted to remind you of what I tried to instill in you last night, Avery." His grip slowly tightens around my hand as he leans forward. Keeping his voice low, he says, "You will answer the phone when I call, Avery. I don't want to be constantly worried about you when I need to have my mind focused on surgery. And I certainly don't want my father making an unexpected visit."

I grimace and feel tears welling up in my eyes as his grip continues to tighten. "Nathan, please. You're hurting me," I whisper, my voice trembling.

"Well, I wouldn't have to hurt you if you would just obey me, Avery. I don't think you understand how a marriage is supposed to work."

I want to stand up and scream at him, but I'm terrified of the consequences. And I'm also terrified that any outburst would cause him not to leave, and I desperately need him gone this weekend. I am always in constant fear when it comes to our relationship. And I think he secretly relishes in my fear of him. "I'll answer the phone," I say urgently. My hand is throbbing under his grip, and I'm worried he might be close to breaking some bones.

"Promise me."

"I promise!" I gasp.

The door to the cafeteria opens, and Nathan instantly releases me and sits back in his chair. I stare down at the table and cradle my hand with my other. It throbs in pain, and I can feel the tears threatening to spill over.

Pam comes to the table with two drinks and sets them down. "I'll be with you in a moment, Dr. Harrison," she calls to the right of her.

My eyes snap up. Max must have been the person who walked through the door a minute earlier. I wonder if he had been watching us from the glass door and witnessed what happened between Nathan and me. As his dark eyes meet mine, I know he saw everything.

He starts walking towards us, but I know things will end badly if he interferes. My worst fears are coming to fruition right in front of my eyes. While Nathan is distracted with the sugar packets on the table, I stare at Max and give him a slight shake of my head. I want him to know now is not the time.

A flare of anger and something else — sadness maybe — wash over his features. He forces himself into a chair at another table. Pam approaches him, and he breaks eye contact with me to relay a short order to Pam in a quiet tone. Then his eyes return to meet mine.

I force my gaze to the table, and I don't look at Max again. Pam brings our sandwiches out after a few minutes. After she walks away, Nathan takes a bite and makes a face. "You were right. The food here is horrible."

I eat with my left hand since my right hand is completely useless at the moment. I don't think he broke any bones, but it's definitely going to cause me some significant pain for a while.

I swallow my emotions and eat in a daze while Nathan goes on and on about the celebrity in California that he's going to be working on. Then before I know it, he's standing and saying my name. "Avery."

Reality slowly returns, and I look up at him.

"I've been saying your name over and over." He moves his hand towards me, and I flinch. I can see the immediate anger in his eyes, but he remains calm. He puts the back of his hand to my forehead. "Are you feeling all right?"

I stare at him. Sometimes it's ridiculous how oblivious he can be after he hurts me. I don't know if he's really that daft, or if he just blocks it out entirely. "I'm tired," I mutter.

"Well, I need to go."

Once again on autopilot, I stand and allow him to pull me into his arms. In my ear, he whispers, "Remember what we talked about. Answer. The. Phone," he says, enunciating each word separately.

I become rigid in his arms. "I will," I promise softly.

He kisses me chastely and throws a fifty-dollar bill on the table. The lunch was probably less than fifteen dollars, but Nathan likes to put on airs. "See you Sunday," he says before disappearing out the exit.

I stand rooted to the floor, unable to decide what I want to do first. I didn't finish eating, but I don't think I can. I feel sick, and my hand is killing me. My purse is on the chair next to me. I search through it until I find a travel container of pain pills. I pop two in my mouth and swallow them down with the iced tea.

Composing myself, I sling my purse around my shoulder and walk through the cafeteria. I feel Max's eyes on me, but I can't force myself to look at him. I will completely break down if he so much as even touches me right now. "Avery," he calls when I walk past him.

I don't stop walking. I push through the cafeteria exit door. I don't want to ignore him, but I know the dam holding back my tears will burst soon enough. I don't want to get Max in trouble. We've been keeping our relationship on the down low, especially at the hospital. I don't want to jeopardize his job or reputation with rumors.

I've already been putting him through enough as it is. I just wonder how much is going to be too much for him to handle.

I know this is difficult for me, but it has to be a living hell for him.

MAX

AVERY ISN'T HERSELF today. She's walking around the hospital in a daze, and it took three times of me calling her name for her to realize someone was talking to her. She told me everything is fine, but I know better. She never met me on the beach last night. I waited hours for her, but she never showed. Something happened last night, and I'm determined to find out what.

I walk into the cafeteria for our usual lunch date, and I stop dead in my tracks outside of the door. Avery is sitting at a table with a man in a suit, and I immediately know it's her husband. He's reaching across the table and clenching her hand in his. I open the door, and he immediately releases his grip on her.

Avery cradles her injured hand in her lap, and it takes every ounce of me not to run over there and punch Nathan in the face.

"I'll be with you in a moment, Dr. Harrison," Pam calls out.

I start stalking towards Avery's table, but the look in her eyes stops me. She stares at me with wide eyes and gives a slight shake of her head. She doesn't want me to interfere. *Damn it!*

I clench my hands into fists at my sides, and reluctantly sit down at a table. I ramble off an order to Pam and focus my attention back on Avery. My eyes bore an imaginary hole in the back of her husband's head; and if looks could kill, Nathan would have died ten times over already.

Avery stares at the table for the rest of her lunch, barely eating, barely speaking and not making eye contact with me again. I watch the exchange between Avery and Nathan as he says goodbye. She looks downright terrified of him, and the bastard has the balls to ask if she's feeling all right. When he places his hand on her forehead after she had flinched away from him, I almost lost my shit. I am so geared up by the time he leaves that I can barely sit still.

And so when Avery walks past me without saying a single word after I call her name, I'm ready to explode. I quickly throw some money on the table and leave without saying a word to Pam. I chase Avery down the hall and pull her into a storage room.

I watch her carefully as she paces back and forth in the small space. She worries her bottom lip between her teeth, and she's still cradling her right hand against her chest. I try to quell my anxiousness and rage, but it's next to impossible. I'm tired of seeing Avery hurt. Something has to change. And then she surprises me by saying, "I can't live like this anymore." She stops pacing and stares up at me with watery eyes. "I want to leave him. I'll do whatever it takes. *Whatever* it takes."

The words are like music to my ears. This is what I have been waiting to hear from her for the past month. She's ready. She's finally ready.

She blows out a long breath between clenched teeth, and my anger instantly dissolves as I stare at her pain-stricken face. I close the distance between us and reach for her hand. I gently pull her hand away from her body, and she grimaces. Some bruising has already appeared, and I tenderly move her fingers to make sure they aren't broken. She's in pain, and it almost breaks me to see her like this. "I don't think anything is broken, but he might have done some damage to your blood vessels," I say quietly. "I'll be right back."

A few minutes later, I return with an icepack wrapped in a thin cloth. I pull a stool out from a table and motion for her to sit down. Once she has, I gently place the icepack on her hand. "This should take down some of the swelling. I'll look at it later." I catch my words and frown. "Well, Monday. I'll look at it Monday."

"No," she says. "Later." When I look up at her in confusion, she says, "Nathan came to tell me goodbye. He's leaving for the weekend. He won't be home until Sunday night."

I'm surprised at how much elation and relief I feel at her words. It's like a ten-ton weight has been lifted off of my shoulders. A whole entire weekend with Avery. Just the two of us. I lean down and place a kiss on her forehead. "You don't know how happy that makes me."

"Me too," she whispers.

After a few minutes of silence, I ask, "What happened last night?"

She looks up at me. "H-how do you know something happened?" she asks, and I can hear the strain in her voice.

"You just haven't been yourself today. I was really starting to get worried."

She stares at the wall, her eyes going unfocused. And then she shakes her head as if dispelling a bad thought. "It just...It was really bad last night," she says before releasing a shaky breath. "And even though I wouldn't ever want to relive last night again...something good came out of it."

When I raise my brow in expectation, she says, "It made me realize that I'm willing to risk it all if that means I can have a life with you." She stands and rushes into my arms. I hold her as she violently trembles. "I know I said I didn't want your help before, but now I'm asking for it. Will you help me, Max?"

I close my eyes, savoring her words. "Avery, I will do everything in my power to get you away from him."

I know in that moment that this has to end. Her pain has to end. And Nathan's hold on her will finally break even if that means losing everything I have worked hard for in the process.

MAX

*I*T'S SATURDAY NIGHT, and I decide to take my girl out for a night on the town. After dinner and a movie, we are planning for another fun night of karaoke at the same little dive bar. Only Avery will be singing, though, of course. I couldn't carry a tune even if my life depended on it.

"So what kind of fundraiser is your father hosting?" I ask on the way to the bar. It's next weekend, and I still haven't decided if I'm going or not. I really want to see Avery at every opportunity I can, but I don't know if I'm ready to see her with Nathan again. It's too easy to lose myself to my temper and frustration. I caught just a glimpse of that in the hospital yesterday.

"Oh, one of those stuffy, over-the-top dinner parties where everyone doesn't actually want to be there but feels obligated to attend. It's mostly going to be men over twice my age talking about politics for four consecutive hours while I try not to pass out from boredom."

"I was hoping for something more lively."

"More lively?" she asks with a cocked brow.

"You know, a raging kegger."

She laughs. "Yeah, I don't see my father hosting a *kegger* anytime soon."

"But you can imagine how much fun it would be. All those old men doing keg stands."

"Keg stands?" She looks at me like she has no idea what I'm talking about.

"Yeah. I'm sure you remember all the frat boys doing them from your college days."

Her smile instantly fades, and she suddenly grows quiet. "I never went to college."

My brows knit together. Avery is so smart. Any college would have been proud to have her as a student. I know she would make a great nurse or doctor. She already has all the basics and the bedside manner down pat.

I glance over at her, and I know she's lost in thought. "Have you ever thought about going to college?" I ask.

She closes her eyes for a moment. "Thought about it more times than I could count. But once I met Nathan, my dreams came to a crashing halt. He didn't want me to go to college. And so I became his *trophy wife* instead." She cringes as she says the asinine title.

I fidget in my seat uncomfortably. "You're still young, Avery. You can still have dreams. You can still go to college." I glance over at her in the passenger seat and give her left hand a gentle squeeze. Her right hand is resting on her lap. It's still a little swollen, but it's healing up nicely.

She shrugs. "I don't even know what courses I would take. I'm not really good at anything."

I frown at her pessimistic tone. "I'm sure there's plenty that you're good at if you tried." Then I add, "You can sing."

"Yeah, I don't think I'm going to be recording an album anytime soon," she says sardonically.

Her negative attitude towards herself makes something inside of me snap. The parking lot for the bar is just up ahead, and I'm thankful for the excuse to pull over and stop the vehicle. What I say to her next needs to be said face to face without her looking away or trying to change the subject.

I pull the SUV into a spot and turn off the engine. Turning in my seat, I grasp her hands in mine. "You're incredible, Avery. And you having not the slightest clue about that fact just does something to me. It makes me hurt for you that you don't even realize how beautiful, talented and smart you are."

She looks away, but I'm not going to let her avoid me. Grasping her chin gently, I make her focus on me. When her eyes lock with mine, I continue. "You are perfect in my eyes. Nothing else and no one else should matter." My thumb tenderly brushes over her soft cheek. "You should have as many dreams as you can grasp onto, and no one should ever be able to take them away. If you want to go to college, then go. If you want to sing, then sing." My fingertips move to the nape of her neck. I weave my fingers through her soft hair. "You never know what the future holds. Everyone is destined for something, Avery, and I think —. No. I *know* that you are destined for so much more. You are destined to do great things in this world and be happy. I just really want you to be happy."

I pull her close to me, and our lips lock in a gentle kiss. I can feel her trembling under my touch. My words have affected her. Good. She needs to wake up and see herself through my eyes for once instead of through the eyes of the monster she's married to.

When she pulls back, her eyes search mine. "I feel like I'm invincible when I'm with you, Max. I feel like everything around us dissolves and nothing else matters."

I smile and kiss her sweetly. "I feel the same exact way." I glance out the windshield at the bar where I first heard Avery's beautiful voice, and I can't wait to hear it again. "Let's go."

We get out of the SUV and weave through the cars of the crowded parking lot. The sign on the way to the front door has Avery's steps faltering. "Open mic night," she whispers with trepidation.

"Hey, you did karaoke a couple weeks ago. Open mic should be a piece of cake," I say in an attempt to encourage her.

She shakes her head slowly. "I don't know, Max."

I pull her in my arms and stare into her beautiful stormy blue eyes. "Hey. Even though I want to be selfish and not want share any part of you, I think everyone should hear your beautiful voice."

She closes her eyes briefly and whispers our newfound mantra, "Only here. Only now."

I give her a gentle squeeze, and she grins. "Ready to knock their socks off?"

She smiles wide and nods.

MAX

I WATCH AVERY speaking with the guitarist that had just played with a band. The guy leans close to Avery and says something I can't hear. She pulls back from him, smiling and laughing. A pang of jealousy courses through me. I hate feeling jealous, but it's so easy to feel that way when it comes to Avery. I know how great she is, and any guy would be lucky to spend even five minutes with her. She's so easy to love. She just doesn't know it.

After a few minutes, Avery takes a seat on the tall stool by the microphone. She suddenly looks nervous, catching her lower lip between her teeth. Her eyes search the crowd and rest upon me. I smile at her and wink, and she smiles back, instantly seeming to relax a little.

The guy on the guitar strums a few bars and says, "Whenever you're ready, Avery."

She wraps her delicate hand around the mic and leans forward. "This is my first time doing this," she says timidly, and the crowd claps to give her encouragement. I whistle and clap loudly, without a care in the world about embarrassing myself. Avery flashes me a crooked grin, and my heart melts. Then she locks eyes with me before saying, "This is for you, Max."

The guitarist plays the short intro before Avery starts to sing. I recognize the song. It's *Bright* by Echosmith, and Avery is doing a hauntingly beautiful cover of it. Without the loud music in the background like when she did karaoke, I can hear her voice much clearer. And she sounds great paired with an acoustic guitar. The guitarist is really good and harmonizes some of the words with Avery, and I'm suddenly envious that he gets to share this moment with her. But I push my jealousy aside when I realize that her eyes haven't left mine even for an instant. She's completely focused on me, and the lyrics couldn't be more perfect.

She's singing about being in love, and my heart pumps a little faster. This is love, isn't it? This is what love feels like, and I am completely head over heels for this girl.

Her voice sounds pure and innocent, but so powerful and controlled at the same time. Once again, she has commanded the audience's attention, and I'm glad I'm not the only one standing there like a fool staring at her. Everyone around me looks amazed and taken with her. I'm sure if they stopped playing and singing right now, you would be able to hear a pin drop in that bar.

They end the song perfectly, as if they had practiced for weeks on it. Avery's a natural. There's no doubt about that.

I listen as the crowd goes nuts with whoops and hollers and people shouting *"more"*. They want more of her, and I know just how they feel. A few minutes with her just aren't enough.

As she talks to the guitarist, I slip to the side of the stage to wait for her. My fingers itch to touch her, and my mouth craves her taste. I am irrevocably in love with this girl, and I'm determined to show her exactly how I feel.

AVERY

I FINISH THE song to an exuberant round of applause and then turn and thank the guitarist a million times. He smiles and asks, "That was really your first time?"

When I nod, he shakes his head in disbelief. "Wow. I have to say, Avery, that you are amazingly talented." He stands and sets his guitar down. "My uncle is a talent scout. I know he would love to hear you sing sometime." He pushes a business card into my hand, and his fingers linger on mine for a few seconds. "Your voice is out of this world. A completely natural and rare gift."

I blush at his compliments. "Thank you." I stare at the card, and I feel tears gathering in my eyes. Maybe there is something out there that I'm destined for just like Max said.

The guitarist nervously rubs the back of his neck and says, "Hey, I put my number on the back of the card just in case...just in case you want to go out to dinner sometime?"

I look up at him. "That's really sweet, but I'm taken." And by taken, I don't mean married. Max owns my heart — completely and eternally.

"Figured I'd give it a shot," the guy says with a chuckle.

The crowd is still going crazy. They want me to sing another song, but all I can focus on is getting off the stage as fast as I can and into Max's arms. My eyes search the crowd for Max, but I don't see him. Then I hear a whistle from backstage. In the darkness behind the stage, I see him emerge from the shadows. I run and jump into his arms, almost knocking us both down. He pulls me back into the shadows and laughs. "You were incredible up there, Avery," he whispers against my ear. "They can't get enough of you." His lips place a soft kiss on my neck, and I shiver. "I know the feeling."

I bite my bottom lip and stare up at him. In the cover of darkness, we stare at each other, and everything and everyone disappears from around us. We are in our own world, and there's only us in this moment. I lean up on my tiptoes and kiss him fiercely. His hands trail down my body and grasp my backside, molding me into his length. He swallows a groan that escapes me as he kisses me. Pulling back, he gazes down at me. "Incredible," he says again.

Grasping his hand, I pull him down the steps and towards the main bar. We are almost to the front door when I hear someone calling my name.

Suddenly, time stands still, and the imaginary bubble surrounding us and protecting us in our own little world shatters into a million pieces. My eyes search for the source of the voice, and I see her moving through the parting crowd. I immediately drop Max's hand and step away from him. A look of confusion and dejection flashes over his features, and I can feel my stomach twisting in knots. I plaster a smile on my face as Barbara approaches us. She is a family friend of the Masons.

She's carrying a mixed drink in one hand and toting her husband behind her with the other. "Avery, hi!" she says with a big smile.

"Hi, Barb," I reply.

She kisses each of my cheeks and steps back. "Nathan never told me how talented you were! You can really sing. I felt like I was at a concert or something," she gushes.

I laugh nervously. I can see Max in my peripheral vision staring at me, but I don't acknowledge him. I'm hoping that Barbara didn't see us together, but I know she probably did. That woman has eyes like a hawk and a mouth that runs a million miles a minute spouting gossip.

"William and I are enjoying a night out. We usually don't come to places like." Her eyes dart around with a sour look on her face. "But I'm glad we did!" She takes a sip of her drink. "I've had about three of these fuzzy whatchamacallits already!"

William rolls his eyes. "More like five," he says with a frown.

Barbara playfully hits in him in the chest. "Oh, live a little, William!" Her eyes roam over to Max, and my heart stops. "I don't believe we've met." She holds her hand out to Max, and he shakes it.

He opens his mouth to speak, but I quickly interrupt him. "This is my...brother. Matt."

Barbara's eyebrows dip low in confusion. "Brother. I didn't know you had a brother, Avery."

"Half brother," Max adds quickly, coming to my rescue at the last second.

She nods and sips her drink. I'm glad that the alcohol is numbing her brain a little so that she believes the lie...or at least I hope she believes it.

"Well, we really should be going," I say to Max.

"I'll see you at your father's fundraiser on Wednesday, Avery," Barbara calls after me as I hurry through the crowd.

I push through the exit and draw in deep breaths of air. My legs feel like jelly as I make my way to Max's vehicle. I can hear his footsteps behind me, but he doesn't say a word and doesn't try to stop me.

I crumble once I get to the Escalade, pushing my forehead against the cool metal of the door. "Oh God," I whisper, panicked. My breathing is uneven and coming in short pants.

"Who was that Avery?" Max asks.

"A friend of the Mason family." I squeeze my eyes shut. "What if she tells Nathan's parents? Oh God. What if Nathan finds out?" I hold a hand to my stomach. I think I'm going to be sick. We've been so careful, but this all might blow up in our face from just one word out of Barbara's mouth to any of the Masons.

Max grabs my arms and turns me to face him. "Breathe, Avery. Just breathe," he soothes. After my breathing has calmed down a bit, Max says, "She was pretty drunk. She might not say anything."

I nod, wanting to believe him, but still not so sure that I'm that lucky. Max puts his finger under my chin and makes me meet his gaze. "We were having such a great night. I hate that it got ruined."

I take a few minutes to compose myself. I definitely don't want to focus on the *what ifs*. I'm done with that. I just want to live in the moment with Max no matter the consequences. I pull him close and smile up at him. "It's not ruined."

"It's not?"

I shake my head, and he grins. His thumb trails over my bottom lip as he asks, "Did I tell you how incredible you were on stage?"

Laughing, I say, "I think you may have mentioned it once or twice."

He pulls me into my arms and whispers into my ear, "Come home with me, Avery."

Home. Such a simple word, but it holds so much promise for a future with Max. I nod, and he opens the door for me. I slip inside. Once he's in the driver's seat, I lean over and pull him to me again. His lips find mine for a smoldering kiss as our hands start roaming. Our passion quickly ignites as my hand trails down his chest and reaches his belt before he breaks away. "We'll never make it home if you keep doing that," he whispers, panting.

Smiling, I sit back in my seat and put on my seat belt. My hand reaches over, and I squeeze his muscular thigh playfully. "Drive fast," I whisper breathlessly.

Groaning, he puts the SUV into gear and pulls out of the parking lot. We have a hard time keeping our hands to ourselves on the way to his house, and I feel like a teenager again. There was a lot I missed out on in my late teens and early twenties, and I intend to make up for it with Max. He makes me feel like the years with Nathan never were, and what a wonderful feeling that is.

MAX

*A*VERY SLEEPS SOUNDLY in my arms. Her dark hair is splayed over my shoulder and arm, and a tiny puddle of drool is on my chest. I crack a smile and kiss the crown of her head. I definitely could get used to this. Waking up with her in my arms is the greatest feeling in the world. She makes me so happy that it's almost like a dream.

My mind drifts to last night, and my cock twitches as I think about how we made hot, passionate love in this bed for hours. I kissed every inch of her body and worshipped her like the goddess she is. We explored and teased and tested our bodies together, and I've never experienced anything like that in my life. Watching her come apart time after time from my fingers, tongue and cock was the sexiest thing I've ever witnessed. An involuntary groan escapes my lips, and Avery stirs beside me.

Her eyes flutter open, and she grins up at me. My heart immediately beats a little faster. "Good morning," she says in that sleepy, sexy voice of hers.

"Good morning, beautiful."

Her eyes travel down my chest and grow wide when she notices the tent in the sheets I made while I was thinking about last night. "I thought maybe it would need a few days rest after last night," she jokes.

I wrap my arms around her and pull her close. "It will never get tired of being inside of you," I whisper in her hair. She smells so good. I just can't get enough of her.

Avery kisses my chest and trails her lips and tongue down my stomach. My muscles quiver under her touch. "Let me take care of you, Max," she whispers.

Well, how the hell can I say no to that? I think to myself just before a moan escapes my mouth.

MAX

AFTER AN AMAZING morning in bed, Avery and I take a shower together. We're quiet as we take turns washing each other. I don't want my time with Avery to end, but I don't feel the overwhelming sadness and apprehension that I usually do whenever she has to leave. This time there is hope at the end of our road.

I have a lunch date with my mother today. My mom has a history of dealing with a domestic violence situation involving her best friend, and both of my parents have a lot of contacts with people in the government. If there is a way to get Avery away from Nathan, I will find it.

After reluctantly letting her go home, I hurry up the highway to the burger joint that Avery and I went to on our first date. My mother pulls in a few minutes after I do.

We're eating on the outside deck when my mother says, "You look happy, Max. Tell me. Did you meet someone?"

I can't stop the wide grin from appearing on my face, and I give a nod of the head to my mom. I didn't tell her why I wanted to meet her for lunch. I just felt like talking to her in person might be best, considering the situation.

She clasps her hands in front of her and looks positively radiant. "Oh, good!" She wipes her hands on a napkin. "So...when can we meet her?"

My grin falters. "Well...it's kind of complicated, mom." I take a deep breath and then hiss it out through my clenched teeth. "She's married."

"Oh, no," she says softly. "Max, what are you thinking? You know those kinds of relationships never end well. Just look at your cousin, Cynthia, and her —."

"Mom," I interrupt her. "It's a difficult situation to explain, but I promise you that she doesn't want to be with her husband. And he certainly doesn't deserve her." My jaw ticks as I think about the abuse he puts Avery through. I look my mom dead in the eye and say, "He hits her."

My mom gasps. She knows firsthand about domestic violence. Her best friend Diane was almost killed by her husband. He left her for dead on the side of the road after he lost his temper and beat her within an inch of her life.

Mom reaches across the table and squeezes my hand tightly. "How bad is it, Max?"

I close my eyes for a moment and squeeze her hand back. "It's bad, mom. It's really bad. I think —. No. I know he would kill her."

She stays quiet for a few moments. Then she nods and says, "Tell me what I can do to help."

MAX

IT'S NOT UNTIL Wednesday afternoon that I finally get the call I've been waiting for. My mom's best friend, Diane, has a horse rescue farm in northern Virginia.

After Diane spent years in therapy rehabilitating her battered body, she wanted to help animals who were once broken just like her regain their way of life as well. The large, picturesque farm is in the middle of nowhere with gated access.

And the best part of all is that there is no direct connection between my mom, Avery or me. Nathan would have no way of finding her. She would be able to file a protection order and get the divorce paperwork started all without him interfering. It's the perfect plan, and I can't wait to tell Avery about it.

As I pull on my suit jacket and straighten my tie, I stare at myself in the mirror. I look happy. I feel happy. I feel like I'm on top of the world right now.

I wasn't going to go to her father's fundraiser tonight, but now I can't stay away. I need to tell Avery in person the good news. I can't wait to see the look on her face when I tell her that she can finally be free from the abuse, free of Nathan...and free to be with me.

AVERY

MY FATHER'S FUNDRAISER for his campaign is tonight. The most prestigious and ridiculously wealthy people will be there, having paid a hefty price for the sit-down dinner's per-plate fee. My heart skips a beat when I think of Max being there. He was on the fence about whether he was going to go or not, but I hope that he'll show up. We won't be able to talk or be next to each other, of course, but just having him in the same room with me is enough to calm my nerves.

Max told me on Monday morning that he has a plan in the works to get me away from Nathan. I just hope his plan comes to fruition soon. I don't know how much longer I can keep up this charade with Nathan.

I stand in front of the mirror in a pink chiffon mermaid style evening gown. The dress is littered with sequins that make me look like I'm sparkling from the chest down. It's strapless and very form fitting through my torso and thighs before flaring out at my knees.

I slip into a pair of nude heels and stare at my reflection. My makeup is perfect. My skin looks flawless. My long hair is silky and shiny with soft waves falling past my shoulders. I look like a living, breathing doll. And Nathan wouldn't want it any other way.

Meticulously, I check every inch of my skin that's showing to make sure I used enough of the tattoo cover-up for the bruises. Since Nathan was gone for the weekend, some of them actually had time to heal. But the fresh ones I received when he got home were particularly difficult to conceal.

I feel hands wrap around my stomach, and I jump. "Easy," Nathan whispers against my neck. I stare at his reflection in the mirror. He's in a designer three-piece suit and looks like a model straight out of a *GQ* magazine. "You look gorgeous," he says before planting a soft kiss on my neck.

I remain calm on the outside, but inside I'm screaming. "T-thank you," I manage to say.

"You're not going to tell me how I look?" he asks, stepping back from me. He holds his hands out and raises a brow for approval.

Turning to face him, I smile and say, "You look very handsome."

He grins. "Everybody is going to envy us tonight." He put his hands on my waist and pulls me close. "Like always," he adds.

Envy. That is one thing that Nathan prides himself on. He has to have the best of the best. Second best definitely isn't good enough. He always has to one-up the other guy.

He leans in for a kiss, and I force myself not to recoil. His lips press against mine. When he pulls away, he's frowning. "You're not still upset about the other night, are you?"

You mean the other night when you beat me? I want to scream at him. Instead, I just shake my head. I missed a few of his phone calls while I spent the weekend with Max, and I paid the price dearly when Nathan arrived home.

"When you didn't answer your phone, I almost hired a private investigator to follow you for the weekend."

His words make me shiver. He would have so easily found out about Max and me. I never thought he would stoop so low as to have me followed, but I should have learned by now to expect the unexpected when it comes to Nathan.

"Next time I go out of town I'll make sure I have someone looking after you." Deep down in my soul I truly hope there isn't a next time. Nathan then kisses me chastely on the lips and says, "Come on. We're going to be late."

AVERY

THE EVENT IS quite spectacular. Whoever my father hired to coordinate it did an excellent job.

As the valet drives away in our BMW, Nathan holds out his arm. I place my arm in the crook of his elbow, and he leads me down the lit walkway to the back of the mansion.

The estate where I grew up was always my most favorite place on earth. I loved riding horses around the property and swimming in the pool that featured a waterfall and slide. I was born into a life of privilege, but I learned something as I got older — money doesn't buy happiness. And that is truer now than it was even back then.

Nathan stops at the gated entrance to the party and hands over our invitations to a security guard. The guard scrutinizes his guest list and then, with a smile, says, "Enjoy the party, Mr. and Mrs. Mason."

We walk through the gate and pause for pictures. Five photographers snap photos, and I have no doubt the gratuitous media coverage is because of the incident a few weeks ago when my father was shot in the arm. His typical parties usually have one or two photographers present, but I have never witnessed this many before.

When a reporter asks about my father's shooting and if there are any suspects, I freeze up like a deer in the headlights. I'm standing right beside the man responsible for the shooting. My husband. Guilt and shame washes over me, and I suddenly hold up my hand up for the cameras to stop flashing.

Nathan digs his fingers into my arm. "What's wrong?" he hisses.

"I can't do this right now."

I pull away from him, knowing he won't make a scene in front of people, especially not the press. I walk the rest of the way to the party by myself, taking deep breaths as I go. Nothing can be changed about what happened. My father is alive, and he will remain that way as long as I don't do anything brash to upset Nathan.

My steps slow as I gawk in awe of the familiar backyard, which has been completely transformed for the gala. There are several large tents draped in ivory chiffon and miniature lights. Under the tents are hundreds of elegant round tables with ivory linens and extravagant centerpieces on top of them. The chairs have matching covers with each chair bearing a black, elegant bow in the back. The yard is illuminated with lanterns, and there are numerous tables set up with more hors d'oeuvres than I have ever seen in my life.

Nathan catches up with me, hooking his fingers around my arm. "What was that back there?" he asks in a hushed whisper.

I pull out of his grip, and my eyes dart around as people walk past us. "You really want to do this now?" I ask, narrowing my eyes to let him know exactly what I'm talking about.

Nathan clears his throat and offers his arm once again like a gentleman, clearly putting on airs for everyone around us. "Shall we?" he asks with an underlying menacing tone that only I would recognize.

Hesitantly, I wrap my fingers around his arm and allow him to lead me towards the party.

"Your father really outdid himself this time," he remarks. Holding up his finger, he stops one of the many waitstaff walking around. He takes two glasses of champagne from a silver tray and hands me one. We both take a sip at the same time. "Delicious," he says in approval.

I nod in agreement as we walk past the enormous parquet dance floor. A string quartet is playing the most beautiful music, and I can't wait to listen to them for the rest of the night.

We find my father on the large wraparound porch of the house. He's in a serious conversation with an older man in a blue suit. When his eyes drift over to me, he immediately excuses himself. "Sweetheart," he says, walking towards me with open arms.

"Dad," I acknowledge, hugging him.

He pulls back and studies me. "You look beautiful. As always," he says with a wink.

"How are you feeling?"

"Totally fine." He leans and whispers, "But don't tell the reporters that. My campaign manager wants to milk this just a little bit longer." I try my best not to roll my eyes. He looks past me and asks, "Have you seen your sister yet?"

"No, but I'm sure she'll be here."

He nods and turns to Nathan. They shake hands, and my dad claps Nathan on the shoulder. "Nice to see you, Nathan. Your parents are around here somewhere. I was just speaking with them."

"I'll keep an eye out," Nathan says. "So how is the campaign going so far?"

I drown out their conversation and glance around at the crowd milling in from the entrance. I'm anxious to find Max. "I'm going to check out the decorations and tents," I announce.

The two of them are busy talking politics and barely notice me walking away. I observe that there are place cards on each table. Nathan and I are at the head table with my father, Allison and her husband and daughter. We are in the biggest and foremost tent that faces all the others along with some immediate family members and the entire Mason family. When I've checked all of the place cards, I frown. Max's name isn't on any of the cards in my tent. Maybe that's best anyway, because I know I will just be more tempted to stare at him all night.

Maneuvering past the tent, I walk to the edge of the yard and stare out over the grounds. A million fireflies light up the darkness with flashing illumination. I sigh and think about how wonderful it would be to be a little girl again. I would give anything to go back in time. And if I could do just that, I would change a lot. I would have never agreed to date Nathan. I would have gone to college like I always wanted to. I'm twenty-three with nothing to show for myself besides being a trophy wife. The term makes me cringe. I don't know how I let myself become so dependent on Nathan. Part of me knows that this was his plan all along. It would make it difficult for me to leave him, and I'm finding out just how difficult now.

"Hey, beautiful," says a voice.

I turn around and squint into the darkness. A figure steps towards me, his back illuminated by the lights from the yard, but keeping his face in the shadows. When I feel his gentle arms around me and breathe in his scent, I whisper, "Max."

"How are you?"

I don't want to answer him. I don't want to cry and risk the chance of ruining my makeup and then having to explain to Nathan the reason behind it. I just sink deeper into his hug. "I miss you, Max. I can't stop thinking about you."

"Ditto," he says with a sigh. His chin rests on top of my head as his fingers trail down my arms. "You look beautiful. I watched you walk in. You took my breath away."

I close my eyes and lay my head on his chest. We dance slowly to the music flowing faintly through the air around us. "I didn't think you'd show up tonight, but I was hoping that you would."

"I wasn't going to, but I got a phone call today that changed my mind."

My body stills in his arms. "Good news or bad news?" *Please say good news. Please.*

"Very good news, Avery." He holds me tighter and whispers in my ear. "Can we meet somewhere private later to talk?"

"Yeah. I know of a place we can go. I'll get a message to you somehow." I hesitate before I say, "But until then...you have to ignore me.

Even meeting like this in the shadows is dangerous." He starts to protest, but I put my fingertips to his lips. "Nathan can't find out about us, Max. If he suspects anything..." My voice trails off, because I don't even want to think about what Nathan would do.

Max kisses my fingertips. "Okay. I'll try to ignore you, but you have no idea how hard that's gonna be." He kisses my lips softly. "I miss you already, and you haven't even walked away from me yet."

"Ditto," I whisper. Then I end the conversation with one word, a promise. "Later."

"Later," he agrees.

Reluctantly, I pull away from him. Even though I'm walking out of the darkness and towards the light, I left the only true light in my life behind me in the shadows.

AVERY

I SIT AT the head table with Nathan, my father, my sister and her husband and daughter. My father is standing and giving a speech into a microphone. His hand sweeps over to us and tears fill his eyes as he raves on and on about his family and how we have been standing by his side ever since the near-miss tragedy that happened weeks ago when he was shot.

Allison leans over to me and whispers into my ear, "Leave it to our father to turn him getting shot into a publicity stunt for his campaign."

I watch her carefully as she sits back and takes a swig of her champagne. That is her fifth glass, and we've only been at the table for a half an hour. Something is going on with her, but I can't put my finger on it.

As she motions to the waiter for a refill, her husband Todd mutters something to her under his breath. Allison's face instantly glazes over with a stony look. She glares at Todd. *If looks could kill.*

"Allison, Avery, stand up," my father instructs. We do as he says, and he's beaming at us both. "These young ladies are my breaths of fresh air, my reason for living. As most of you know, I was a single father for years after my wife Olivia died from ovarian cancer. These girls were my sole reason for carrying on." His voice cracks as he speaks, and he quickly clears his throat. "I love you both so much."

The crowd claps, and Allison and I plaster fake smiles on our faces as some of the photographers snap a few pictures. I hate being the center of attention, and these kinds of events always call for that.

"And let's not forget about their wonderful husbands, Nathan and Todd, and my beautiful granddaughter Sophia." We all stand together as the photographers snap pictures.

"One big happy family," Allison mutters sarcastically.

My father scoops down to pick up Sophia. She giggles in his arms, and he beams at her. "I hope to have more grandchildren soon," my father says as he gives a proud look to Nathan and me.

"Very soon," Nathan replies with a big grin.

My stomach turns, and I grab the edge of the table for support. Perhaps sensing my discomfort, my father quickly turns his attention to another topic. We all sit down, and I am thankful for the focus to be anywhere but on me.

"What is going on with you tonight?" Nathan asks in a hushed whisper.

"I have a headache," I lie.

"They should be serving the food soon. Maybe you just need to eat," he replies. He leans in close and says, "I can't wait to get you out of that dress when we get home. Every man in this place has been eye-fucking you all night. They want what they can't have." He kisses my earlobe, and I want to throw up. "If anyone so much as touches you tonight, I'll kill them." He hisses the threat, and a shiver runs up my spine.

It takes all of my willpower to stay seated at the table and not run out of there as fast as I can. My eyes search the sea of people, and I lock onto a dark gaze in one of the rear tents. In those eyes I see my future, and they instantly calm my nerves. I don't stare at Max for very long, but in those few seconds he gave me enough strength to carry on for a few minutes more.

I'm so anxious to hear Max's good news that I can barely sit still through the meal. My mind races as I consider all of the possibilities.

Maybe there is someone who can finally help me.

Maybe I will finally be able to leave Nathan for good.

The maybes are piling up, but as long as there is even a glimmer of hope, I can hold on for another day. It will all be worth it in the end if it brings me to a life where Max and I exist and are happy together.

MAX

I'M STARTING TO regret my decision to accept the invitation to this party. I know I wanted to be able to talk to Avery as soon as possible about my plan, but I wasn't counting on the fact that seeing her with Nathan would destroy me. I try not to stare, but my eyes constantly find her in the crowd. Nathan barely leaves her side. His hands are constantly straying to hold her by the waist or touch the nape of her neck or drift down her arm to hold her hand. He's staking his claim, showing everybody that she belongs to him. She is only a pretty thing to possess in his eyes. And every time I see him touch her, I find myself having a tougher time not exploding from all the pent-up anger inside of me.

I watch her mask fall into place. The happy wife to the perfect husband. The perfect daughter to the soon-to-be governor. But it's all a sham. It's in the moments when the cameras aren't flashing that I see the mask slip. I see a hint of her unhappiness. And it's all I can do not to go to her.

I'm careful in my watching of Avery. I never stare at her or in her general direction for too long. I always try to keep her in my peripheral vision even when I'm speaking to someone. And in all of that time, she never once glances my way.

As the night goes on, I grow more and more desperate for her gaze. My only solace is the champagne that seems to be dispersing through the crowd in absurd abundance. By my tenth glass, I am finally tipsy enough to numb myself to the point that I no longer have the pressing urge to walk up to Nathan and punch him square in the jaw.

I'm buzzed on alcohol, and it helps the pain I'm feeling deep within my chest. My soul is crying out for its counterpart and is being totally ignored.

I'm counting the empty flutes in front of me at the table when a waiter stops in front of me. "Champagne, sir?"

I don't even acknowledge him and attempt to wave him away. I know I shouldn't drink any more. I've had enough already.

"Sir?" he asks again.

I look up at the young man and notice he's holding out a flute with a note tucked around the stem. He leans down and whispers conspiratorially, "A woman asked me to deliver this to you."

I don't need to ask who the woman is. I know it's from Avery. I quickly take the items from his hand and secure the note in my palm. "Thank you."

He nods and walks away. Once I know it's safe and I'm alone, I unfold the note and read it several times.

Meet me in five minutes by the guest bathroom.

I take a long drink from the flute, draining it, and add the empty glass to my collection on the table in front of me. I stand and make my way across the lawn. On the way, I spot Nathan boasting amongst a group of ten other men. They are hanging onto his every word, and he plays the part of a gentleman all too well. The men laugh at his jokes and smile up at him like he is a god. If they only knew the kind of man they were really worshipping. He's nothing but a piece of shit, a wife beater and a cold-blooded monster living in a fancy life of deception.

Disgusted, I walk past them quickly and make my way into the house. The inside foyer and hallway are illuminated, and I follow the signs for the guest bathroom. The rest of the house remains dark, signifying that guests should not venture beyond that point.

I stand there, waiting, when I hear someone call my name. I turn, and my eyes narrow as I stare into the shadows of the adjacent room. I can see a silhouette of a woman. Blinking, I wonder if I did, in fact, drink too much champagne.

"Max," Avery whispers. Then I see her delicate hand as it reaches out of the darkness towards me.

I place my hand in hers and allow her to lead me through the darkened downstairs and up the grandiose staircase. She doesn't say a word as we walk down a dimly lit hall. We stop at the last door on the right, and she pulls me through, closing the door behind us. A lamp clicks on, and I squint until my eyes adjust to the sudden brightness. Glancing around the room, I realize this is Avery's childhood bedroom. The walls are pink and purple and plastered with posters of boy bands from the nineties, horses, butterflies and flowers. Numerous trophies and awards line every shelf in the room for cheerleading, tennis, swimming and horseback riding competitions. Several pictures of her with horses litter the room, and her love for the animal has me smiling. She's going to absolutely love it at Diane's ranch, and I can picture her there in my mind already.

I walk over to a small white dresser and stare at a picture of her and her mother Olivia. They both share the same long, reddish-brown hair and beautiful blue-gray eyes. Olivia is sans all the makeup and costumes like she had been wearing in her movies Avery and I watched together. She's stunning. "You're the splitting image of your mom," I comment. Glancing at her, she smiles, and I know she finds that to be a huge compliment.

A large photo album rests on the edge of her dresser, and I open it. My fingers flip through pictures of her on the back of a motorcycle, standing at the top of a waterfall and getting ready to jump off and photos of her partying with her girlfriends. I take my time looking at every picture of her. I'm getting a glimpse of Avery years ago before she met Nathan, before he started to break her spirit. She looks so carefree and happy and was clearly a knockout even back in high school. I chuckle and say, "You look like you were a handful back then."

"My dad threatened me with boarding school on more than one occasion," she says with a mischievous grin.

I turn and pull her into my arms. I kiss the crook of her neck and linger there, breathing in her sweet scent. "Rebel," I whisper against her skin.

She lets out a small sigh, and it turns me on. "I miss you," she confesses. I can hear the catch in her voice, and it makes me hold her tighter.

"I miss you too," I whisper. I lean back and stare at her for a few moments. No words can describe how much I miss her and think about her and want to be with her every second of every day. So I let my mouth do the talking and crush my lips to hers. Her hands slowly trail up my chest and wrap around my neck, pulling me even closer to her. When we eventually part, she says, "You taste like champagne."

"Well, I probably drank enough for the both of us." I frown. "The alcohol is the only thing keeping me sane tonight." Sighing, I shake my head. "I can't stand seeing you with him, Avery. It's driving me crazy."

"I know. I'm sorry." She slowly pulls back from me.

I open my mouth to tell her about Diane and the farm, but all of that goes out the window the moment she starts to slowly unzip her dress. My mouth goes dry as the material falls to the floor. The sight of the black lacey corset with matching thong, garters and thigh highs is almost too much to bear. I can feel my cock painfully straining against my zipper.

She steps out of her high heels as my eyes drink her in. She planned this. She wore this just for me, and it turns me on even more.

"I need you, Max," she says quietly. Her voice sounds hot and sultry, and I swallow hard.

I pull her to me, molding her luscious body against mine. A perfect fit. My hands roam all over her soft skin, wanting more, not being able to get enough of her. My fingertips skim from her stomach down to her hips and touch the top of the stockings. My hands stop as I wonder if Nathan will get to see her in these tonight. She's going home with him after all. Not me. I frown and pull back from her as the idea invades my thoughts.

I rake my fingers through my hair. "Fuck...Avery...I can't stop thinking about how I'm not the one you'll be going home with at the end of the night." She stares at me with apprehension written all over her face. Her eyes look fearful, but what is she afraid of? Afraid of losing me?

"I want you to make love to me, Max," she whispers.

I close my eyes, savoring her words. Whatever needs to be said can be said later, because right now I need her too...more than anything. I close the distance between us and crush my mouth to hers in a fevered kiss. A moan escapes her, and I swallow it down.

Without breaking the kiss, I remove my clothes as fast as I can, our lips only parting when I have to pull my shirt over my head. Naked, I push her backwards until she falls onto the mattress. I kneel at the end of the bed and lock my gaze with hers as I dip down between her legs and breathe in her scent. A satisfied groan erupts in my throat as I lick her through the lacey material of her thong. She lets out a low moan and bucks her hips. Pushing the material aside, I lick the length of her slit before focusing my attention on her swollen, little clit.

Her hands fist in the sheets as she tries to hold back her cries. Placing my hands under her hips, I bring her closer to my mouth and begin sucking and licking her hard and fast. Within minutes, she comes apart in my hands. Her hand clasps over her mouth to muffle her cries as her body quivers under my tongue. It's one of the hottest things I have ever witnessed.

She slowly stands and pushes my chest gently until I fall onto the bed. I watch her as she unsnaps her garters and slips out of her thong. I sit up on the bed, stroking my length in my hand as she removes her corset, tossing it on the floor.

Avery straddles my lap and grinds her wet slit over me. I'm rock hard, and my cock is practically weeping to be inside of her again. I groan out in frustration when I realize I didn't bring a condom with me. "I don't have a condom," I say, and it sounds like a curse.

She hesitates, but only for a moment. "It's okay." She kisses me sweetly. "I need you, Max. Now," she begs.

The thought of being bare inside of her makes my cock pulse and my heartbeat quicken. No boundaries between us. "Fuck," I groan as she impales herself down onto me. I sink my teeth into my lower lip to keep from screaming out. It feels like heaven being inside of her. We fit together so well. It's like she was made for just me.

Once she has totally sheathed my length, I release a hiss of air between my gritted teeth. "You feel so good. So tight. So wet." I start to slide in and out of her, savoring every inch of movement. My mouth moves to hers, and I kiss her deeper than I ever kissed her before. My tongue invades her mouth, sweeping along her teeth and devouring her. I want her to know how much I've missed her, how much I've missed being with her like this. She moans against my lips.

My pace is slow and steady, and I feel her grinding down against me. "Faster, Max," she pleads.

I look up at her. We've never taken it fast and hard before, and I don't want to hurt or scare her. "Are you sure?" I ask.

"Yes. Please," she begs. "I trust you."

I grip her hips and pump up as she comes down, and the feeling is euphoric. We have the perfect, torturing rhythm, and I wouldn't be able to stop even if I had to. Avery rides me fast, as if she can't get enough. I know I can't get enough of her.

The soft sounds of our lovemaking fill the room, and every one of her moans has me climbing to the edge faster and faster. My fingers dig into her hips as I thrust into her hard. Avery cries out one last time before collapsing onto my chest. Her core spasms and grips me over and over again as wave after wave of pleasure travels through her body. She's panting against me, whimpering through the orgasm, and I hold her close, savoring the feeling.

I pump into her one last time before gasping her name. I can feel my warmth spreading inside of her and the thrum of her heart against my chest. I hold her close, burying my nose into her hair, breathing in her flowery scent. "Avery," I sigh. She raises her head to gaze into my eyes. "I love you," I say before leaning up to kiss her softly. "You don't have to say it back. I just wanted you to know," I whisper against her mouth.

Tears fill her eyes, and she kisses me so deep, pouring all of her emotions into that kiss. She doesn't tell me she loves me too, but that kiss tells me exactly how she feels. I know she loves me.

We clean up in the adjoining bathroom and start to sort through our scattered clothes around the room. I'm completely dressed by the time she's slipping back into her gown. I watch as she pushes the material down over her curves until it molds to her body. She is so beautiful she takes my breath away.

I push her long hair to her right shoulder and carefully zip the dress. I allow my fingers to touch her skin while I do it, and I feel her shiver beneath my touch. I stare at her reflection in the vanity mirror. She looks sad again, and I know it's because she's thinking the same thing I am. In a few minutes, we'll leave this room, and she'll go back to Nathan, and I'll go back to being alone. But if she agrees to the plan that my mom and I concocted, then she doesn't have to stay with Nathan for very much longer.

AVERY

MAX TELLS ME about the farm and Diane and how she's willing to let me live there to get away from Nathan. I can barely contain my excitement as he goes through every last detail. I can't believe that after all this time I'll finally be free. This could work. No. This *will* work. It has to.

"He'll never even think to look for you there. He'll never find you, Avery. You can put everything into motion — the protection order, the divorce papers, just like you planned. You can finally be free of him. This is your chance. Our chance," he says with an eager expression. "Say yes."

My entire body shakes as excitement and happiness floods through me. Free. I'll finally be free. I run across the room and jump into Max's arms. "Yes," I whisper into his ear. He picks me up and spins us around. I squeal in delight and press a million kisses to his face. When he puts me down, I stare up at him. "Thank you, Max. I don't know what I would do without you."

He stares down at me with pure adoration. "We need to pick a day to leave. I was thinking this weekend. That way I could drive you up to the farm, stay with you and come back to work Monday."

I think about this week's schedule. "Nathan has a business meeting Friday night. He had marked it on the calendar. That should take hours."

Max nods. "That will give us a good head start." He squeezes me tight before letting me go. "We better get back to the party before he starts wondering where you are."

I nod in agreement, but I don't want to leave Max's side. I want to stay with him always. After Friday, it won't be so tough to be together. "Will you come and visit me?" I ask as I open the bedroom door.

"Every weekend," he promises. "And then when the divorce is final, we can talk about our future together. Maybe find a place of our own in another state where Nathan will never find you again."

I close my eyes and sigh happily. "I can't believe this is really happening," I say, bursting with excitement.

"Believe it," he says. He gives me a soft, lingering kiss before saying, "You go first. I'll wait several minutes before I come down."

"Okay." I make my way down the hall and look back at him one last time before walking down the stairs. I didn't tell Max that I love him, but I know that I do. And when I step foot on Diane's farm and actually feel safe, I will tell him how I truly feel. I'm always expecting the rug to get ripped out from underneath me, but I know Max would never hurt me. I just need that sense of security before I can release my true feelings.

I step outside of the house, and my eyes rest upon Nathan and Allison dancing together. I have no idea what's going on with my sister as of late. First she rats me out to Nathan, and now she's cozying up to him on the dance floor. Nathan's hands are resting low on her back, and Allison looks like she's on cloud nine. Her eyes glitter in the light as she looks up at him with a huge smile on her face. Something is going on between them. I just wish I knew what.

My father makes his way onto the porch, and his face lights up when he sees me. His smile slowly fades, however, when I don't return the cheerful expression. "You don't look happy, sweetheart," he says.

"That's because I'm not," I blurt out.

He raises a brow. "What's wrong?"

I sigh heavily. "I already tried to talk to you once about this, Dad."

"About the divorce?" he asks in a hushed whisper.

I nod.

"Oh, Avery, let's not talk about that here with so many Masons traipsing about." He gives me a peck on the forehead and says, "Go and find Nathan. Talk, dance, drink some champagne." He smiles. "Have some fun."

I wonder when my father will finally open his eyes and see the truth. I'm starting to think that day will never come. "Dad, there's something I need to tell you." I need to tell my father about what's going to happen this weekend. I'm not going to tell him where I'm going or any of the specifics, but I want to make sure he knows that I'll be okay when I suddenly disappear. I don't want him thinking the worst and wondering if I'm okay or not. But before I can utter a single word of my plans, I see Nathan walking towards us. I mutter a curse under my breath. Turning to my father, I quickly say, "Can we meet for lunch before Friday, Dad? I really need to talk to you."

He gives me a puzzled look, but then nods and says, "Sure, sweetheart. I'll call you as soon as I get a chance to check my schedule and let you know which day works best for me."

I want to tell him how sick I am of being penciled in, but all words escape me when Nathan climbs the steps of the porch. "Dance with me," he says with a devilish grin, holding out his hand. I tentatively put my hand in his, and he escorts me to the dance floor.

My dad grins. "Save one for me, darling!" he calls after us.

"Try to pretend you're having a good time at least, Avery," Nathan whispers as he pulls me close to him. "I know how much you hate these parties."

I don't hate the parties. I hate having to pretend for hours at a time that I'm in a happy marriage. It's utterly exhausting. I put on a brave face and an artificial smile as Nathan moves me around the dance floor. He's a good dancer. Always has been. It's just one more of the deceiving qualities about him.

After a few minutes, I say, "I saw you were dancing with Allison. You two seemed pretty close."

Nathan stares me down. "What are you trying to imply, Avery?" he asks through gritted teeth.

"Nothing. I was just —."

"You were just what?" he snaps quietly. His mouth is at my ear as he hisses, "I will drag you out of here by your hair if you keep this shit up."

I can feel his fingernails digging into my back, and I try to control the emotion on my face. I try to pretend that he's not hurting me.

My eyes catch a glimpse of Max walking towards us. He looks upset, and I don't doubt that he was watching us and witnessed Nathan's mood swing. I think of the pool man that Nathan put in a coma just for winking at me. What would he do to Max if he comes over here? What if Max tries cutting in? My eyes widen with fear as I look over Nathan's shoulder at Max. Max stops walking and just stands there, staring at me. I shake my head infinitesimally and breathe a sigh of relief when he reluctantly walks away. I don't want Max to get hurt. And anyone who tries to come between Nathan and I always gets hurt.

MAX

I WATCH HER dance with Nathan. If I didn't know her, I would say she looked happy. But I can see right through the mask she's wearing. The big smile with the perfect amount of teeth as she gazes up at her darling husband.

Any onlooker would think what a great couple they make. But I know better. Her eyes tell me everything I need to know. Her smile doesn't touch them, and she looks like a doll posed for perfection.

I squeeze my eyes shut, and the memory of the moment we just shared not even half an hour ago fills my mind. Her beautiful, naked body trembling as we made love. The expression on her face as she let go and came apart in my arms. I would never be able to get my fill of her. Once she's mine, I'll treasure every single moment I have with her and make her feel loved and cherished like she deserves.

My hands curl into fists at my sides as I watch Nathan twirl her around the dance floor. Avery says something to him, and then the look on his face turns from kind to murderous. He holds her tightly, a little too tightly. He pulls her close and whispers something in her ear.

I can see Avery's entire body tense as his fingernails bite into the bare skin of her back. Her fake smile falters, and she grimaces in pain.

I can't stand it any longer. I walk towards them with the intent of cutting in. His back is towards me, and he doesn't even see me coming. But the look in Avery's eyes halts my steps. She's silently pleading with me to not come any closer. Her eyebrows rise up and then dip as she gives a slight shake of her head.

I stare at her for a fraction more before turning and walking the other way. Would he punish her for dancing with someone else? I don't need her to answer that question. Yes, he would. That is why he has kept tight tabs on her all night. He is allowed to dance with other women, but it would simply be out of the question for her.

I saw him dancing with Avery's sister. He was joking and laughing with her.

Obviously he's not mean with every woman he comes across, so why Avery? Why hurt Avery, one of the kindest and sweetest girls on the planet?

Fuming, I walk around one of the tents in the darkness. Wanting to scream but not wanting to draw attention to myself, I instead breathe out a heavy sigh through my clenched jaw.

I need to focus on Friday. Friday is the end of this very dark, depressing tunnel. After Friday, her life and my life will change for the better.

I told myself I would keep on the down low until we can get her away from him, but I have this overwhelming need to protect her. Soon I'll be able to keep her safe from him. Never again will she know what it's like to live in fear.

AVERY

THE SONG ENDS, and I have every intention of going to find Max when an older man approaches us. My stomach drops when I recognize him. William. He and his wife Barbara were in the karaoke bar when I was there with Max Saturday night.

"Nathan and Avery," he says with a big grin.

My breathing picks up, and I try to hold myself together. I slowly start to relax when William starts talking about the upcoming elections. My eyes dart around, but I don't see his wife anywhere. I don't want to be here when she decides to show up in case she attempts to bring up that night. I slink back from Nathan in an attempt to escape the conversation, but he reaches out and grasps my arm. He smiles down at me sweetly and says, "We'll go soon. I promise." Then he turns his attention back to William.

I nod and plaster a fake grin on my face.

After several minutes, I finally feel calm. No sight of Barbara. Perhaps she didn't show tonight. Hoping that Nathan will relinquish his hold on me, I ask, "Why don't I go get us a glass of champagne?"

Before he can answer, a shrill voice yells my name. I turn, and my heart stops. Barbara is waving her hand in the air and coming towards us. I try to pull away from Nathan, but he keeps a steady grip. His eyes narrow as he stares down at me. "What's wrong, Avery? You seem a little jumpy," he says quietly.

Barbara rushes over and pants, clearly out of breath from practically running across the lawn. "Oh, Avery, I'm so glad I got to see you tonight. We didn't really get a chance to talk much on Saturday night."

Nathan stills beside me, listening intently. I try once again to pull away from him, but his grip is locked tight on my arm. His fingers dig into my skin as Barbara continued to talk.

"I wanted to tell you what a lovely voice you have. You should sing more often. William and I just adored watching you that night."

I stare at the woman with wide eyes. I can feel Nathan's glare on me. The muscle in his jaw ticks as his teeth clamp down in anger. Then he turns his attention to Barbara. "What night was that again?"

"Saturday night. William and I were so bored that we stopped at a bar for some drinks. We were all the way in the back." She smiles wide and looks at me. "We haven't been to a bar in ages! Of all places to run into you and your brother —."

"Brother?" Nathan interrupts.

"Oh, yes. Avery introduced us to her brother. He's just as charming as your wife here, Nathan," she says with a wink.

I can feel the anger radiating off of Nathan in waves. His hand clamps down on my arm, and it takes everything in me to not cry out in pain. "Well, I hate to cut this short," he says, "but Avery and I really must be going."

"Oh, so soon?" Barbara calls after us.

Nathan practically pulls me towards the valet. He fishes his ticket out of his pocket and hands it to the young attendant. Once the kid disappears into the field of parked cars, Nathan grabs my arm and turns me to face him. He glares at me with a bitterly cold stare, and an icy terror quickly spreads through my veins. "All these years and you've never introduced me to your *brother*," he says, emphasizing the last word, because he knows I was lying. "I guess I now know why you didn't answer your phone when I was gone this weekend." He shakes his head slowly.

"Nathan, please, I —."

He growls at me, and I instantly clamp my mouth shut.

The BMW pulls up the curb, and Nathan barely gives the valet a chance to put it in park before he heaves the door open and pushes me into the backseat. I fall onto the seat and quickly scramble to the door handle, but Nathan is in and locking the doors before I even have a chance to escape.

He glares at me in the rearview mirror. "You lying, fucking whore," he spits before putting the car in drive and pressing on the gas.

The tires spin, kicking up gravel as we speed off into the night.

MAX

I'M IN THE middle of a conversation with someone, but my thoughts and eyes constantly stray to Avery. Nathan and her are talking with another couple. I recognize the couple from somewhere, but I can't seem to place them.

The next time I look up, I see Nathan leading Avery towards the exit. His expression is murderous, and Avery looks panicked and terrified. "Excuse me one moment," I tell the man beside me.

I walk quickly, my eyes staying on Avery. I can tell by her body language that something is definitely wrong. I push past other guests as I try to catch up with them. They are waiting for their car by the valet. I wonder why they're leaving already.

When the vehicle stops in front of them and the attendant gets out, I watch Nathan grab Avery and roughly push her inside. My feet are moving before I can even think, and I run through the yard towards the car. Before I can reach them, the car takes off down the driveway. "Avery!" I call. The car vanishes into the night within a matter of seconds. I'm too late. I'm too late.

I push my hands through my hair, pulling at the ends in frustration. I do a full turn, looking for help. Someone. Anyone. No witnesses. No one is around.

Walking back to the lawn, I spot the couple that they were just talking to and walk up to them. The woman immediately grins when she sees me. "We were just talking about you," she says. "I was telling Avery's husband about how lovely her voice is."

I stare at the woman with a puzzled expression.

She chuckles. "You must not remember me. My husband and I were at the bar Saturday night when Avery was singing. Aren't you her brother?"

I nod and swallow nervously. That's why I recognized them.

"I thought so," she says with a smirk.

"Did you tell Nathan that you saw me there too?" I ask even though I already know the answer.

She nods. "I told him that you are just as charming as your sister," she remarks.

Nathan knows. He fucking knows.

"Excuse me," I murmur, making my way past the couple.

I return to the heart of the party and pace the lawn, looking for a cop or security. But then I think back to what Avery said. Nathan's dad is the chief of police. What would he do if I went to him for help? Would he lock me up if I accused his son of being a wife beater? If I get arrested, I wouldn't be able to help Avery at all. I could go to her father, but he's surrounded by people, strangers. How do I know I can trust any of them? Can I even really trust her father? Her sister Allison was dancing with Nathan earlier, so how do I know that she would help me and not turn around and tell Nathan everything?

Fuck! I scream in my head.

I collapse into a chair and put my head in my hands. I can't go to her family or the cops. Who else is left? Who would even believe me considering the reputation and power that the Mason family has? The realization of how dire the situation is hits me like a thousand bricks. Now I know exactly how Avery feels — completely alone and vulnerable with no one to turn to.

Standing, I make my way to the valet. At least now she does have one person she can count on.

She has me.

AVERY

I'VE BEEN TERRIFIED before. I've been terrified to the point where I've been so scared that my heart feels like it's going to seize up and stop beating. I don't know what I'm feeling right now. I am so frightened that I can barely move, barely breathe and barely even blink. I am completely paralyzed with fear, and I feel like I'm going out of my mind. I know what's coming, and my brain is kicking into fight or flee mode. I don't know what's going to happen, but it's going to be bad...really bad.

Nathan shuts off the engine to the car. We're parked in the driveway of one of Nathan's vacation properties. It's a modern two-story log cabin secluded in the woods and overlooking a lake. It took us a half an hour to get here, and I had been trembling with fear with every passing second.

His shoulders raise and lower with each deep breath he takes as we sit in silence. I know he's trying to rein in his anger, but it doesn't seem to be working. Will he kill me? I shudder at the notion that he possibly could kill me tonight. Why else would he bring me to this cabin that's in the middle of nowhere?

His hands are wrapped around the steering wheel in a white-knuckle grip. He slowly twists his hands, making an awful screeching sound against the leather. "Who is he?" he asks in an eerily calm tone.

I'd rather die than say Max's name. "It was just some guy who bought me a drink."

"Did you leave with him?"

"No," I lie.

"Did you sleep with him?"

"No," I whisper.

"YOU...FUCKING...LIAR!" he roars, turning around in his seat to glare at me.

I don't even have time to flinch before his fist connects with my face. Bright stars swirl in my vision as I slump against the backseat. The world is spinning on its axis as I fumble for the lock and then the door handle. I manage to open the door and fall out. Gravel digs into my knees as I crawl away from the car as fast I can.

A piercing scream emits from my mouth as I call out for help. I know there are no houses within miles, but maybe somebody is boating on the lake or taking a late night stroll. That is the only shred of hope that I have, and I cling to it with every ounce of strength I have left.

I try to stand, but my legs suddenly forget how to work. I have no doubt in my mind that he's hell-bent on hurting me to the fullest extent right now. I think about what happened after the pool man flirted with me. He broke my arm, and I hadn't even done anything then. This time he thinks that I cheated on him. The punishment will be worse than anything I have ever been through before, and mentally I don't think I can handle that.

I can hear his footsteps behind me. Tears stream down my face as I continue to scream. "Somebody please help me!"

"No one is going to help you, Avery. No one is going to save you. And no one can fucking hear you." He plants his shoe on my back, pushing and holding me to the ground. The gravel digs into my skin, and I struggle to catch my breath. "Do you really think I would let you scream if I thought someone could hear you? How stupid do you think I am?" He scoffs and shakes his head. "Well, you must think I'm pretty stupid actually, because you've been sneaking around and fucking someone else behind my back."

"It was just a guy at the bar who bought me a drink!" I say again, continuing to lie.

His hand fists into my hair as he hauls me up to face him. "You will tell me the truth even if I have to beat it out of you," he says through clenched teeth. Pain tears through my scalp as he drags me towards the cabin. I can feel chunks of hair being ripped out by the roots, but I continue to struggle against him. "No!" I scream. If we go inside the cabin, he'll be able to do whatever he wants for as long as he wants. I can't let that happen. Reaching up, my fingernails dig into his wrist, drawing blood.

"Fuck!" he yells, releasing me.

I turn to run, but his hands are already on me, pulling me back. I struggle against him, but he's too strong. He eventually forces me inside. The foyer lights come on automatically as we enter. I had loved coming to this cabin at one point in time. Now I envision it as a lavish tomb for my soul when Nathan kills me tonight.

His grip on me loosens, and I drop to the floor. He slams the front door shut, and I hear the locks on the door ominously click into place. He has me right where he wants me, and there's not a damn thing anyone can do about it.

Nathan walks into the kitchen and grabs a pair of shears from the knife block. Panic rushes through my system as he stalks towards me, and I push myself backwards until I'm up against the wall. I kick at him as he reaches for me. He manages to grab my ankle, and he squeezes until I cry out in pain.

"You would be wise to stay still, Avery," he says so calmly it causes a shiver to run up my spine. And then he begins to cut through my dress. "This dress cost me over a thousand dollars," he mutters, disdain lacing his voice. "You don't deserve it. You don't deserve me. You don't deserve anything!" The blade nicks my skin here and there, but he manages to cut a jagged line up the middle of the material without gutting me like a fish. The fabric falls to the side, revealing my sexy lingerie. I curse myself for wearing it. I had solely worn it for Max, knowing that I would probably see him there and knowing that I would try to get him alone.

Nathan stands up as his eyes roam over the length of my body. "I've seen a change in you lately, Avery. You're getting less compliant." He points the shears at me. "And now this whole thing with going to the bar and picking up strange men." He glares at me. "I don't even know what another man would see in you other than a good lay. That's all you would be good for."

With all the courage I can manage to muster, I look up at him and say, "Go to hell."

His head tilts and his eyes narrow. "What did you just say?"

"*Go to hell!*" I scream.

In an instant, his hand snatches my hair, and he hauls me off the floor. Pain instantly throbs at the base of my skull, and I fear I'll pass out. He pushes me against the wall, pinning me there with his forearm jammed against my throat. I gasp for air as he brings the shears close to my face. "I'm going to make sure no one ever wants to look at you again."

I squeeze my eyes shut, fearing the worst. Would he really scar me for life?

Snip. Snip. Snip.

The blades of the scissors slice through my hair, dark strands falling to the floor in huge clumps. When he's done butchering my hair, he slaps me hard on the cheek. I fall to the floor, hitting my head against the unforgiving tile and gasping for air. My vision blurs, and a high-pitch ringing in my ears muffles the noise surrounding me.

I can only sense what happens after that. My body is lifeless. My brain is numb. I know he's kicking me, but I can't feel it anymore. Darkness creeps up on the edge of my vision.

It's waiting to take me.

I don't want to hurt anymore.

So I let the darkness consume me.

MAX

I'M GOING INSANE. I went home after the fundraiser and waited for the black BMW to pull into the driveway next door. It never did. All night and early morning I sat, watching, waiting. I had already made my mind up that I was going to rush over there and take her away from him no matter what I had to do. However, they never came home.

I tried knocking on the door several times, but no one answered. I called the cell phone I gave Avery a hundred times, but she never picked up. And the number of voicemails I left is so innumerable that I lost track. I left messages with her father as well, but so far he hasn't called me back even though I specifically told him I had an urgent matter regarding Avery.

I watched their house like a hawk until I had to leave for work, but I never saw any movement. No one came home, and no one left.

Now I'm sitting at the hospital attempting to reign in my emotions as I stare down at a patient's chart with a blank expression. Avery never showed up to volunteer this morning. I have no idea what happened after the fundraiser, but the look in her eyes still haunts me. What if he hurt her? What if he...killed her?

I push the thought to the back of my mind and shake my head. I can't think about that. Not now. Not ever.

During my lunch break, I call my mother. I ramble off to them what happened last night as I pace back and forth outside of the hospital. "I don't know what to do, Mom. I don't know where she is. She could be lying in a ditch somewhere, and I wouldn't even know." I swallow hard and close my eyes. "He could have already killed her." My voice breaks as I utter, "I can't lose her. Not now. Not when we were so close to saving her."

My mom does the best she can to soothe me over the phone, but I am utterly and completely broken, lost and exhausted. I didn't know how deep my affection for Avery ran until she disappeared. And now I know how much I love her, how much I want to take care of her and never let her go.

"And you said you can't contact the police department?" she asks.

"No. Her husband's father is the chief of police, and Avery had told me she couldn't trust him. I called every other police department in this state, and they all told me that their hands are tied since it's not their jurisdiction. I don't know what I can do. Avery's own father won't even return my calls."

My mother is silent for a long time. Then she finally says, "That poor girl. No wonder she couldn't run before. This husband of hers has a lot of power, more power than I could've ever imagined."

I stop pacing and press my back against the wall. "I have to find her, mom. I have to help her. I'm the only one who can save her now."

"We'll figure it out. Your father has a friend from college who works in the public safety department in North Carolina. We'll give Eric a call and see what he can do."

"Thanks, mom. I really appreciate it. I'm at my wit's end here."

"I know, Max. I know. Just hang in there. We're going to do everything we can," she says reassuringly.

We end the call, but I don't feel any better. It's been fourteen hours since I last saw Avery, and I can only imagine what kind of hell she's experiencing right now.

AVERY

⚜

THERE IS A buzzing in my ears that won't stop. It's like a nagging fly that just won't go away. I try to open my eyes, but the right one stays closed. My fingers fumble to touch my face, and I wince as my fingertips touch the puffy skin around my eye. It's swollen shut. And then I suddenly remember why.

The memories of the beatings I took from Nathan flood my mind, and I sit bolt upright. The quiet room is filled with my ragged breaths as I take in my surroundings. I'm still in the cabin and in the upstairs master bedroom upstairs. And Nathan is nowhere to be found.

I swing my legs off the side of the bed, and the movement is almost too much to bear. My body is trembling with pain. I hurt everywhere, and I feel like a truck ran over me, backed up and ran over me again. My good eye catches the phone on the end table, and I struggle to reach it. Every bit of movement causes a whole world of pain.

I hiss through gritted teeth and manage to grab the receiver. I push the on button and hold the phone to my ear. No dial tone. I pull at the base, and that's when I see that the phone line is not connected. I strangle the phone hard in my hand to keep from crying out in frustration. Nathan must have known I would try to call for help. He's always one step ahead of me.

With more effort required than it should, I manage to stand, my feet sinking into the plush carpet. Bracing myself with the end table, I walk over to the window. I look down at the twenty-foot drop and grimace. Even if I managed to survive the fall without breaking anything else, there is no way I could run from him. My current condition is not leaving me with very many options.

The bedroom door abruptly swings open, and all my hopes for escape are suddenly extinguished. I instinctively cower in the corner of the room by the bed. Sobs and gibberish come flooding out of my mouth as Nathan's heavy footsteps approach me. I feel his fingers in my hair, which he had ruthlessly chopped when we first got here. He strokes me like a wounded animal and hushes me.

"This can all be over, Avery."

Those same words have been spoken over the last two days. Over and over and over again.

"Just give me his name," he says calmly.

He wants the name of the man from the bar. He wants Max. Well, he'll have to kill me first. "There's no one else," I whisper through a sob. "It was just some guy at the bar. I don't even know his name," I cry.

"You're lying again." He clucks his tongue in disapproval and shakes his head. "I guess you haven't learned your lesson yet. It's only Friday, Avery, and we're not leaving until I have a name." His fingers in my hair suddenly tighten and pull, causing a searing pain to erupt in my scalp. "Let's go downstairs, shall we?" he asks while dragging me behind him. "Blood is so hard to get out of carpet."

MAX

It's Friday afternoon when I'm finishing up my rounds at the hospital. It's hard to concentrate, but I try to keep my thoughts of Avery towards the back of my mind for the sake of my patients. But during lunch, walking down the hall and any free time in between patients, my thoughts are consumed by only her. I walk into Jacob's room, and I feel an ache in my chest that Avery's not here.

He looks up as I walk in. His face falls, and I know it's because he was expecting Avery. "Hello, Jacob."

"Hi, Dr. Harrison."

"How are you feeling?"

"Okay I guess," he answers solemnly.

I check over the nurses' notes and his vitals. "You seem down. Something wrong?"

"Avery didn't come to visit me yesterday or today. She always comes to visit me at the end of the day." His bottom lip puffs out as he frowns.

"It's not because she didn't want to see you. She's just...not feeling well," I lie. I feel bad lying to the kid, but the truth is far too harsh for me to tell anyone, let alone a six year old.

"Oh," he says softly. "Well, if you talk to her, tell her I miss her and that I hope she feels better."

His words break my heart, and I have to choke back my emotions. "I will. I'll tell her."

He stares out the window for a few moments before turning and asking, "She is coming back, isn't she?"

I close my eyes and desperately try to keep my voice calm as I say, "Yeah. She's coming back." I tap the edge of his baseball hat like I've seen Avery do so many times before, and that elicits a small grin out of him. "I'll make sure of it," I promise before leaving his room.

My cell phone buzzes in my pocket, and I am quick to answer it. "Dad," I say. "Tell me you have some good news."

"I do. I pulled in a favor from an old college buddy of mine. His name is Eric Jones, and he works for the state's Department of Public Safety. Eric and a colleague of his are on their way to Nags Head right now. Can you meet them at five o'clock?" He rattles off an address of a local café.

I grab a pen and paper from the nurses' desk and jot down the time and place. "Sure. Do you think they will be able to help me?"

"I think they are your best hope at finding her at this point, son."

~

I SIT IN the small café with two men across the booth from me. My dad's contacts paid off. Eric Jones, my dad's friend, is from the Department of Public Safety. The man next to him is Lance Romero, who is a Special Agent in Charge with the State Bureau of Investigation. The men are complete opposites. Eric is short and stout whereas Lance is tall and muscular. Eric is jovial and talkative, and Lance is quiet and hasn't spoken more than a few words since they arrived. Eric has blond hair, blue eyes while Lance has brown hair and eyes. Lance is definitely more intimidating, but

Eric claimed earlier that he's all bark, no bite. So far, I'm not totally convinced.

Eric takes notes as the three of us talk over coffee. "So the last time you saw her was Wednesday night?"

"Yes. And there has been no sign of her since then." I stare down at the dark liquid in front of me. I didn't even bother putting cream or sugar in the coffee. I need it as strong as I can get it. I have barely slept a wink the past few days. I'm a nervous wreck, completely on edge. All I can focus on his Avery and imagine the horror she must be experiencing. It's literally driving me insane.

"You said his father is the Chief of Police?"

"Yes. Richard Mason."

Eric continues to jot down notes and talk while Agent Romero sits there in silence. I look up at Lance and take in his quiet demeanor. He looks calm and collected as he sips his coffee. After Eric's finished with the interview, Lance sets down his cup and says, "Now, the local department didn't ask for our involvement, so I'm sure Chief Mason is going to object to us storming into his barracks." He smirks. "Quite frankly, I don't give a damn what he objects to. You're the key witness to abuse and a kidnapping. And in a case such as that, the jurisdiction he has won't matter. The Bureau will hold precedence, and I'm going to do everything in my power to make sure that Avery is all right."

His words sink in slowly, and my hands shake as I wrap them around the warm mug. I chuckle, but it comes out like a sob. My emotions have been running high over the past couple of days. It feels like I've been waiting forever for some kind of light at the end of this very dark tunnel. And now, finally, there is hope, a ray of light breaking through the darkness. "Thank you," I say, my voice wavering. "I was at the end of my rope trying to figure out who else to turn to."

Eric speaks up with, "Well, I knew your old man back in college. Let's just say he bailed my ass out of some things back then, so I definitely owed him a favor." He claps a hand on Lance's shoulder. "And I knew I could count on Romero here to help me."

Lance slowly nods. His features darken as he says, "My sister was killed by her abusive boyfriend. I was only a kid back then and couldn't stop it. But now I make it my mission to find assholes like Nathan Mason and see that they get the justice they deserve."

I nod my head solemnly. Nothing more needs to be said. He understands my frustration and anxiety. He gets it. "So where do we start?" I ask.

Eric looks up from his notes. "We start with the father, Chief Mason. If Nathan has been in contact at all, we'll find that out. Then we'll move from there until we can find out where Nathan might be holed up with Avery."

I swallow hard. Facing Nathan's father face to face and having the truth about his son divulged is not going to be easy. But at this point, there is no other way. He will have to listen to the truth whether he wants to hear it or not.

~

CHIEF RICHARD MASON stands up from behind his desk to shake our hands. "Have a seat, gentlemen," he says, motioning to the chairs in front of the large oak desk.

Lance, Eric and I comply as Chief Mason sits back down in his scarred leather chair. "I usually don't have people barging in here at five o'clock on a Friday evening flashing badges." His voice is cordial, but his expression is anything but. "I have to say I'm intrigued considering I haven't gotten any calls from the State Bureau of Investigation telling me that I was to expect some visitors." He eyes Agent Romero as he speaks.

"We have reason to believe there was a possible kidnapping Wednesday night." Lance leans forward in his chair. "Do you know where your son is, Mr. Mason?"

Richard drums his fingers nervously on the armrest of the chair. "What exactly is this about, and why does it involve Nathan?"

Eric pulls out his notepad and flips to the first page. "Wednesday night your son and Avery Mason were at a fundraising campaign for her father. We have a witness who says Avery was forced into a car and taken against her will. Have you heard from Nathan since Wednesday night, Mr. Mason?"

Nathan's father suddenly looks flustered. "What in God's name are you talking about? My son would never kidnap his own wife!" He stands up and paces behind his desk.

Eric continues. "Your son has been physically and mentally abusing Avery for quite some time. Were you aware of that?"

Richard stops and looks pointedly at Eric. "You have some nerve coming in here with these ridiculous accusations! My son would never hurt anyone. He is a respected member of the community. He is a plastic surgeon. He is —."

"I don't give a fuck what he does for a living or how he pretends to act in front of members of society," Lance interrupts. "We want to know if you were aware of the abuse. It's a simple yes or no answer."

Richard shakes his head. "Nathan would never —." His voice trails off, and I can see that he's in deep thought. He sinks down into his chair, and it's several minutes before he finally answers. "There was a girl in college that accused Nathan of hurting her, but she dropped all charges as soon as she saw the cash settlement. How do I know the same thing isn't happening here?"

I shake my head slowly. So Nathan has a history of abusing women. Just because they shut her up with hush money doesn't mean he didn't hurt the girl. "I saw the bruises," I say, speaking up. Eric gives me a sideways glance, but I ignore him. "He hit her. He abused her physically and mentally, and now he's holding her somewhere against her will. We need to find her before it's too late."

Chief Mason raises his gaze to me. "I haven't spoken to him since Tuesday," he says quietly. "I don't know where they could be."

Lance stands and puts his palms flat on his desk. He looks tall and menacing, and I'm so grateful that he's on my side. "Try calling him. Now," he orders.

Richard pulls open a desk drawer and retrieves his cell phone. He dials the number while we all wait in suspense. After several tries, Richard finally says, "He's not answering his phone." He frowns. "That's not like Nathan. He always answers when I call," he says, his voice distant.

Eric pulls out a pen. "They're definitely not at their house, so any idea where he could have taken her?"

Chief Mason places a hand on his desk to steady himself as he stands. "Our family owns numerous vacation homes and rental properties." He sighs heavily. "There are a lot of places that he could have taken her."

Eric readies the pen. "Start with the most likely possibilities, and we'll go from there."

As Eric and Chief Mason go over the numerous properties, Agent Romero and I step out into the hallway. "We need to split up to cover more ground. I'm going to ask the chief to lend us some of his men to help."

I like Lance's way of thinking. Every hour that goes by without finding Avery is another hour that she could be getting hurt...or worse. I shudder at the thought. "He has a plastic surgery practice on Eighth Avenue. I'll swing by there and ask his staff some questions."

"Good idea," Agent Romero replies. "Eric and I will start on this list and see if we can come up with any new information. Call me if you find out anything."

"Will do."

~

NATHAN MASON'S OFFICE is exactly how I pictured. Numerous posters line the sterile, white walls as I walk to his secretary's desk. The posters claim that if you are an ugly duckling, Dr. Mason can make you beautiful. There are before and after photos of lip injections and face lifts. It's his job to make beautiful people feel horrible about themselves so that they will consent to excessive and expensive surgery. He makes people feel as if they're not good enough for society and that they need to change. If only his professional life didn't mirror his personal life.

Nathan Mason's secretary is exactly how I pictured as well — a buxom blonde with full lips and dressed in one of the shortest skirts I have ever seen a woman wear. She looks up at me with bright blue eyes as I approach the desk. "Hello. How may I help you?" she asks. Her mouth barely moves when she talks, and I wonder briefly if she gets a discount on surgery.

"Is Nathan Mason here?"

"Dr. Mason is on vacation."

Vacation. I curl my fingers around the edge of the desk. So he contacted his secretary. I need to know everything she knows. "Was this a planned vacation?"

She shakes her head. "Oh no. It was quite sudden actually." She rolls her eyes. "In fact, so sudden that I have had a terrible time rescheduling all of his appointments."

"Did he say when he was going to be back?"

She nods. "Yeah. He said not to expect him back until Monday." Her eyes narrow as she stares at me. "Are you a friend of Dr. Mason?"

I decide the best choice here is to lie. "Yes. I'm a friend of the family. We've been trying to reach Dr. Mason. His father is in the hospital."

Her blue eyes widen. "Is his father all right?"

"It's not looking good. We really need to reach Nathan, and he's not answering his phone. Any way you can help me out?"

She glances down at the desk and rummages through some papers. "I only have his cell phone and house number. I don't have any other number to reach him."

My hands tighten around the desk. "Did he happen to mention where he was going?"

She holds up her finger as she rummages through the notes on her desk. "Yes, he did actually. I know I wrote it down somewhere. I write everything down since I'm so forgetful." She smiles and pulls out a slip of paper. "He said he was going to the cabin on the lake to do some fishing."

"Address?"

She shakes her head. "I'm sorry. I don't know the address."

I curse silently in my head and then tell the secretary, "Thank you." I pull my cell phone out of my pocket on the way to my car.

Lance answers on the first ring. "Romero."

"I think I know where they are. Nathan told his secretary that he's at the cabin on the lake."

"Cabin on the lake," Lance says to whoever's in the room with him. He rattles off an address, and I jot it down on a piece of paper. "The chief said it's about a thirty-minute drive from here."

I pull the car out of the parking lot and hop onto the highway. "I'm on my way."

"Now, just wait a minute, Max. You need to let us do our job. We're going to get a tactical team ready. When we know it's safe, then you can —."

"I'm sorry, but it might already be too late. I'm not wasting another damn second without finding out if she's all right."

"Nathan could be armed. You can't just go barging in there!" Lance yells.

"Then I suggest you hurry," I say before hanging up the phone. I'll make it to the cabin before the police, but at this point I don't care. Nothing matters right now except for Avery. I need to find her. I need to get her away from that monster before it's too late. My foot pushes down on the gas pedal as I speed down the highway. "Hang on, Avery. I'm coming."

AVERY

PAIN WRACKS MY body, and I shiver uncontrollably in the dining room chair. The seconds, minutes and hours blur together, and I'm beginning to wonder if I'll ever get out of this hell.

Nathan sits across the table, calm as ever, as he eats dinner. "Eat, Avery," he demands, before bringing a spoonful of soup to his mouth. "You'll need your strength for what I have planned for you tonight."

His words chill me to the bone. If I thought he was cruel and sadistic before, I'm getting a look at a whole other side to him that I didn't know existed — that I never could have fathomed existing. The person on the other side of the table from me is a sick and twisted monster. I can't even see a glimpse of who Nathan once was. This person is a complete stranger to me.

I stare down at the bowl, and the smell of the food sickens me. My heavy eyelids droop. My body wants to keep succumbing to the cold and numbness, and I wonder briefly if I'm dying.

"Eat!" Nathan yells. "Don't make me force you, Avery, because I promise you won't like it."

His voice brings me back to the present, and I stare at the soup through narrowed eyes. With an exorbitant amount of effort, I manage to grasp the spoon. My hand trembles, and the metal clacks against the bowl as I try to gather a spoonful.

A buzzing sound distracts me, and my eyes snap up. Nathan pulls his cell phone out of his pocket, and I eye it greedily. While I'm trying to formulate a plan in my head on how to steal his phone, he begins to chuckle to himself. "Your sister sends a lot of texts," he remarks.

Allison is texting Nathan. A feeling of hope blooms in my chest. Does she know I've been kidnapped? Maybe my family and Max are looking for me.

"And she sends a lot of nudes," Nathan says with a smirk. He eyes me carefully from across the table, waiting for my reaction.

My head is too foggy from the pain to even comprehend why my sister would be sending him nude pictures. I look up at him with a questioning look on my face.

"Oh, come on, Avery. You're not *that* stupid. Figure it out," he says with a dismissing wave of his hand.

I think back to when I met Allison over lunch to talk about divorcing Nathan. She was clearly on team Nathan for a reason I couldn't fathom at the time. And then I remember the way they were dancing together at my father's campaign event, how close they seemed, how carefree and happy together.

My fingers clench around the spoon. Allison wouldn't help me because she was too busy sleeping with my husband. She believed *him* over me, her own sister. A spike of adrenaline courses through my body, and I stand up quickly, knocking over my chair in the process. My hands grip the bowl of soup, and before I can even think about what I'm doing, I launch the bowl across the table at Nathan.

The hot soup splashes over him, and the bowl strikes him in the forehead before crashing to the floor. A cry of triumph erupts from my throat. So many times I have dreamed of hitting him, hurting him like he has hurt me. But the joy is short-lived, however, when he slowly stands and glares at me with an intense and blistering gaze.

His fingertips go to the bump forming on his forehead, and he swipes at the blood seeping from his head wound. He lowers his hand and stares at the blood on his fingers for a long time. "You're going to pay for that," he says with an eerily calm voice.

With one swift move, he knocks the table over and stalks towards me. I make the front door my goal, but I can't move fast enough. My feet don't want to cooperate, and my legs feel like jelly. I only make it as far as the next room before Nathan tackles me to the hardwood floor. A powerful scream erupts from my lungs as he turns me over so that I'm on my back. His hands hold down my arms when I try to fight him off.

"You will not defy me!" he shouts. His hands move from my arms and latch around my throat.

I claw at his arms as I struggle to breathe. He squeezes tighter and tighter, the wicked grin on his face widening as I gasp for air. My body bucks under him, but he's too big, too strong. I launch my knees into his back, but he doesn't budge. He's firmly planted on top of me with a crazy look in his eyes. He's going to kill me this time. I just know it.

Gradually, my limbs start to go limp, and shadows creep into the edge of my vision. I gasp desperately for air, but my lungs are painfully denied a single breath. I'm on the verge of passing out, but I continue to struggle. I don't want to go into the darkness. I want to go towards the light, towards Max. But Max isn't here to save me. No one is.

I try to drag in a breath, but his grip is too tight. My vision blurs as I start to slip into unconsciousness.

Max.

I love you.

Max is the last thing on my mind as my mouth gapes open for one last unsuccessful gasp. And then I do the one thing I promised myself I would never do.

I stop fighting.

MAX

It only takes me twenty minutes to make the drive to the cabin. My GPS alerts me that the destination is just right ahead, and I curl my hands around the steering wheel in a white-knuckle grip. The woods are so thick along the gravel driveway that I can't even see the house yet.

My foot presses down on the gas pedal as my anxiety builds. Dust and gravel kick up on the road behind me as I accelerate a little more. If Avery isn't here, then this is just time wasted in my efforts to find her. But something in my gut is telling me that this is right. She's here. I can feel it.

And when the black BMW comes into view in the driveway, my stomach twists into knots. They're here, but is Avery still alive? I banish the thought from my head before I can even dwell on it. I have to believe that she's okay. Until I see otherwise, I have to believe that.

I pull off the gravel road and park where my vehicle is almost invisible amongst the trees. I slowly climb out of the SUV and close the door as quietly as I can. Checking my watch, I bite my lower lip nervously. The team is probably ten minutes behind me. Maybe more. Maybe less. But I can't wait.

Staying crouched down low, I make my way towards the large cabin. I slowly climb the steps to the porch and wait. No movement. No sounds. I press my ear to the door, and I hear a loud noise. It sounds like something was knocked over. And then I hear Avery screaming. It's a blood-curdling scream that pierces me right down to my very soul and turns my blood to pure ice.

Adrenaline courses through my veins. I reach for the doorknob. It's locked. I run to the window and try to lift it, but it won't budge. Fuck! Panicked, I look around for something, anything. I grab one of the metal patio chairs and turn it so the legs are facing away from me. With all of my might, I ram it against the window. The glass shatters.

I don't even take my time making my way inside as shards of glass cut me all over, ripping my shirt and jeans and skin in the process. I take in the scene before me. The table is overturned, and Nathan is on top of Avery with his hands on her throat. Nathan glances up at me, and the look in his eyes is pure evil.

My gaze flickers to Avery. She's lifeless on the floor. I'm too late. *He killed her.*

Nathan stands and makes a move towards me. "You son of a bitch!" I yell. I take off in a fast sprint and drive the chair legs right into his chest. He grunts and stumbles back into the wall.

Tossing the chair to the side, I throw a hard punch that connects with his jaw. God, it feels so good to finally do that. He falls to the floor in a heap. I want to make him feel the pain he caused Avery. I want to kill him. My hands run through my hair in frustration, pulling at the ends. No. I have to focus on Avery first. I'll deal with that piece of shit later.

I rush over and kneel down at her side. My fingertips are at her bruised neck, trying to locate a pulse while I lean down to her mouth to check if she's breathing. "Please," I whisper. I wait. I pray. I try to hold myself together during those excruciating seconds. And then I feel a faint beating of her heart against the pads of my fingers and a light wheeze as she takes a shallow breath. "Oh, thank God!" I cry with relief.

I don't want to move her in case her neck is broken, so I pull her hand into my mine and hold it tightly. "I'm here, Avery. It's going to be okay. Just hold on." I yank my cell phone from my pocket with the intent to call 9-1-1.

"I wouldn't do that if I were you," Nathan says from behind me.

A clicking noise fills the silence of the room, and it takes me a moment to register the sound. When I turn and drag my gaze upwards, I see Nathan standing ten feet away with a gun pointed at my chest. Blood is dripping from his lopsided mouth, and I have no doubt that his jaw is broken. His lips are curled up in a misshapen sneer. "So you're the guy who's been fucking my wife," he slurs.

I slowly stand, putting myself as a barrier between the gun and Avery. He won't hurt her anymore. I won't allow it. But if he does shoot me, I won't be able to protect her. And that thought kills me more than any bullet could.

I watch with curiosity as he picks up the house phone and dials 9-1-1. When the operator picks up, Nathan says, "I need the police right away! I came home to a man assaulting and strangling my wife. He attacked me, and I shot him." He musters up the best shaky voice he can as he says, "I think my wife is dead. Please hurry." He rattles off the address before ending the call.

"You're a real piece of work, Nathan," I say. He has no idea that the cops are already on their way. They won't believe his story, but I don't let on that I know anything different. The ambulance is going to be on its way as well as even more law enforcement, and Nathan doesn't have a clue that it's for Avery and my benefit, not his.

He nods in agreement. "Hey, I'm going to kill two birds with one stone. I get to kill my wife and my wife's lover and get away scot-free. It can't get any better than that." He spits blood onto the floor. "You're the one who broke into my home after all. You attacked me, and I had no choice but to defend myself and shoot you. It's too bad I wasn't able to save Avery."

I listen to his fabricated story that he's going to tell the cops. He has every intention of killing me and then finishing what he started with Avery. Panic surges through my veins. I have to do something or he'll kill not only me, but Avery too. I need to stall until the police can get here. "Tell me something, Nathan. Did you enjoy hurting her?"

He hesitates for a moment. "Yes," he says finally with complete coolness. "When I first met Avery, she was a wild and free spirit. And the more I was around her, the more I just wanted to break her will and make her mine." He takes a step closer to me as I take a step back. "She was hard to break. Much harder than the girls before her...and after her," he adds. "Avery was quite the conquest."

He really is a sick bastard. "But you never did break her completely, did you?"

A crooked smile appears on his face. "I almost did. I knew something happened after I went to Seattle for a week. Avery was different. She was...defiant again. I didn't know why at the time, but I eventually found out. She found someone new." He hesitates and then says, "You." His fingers clench around the gun in frustration. "But she wouldn't give me your name...not even after I spent three days trying to beat it out of her."

I cringe at his words. "You never deserved her."

He cocks his head to the side. "Maybe not. Maybe you think that you deserve her, but you'll never have her. The only person who isn't leaving this room in a body bag is me." He aims the gun, and I watch as his finger starts to pull back on the trigger.

Instinctively, I drop down low and quickly move to the left. The first shot rings out, and I hear the glass breaking in the window just behind me. He missed. Huddling behind the kitchen island, I listen to his footsteps. Right now I'm delaying the inevitable. I'm not leaving Avery alone in the house with him, but I don't want to get shot either. The only thing I can hope for is that Romero and his team arrive here soon.

I dart out from behind the island and run for the living room. Another shot rings out, but this time Nathan doesn't miss. I instantly feel a spike of pain spiderwebbbing out from my arm. I skid to a stop behind the sofa and try to catch my breath as I quickly assess the damage. It looks like the bullet grazed me. I'm bleeding, but not profusely. I'm hurt, but I'm still alive, and I can still save Avery. That's all that matters. I need to stay alive for her.

After a few seconds, I hear his footsteps. He comes to a complete stop, and my heart stutters. I know exactly where he is. "Come out now or I'll shoot her."

I peer out from behind the couch. Nathan is standing over Avery with the gun pointed right at her head. My blood runs cold. "Okay!" I call. I stand and slowly move into his view. "Kill me. Take your anger out on me, Nathan. Not her."

"How noble of you," he says sarcastically. "No wonder she fell for you. You're the exact opposite of me," he says with a crooked grin. Nathan raises the gun, and it feels like everything is happening in slow motion. I close my eyes and hold on to the image of Avery. I just pray that the paramedics make it in time to save her.

"Freeze!" a voice calls from behind me. "Drop the gun!"

My eyes snap open, and I glance behind me to see two uniformed police officers stepping through the window I had broken through earlier. Their guns are drawn as they step towards Nathan. The look on Nathan's face is priceless — shock, terror and despair all at once. "Officer, this man broke into my house and assaulted my wife!" he protests.

One of the officers says, "We'll figure all of that out later, but right now you need to drop the gun."

Nathan seems reluctant, not bothering to loosen his grip on the weapon. "I'm Nathan Mason. My father is Richard Mason. He's the Chief of Police at —."

"I don't give a fuck who your father is right now. Drop the gun now or I will shoot you!" the other cop yells.

The standoff seems to last hours, but I know it can't be more than a few minutes. The thundering sound of my heart beat pulses in my ears as the blood runs from my shoulder. The room is quiet, and I can hear the steady drip of blood from my index finger to the floor below.

Chief Mason enters the room with his hands up in a supplicating gesture. "Nathan," he says with a commanding voice. "Put down the gun."

Nathan shakes his head. "Dad, you don't understand." He takes a step closer to me, his finger pressing against the trigger.

"You can make me understand later, but right now I want you to put the gun down."

"I can't do that." Nathan's hands begin to tremble as the gun shakes in his grip. "I have to end this."

"Nathan," his father says sternly. When Nathan's eyes dart up to meet his, he continues by saying, "You don't have to do this, son. We'll work through whatever is going on here." When Nathan doesn't budge, he slowly says, "Don't make me do something I'll regret."

I watch as Chief Mason raises his own gun and points it towards his son. A myriad of emotions wash over Nathan's face, a mixture of resentment and disbelief.

Nathan returns his gaze to me. "I'm ending this. Now."

Without having time to react, two gunshots ring out almost simultaneously. I watch Nathan stumble backwards at the same time I do. He falls to the floor, crying out in pain. His father shot him in the arm, and the gun in his lifeless hand goes skittering across the hardwood floor.

It's over. It's finally over.

I press a hand to my chest as a sudden overwhelming pressure erupts inside of me. My fingers feel numb, wet. And when my eyes dart down to my hand, I realize it's covered in blood. Was I shot? My brain is too foggy to focus on anything at the moment.

An officer yells into his scanner, "Two gunshot victims. We need an ambulance here STAT!"

Two gunshot victims. Two.

Feeling weak, I turn and fall to my knees beside Avery. The blood is pouring from the wound in my chest and slowly pooling on the floor around me. "Avery!" I call out, but my voice sounds frail, disconnected.

I can hear people around me yelling out instructions, and two officers are wrestling Nathan to the ground. He's putting up a fight even with an injured arm. I blink, and I'm suddenly lying on the floor next to Avery. Pulling her hand in my mine, I hold onto her with every ounce of strength I'm able to muster. Her skin is so pale, and I can't tell if she's breathing anymore.

"Don't you dare give up, Avery." I grip her hand tightly. "Stay with me, baby." Tears trickle down my cheeks. I need her to be okay. I can't lose her. Not like this. Not to *him*. I'm starting to feel lightheaded, but I refuse to close my eyes and slip into unconsciousness.

People are rushing around me, putting pressure on my chest, but I can barely feel anything.

Agent Romero yells, "Stay awake, Max! The paramedics are on their way!"

I never break my grip with Avery; never turn my attention away from her. "You're going to make it, Avery. Do you hear me? You have to make it." I cough as blood fills my lungs and spills out between my lips. A sob escapes my throat as I realize I'm losing the fight against staying awake and that I may never see her beautiful eyes again. I don't want to leave her, but I don't have a choice now. The pain is taking over, and I can't stop the darkness from overtaking me. My grip on her loosens against my will. I stare at Avery until I can no longer keep my eyes open. The image of her beautiful face is forever etched into my brain...and it slowly fades to total darkness.

AVERY

MY MOUTH FEELS like I've been walking for ten years through the Sahara Desert. My dry and cracked lips slowly part as I attempt to ask for water, but the only sound that comes out is a strange groan that reverberates down the column of my neck, sending a sharp pain through my throat. The groan is cut short by the immediate pain. I try to swallow, but my lethargic tongue thickly sticks to the roof of my mouth.

"She's waking up," someone says.

The voice sounds so familiar.

Rosie.

Rosie is here. But where is here?

My eyelids flutter as memories start rushing back to me. *Nathan.* The last thing I remember is him on top of me, his hands around my neck squeezing the life out of me. I scream in my mind for help, and eventually the noise escapes my lips. It's a loud, strangled cry that sounds feral.

My eyes snap open. I hear the fast beeping of the heart monitor behind me as my chest rapidly rises and falls.

"Calm down, Avery," Rosie commands, rushing to my bedside. "You're at the hospital. You're safe, honey."

My eyes dart around, assessing my surroundings. I'm in a hospital bed wrapped in bandages with an IV sticking out of my arm. My gaze catches Rosie as she moves her hands up and down slowly, instructing me on how to slow my breathing. "That's it. Nice, steady breaths," she says as the monitor gradually returns to a normal rhythm.

Dr. Benson, who I've known since I started volunteering at the hospital, enters the room. He has a short, hushed conversation with Rosie before he walks over to me. His face is pinched with concern as he raises a penlight to check my pupils. "Hello, Avery. Do you know who I am?"

I try to answer him, but my voice comes out in a raspy, fragmented whisper. I swallow hard, and a sharp, stabbing pain flows through my neck. My fingers reach for my throat, and I realize I'm wearing a neck brace.

"That's okay. Don't try to speak. Nodding or shaking of the head works just as well. Do you know who I am?" he asks again.

I give a small nod.

"Good. That's good." He motions to Rosie, who brings over a few items and places them on the overbed table. There is a small whiteboard, a black marker and an eraser. I stare at the things before me in uncertainty.

Dr. Benson notices my confusion and explains, "We want you to use these to talk until your throat has some time to heal. You've had massive trauma to your cervical spine. Based on your symptoms when you tried to speak, I believe you are suffering from vocal box paralysis. We won't know the full extent of the damage until we can assess after the swelling has gone down and you have rested." He points to the board. "The key word here is *rest*. Don't try to talk. Write it down. Understood?"

He stares at me until I nod in response. Then he continues. "Do you remember how you got here?"

My brain is foggy, and nothing seems to be coming into focus. I shake my head gently, as every bit of movement seems to be causing me pain.

"What's the last thing you remember?"

I grab the board and marker and slowly write my response with a shaky hand. *My husband strangling me. Then everything went black.*

He nods slowly as a deep frown slowly sets on his face. "You might remember more of what happened. Just don't try to force the memories." He hesitates before he murmurs, "Some things are better left in the dark."

I swallow hard, the pain searing through my throat once more. I erase my words on the board and scribble the word *water*.

"Rosie, will you get us some ice chips, please?"

"Sure thing, Doctor," she says before leaving the room.

Dr. Benson makes a few notes in my chart until Rosie comes back into the room. "I have some more patients to check on, but I'll be back, Avery. Get some rest."

I nod and watch him leave. Rosie puts a small ice chip on a spoon and feeds it into my mouth. "Let it melt on your tongue, Avery," she instructs.

I almost groan in pleasure. I have never been so thirsty before in my life, and the ice melting on my tongue is almost euphoric.

She carefully takes a small sponge stick, wets it and gently rubs it over my cracked lips. Tears fill my eyes as I stare up at her. She has no idea how thankful I am for her kindness.

"Don't cry, baby girl," she whispers. "You're safe now." She hesitates and then nods to herself as if deciding an inner turmoil. "Nathan is in jail. They locked him up. He can't hurt you any more."

The corners of my mouth lift up. At least he isn't getting away with hurting me this time. I have waited so long for this moment. My eyelids grow heavy, and I faintly hear Rosie telling me it's the medicine in the IV making me tired. The moment my head falls back on the pillow, I'm asleep.

I wake up hours later. I don't even know how long I've been asleep. The pain in my body hasn't subsided, but the drugs in the IV are definitely helping. There is a tall, burly man sitting on the other side of the room. His long legs are crossed at the ankle, and he sips his coffee and stares at the television in the ceiling by my bed.

When his gaze flickers to me, he sits up quickly, almost spilling his coffee. "It's nice to see you awake," he says before standing. "I'm Agent Lance Romero with the State Bureau of Investigation."

I stare up at this large man as he makes his way over to me. He's intimidating, but I have a feeling deep down he's a gentle giant. I point to my neck to let him know that I can't talk.

"Oh, yeah. The doctor told me you wouldn't be able to talk for a while."

I grab the whiteboard and marker in front of me and write a question on the board before holding it up to him. "How did I get away from Nathan?"

"You don't remember?"

I shake my head.

"Well, it all started when Dr. Harrison alerted his parents to your situation. His father got in contact with a friend of mine, Eric Jones, in the Department of Public Safety. Jones contacted me, and we went to work on trying to find you. Max..." He seems to get choked up for a minute, but then he clears his throat and continues. "Max saved your life. He went ahead of the team...against my orders," he says with a small grin, "and he confronted Nathan. The rest of the team arrived shortly thereafter, and Chief Mason shot Nathan, taking him down."

My heart swells with pride. Max saved my life. He was my knight in shining armor after all, as I always knew he would be. If he wouldn't have got the ball rolling, I would be dead. Nathan would have killed me that day. I have no doubt in my mind about that.

I press a hand to my heart, feeling overwhelmed with emotion.

Romero watches me carefully. Then he says, "I should go. I know the doctors don't want any of us in here while you're supposed to be resting. I'll be back, though, if that's okay?"

I nod. I quickly write a note on the board. *Thank you.*

Romero grins, but I can see sadness behind his eyes. "You're welcome. I'm just glad we could save you." He says it as if there was someone else he couldn't save, but I don't question him about it. He shakes his head as if clearing his thoughts and then says, "Okay. You get some rest, Avery."

I watch him leave and then sit back in bed. The medicine is making me so foggy, and time is just flying by without me being aware of my surroundings. Every time I blink it feels like I'm losing minutes of time. I wonder if Max has visited me yet and I just wasn't awake when he did. A smile creeps over my lips. I can't wait to see him. First, I'm going to tell him how much I love him. I never got the chance to say it back, and I regret that more than anything. I want him to know how I feel and how I've felt ever since the first time I met him.

I drift off to sleep and dream about Max...my Max.

AVERY

THE NEXT DAY I'm bursting with questions. I want to know what happened. I want to know where Max is and why he hasn't come to visit. My thoughts linger back to Agent Romero and what he said. He said Max went ahead of the team and confronted Nathan. Did Max get hurt? The thought of Max being injured sends a chill up my spine. That would explain why he hasn't visited. But I quickly push the thought aside. I've been so out of it because of the drugs that maybe Max has been here every time I've been asleep. Rosie said my father has visited me several times, but I was never awake when he was here. Besides, if Max were hurt, someone would have told me...right?

By the time Rosie comes into my room, I already have Max's name written on my board. I hold it up to her when she walks in. Her expression instantly changes from cheerful to distraught in an instant. My heart falters as I point to his name and raise my brow at her. She shakes her head, but I reach out and grasp her hand. "M...a...x," I whisper. I try to say more, but a sharp pain erupts through my throat, and I instantly regret trying to speak.

"No talking. Write it," Rosie says quickly.

My fingers move feverishly as I write, *Did something happen to him?*

"Yes." After a few moments, she asks, "You don't remember, do you?"

Remember what? I wrack my brain for answers, but come up empty handed. I don't remember what happened after Nathan tried to strangle me.

Hurriedly, I erase the board and scribble, *Is he okay?*

"Avery...he was shot."

I wave the board frantically in front of her. *Is he okay?*

"He had emergency surgery." She hesitates and takes a deep breath before saying the rest. "He's in the ICU and hasn't woken up yet, Avery. I'm sorry."

My world crashes down around me, and I instantly feel the hot tears stream down my face. I try to cry out, but I can't. I can't even voice my own panic, my own fear and grief.

Suddenly, I push the sheets down and swing my legs to the side of the bed. Rosie attempts to hold me down, but I struggle against her grip. I stand and stumble into the nightstand. The vase holding a bouquet of flowers goes crashing to the floor.

The sound of the glass breaking resonates through me to my very soul. My head pounds as the memory comes flooding back to me. I wasn't awake at the time, but I heard everything even if I didn't see it happening.

And the memory plays out in my mind like watching a movie with no picture, just sound. Max crashed through the window and attacked Nathan. There was a struggle. Gunshots. I remember Max holding my hand and talking to me.

My knees give out as I crumble to the floor. A strangled cry rips from my throat as I grab onto the bed for support. My hands twist in the sheets tightly as I sob. He saved me, but almost got himself killed in the process.

"It's okay, Avery," Rosie says in an attempt to calm me. "He'll make it. He'll pull through. You'll see."

But her words don't help me. I need to see him. I need to hold his hand and comfort him like he did with me. I grab the stupid board and scrawl on it. *Take me to Max.*

"Avery, I can't. The doctor said —."

I shake the board at her with tears spilling down my cheeks. I have to go to him. I have to see Max.

"Okay. Let me get a wheelchair," Rosie concedes.

~

The ICU is only fifty feet from my room, but it feels like miles. I am so close, and yet so far away from Max. Rosie hasn't said a word since she agreed to take me to him. I know she's breaking rules and could get in trouble, but I'm prepared to take all of the blame. If she wouldn't have helped me, I would have found another way anyhow.

We enter the room, and I can instantly feel my breathing pick up as I try not to panic. I should have expected the worst, but I was hoping for the best. I'm not prepared for Max's condition when we enter his room. Rosie parks the wheelchair by his bedside, and I silently sit there, my eyes wide and unblinking. Tears steam down my face, but I don't make a sound.

He looks so pale and fragile, and it makes my chest ache for him. There is a breathing tube in his throat, and the ventilator hisses as it forces air into his lungs. His chest and shoulder are wrapped in bandages and gauze. He has an IV and tubes everywhere, so I'm extremely careful when I reach to take his hand into mine. His skin feels cool to the touch, and it takes everything in me not to breakdown.

This was my worst nightmare. Deep down I knew I would be putting him in danger if he helped me, but I let him help anyway. I feel so much guilt it almost feels overwhelming. This is all my fault. It's all my fault.

I grasp his hand. I can't even tell him I love him. I can't speak the words I so desperately want to tell him. My forehead presses against his hand, and I sob silently. *I'm sorry. I'm sorry. I'm sorry.* I repeat the words over and over and over in my head.

After a while, Rosie says, "That's enough for one day, Avery. You can come back later when you feel better."

I'm hit with the realization that there might not be a later. Max could die while I'm down the hallway, and he would be all alone. I have every intention of coming to see him as often as I can. And when I feel well enough to walk, I will be by his side every minute of every day until he gets better. And he *will* get better. I won't let him leave me like this. I need him. I love him.

I kiss his hand and, reluctantly, let Rosie wheel me out of the room. I look back at him one last time, and my heart shatters into a million pieces all over again.

AVERY

OVER THE NEXT few days, I will myself to get stronger, to fight harder. And it's all because of Max and my need to see him and be there for him. My throat eventually heals well enough to allow me to talk in a whisper, and I sneak off to Max's room as often as I can. The nurses learned quickly that if I'm not in my room, I'm with Max. I've been reprimanded and brought back to my room more times than I can count, but I don't care. Nothing can stop me from going to see him.

It's in the afternoon the next day when Dr. Benson goes over my x-rays with me. "There isn't as much damage to your cervical spine as I once thought, which is a good thing." He holds the films up to the light once more. "I still want you to wear the neck brace as a precaution for a few more days. After that, I'll reassess your condition and any damage to your vocal chords."

"When am I going to get out of this bed?" I ask him in a hoarse whisper.

"From the nurses' notes, I would say that you've barely been in it," he says with a grin.

"Sorry," I mutter.

He pats my hand reassuringly. "We're all worried about Dr. Harrison. And I know you're worried most of all." He tucks the x-ray films into a folder and says, "As long as all the test results come back okay, I should be able to discharge you tomorrow." He holds his finger up, and I can feel a big *but* to his statement coming on. "But I want you to go home and rest. You can't do anything here for Max, and I know he would want me telling you the same exact thing."

I nod in agreement, but I have no intention of going home and resting. When Dr. Benson sighs, I know he knows exactly what my intentions are. "Thank you," I tell him.

"You're welcome. I'll see you tomorrow, Avery."

A few minutes after he leaves the room, my father enters the room. My father has been by my side almost twenty-four seven the past few days. He had been in another part of the state when he received news that I was hurt and in the hospital. He immediately dropped everything and came to see me, much to my surprise.

He's holding a cup of coffee in his hand, and I frown at the bags under his eyes. He's barely slept, and even though I want to tell him to go home, it's been so nice having him here. "Dad, you look tired."

He waves his hand dismissively and shakes his head. "I can sleep when I'm dead," he remarks. He sits down in a chair beside my bed. "What did the doctor say?"

"He said there isn't as much damage to my neck as they thought, but I have to continue wearing my lovely new necklace," I say, indicating to the hideous neck brace.

Dad flashes me a lopsided grin. "I'm just glad you're all right, sweetheart."

A knock on the door has us both turning our attention towards it. A woman in a black pantsuit sporting a police badge clipped on her pocket stands in the doorway. "Hello. I'm Detective Sheila Waters. May I speak to you, Avery?" When I motion for her to come in, she says, "Thank you." She walks to my bedside and turns her attention to my dad. "You must be Avery's father."

"Yes. Andrew Bennett," my dad answers as he shakes the detective's hand.

"I would like to ask Avery some questions about the events that took place a few days ago."

My father glances at me with a raised brow, and I nod in approval. I'm willing to do anything to keep Nathan locked away for a long time. My trembling hands reach for a cup of ice water, and I slurp noisily through the straw. It's still very difficult to drink and swallow. Water dribbles down my chin, and I fail miserably at trying to prevent it. My father is quick to wipe up my mess with a napkin. I look up at him with an appreciative gaze, and he gives me a small smile.

I push the button to move the bed into a better sitting position as the detective opens up her briefcase and pulls out a recorder, a notepad and a pen. "Is it okay to record our conversation, Avery?"

I nod, wanting to save my voice for the more important answers.

The detective eyes my father and then glances back at me. "Are you comfortable with your father being here?"

I turn to my father. "You can stay," I whisper. My voice still sounds like I swallowed gravel. "Just leave if it gets to be too much."

He nods solemnly, squeezes my hand gently and then goes to take a seat by the door.

Sheila takes his vacated seat, presses the record button and readies her pen. She spouts off the date, time, location and hospital room number. Then she asks me, "What is your name?"

"Avery Mason." I cringe at my last name. I have every intention of changing it as soon as I'm discharged. I don't want to be associated with that name ever again. "Please just call me Avery," I suggest.

Sheila nods and gives me a sympathetic smile. "Avery, we're here to talk about the events that occurred between Saturday the 27th and Tuesday the 30th, when you were found by police. Were you at the cabin by your own free will?"

"No."

"Did your husband Nathan Mason kidnap you?"

"Yes."

"Did he abuse you in the past?"

"Yes."

"Was that the first time he ever hit you?"

I swallow hard and pinch my eyes closed. It seems like forever ago that he first hit me, and my mind is cloudy from the drugs. I shake my head to clear my thoughts.

"Do you remember the first time he ever laid a hand on you?" the detective prompts.

"Before we were engaged." I hear my father take a sharp intake of breath, but I don't dare look at him.

"You were married two and a half years ago. So the abuse has been going on for years?"

"Yes."

"Physical and mental?" she asks.

I nod, and then realize I have to answer for the recording. "Yes."

She pulls a camera out of a bag, and I swallow thickly as I eye the piece of equipment. Sheila, perhaps sensing my apprehension, says, "We need to document the abuse to build a case against your husband. I'll be snapping some photos while I ask you questions, if that's all right."

"Okay," I agree quietly.

The questioning continues, and I can almost feel the tension in the room from my father's discomfort. He truly had no idea what I was going through. Nobody did. Except for Max. Tears form in my eyes when I think of him struggling to live right down the hall from me.

The flash from the camera brings me back to the present. Detective Sheila looks at me expectantly. "I'm sorry. What was the question?" I ask.

"I asked if you ever tried to get help. Did you ever try to leave him, Avery?"

The question has me flustered. At that moment I wish I had asked my father to leave earlier. "I tried to leave many times. I tried to ask people for help...but nobody would listen." I ramble through the countless times I tried to leave, the shelters and hotels I stayed in, the bus incident, even the suicide attempt, everything. It's all out in the open now.

"She asked me for help," my father says distantly. "I didn't help her." He stands and looks at me. "I'm sorry, Avery. I'm so sorry, sweetheart," he says, his voice breaking on a sob.

"You didn't know," I tell him. "Dad. You didn't know."

He shakes his head. "I should have listened to you. I didn't listen." He continues to shake his head in a daze.

"He would have just hurt you too." Then I realize he did try to hurt my dad. The drugs fogging my mind almost made me forget about the shooting incident entirely. I turn to the detective. "Nathan paid someone to shoot my father. He told me about it the morning it happened. It was just another one of his tactics to get me to comply, to get me to stay."

My father stares at me in disbelief, and then he hangs his head in shame. "I had no idea what kind of sick monster Nathan was. I was so blind," he mutters.

Detective Walters makes some notes and nods. "I'll need to look into this further. I might be able to book Mason on a conspiracy for murder charge." She pushes a button on the recorder and stands, slowly packing her things away into the briefcase. "I think that's all we need for today, Avery. I'm going to need a statement on that hit for hire when you're feeling up to it."

"Sure. Whatever I can do to help the investigation," I say softly.

"I'll be in touch."

After the detective leaves, my father walks over to my bedside. "Avery," he says, but he can't finish what he was going to say.

I've never seen my father cry before this moment. He never even shed a tear at my mother's funeral. I understand now as an adult that he had to be strong for Allison and me. "It's okay, Dad," I say reassuringly.

"No. No, it's not."

He takes my hand in his and pulls it to his face. He rests his forehead against my hand as he sobs. "I didn't know. I didn't know," he repeats over and over. "I'm sorry, Avery. I'm so sorry."

A soft knock breaks through my father's sobs. We both turn to see Allison in the doorway. She has a big smile plastered on her face, but it quickly falters when she sees me. "Oh, my God. Avery," she says. Her fingers cover her mouth in shock as she stares at my battered body.

"Get out," I say through clenched teeth.

Allison takes a few steps into the room. "Avery," she starts.

My hands curl into fists as I tremble with rage. "Get the hell out of here!" I yell.

My father glances back and forth between the two of us with a confused look on his face. "What's going on?" he asks my sister.

Allison has the nerve to shrug her shoulders as if she doesn't know, as if she didn't sleep with my husband and refuse to help me when I needed her the most. As if she wasn't sending him text messages and pictures while I was being beaten and tortured by the man she was sleeping with. She has the nerve to pretend like she didn't choose Nathan over me. Her eyes slowly fill with tears. "Avery, please," she sobs.

"GET OUT!" I scream at the top of my lungs. A burning pain runs through my throat, but I ignore it. I want her gone. Now. I can't bear to even look at her.

My father steps towards Allison. "Maybe you should just come back later, Allison."

She stares at our father and then at me with tears falling down her cheeks. "Avery, I didn't know. You have to believe me. I didn't now what Nathan was doing to you!"

I grab the nearby eraser board tightly in my hands. I watch her crocodile tears, and it makes me sick that she is the one who is upset right now. She has no right to be upset. Angrily, I chuck the board at her. It hits the door right beside her head, and I am infuriated that I missed. A loud sob emits from Allison's mouth before she flees the room.

My dad looks down at me and raises a brow as if to ask what was that about. I just shake my head; and, thankfully, he doesn't try to broach the subject. As far as I'm concerned, Allison is dead to me just like Nathan. My father and Max are the only family I need. And I pray that Max gets better so that I can be there for him just as he's been there for me all this time.

AVERY

*D*R. BENSON STAYS true to his word and discharges me the next day with a two-page list of restrictions and medications. I ignore the pieces of paper entirely and make my way to Max's room once I'd changed out of my gown and into some clothes my father had bought for me.

A nurse is changing the bandages on Max's shoulder. Anthony looks up and smiles as I enter the room. He's been one of my co-conspirators in the hospital, not telling on me when I snuck into Max's room so many times this past week. "You're not rocking the gown anymore, Avery. Does that mean you're officially out?"

I nod and give him a small smile. I immediately go to Max's bedside and gently kiss his cheek. "Hi, Max. I'm here." I glance up at Anthony and ask, "Do you...do you think he can hear me?"

Anthony nods. "I like to think so. I mean it can't hurt. Right?"

"Right," I say before turning my attention back to Max.

After Anthony leaves the room, I settle into the chair next to Max's bed. The beeping of the machines is hypnotic, but I refuse to fall asleep. My body aches with pain, and I know that eventually I will have to leave and fill a bunch of prescriptions, but right now I just want to be with Max.

Pulling Max's hand into mine, I say, "I love you, Max. I never got the chance to tell you that. I should have said it back that night. I shouldn't have held my true feelings for you inside. It wasn't fair." I swallow hard. "And now you might never get the chance to hear them." I grasp his hand tightly between mine. "I can't lose you. I just...I can't. I need you, Max. Please. Please come back to me." I place a soft kiss on his hand.

I look up just as an older woman and an older version of Max walk into the room. I've never met Max's parents before, and I actually never thought I would get the chance to. I stand as quickly as my body allows, and I make a futile attempt to make myself presentable, which proves to be impossible. I'm covered in cuts and bruises and I'm wearing a neck brace. Not much room for improvement here.

I take my mother's advice to heart and put the biggest smile I can on my face. She always told me the most beautiful thing I could wear was a smile, and so I wear it proudly and hope that it diverts some of their attention away from my appearance.

His mother's eyes are fixated on Max for a few moments before she even realizes I'm in the room. When our eyes meet, hers instantly become glassy. I wish we could have met under other circumstances, in a setting that wasn't so dire. But it is what it is. Her lips turn up into a smile to match my expression. "You must be Avery," she says in a soft voice. "I'm Caroline, and this is my husband Daniel." Her petite legs carry her over to me, and she outstretches her arms. Hugging me tight, she says in my ear, "Max told us so much about you." She pulls back and holds my face gently in her hands. "You poor girl. How are you? How are you feeling?"

"I'm doing better now," I respond. "Thanks to your son," I add quickly.

Caroline nods and looks over at Max with adoration in her gaze. "We're so proud of him for what he did." Her hands fall from my face and grasp my hands tightly in hers. "We're just hoping for the best possible outcome now. We just want him to come back to us."

I nod as tears fill my eyes. "I want that too."

～

I spend the next few hours talking with Max's parents about his childhood. I find out firsthand what a daredevil he was, riding his bike down a set of stairs when he was only four and breaking his arm from jumping too high from a swing when he was eight. The stories make us all laugh. But after the laughter dies down, the sadness creeps back in.

My father appears in the doorway and smiles when he spots me. "I thought I'd find you in here. The doctor told me you were released hours ago, but you never came to the house. I got worried."

Frowning, I say, "I'm sorry, Dad. I didn't mean to worry you."

I make introductions for Max's parents, and my father shakes hands with them both. Then his eyes settle on me, and he frowns. "Avery, you look like you're in pain. Let me take you home."

Slowly and carefully, I stand from my chair. I am in desperate need of pain medicine, but I was enjoying the time with Max's parents so much that I pushed the pain aside. My father extends his elbow, and I hook my arm around it. I look at the Harrisons and say, "It was so nice to finally meet you."

"Same here, Avery," Max's dad says.

"I'll be back as soon as I can," I tell them.

His mother shakes her head. "You go home and get some rest. We'll make sure to call if anything happens."

"Thank you."

"Ready to go, sweetheart?" my dad asks.

I look longingly at Max one last time before nodding. I don't want to leave him, but I silently promise to be back as soon as possible.

AVERY

THE NEXT DAY at the hospital is rough. The pain medicine keeps making me drift asleep, but I try my best to stay awake. I stay by Max's side, holding his hand and talking to him. I don't know if he can hear me, but I like to hope so. I want him to know that I'm here for him.

After a while, I rest my head on the cool sheets of his bed and stare up at him. My eyes only close for a moment before I hear someone whispering my name.

"Avery."

I slowly open my eyes. Max is staring down at me. "You're awake," I say in surprise.

I look around the room and realize we're not in the hospital anymore. We're in his bed at his house. I reach up and tentatively touch his rough cheek. "Max," I say softly. "I was so worried about you."

He starts to talk, but I can't hear him. There's a loud alarm filling the room, and I quickly cover my ears to block out the noise.

I sit up quickly as the blaring sound cuts through my dream, shattering me awake to the present. My eyes find the source of the alarms, and his heart monitor is showing a flat line.

"No!" I cry. "Max!" My throat is raw, but I blink past the pain. "Max!" I squeeze his hand tightly.

Two nurses rush into the room. One checks Max's vitals as the other grabs a nearby phone, waiting for instruction. "Unresponsive. Call the code," the assessing nurse says.

"Code blue, ICU, room number three. Patient is unresponsive," the other says quickly into the receiver.

Seconds later a voice comes over the intercom system. "ICU room three. Code blue. Code blue team needed in ICU room three."

I stand and reluctantly surrender my grip on Max's hand. I move into the corner of the room as the nurses begin to perform CPR. My arms curl around my waist, and I hold myself tightly as silent sobs wrack my body. "Please," I plead, but I don't know whom I'm even asking for help.

Within a few moments, nurses and a doctor are rushing into the room. Numbers are being shouted out left and right as they check his vitals and administer medicine. Everything happens so fast that it almost blurs together in my mind.

The heart monitor continues to show no response, and my own heart wants to cease beating. This can't be happening. It wasn't supposed to end this way. He was supposed to wake up and get better. We were going to have a life together. We were going to be happy, *finally happy*.

"Continue chest compressions. Place and charge the defibrillator pads," a doctor commands.

Two nurses hustle to place two large pads on Max's chest, and then one pushes a button on the machine they're connected to. The sound of the machine charging sends a shiver through my spine. Within a few seconds, it starts to beep.

"Clear!"

Everyone takes a step back.

"Shock."

A button is pushed, and electricity surges through Max's body. An intense moment passes as all eyes are glued to the heart monitor.

"No response," a doctor says. "Resume chest compressions."

My vision blurs as I silently pray. "Please, Max. Please," I plead.

"We're not giving up on you, Dr. Harrison, so don't you dare give up on us," the doctor says through gritted teeth. He raises his head to one of the nurses. "Charge the pads again."

"Max!" I cry out.

Anthony walks over to me and gently puts his hands on my shoulders. "Avery, you can't be in here right now."

I struggle against him as he pulls me towards the doorway. "Max!" I scream.

Anthony all but picks me up to get me out of the room. "They're going to help him. Let them do their job."

I stand in the hallway with my back pressed up against the wall as the nurses and doctors race to save Max's life. I stare at Max's lifeless body as they do chest compressions and force air into his lungs. The heart monitor shows no sign of life. He's dying. *He's dying.*

I look up to see Daniel and Caroline rushing through the double doors, and their faces fall as soon as they see how upset I am.

Caroline runs to me. "What happened?"

I open my mouth, but I can't speak. The only sound that comes out is a sob. She grabs me and holds me, and I grasp onto her for support.

Max's father stands in the doorway, watching the crew work on his son. Tears fill his eyes as he whispers, "Come on, Max. You've always been a fighter. And we need you to fight right now."

After a few nerve-wracking minutes, the doctor calls out, "We've got a heart rate!"

Caroline, Daniel and I wait with bated breath as they continue to work on Max. And then finally the doctor walks out to talk with us. "Max has a good rhythm. We're going to continue monitoring him closely for the next twenty-four hours, but I think he's out of the woods for now."

"Oh, thank God," Caroline says in a hushed whisper.

The three of us are huddled together crying when a voice asks, "What's going on?"

I look up to see a girl around my age standing a few feet away. She has dark hair and dark eyes just like Max, and I know instantly that this is his sister.

"Oh, Megan," Caroline says, cupping her daughter's face in her hands. "We almost lost Max, but he's okay now."

Megan's bottom lip quivers as she asks, "He's okay?"

"Yeah."

I watch them hug, and I realize how much I miss my mom. New tears fill my eyes, but I quickly dash them away.

Daniel wraps his arm around my shoulder and pulls me in close. "Megan, this is Avery, Max's girlfriend."

Megan pulls away for her mom to assess me. A big grin breaks out on her face, and it reminds me of Max so much. "It's nice to finally put a face to the name," Megan says. "Max seriously wouldn't shut up about you."

I can't help but smile at her words. All this time I was trying to keep Max a secret, and he was telling his family all about me. But that's just Max. He's open about his feelings. You never have to question how he feels about anything or anyone.

"Nice to meet you, Megan." I hold out my hand, but she pulls me in for a big hug.

"Thanks for being here for my brother," she whispers in my ear.

I'm too choked up to respond, so I just hug her back and stay quiet. Max's family is so loving and caring. I can see why he possesses those same characteristics. They've made me feel so welcome and wanted, and I am so thankful for that, because it's just what I need right now.

When we part, Megan says, "Let's go down to the cafeteria and get some coffee. I want to know everything about the girl who has stolen my brother's heart."

AVERY

IT'S BEEN THREE days, and Max's condition has slightly improved. He still hasn't woken up, but two of the nurses reported eye movement and some audible groans. The doctor says this could be a sign that he is going to wake up, and we're all hanging on by a thread in hopes that that's true.

I wake up early and get ready for my daily visit to the hospital. With some strategically placed clothing, makeup and a hat, I am able to pull off the appearance of looking almost back to normal. When I get to the hospital, I spend some time in the activity room with various kids. It's nice to see the children's faces light up when they see me. I had been a constant in their lives, and then I just kind of disappeared. It's good to be back, and I can't wait until Max is better so we can both get back to living our lives.

After a quick stop in the cafeteria for chocolate pudding, I make my way to Jacob's room. An unwavering smile is on my face in anticipation of seeing him. Rosie told me that he asks about me every day.

I knock softly before entering. Jacob's eyes instantly light up when he sees me. "Avery?" he asks almost as if he can't believe I'm actually here.

His eyes scan my face and the baseball cap on my head. "Hey, Jacob. How have you been?"

He shrugs, and his lower lip begins to tremble. "I missed you," he whispers softly. He swipes away a stray tear with his forearm and stares up at me. "Where did you go?"

"I was sick," I say with a small sigh. He gets a concerned look on his face, so I quickly say, "But I'm better now."

"So you'll be here every day again?" he asks.

I bite my lower lip and shake my head. "Not yet. I have to get some more rest first, and then I'll be back."

"Promise?"

I nod. "Promise." From behind my back, I produce the chocolate pudding.

A huge grin appears on his face. "Will you read me my favorite story while I eat this?" he asks, taking the pudding and spoon from me.

"Sure, Jacob." I retrieve the big fantasy book from the shelf and sit by his bedside. My emotions are running high, and my voice wavers a little as I start to read. I missed this. I missed spending time with the kids and reading to Jacob.

"Are you okay, Avery?" he asks.

I smile up at him and nod. With as much effort as I can muster, I steady my voice and nerves and continue to read. And Jacob, for the first time ever, stays up until the very end. I close the book and look at him. "You finally got to hear the end of the story," I comment.

He nods and puts the finished pudding cup and spoon on his nightstand. "You know, that story reminds me of you and Dr. Harrison."

The mention of Max's name has tears instantly pooling in my eyes, but I keep them at bay for Jacob's sake. "Oh yeah? How so?"

"Well, you would be the princess, and Dr. Harrison would be the knight. The dragon is whatever has been keeping you two apart. But the knight slayed the dragon and saved the princess." He puts a finger to his chin as if he's deep in thought. "I think that you and Dr.

Harrison will live happily ever after too just like the princess and the knight. Maybe not in a big castle like they did, but at least you'll be happy," he says with a toothy grin.

I place my hand over my thumping heart and do my best to quell my emotions. "That sounds so nice, Jacob." At this point I don't know if Max and I will get our happily ever after. If only life was as easy as a children's fairytale.

After placing the book back on the shelf, I tell Jacob, "I have to go visit with Max now."

"You'll come back soon?" he asks eagerly.

I lightly tap the brim of his baseball cap, and he smiles wide. "I will. I promise."

I walk out of his room with a heavy heart, and it grows heavier with every step to the ICU. Just a few days ago when I was in here, Max almost died. That memory will haunt me forever. I thought I had lost him, and I realize that I wouldn't be able to bear it. I love him too much to lose him now. But his fate is not up to me no matter how much I wish it were.

Sitting down in a chair by his bed, I pull his hand into mine. "I just saw Jacob," I tell Max. My eyes scan his face for any sort of reaction, but, of course, there is none. Sighing softly, I say, "I read him his favorite story. He said it reminded him of you and me. He said that you're my knight in shining armor; I'm the princess, and that you slayed the dragon keeping us apart. If only he knew how true that was." I smirk. "Jacob said we'll get our happily ever after." I squeeze his hand. "I want that more than anything, Max. I want to be with you more than anything in this world." I kiss his hand gently and rest my head on his bed. I close my eyes and savor the warmth of his hand on my cheek. "I love you. I love you," I repeat over and over again. "Please come back to me, Max." I watch him for what feels like hours. My head grows heavier with every passing second, and I curse the drugs running through my system. I just want to be here for him. I want to be the first person he sees when he wakes up.

I must have fallen asleep. I feel something tickling my face, and my eyes slowly open to find the source. Max's fingers are gently brushing against my cheek. *Oh no. Not again.*

Panicked, I bolt upright in my chair and stare straight into the dark gaze of Max. Tears fill my eyes and quickly spill over my cheeks. "Max," I choke out. "Am I dreaming?"

He gently shakes his head. His movements are restricted from the tubes and machines he's hooked up to.

My hand fumbles with the nurse call button as I hold his hand fiercely in mine. "The nurse is coming." I stand, and his hand grips mine. He's trying to tell me something, but he can't talk with the tube in his throat. "Don't try to talk." I place my palm against his cheek, and he leans into my touch and closes his eyes. "I love you, Max." His eyes open and meet mine. "I love you. I love you so much. I'm sorry I didn't say it back, but I'm saying it now," I say with a sob.

He tries to reach for me to wipe my tears away, but he grimaces from pain as his arm falls back to the bed.

"Dr. Harrison," the nurse says as she enters the room. "My name is Patricia. You need to lie still so we can get that tube out of your throat. Okay?"

He nods once in response as a few other hospital personnel enter the room. I move to step away, but Max quickly grabs my hand and holds it tight. I raise his hand and press my lips to his skin. "I'll be right back. I need to get out of the way so they can help you. Okay?"

His eyes look pleadingly at me for a long moment before he finally nods in agreement.

I step out into the hallway as the nurses work on him. I press my back against the wall and sink to the floor. My emotions are running wild with relief, and tears freely stream down my cheeks. He's awake. Max is awake. I take a few minutes to compose myself and then make a call to Max's parents. They barely let me get the words out before his mother cries out in happiness and hangs up the phone.

They've been staying in a nearby hotel, so I'm sure they'll be here within a few minutes.

The nurses are talking to Max and asking him questions, but he doesn't seem to be cooperating. My brows dip as I hear a few mumbled words come out of his mouth. And then I can make out what he's saying. My name.

"A...v...e...r...y." His voice is deep and gravelly. "A...Avery."

I rush into the room. His eyes lock onto mine, and he instantly reaches for me. He pulls me into his arms and holds me so tightly. I melt into him. It's as if the past few weeks haven't happened. We're here. Together. Just like it was always meant to be.

"He really shouldn't be making any sudden movements," one of the nurses says, scolding us, but she doesn't make a move to separate us. In fact, no one does.

I eventually pull back, and Max stares up at me as if I'm his sole reason for breathing. "Say...it," he says.

My eyes fill with tears once more as I whisper, "I love you."

He pulls me back into his arms just as his mom, dad and sister rush into the room. They gather around Max and I, and we share a group hug with hushed whispers of affection and prayers.

MAX

I AM ALIVE.

The past couple of weeks now seem like a dream. I can remember little tidbits of Avery's conversations with me. Having her by my side gave me hope. It made me want to live.

I blink up at her. I must have fallen asleep from the medicine again. After going through a battery of tests earlier in the day, everything so far is coming back normal. No brain damage. Thank God. But I did suffer some nerve damage in my shoulder. I don't know if physical therapy will ever get me back to normal, but I'm going to try. I'm going to try for Avery.

I reach up and brush away the tears on her face. She hasn't stopped crying since I woke up yesterday, and I'm tired of seeing her cry. I want her to be happy. "No more tears," I say.

"These are happy tears. I'm just so overwhelmed that you're awake, that you're okay."

A lopsided grin appears on my face, and it makes her smile. "You didn't think I'd miss the chance to finally be with you, did you?"

My words make her cry even harder, and she leans over, placing kisses over my cheeks and lips. "I love you. I love you. I love you," she repeats, and I know I'll never get tired of hearing those words come out of her mouth. "Promise me you'll never leave me again."

"I promise. I promise to cherish you every single moment of every day for the rest of our lives."

She kisses my lips gently one more time. "I finally have my happily ever after."

EPILOGUE

AVERY

AFTER THE DJ announces the newlywed's first dance, *At Last* by Etta James pumps through the speakers. Max leads me onto the dance floor and holds me close. "This song brings back memories, Mrs. Harrison," he says with a big grin.

He's been calling me Mrs. Harrison nonstop ever since our wedding ceremony ended two hours ago. I will never get sick of hearing it, though. "Yes, it does, Mr. Harrison," I say and rest my head on his shoulder. I breathe in his spicy, clean scent and sigh contentedly. Everything about Max makes me feel safe and warm.

As I look around the beautiful hall with the glittering winter decorations, it takes my breath away. I still can't believe I'm not dreaming. The winter themed wedding just seemed fitting since we are both looking for a fresh start. And like a fairytale come true, on the twentieth day of December, it snowed, covering the ground with sparkling snow as we welcomed our guests into the church.

It was a long, hard road that we had to travel to get us here. There was a lot of physical therapy to get Max to where he is today and a lot of psychological counseling to get me where I am today and a lot of court testimony to make sure Nathan stays locked up for a long time.

But the most important thing is that we made it.

We've been through a lot, and Max held my hand every step of the way. I don't know what I would do without him. And when he proposed one sunny day in the park four months ago, I said yes without any hesitation in my mind, body or soul. He is mine, and I am his. Finally.

He glides me effortlessly around the parquet dance floor. We have hundreds of guests, but it feels like we are the only two people in this room — maybe even in the whole universe at this moment.

As the song comes to an end, Max gracefully dips me low. That move elicits a lot of applause from our guests, and I can't help but smile. I've been smiling a lot these days.

The DJ plays another slow song, and Max holds me close. "I don't want to let you go," he confesses.

"I don't want you to let me go," I whisper.

He leans in to kiss me, but stops short when a small voice asks, "May I cut in?"

We turn to see Jacob all dressed up with a big grin on his face. His leukemia went into remission a few months ago, and his red hair is growing back in all its glory. It's spiked in all different directions, and he looks happy and, most importantly, healthy.

"I'll let Jacob dance with you, but he is the only exception," Max murmurs with a wink.

"I have to dance with my father."

Max sighs and jokingly says, "I guess I'll let him dance with you too." He kisses me chastely and says to Jacob, "One dance, Jacob, and that's only because I like you so much."

Jacob sticks his tongue out playfully and then looks up at me. "I never danced to a slow song before," he says, suddenly unsure of himself.

I smile and take his hands into mine. "Then I'll lead."

～

*A*fter dancing with Jacob and, much to Max's dismay, several other wedding guests, Max pulls me back into his arms. "Not letting you go this time."

I bite my lip to hold back a grin. "I still haven't danced with my dad."

"Damn it," he mutters.

I laugh and give my husband a kiss. I never thought I would ever be this happy. Just when life has knocked you down to the bottom rung, fate has a way of bringing you back up the ladder.

My fingers graze over my *something new* — a necklace that Max gave me last night. He said it symbolizes our relationship. It's a locket with charms that signify different steps in our relationship — a karaoke microphone and music notes, a sailboat, a crystal heart and finally...a bird with its wings spread and an empty birdcage.

He told me that the last two charms represent me. I'm no longer a bird trapped in a gilded cage. I'm free to love. I'm free to live. And I'm free to choose my own path in life. And I want to do all of those things with Max by my side.

I went through hell and back only to be saved by the one true love of my life. And I would do it all over again if it meant meeting my soul mate, my savior, my hero.

"I love you," I whisper to Max.

"I love you more than anything in this world," he whispers back. His hand ventures down my side and pauses at my barely protruding belly. A big smile forms on his lips as he gazes down at me like he's the happiest man on earth. "And I love our little boy...or girl."

I grab his hand and move it back up to my hip. "If you keep touching my belly, people are going to know I'm pregnant," I hiss into his ear. I'm only twelve weeks along. If the wedding had been planned any later, I might not have been able to fit into my wedding dress.

"Is it a big secret?" he asks, and the look on his face tells me that the cat's already out of the bag.

"You told your parents, didn't you?"

He shakes his head. "My mom has this weird sixth sense or something. She knew before you even took a test."

Smiling, I say, "That's because she's around me so much. She probably noticed a change in me or something. Mother's intuition." Max's mom has really become a second mother to me, and it's so nice to have that maternal bond again.

Max's hand returns to my belly, and I don't pull it away this time. He looks so happy, and I want him to always feel that way.

As I gaze up at my husband, I think to myself how perfect my life must appear to an outsider. I'm twenty-four years old. I married my soul mate, someone who would do anything for me and go to the ends of the earth to save me. Our child growing inside of me will get more love and affection than anyone could even imagine. A few weeks ago, Max and I bought a house in the suburbs across the street from a park where our kids will be able to play. And I get to spend the rest of my life with a man who completely adores me.

I have the kind of life women dream about. I have the kind of life that women envy.

Anybody on the outside looking in would say I have the perfect life.

And they couldn't be more right.

THE END

ABOUT THE AUTHOR

Thank you for reading! If you enjoyed reading *Saving Avery*, please consider telling your friends and posting a short review. Word of mouth is an author's best friend and much appreciated. Shouts from rooftops are great too.

If you'd like to be notified of all of my new releases, giveaways, sneak peeks, freebies and more, please sign up for my newsletter: http://eepurl.com/cNFoo5

Made in the USA
Middletown, DE
12 June 2025